KINGS OF THIS WORLD

Peter Bailey

KINGS OF THIS WORLD

DOUBLE DRAGON

Chapter One
Theatre

By nine thirty, Matthew knew that the evening couldn't get any worse. The play that had started well had turned out to be dull, amateurish and, worst of all, predicable. He'd mentally written the review after just the first half hour and nothing that had happened since then had changed one word.

The Eternal Banker *is the latest big budget play to hit the West End and comes complete with all the things necessary to make it a hit. Big names direct from Oscar-winning films? Check. Flashy special effects? Check. But somehow all of this adds up to a third-class production of a second-rate play with only one flaw. Unfortunately, this is the cast. {name} might have performed the role of Billy ably, but without panache, but {name} as Nadia appeared to be labouring under the misapprehension that a flash of cleavage is any substitute for acting. The production was nearly as wooden as the scenery and the whole thing would have been much improved by at least one person knowing all their lines.*

All he had to do was fill in the names, add some anecdote about the rumoured-to-be-coke-addicted soap star who appeared naked for exactly five seconds in the second half and tomorrow's copy would be ready. This might be his only chance to have a review appear in a national paper before Stephen recovered from food poisoning and he wanted it to make an impact.

At nine thirty-five, he decided it wasn't really going to get any better, looked around for an exit and saw the faces staring at him in amazement. There was a moment of panic and half-forgotten dreams of being naked in public. Then he realised that he was not the object of their attention and looked at the woman on his right. She was very slim, dark-haired and slumped low down in her seat with her dress pulled up high. Her head was twisted back, looking at the ceiling with wide, staring eyes. But what Matthew mainly saw were her hands rhythmically moving between her thighs. He told himself that she was just vigorously scratching an itch or harmonising badly to the music, but he could see a dark tuft of pubic hair, her glistening fingers, the folds of her sex parting under probing fingers. She was very enthusiastically masturbating to an audience of hundreds of people.

Matthew's belief that he was broad-minded vanished in that moment. He felt more shocked than if he'd stuck his fingers in an electric socket. He couldn't breathe, couldn't move. The sight of a complete stranger doing something so private in such a public place shocked him more than he could believe.

It was the sound of camera shutters that snapped him out of his fugue. All around him a tidal wave of men, and women, were aiming phones towards her, standing on seats for a better view, whooping and whistling, "More!" "You go, babe!" None of this seemed to bother Matthew's neighbour. Her head rolled from side to side, watching her audience and licking her lips. Then she slid further down in her seat, opened her legs as

6

wide as possible, wider than possible, hands moving faster over her sex. Matthew looked longingly at the aisle beyond her. But to get there he'd have to step over, between, her wide-spread legs. Then she stopped suddenly, screamed so loud it hurt his ears and curled into a foetal ball. Her knees snapped up tight to her chest and there were sudden tears in her eyes. Matthew was still wondering if he should cover her with his jacket or something equally chivalrous when she solved that problem for him by rolling to one side and punching him in the face.

***

The manager's office was a long, thin room at the top of a meandering set of stairs. The faded opulence of the theatre stopped abruptly at its door and the carpet inside was threadbare and had been patched with tape. The walls were a jigsaw of crumbling plaster decorated with fading posters for plays that Matthew had never heard of. A battered desk faced a row of small windows that looked out over the frozen waves of red velvet cheap seats. Matthew wondered if someone had been watching just half an hour ago when the evening had come completely off the tracks. Perhaps the same someone had also called the police, after they'd taken several photos for later detailed examination.

PC Ward showed Matthew to the only visitor's chair. When the police realised where Matthew had been sitting he had been gently, but very firmly, taken to one side by a reassuringly solid policeman whose gaze believed nothing. On the way to the manager's office he had grudgingly revealed that his name was PC Ward. If he had a first name other than PC he hadn't offered it.

"And you never saw this woman before she sat next to you?" PC Ward asked.

"Never. She sat down a few minutes after me. We chatted for a few minutes. Well, she did most of the talking. She complained about the seats; it was too hot then, a moment later, it was too cold. Kept taking photos, gibbered on about uploading them to Facebook. She went quiet when the curtain came up but she was still jabbing at her phone and bopping around in her seat."

"And you were on your own tonight, sir?"

"Yes." Matthew saw the doubt on the policeman's face and quickly added, "I'm with *The Bulletin* reviewing the opening night."

PC Ward lowered his notepad and pointedly looked Matthew up and down. He was a fresh-faced young man that might have been handsome – if ever he smiled. The bags under his eyes from lack of sleep and the disappointed set of his mouth implied that smiling was something he didn't do much of. His hair was too long and he pulled it away from his eyes in a nervous tick that he was completely unaware of. His grey business suit had once been a *smart* grey business suit, before months of overcrowded tube trains and lunch a la desk had left their mark on it. If the call had come any earlier he could have rented a smart suit, maybe a bowtie to complete the ensemble. But if the news of Stephen's sudden need to be no more than three feet from a toilet at any time had come any earlier then the job would have gone to someone else. He was only here because there was no one else. As the office junior he was the lowest of the low and Philip had made his role tonight very clear. *Don't fuck up.* Matthew wasn't sure he had achieved that. Matthew realised that PC Ward was still staring at him intently and hastily produced a business card and passed it across.

PC Ward took the card and squinted at it. "Sorry, sir, the printing's not very clear. If you could just give me your name and address?"

"Matthew Rowe, 256A Ailward road, Brent Park," he said, dejectedly. When he'd got the job with the paper he'd paid £20 for the cards. And now he had a chance to actually use one of the dammed things it was useless.

PC Ward carefully noted down his details, tongue sticking out from the corner of his mouth.

"Did she stay in her seat at the interval?"

"No, she said something about popping out for a moment. I thought she went to the bar." But now Matthew thought about it, she had been gone for the whole twenty-minute interval and when she got back she had looked very flushed.

PC Ward made some more ant tracks of Pitman shorthand in his notebook. His hand shook while he was doing that. It had taken three police and one security guard to carry her kicking and screaming out of the theatre.

"I believe she punched you, sir?"

"Yes, just here." Matthew touched his cheek and found that it was still wet and sticky. The first thing he'd do when he got out of here was wash his face. The second thing would be to find a large drink. "But I don't think she really meant to. It was as if she had just woken up and realised what was happening."

"That's very generous of you, sir, but I don't think that's any defence in law. We'll contact you later to make a separate complaint of assault that we can add to the charge sheet. But failing that, I think that's everything for now, sir."

"What's going to happen to her? Will you charge her with some sort of public order offence?"

"Officially, sir, she's been held for questioning." His voice dropped to a whisper and he looked around furtively. "Unofficially, she's probably going to be sectioned, admitted to a psych ward for her own good."

"No indications of drink or drugs?"

"I couldn't say, sir. But thank you for your statement. It's been very useful."

PC Ward came to his feet and stepped around the desk, arm outstretched to shake Matthew's hand. And the moment he came to his feet PC Ward shook his hand briskly, gripped his forearm and steered him to the door. As they walked downstairs PC Ward talked as if he couldn't stop.

"We'll be in contact in a few days' time for the assault statement. But in the meantime I really wouldn't worry about tonight's events. London is still one of the safest cities in the world with a year on year decreasing crime rate with ..." He took a deep breath. "... neighbourhood teams utilising our corporate objectives and close working relationship with the Crown Prosecution Service to maximise security of people and property."

At the bottom of the stairs he shook Matthews's hand even more briskly and reached past him to undo something. "It's been a pleasure meeting you, sir," he said and stepped forward, moving Matthew back through the door behind him and outside. The door closed with a solid thud and an icy rivulet of rain crawled down Matthew's neck. He retreated under cover of the theatre's canopy as he pulled his jacket around him. At some point during the evening it had started to rain and forgotten how to stop. Silvery curtains of rain chased rubbish down the street and reflected neon-scrawled, unreadable messages across slick pavements. The crowd that had flooded out of the theatre when the police arrived had already disappeared into the nearest pub or were on their way home, all of them probably making phone calls containing some variant on, 'Well, you'll never guess what happened tonight.'

Once, Matthew would have been saying something very similar; instead, he mopped his face with a tissue and headed towards the nearest pub at a fast walk. And because the theatre was on the edge of Soho, AKA London's party ground, the nearest pub was a hundred metres left, about the same right or straight across the road. A taxi blared its horn at him as he crossed the road. Drinking alone had never been his idea of a good time, but after what had happened in the theatre he needed a drink, or two.

The pub was an anonymous, corporate clone that had started out life as an eighteenth-century tavern, before being renovated, restored and reinterpreted into a plastic replica of the place it once was. It probably made sense to someone. Outside it was high-impact, plastic oak beams on pre-stressed, pre-rendered walls under a thatched-glass, fibre roof. Inside it was a wall of heat and noise. Matthew pushed himself into a densely packed throng of people who all seemed to be having 50% more of a good time than usual. Shouted conversations competed against over-amplified guitars. In the corner, a middle-aged woman was dancing on a table, badly as it turned out, when she disappeared with a crash. Matthew guessed one of the banks had celebrated some dodgy deal by handing out bonuses that the staff were trying to spend before the Government found out.

A wall of people hid the bar and it was only the brief opening as someone pushed their way out, clutching three pints in two hands, that let Matthew reach it at all.

"Pint of lager."

"What?"

He repeated his order, shouting it this time directly into an unwashed ear. The glass he got in return came with a thick head of foam, but it tasted delicious and he let the motion of the crowd shove him into a corner.

He wondered what the woman would think in the morning. How could she ever look people in the eye knowing that she was probably starring on several amateur porn sites? Did she have a husband, a boyfriend that she would try to explain the unexplainable to? Because nothing that had happened made any sense. One moment she had been aware of her audience but they didn't matter. The next they were the only thing that mattered. When the police dragged her out she had been a spitting, clawing hell-cat, using words that would have made a twenty-year sailor blush. He had asked about drink or drugs out of routine, but as far as he knew none of those things could explain her sudden changes of behaviour.

He lifted his glass and was surprised to find it already empty. He pushed his way back to the bar, opened his mouth to order and the barman saved him the trouble by slopping a full pint glass at him, plucking the note from his fingers and turning away to serve another customer. Matthew stared at the greasy ponytail at the back of the barman's head for a long minute before deciding that he really wasn't going to turn back and said, "Excuse me." And then shouted the same before the barman looked around at him. "My change?"

"Sorry, sir." The barman shoved a £20 note in his hand and turned away again. Matthew had only given him a £5 note. A flying wedge of thirsty customers forced him away from the bar while he was still considering the ethical problem the note presented. Then he shrugged his shoulders, took a drink and instantly decided that whatever the pint had cost he had still been overcharged. The contents of the glass tasted like some horrible melody of real beer and washing-up liquid. He spat the liquid back into his glass just as there was a crash from the direction of the bar that sounded like a whole tray of glasses hitting the floor. The crowd surged towards the bar like iron filings to a magnet, leaving an empty path between Matthew and door. A hand wearing a red washing-up glove waved jauntily above the sea of heads and Matthew decided that this was the perfect time to leave. A bray of cheers was cut off abruptly as the pub doors swung shut behind him. At the corner he stopped and looked back at the glowing windows of the pub. He had told himself that the waving hand had been wearing a red glove. But it had looked a lot like blood.

***

The underground station was crowded as the pub had been, only all the people here wanted to test its acoustics by singing as loudly as possibly. A teenager trying to crowd surf along the length of the platform made it as far as the sign announcing the time to the next train before disappearing with a dull gong-like sound. Everyone was having a good time. Matthew just wished he was one of them. His bladder was a hot and heavy bag low down in his groin, and just above that his stomach gurgled and moaned; the former thanks to the first pint, the latter to the second. When a train pulled in there was plenty of room to sit, but that would have only increased the pressure on his bladder, so instead he stood by the doors.

A woman dancing excitedly to music only she could hear caught his eye and blew him a kiss. For a moment Matthew saw himself struggling across the carriage, getting her number, offering to buy her a drink, but what then?

He left the train at the next stop and moved two carriages down.

At Matthews's's station the train nearly overshot the platform and three of the carriage's four doors opened onto dark tunnel wall. Matthew quickly left via the remaining door before the train might jerk forward, cutting him in two. The train doors closed behind him and opened immediately. Closed again and opened. A garbled announcement containing the words 'doors' and 'away' echoed down the platform but as Matthew started up the stairs the train was still futilely opening and closing its doors.

After the stifling heat underground the cool street outside was almost pleasant. As he crossed the street a very tall woman wearing a very short skirt caught his eye – *See anything you like, honey?* – and lifted the skirt high enough to prove conclusively that she had no underwear, and that *she* was a *he*. Matthew crossed the road and walked very quickly. Most of the streetlights were working, which was an unexpected plus, but this was more than outweighed by the fact that the street was completely empty.

When they had bought into the area they had been sure that it would be the next up and coming part of London's sprawl. But the wave of gentrification had stalled three streets away and most nights the distance between station and home could be counted not by feet and inches, but by the number of offers for drugs, sex or violence. But not tonight. Tonight Matthew felt very exposed and without noticing he lingered under the tent of light from each streetlight before hurrying to the next until he saw a short row of shops and the squat shape of the flat above.

The *For Sale* sign that had been strapped to a drainpipe had fallen over again. He didn't think that would make any difference. The flat had been up for sale for six months and the best offer had been exactly half of the asking price. That was starting to sound like a good deal. Kirsten had said there was no hurry for the sale. It would give him time to sort himself out. He didn't think either of those things would be happening anytime soon.

The stairs to the flat were hidden at the back like an embarrassment and Matthew climbed them very slowly. He opened the front door against a snowdrift of mail that he pushed to one side without opening. Just from the envelopes alone he knew that the dominant theme in most of them would be *Your minimum payment is now overdue*. Although there be would an increasing number that had gone up to DEFCON 2 with *Your account will be passed to a debt collection agency*. He thought he might have as much as another two or three months before bailiffs started knocking on the door, and then it would be easier to post the keys to the mortgage company and hope they never catch up with him.

The flat had been mainly Kirsten's idea, but for a while it had been a good idea. They had met during a drunken housewarming – as if 'met' could ever be an adequate way to describe being completely, life-changingly captivated. She was literally so beautiful that it was several hours before a combination of cheap wine from the open bar and Spandau Ballet from the stereo let him talk to her. Using the confidence of alcohol, he soon discovered her name, that she was from Norway and that her favourite band was an obscure darkwave band called SITD. And then it was a complete coincidence that he had two tickets to their next gig (he didn't and making that happen cost him lunch for a week). The gig became a first date and then later on he showed her London, she taught him a few words of Norwegian and very quickly they fell in love.

They found a flat based on the intersection of house prices, transport links and areas that Kirsten thought sounded nice. In a former life it had been a rabbit warren of cheap bedsits for the labourers that built the North Circular. The moment they took possession they unleased an orgy of builders and painters to transform it into an inner-city haven of stripped pine, concealed lighting and colour coordinated furniture. When they finally moved in, they had laughed like little children and made love in every room, even the airing cupboard. The almost affordable weight of the mortgage meant they got very good at spotting special offers and the last-minute bargains before the shops closed. Evenings out were a rare luxury. But they were happy. Sometimes they would sit watching TV with the sound off, adding their own dialogue. Sometimes they would just sit and hold each other. And then everything changed. Even in retrospect, he could never quite see where things had gone wrong. Suddenly there was a distance between them, something subtly wrong. The realisation that she was seeing someone else had crept on him like standing in rising, ice-cold water. But once the idea had come to him the evidence was plain to see: the unexpected late nights; the slight disarray of her clothing when she got back from the library. The knowledge had cut like a knife and when it became too much he had confronted her. He knew everything. There was nothing left to hurt him anymore. Then she had told him the name of her lover.

Janice.

Kirsten, the woman he had made love with, laughed with and adored, had become a lesbian.

She had been very kind and that kindness had been more than he could bear. Nothing had been planned. She had never touched another woman like that before. She had probably been more shocked than Matthew was right now and she had laughed. She had just turned a corner in her life. What had happened was nothing to do with him. And yet it was. He spent a week in a fog of alcohol and memory, revisiting every time they touched, every gasp as she orgasmed, and still could not see the flaw that had set them apart.

After a month he decided to move on, installed Tinder on his smart phone and threw himself back into the dating pool. He met pretty women, sexy women, women that made him arrange sudden phone calls that his grandmother had just died. Sometimes his dates had grandmothers that died instead. Then he met Cyndy – pretty, funny, sexy – and on their third date she invited him to stay the night. But in the bedroom he held her and nothing happened. The part of him that should have been excited was limp and the part of him that should have been ecstatic was embarrassed. She had been very kind and said that it didn't really matter. She'd talk to him again in a few days' time. He never heard from her again.

And if his body had turned against him then so too did his job. Because it was only after that disastrous evening he discovered that Cyndy had a brother and he worked for the same newspaper. And suddenly everyone knew. The women were very nice, one or two even offered to 'help him out', but the men thought it was the funniest thing ever and every day the internal post delivered pornographic magazines, DVDs with handwritten labels and strange herbal tablets. One or two of the men had offered to 'help him out' as well.

A scream from outside interrupted a too-vivid flashback of fending off Greg from the art department. Matthew pulled aside the net curtains and looked down to the sodium-lit street. The car across the road was long and black and the face of the woman bent over its bonnet stood out very clearly. Her mouth was open in a perfect O of either passion or pain. Her dress was pulled up over her hips and the man standing behind her was jackhammering away like a rabbit. She screamed again. Definitely not passion. Matthew lunged for the phone, but before he could dial the first nine there was the screech of tyres and blue strobe lights swept the ceiling. He dropped the phone and dashed back to the window. A police van had skewed to a halt across the front of the long black car. Both doors were already open and two policemen had Jackhammer Man trapped between them. One of the policemen said something, but he never even looked around. Both policemen did something complicated with one hand and they both had gleaming three-foot batons. The first blow caught Jackhammer Man across the shoulders with a dull, heavy sound. The second blow landed with a brittle, crunching sound as he fell away from the woman. Then the police literally threw him into the back of the van. He was at least six feet tall and built to scale but the police simply picked him up at collar and waist, swung once and threw him headfirst into the back of the van. There was a wet sound as he disappeared. Both police repeated the complicated motion and their batons disappeared. One bent to look at the woman slowly sliding off the car bonnet and then both held her and threw her into the back of the van. The van pulled away in a haze of tyre smoke and Matthew watched it take the corner, backend wagging like a dog. Then the street was empty again.

Matthew watched the spot where the van had disappeared. The TV had shown him lots of reasons for what he had just seen, but none of those programmes finished with the police putting both assailant and victim together in the back of a police van.

He dropped the curtain and began the much more important job of seeing how much more beer he could drink before falling asleep. Between his second and third can he owlishly examined the stack of business cards he had offered to the PC. They looked perfectly clear to him. The top one must have been smudged in his pocket and he made a mental note to buy a case.

Chapter Two
Interlude, Australia

"Unexpected item in bagging area."

Lucas swore at the self-service till and put the beer back in his shopping basket.

"Item removed from bagging area. Replace item in bagging area."

Lucas swung the pack at the display. The screen exploded in a spray of foam and shards of plastic. He was instantly horrified; he'd never meant to do that. They'd call the police. His name would be in the papers.

A hand grabbed his shoulder.

"What are you doing? Stop that!"

He brought his elbow back as hard as possible and someone screamed in his ear. He turned and swung his fist into the stomach of a young checkout assistant. She stumbled back, doubled over in agony. He felt sick; he'd never punched anyone since school and now he'd hit a woman in public.

The assistant tripped over a plastic bag and fell backwards. He saw a glimpse of white panties and was instantly hard. He pulled his trousers down over a rock-hard erection and stepped out of them. A tin of peas hit him between the eyes and blood sprayed his cheek. He looked around, realised that he was the centre of a circle of horrified attention and his erection promptly disappeared. He felt that he was losing his mind, perhaps someone had laced his tea, and instantly he was angry. He'd go back to work and find out who they were. He'd smash faces and hurt them until he knew.

He grabbed his trousers for the car keys there and ran. Between Customer Services and the cigarette desk he realised the absurdly of the situation. A half-dressed, middle-aged man running through a supermarket clutching his trousers. He stopped running and waited for security. The doctors would agree that it was a mental breakdown and he would be a soon-forgotten half inch on the front page. He'd take the pills they gave him and confess everything in group therapy.

Through the supermarket's floor-to-ceiling windows he saw a red Audi pulling out from its parking space and for just a second its driver made eye contact. And Lucas just knew that he was laughing at the fat old man standing there without his trousers. He was probably having a good laugh at the size of his manhood, but he'd show him. He'd teach him what respect meant.

Lucas charged through the supermarket doors and a white van doing sixty across the car park hit him head on and threw him through the windscreen of a Jaguar. His last thought was *Nice seats*.

Chapter Three
Interlude, New York

The meeting room was too warm and the hum of the projector almost hypnotic. David rested his head on his hand and started another doodle. Barnaby clicked the remote and the PowerPoint slide on the screen swirled like water draining away and was replaced by a 3D bar chart with tiny unreadable labels.

"And in slide thirty-three you can clearly see the relationship between the increased volume of service desk calls and the rollout of service pack four. There have been multiple issues around end user experience and slow performance. David, this is your area."

David sat bolt upright, suddenly fully awake. Barnaby pointed an accusing finger at him.

"These issues are the responsibility of your group and should have been addressed during ITC testing as they are wholly preventable. What can you bring to this meeting to reassure us that you have an action plan in place?"

David felt the blood pounding in his head. His hands closed into fists. All he could see was Barnaby's fat, self-satisfied face. He stood up so suddenly that his chair flew out behind him and lunged across the table. His elbow caught the projector and his face was briefly painted in multi-coloured bars. He clawed for Barnaby's throat and his momentum carried them both to the floor. He sat astride Barnaby's expansive stomach, lifted the projector with both hands and smashed it down on his face.

A scream from behind him made him look up. David saw pale, shocked faces staring at him as they fought to get out of the room. He stood up, swung the window open and dived out all in one continuous motion. He fell for twelve seconds and screamed all the way down.

Chapter Four
Interlude, Buenos Aires

Carlo swerved and hit the traffic warden at eighty. He skewed to a halt in a cloud of tyre smoke and looked back at the broken figure on the pavement. He undid his seatbelt and accelerated towards the solid brick walls of the library. The fireball was visible all over town.

Chapter Five
Office

In the morning, Matthew felt like crap. Despite the two paracetamol and half a pint of water he'd taken before bed his head pulsed slowly and his mouth felt furry, as if it had begun to moult overnight. He took another two paracetamol and stood under an ice-cold shower for as long as he could bear. It didn't really help. When he closed his front door behind him everything seemed too bright and he felt vaguely sick.

The streets were still completely empty, but this at least was an expected emptiness. Matthew had long ago realised that most people in the area worked to a different clock, one where mornings did not exist.

The sun was out and he started to feel human again as he walked to the underground station. He hummed a few words of the song that had been on the radio as he left the flat and, after a few minutes, he felt almost happy, as if he had taken the first step to moving on with his life. He started down the stairs to the station but then stopped as if he had walked into a wall.

He had told himself that what had happened at the theatre and afterward was perfectly explainable, if only he could find the key. But this was beyond explanation. Matthew took an unwilling step forward. In a corner, litter danced to a breath of air coming up from the escalators. To his right, a torn poster waved excitedly but the great hall that should have been bursting with people pushing to make a nine o'clock start was completely empty. The clock overhead ticked off another minute while Matthew looked around hopefully. Very slowly, he turned back to the stairs that would lead to normality. Then he turned back to the moving band of the escalators like a weathervane driven by indecision. More than anything he wanted to go home and phone in sick. No one would really miss him. He could spend the day watching daytime TV and tomorrow would be different.

The low roar of a train arriving echoed across the hall and Matthew squared his shoulders and walked quickly to the escalators. He told himself that even this was somehow explainable – a local business had declared an unexpected holiday or a connecting line was down and lots of people had walked to the next station – and as long as he carried on as normal the world would fall into place around him.

There was a train waiting on the platform and that at least was satisfyingly normal. It was half-filled with other commuters either slumped over, reading the paper or eyes closed with headphones blocking out the world. One jeans and T-shirt-clad teenager was so engrossed in a technical-looking manual that he never looked up. It must have been a very good book; he was still reading the same page when Matthew left the train.

When he had got the job with *The Bulletin* he had walked the short distance from the underground station, gawking at each multi-storey eruption of glass and steel, wondering what took place behind those innocent brass plates and who might be looking down on him, knowing that they controlled the smallest possible aspect of his life. This morning, he kept his head down and walked as quickly as possible.

"Morning, sir." The office security guard snapped off a very smart salute, slightly spoilt by the fact that he was wearing a pink, glittery T-Shirt with the message *Dirty Bitch*. Matthew thought it was probably some charity thing. Perhaps he'd missed the memo.

A misspelt sign informed him that the lifts were 'out of odour' and his head pulsed with each step to the second floor.

His office was a square, open-plan space, divided by waist-high partitions into a corporate cubicle farm. As the lowest of the low, his desk was at the exact centre of the office, the maximum possible distance from any natural light and completely anonymous. Except this morning, because this morning it was easy to see which desk was his. It was the one with a crowd gathered around it. He froze the moment he saw the reception committee, but that was too late and a chorus of cheers broke out.

"Come on in! Don't be shy! This is your big moment. Give him a big hand."

And they did. Helping hands dragged him forward while Carl, his cubical neighbour, stood on a chair and waved his hands.

"Ahem! It falls upon me to welcome our conquering hero. Last night you faced one of nature's most deadly predators and as a mark of respect a special edition of the paper has been printed just for you. Gentlemen, show our mighty hunter his prize."

The crowd around his desk open up and Matthew saw the mock-up of a front page tacked above his desk. Under a headline *Matthew Spies Forgotten Species* was a photo of him staring open-mouthed at the crotch of the half-naked woman next to him.

"We thought you might have forgotten what one looks like. So we wanted to preserve the memory just for you."

Matthew looked around at his waiting audience. He could either rip down the page and tell them to bugger off or he could join in the joke at his expense. Everyone looked slightly flushed, their smiles too wide, their applause uncoordinated. If it had been later in the day he'd have said they had been in the pub. It was their smiles that made the decision for him.

"Gentlemen, I thank you for the honour and you must know ..." He paused for dramatic effect. "... that I rose to the occasion!"

The applause went on for a lot longer than he had expected and hands slapped him on the back as the crowd broke up. As soon as their attention was diverted he'd rip the loathsome thing down. Not only was it far too graphic to have in a public area, but it made him look like some sort of pervert.

Philip's arrival gave him a chance to slip away from the crowd. He was Matthew's line manager and ruled the office like his own little kingdom. On Matthew's first day he had introduced himself as tough but fair, but since then Matthew had only ever seen tough. Normally so precise about everything, Philip was not only late, but he looked a mess. As ever, he wore a three-piece suit, but the jacket and waistcoat were blue pinstripe and the trousers black. His shirt was done up wrong and one unmatched buttonhole flapped open every time he moved.

"Sorry about the fuss. Some of the office wanted to remind me about last night," Matthew said.

"Night! Yes! Last night!" As Philip took his jacket off it got caught on something and he flailed ineffectively until Matthew helped.

"Should I write up my account of what happened? Might make a nice human interest story in the style section."

"Section! Yes, write it up. Send it to … when it's done." Philip sounded strangely vague and confused as if he were still waking up. Perhaps he was. He didn't seem to have shaved. He lowered himself into his padded, leather chair in slow motion and Matthew wondered if he'd had too much to drink last night. It would explain a lot of things.

The crowd around Matthew's desk had finally dispersed and he edged back towards it. "I'll make a start then."

"Then!" Philip turned towards his monitor and ignored Matthew completely. This was a new side to Philip that Matthew had never seen before. Normally Philip's idea of scheduling was to give him three pieces of work and immediately demand to know why none of them were complete. Whatever he had been doing it must have been a hell of a night.

***

30

The article took shape slowly. Matthew had decided to frame it as a sad indictment of NHS cuts that proper support was not given to those in maximal need. He was just looking up the latest figures for mental health funding when someone swore very loudly and profusely behind him.

"Stupid computers!" Freddy stood up from his desk and kicked something under it. "Stupid, buggering, useless, fricking machines!" He punctuated each word with another kick. The first kick had been a dull thud; by the time he reached 'machines' the sound had become the loose jangling sound of broken components in a tin box. "Bugger this for a game of soldiers; I'm going down the pub. Anyone else coming?"

There was a brief pause, an exchange of glances and then most of the office followed him out of the room. And Philip, master of his domain, did nothing. That meant whatever he was so intent on was more important than a few people going to the pub early. That meant big, corporate, something so vital that it had kept him up all night working on Gantt charts and manpower projections. The possibilities were endless. Someone was buying us out. We were buying someone else. All their jobs were being outsourced to India.

Matthew casually angled his monitor so that Philip couldn't see what he was looking at and began to search the internet. If he was going to be looking for a job in a few months' time he needed a head start before the more experienced reporters started looking.

The internet was weird.

Lots of sites were either down or just strange. According to *The New York Times*, the president was a 'big ol' poopy head'. An article in *The Guardian* started with *The failure of neoliberal laissez-faire economic policy* and ended with a hundred-line poem that tried to rhyme 'bollocks' with 'hydraulics' and 'Thatcher' with 'chancer'.

Matthew sat back in his seat so he could simultaneously watch Philip and the porn video that was the only thing available on the Forbes website. The scene was shot in an office very like this and he was sure he recognised the focus of a particularly inventive threesome from corporate presentations.

The internet was weird, but did that really mean anything? Computer viruses appeared at exponential rates. Every day there was another threat that was worse than anything ever seen before. This time some teenage hacker from China had just been more successful, but there was nothing about *The Bulletin*. That left only one way to find out what was so important that Philip had barely looked up all morning. Matthew checked the time, 12.15 p.m.; it was a plausible excuse. All he needed to do was look at the right point.

He stood up, theatrically stretching his back as he walked towards Philip's desk. "I'm just going to get a sandwich. Do you want anything?"

"Thing?" Philip said slowly, never looking away from his monitor. "No."

"Okay, see you in a minute." And then the obvious route to the door was past Philip's desk. Matthew took three steps and then looked over his shoulder to see the vitally important documents Philip had been working on all morning. And all there was on Philip's screen was the screensaver with its corporate logo bouncing slowly from edge to edge. No PowerPoint presentations. No multi-tabbed Excel spreadsheets. Just the endlessly repeated motion designed to stop screen burn on their old-fashioned CRT monitors.

Matthew stopped as abruptly as if he had walked into a wall and turned back to Philip's desk, expecting any moment that he would spin round, shout, "Gotcha!" and issue a formal warning. But his head continued its tiny corrections to track the onscreen motion as if it were the only thing in the world.

Matthew took another step back to Philip's desk and his foot caught a carelessly placed bin with a dull gong-like noise. Philip's head twitched the slightest possible amount and resumed its hypnotic tracking of the bouncing logo. Matthew had the horrible feeling that he could tap him on the shoulder with no effect, that he could pull Philip's chair away from the desk and he would just turn to see the monitor.

Matthew turned away so quickly that the bin went flying across the room. He'd always thought Philip was a bit tightly wound, ready to jump at the slightest event. Well now one of his cogs had stripped its gears and was out of the box. All his paddles were not in the water. He'd had a breakdown. Perhaps it would turn out that there was a drugs problem or he was unsure of his sexuality, but for now it was Matthew's problem and he didn't want it. If he was the one to contact HR then there would be questions. What had he been doing all morning? Why hadn't he noticed before that Philip was having a breakdown? But on the other hand he could casually drop into conversation that while everyone else was at the pub he'd been working on an important article when he realised that something was very wrong with poor old Philip.

By the time he reached the street he had made his decision (someone immediately walked into him and told him to fuck off, but this was London; it was nearly expected behaviour). He'd get a sandwich and if Philip was still catatonic when he got back to the office, he'd make the phone call and be the hero of the hour. It might do him some good at pay review time.

The pub on the corner was doing a roaring trade with a crowd spilling out to the pavement, but, amazingly enough, there was no queue outside the deli across the road. He'd order his usual beef and horseradish on white and be back at work in a few minutes, ready to play either concerned bystander or hero of the hour.

A couple kissing each other with enthusiasm moved reluctantly out of the way as he crossed the street and Matthew saw inside the sandwich shop. The counter was thick with customers waving money at besieged assistants, screaming at them to take their order, pounding on the counter to speed things up. More people flooded into the shop, pushing Matthew into the sea of madness. Elbows jabbed him in the ribs, feet crushed him underfoot. A hand fumbled at his crotch, grinding his testacies together. There was the sound of breaking glass and someone screamed. The crowd swept Matthew inexorably towards to a window. His feet scrabbled on broken glass and the crush of the crowd abruptly disappeared. He backed away from the shattered window of the sandwich shop using a lamppost then a padlocked bicycle to stay on his feet. A woman, impaled on the razor sharp jags of glass left in the window, jerked a few more times and spurts of arterial blood wrote across the pavement. A pretty woman scooped up a sandwich with a look of extreme cunning, turned away and a smartly suited businessman stuck a shard of glass into her throat, pulled the sandwich from her twitching hands and walked calmly away.

Matthew looked up the street. The pub on the corner was the centre of a mob of people kicking, gouging and biting each other to get to the bar. An upstairs window shattered and a stream of people fell twenty feet to the hard concrete pavement. The courting couple lay in the middle of the junction having loud and enthusiastic sex, the crowd around them either openly masturbating or dropping to the ground in groupings of naked limbs.

Matthew backed away from the madness, trying not to look but unable to stop his eyes capturing small events: the woman slashing at her face with a piece of glass; the man roaring like a bull and repeatedly smashing his head into a brick wall. He then realised that he was clutching the access card that opened the office turnstiles so tightly that its edges were cutting his hand. The turnstiles were a floor-to-ceiling revolving door made from very solid steel bars that had been installed during a series of terrorist attacks. Only authorised card holders could enter the building. He was an authorised card holder. He could get into the building. The maniacs on the street could not. He could wait there ("Hide there," a small voice said) until the riot police turned up with their water cannons and CS gas. They were probably on their way already.

A hand gripped his shoulder and pulled him back. He lashed out, felt something crunch and ran. Hands reached out to him, some just touching him, some holding him for a second before he could break free. A genial old man with white hair held out his arms wide and Matthew ran straight into them.

"You think you're smart! So fucking smart! I'll show you!" Matthew brought his knee up as hard as possible, felt vulnerable flesh pulp and the old man jack-knifed over to be sick.

The office doors began to slide open automatically when he was a few feet away and Matthew pushed them further apart until he could slip through. The reception area was brightly lit, dressed with vases of real flowers that looked artificial, and was completely empty. There was no one here having sex or waiting to attack him. His hand shook so much that the card reader didn't recognise his presence and the steel bars of the turnstile remained locked in place. Using both hands, he pressed card to reader until he felt that the plastic would break and his hands would slip into fragile circuit boards. The click as the turnstile unlocked was very quiet. The bars revolved and Matthew fell to the floor inside.

He lay there for what seemed a very long time, watching the madness outside with no more understanding than a camera. People ran, but from what or to what he could not see. A man howling like a wolf left bloody footprints behind him. The glass doors shook with an almost musical note as someone ran full pelt into them, bounced back and disappeared from sight.

Matthew walked back on his elbows until he was propped up against the wall. The glowing digits of the LED clock over the turnstiles made no sense at all and he read them twice until he was sure. It was 12.35 p.m., just twenty minutes since he had left the office and walked into an insane asylum. Another thump on the glass doors made him look up, but he was safe here. They were outside. All he had to do was wait until the emergency services restored order.

And then he looked up. Because not all of them were outside. He had left Philip hypnotically watching the screensaver on his monitor. He had been passive then, but perhaps the smartly dressed businessman had been passive just before he put a shard of glass into the woman's throat. Matthew held his breath, trying to hear small office sounds above the rhythmic whoosh of his pulse, ready to hear footsteps closing on him. He looked from the certainty outside to the possibility above and his mind took the possibility and spun it into a widescreen epic of an army of maniacs looking questioningly in his direction. Soon they would fill the stairwells in a wave that would rip him apart.

He edged closer to the turnstiles, closer to the known madness. But what if he were safe here and was about to run screaming from an empty office block?

12.45 p.m. He would very quietly go upstairs and prove to himself that Philip was still watching

37

the simple shape on his monitor and that they were alone in the building. And if not, then the fire extinguisher he unclipped from the wall felt comfortingly solid. It would make an excellent weapon.

Matthew edged closer to the stairs and the sound of his shoes on the marble floor was far too loud. Each step shouted out, 'Here I am! Come and get me!' He imagined heads triangulating his position, lining up in wait for him. He left his shoes lined-up neatly at the bottom of the stairs. His feet slipped on the smooth marble, but now each step was completely soundless.

At the first landing he stopped, looked up and down and, most importantly, listened carefully, expecting to hear the tramp of feet closing in on him – but there was only silence. On the second landing he paused and listened. By the third landing he knew Philip would still be hypnotically watching his monitor, no more aware of what was happening around him than the photocopier.

Matthew began to feel rather silly walking around in his stocking feet. He strode confidently into his office and skidded to a halt when he saw that Philip's chair was empty. He took another step towards Philip's chair and realised that he had certainly gone, but he had left something behind. He told himself that the dark patch on the padded seat was just shadow, but the ammonia tang in the air told him the truth. Philip had sat watching the screensaver until he had wet himself.

Matthew backed away, trying to link the sharp, quick-witted Philip, who had sarcastically drilled into him the importance of the Oxford comma, to the blank-faced dummy he had seen before. Then the other, much more important question occurred to him: What had happened to Philip? If the need to use the toilet hadn't moved him, then what had?

Matthew looked back towards the entrance and a crunching blow from behind forced his thighs against the top of Philip's desk. A forearm slipped under his chin and pulled back hard. He tried to breathe but couldn't. He pulled at the forearm but it didn't move. He whipped his hand back over his head, but the hand that should have held the solid mass of the fire extinguisher held nothing at all now. He jerked both elbows back. There was a solid impact, a grunt from behind, but the forearm only tightened against his throat. Lungs pumping uselessly, he fought for breath, the room pulsing with each heartbeat. He thrashed wildly, clawing, kicking – anything for air. His knee thudded into the desk, pushing him off-balance and the weight of his attacker pulled them both down. They landed with a heavy thud that snapped Matthew's teeth together, but the arm around his neck went loose and he rolled away from under it.

Climbing to his feet, he pulled in great lungfuls of beautifully cool air. From behind he heard a groan and looked back. Two hours ago, Carl had been the cheerleader for his big welcome; now, he was snarling like a wild animal, clawing at the floor with broken fingernails to get to him.

Matthew turned away and a hand gripped his ankle, pulling him back. He grabbed the handle on a filing cabinet that rocked wildly as Carl reeled him in. The grip on his ankle disappeared, but was instantly replaced by two hands on his belt pulling him down, pulling the filing cabinet over. Carl pulled again and 400 pounds of third-quarter expense reports slammed down on his head. The crashing sound filled the room, but didn't go away. The wet sound of metal on flesh was replaced by familiar sounds: doors opening, footsteps on stairs. Matthew sprinted towards the stairwell. From above, he heard wolf-like howling. All the people he had so foolishly thought were outside were inside as well.

He bounded down the stairs, barely touching each step, and passed his shoes at the bottom. He covered the distance to the turnstiles in one galvanic jump, repeatedly pressing the release button until the gate unlocked, and he pushed his way through and ran.

The concrete pavement was cold and strangely inflexible under his stocking feet. His jacket flapped behind him like damaged wings. The entrance to the underground was just fifty yards in front of him and he kept on running right past it. There was no way that he was going to exchange one confined space for another.

Ahead of him, two men moved to block his path and Matthew dropped his shoulder and aimed for the small gap between them. There was a bone-crunching impact and they flew apart like same pole magnets repelling each other.

At the corner, Matthew turned left and was gone.

Chapter Six
Running

After his initial headlong flight, Matthew settled into a fast jog and, for the first time, was pleased that Kirsten had dragged him to those interminable circuits of the park. To begin with, running in stocking feet was just strange. Then it hurt. Each footfall was a solid impact on the pavement, then a grinding sensation as the ball of his foot rolled over unforgiving concrete, and finally a blissful moment as he lifted his foot ready for the next step.

London streets acquired a new topology that he had never appreciated before. Pavements were like hard-packed sand to run on: smooth and gritty – except for the evidence of dogs that he came to hate. But crossing roads was an exercise in pain. The high-friction surface that was so good for cars was like stepping onto a thousand tin tacks. A traffic island in the middle of the road was a brief respite from pain.

The madness that he had found outside the office seemed to be slowly following him like a reluctant child behind its parents. As he crossed Tottenham Court Road a black taxi suddenly changed direction to run him over, missed and hit a lamppost in an explosion of abuse and steam. As he passed the sex shops on Brewer Street a car tried to leave its parking space at the side of the street by alternately ramming the car in front and then behind. The front of the car hissed steam and at the back the boot had strung open and glossy magazines showing pert, thirty-year-old schoolgirls littered the street. But the driver's expression was completely neutral, as if he were doing nothing more than listening to the radio.

Very slowly, two sharp blades of pain began to slide under Matthew's ribs. If Kirsten were here she would have called it 'just a stitch' and goosed him along until the pain passed. But now the pain from his feet began to merge with the pain over his hips and his fast jog became a slow jog, became walking. He rested for a moment on the lip of a concrete flower planter and looked around. The streets here were very quiet, but judging by the expensive parked cars and the trendy mews houses, this was Mayfair where quiet was the norm.

He stood up and staggered a few steps on legs that were just pillars of pain. For a moment he considered just hiding in a quiet corner, but any house that didn't have a pedigree, but very large, Doberman would be sure to have a matching pair of Purdey and Purdey shotguns that would blow a very large hole in him.

The scream of an over-revved engine brought his head around. The low-slung, shark-like profile of a high-performance car shot across the end of the road and a second later there was the squeal of tyres and the crunch of metal on metal. Matthew discovered he could run just a few more steps. He looked around the corner and stopped, trying to put it all together. On his right, the back of a Porsche stuck out from the glittering remains of a shop window. But on his left, a much smaller convertible was bent into an almost U-shape. It was only the skid marks on the road that filled in the blanks. The

Porsche had tried to take the corner far too fast, hit the convertible and bounced off into the shop.

Flames began to lick out from under the Porsche. Matthew saw something move under the grey curtains of its deflated airbags and realised that its driver was still alive. But not for long.

He turned away. The Porsche had been driven like a maniac. Its driver was probably just another manic who'd sooner cut his throat than thank him. But then he turned back, because it was that word – probably. What if the driver had been just trying to escape the madness behind him? Just like him in fact. Leaving the driver to burn to death would be a horrible way to die. Matthew looked across the road at the spreading pool under the convertible. And if the fire didn't kill him, the moment a spark reached the leaking petrol, the explosion certainly would.

The fire was still small and only on the left of the Porsche. He might have only a few minutes. Before he could reconsider, he scrambled up a heap of blocks that must have been a low, decorative wall in front of the shop. Most of the glass had been pushed in, so instead of climbing over razor-sharp edges he only had to endure bare feet on broken brick. There was a gap between the edge of the window and crumpled Italian coachwork so narrow that he had to turn sideways to squeeze through it. The inside of the shop was thick with the scent of flowers and a display of roses was embedded in the Porsche's windscreen. Matthew pulled at its door handle. It didn't move. Bracing himself with one foot on the car's body, he tried again and the door grated open an inch. The face of the car's driver pushed aside deflated airbags. Matthew saw his lips move but all he could hear was collapsing masonry.

"It's stuck! Push!" he shouted.

No indication that the driver had heard him, but the head disappeared and the door began to shudder from repeated blows from inside. The door jerked open another inch. Matthew pulled the handle again, strained until he saw bright flashes of light and the door popped open.

The driver was a large, fleshy man who seemed origami-folded behind the Porsche's black, leather steering wheel. Matthew grabbed a sleeve and pulled. He felt stiches part and then he popped out like a cork from a bottle. Flames began to pour out from under the car and Matthew towed the driver through the gap between the edge of the window and out of the shop. The moment they were a safe distance away, Matthew released him.

The driver was a tall, heavyset man wearing carefully faded, blue jeans stretched over a soft pillow stomach with a crisp, white shirt ripped at one shoulder. His shoes were expensive-looking trainers that looked too pristine to have ever trained. His watch was a half-pound lump of stainless steel that probably had enough dials to tell the time in three countries and the weather forecast in two. He looked like the sort of man that might have owned the Porsche. Perhaps he was just somebody trying to escape. He looked normal enough. But Matthew couldn't forget that the businessman had looked completely normal just before he pushed a glass shard into a woman's throat.

Something in the burning shop popped and a fat spark landed on the torn fabric at the driver's shoulder.

"Watch out!" Matthew said. "On your shoulder."

The driver didn't look at Matthew, didn't look at the haze of smoke rising from his shoulder. He looked at the car, at Matthew, up the street and back to Matthew. "This is all your fault," he said. "You distracted me. Look at the car. It'll never be the same again. The shop's ruined. It had nice flowers. It's cold out here. I should have worn a jacket. I'm hungry. Why haven't you got any shoes on? You tore my shirt pulling me out."

And while Matthew was trying to process that stream of consciousness, the driver waded in. He pulled Matthew close and held him for a roundhouse punch that took his breath away. Matthew tried to bring his knee up but the driver knew that move and his thigh was already turned in to protect him. The driver swung again and Matthew tasted blood. He flailed uselessly against the grip holding him, stopped fighting and let the driver pull him close. He held both of the driver's shoulders as if he were going to kiss him on the cheek, pushed forward off his back foot and snapped the dome of his forehead down onto the tip of the driver's nose. A bolt of pain slammed into Matthew's head. He reeled back, trying to hold a head together that felt as if it were exploding like an over-inflated balloon. There was something soft in his hand and he forced his eyes open, just knowing that he would be holding a handful of grey brain tissue that had leaked from the crack in his skull.

His eyes refused to focus; he saw everything double. He closed and opened them several times until he could see a long strip of fabric in his hand. A moan brought his head up. The driver was sat on the ground with his feet splayed out in front of him like a toddler. Both hands were clasped to his face with blood spurting between spread fingers. There was something wrong with his left arm and for a horrified second Matthew thought he had ripped his arm away like a child's toy. But the driver was certainly holding his face with two hands and Matthew realised that he had just finished ripping his sleeve away from the shoulder. He started to drop it as the driver waded back in and he flicked it towards him like cracking a whip. The ragged end of the sleeve was already smouldering and it glowed as it snapped. The driver dropped back, actually foaming at the mouth now, ducked left and came in again. Matthew cracked the sleeve and this time he left a shower of sparks behind like a circus showman cracking an electric whip.

Matthew looked behind him as he backed across the street. The corner was only a few feet away. All he had to do was get a bit of space between them and then he could run. He looked back just in time to see the driver snap out his arm and a brick caught him under the ribs. Everything went grey and he stumbled back. The driver charged in and Matthew only just managed to flick the burning end of the sleeve in his face to drive him back. He crouched down and reached for another brick, and when he found it he laughed hysterically. Matthew realised that he didn't have time to reach the corner. Didn't have any time at all. The driver's arm snapped out, there was a flash of pain on the left side of Matthew's head and he was briefly deaf on one side. He changed direction, sliding sideways now, constantly checking distances and angles. The driver brought up his arm to pitch again, Matthew flicked the sleeve and it flew from his grasp and landed behind him.

Matthew dived into the shelter of a concrete planter as the driver came forward. There was a moment when he thought that Hollywood had lied to him. Then there was a long foghorn sound and suddenly it was much too hot. He brought his hands up over his face and felt exposed skin blister. The ground hummed under him like a jet engine and just as suddenly the heat went away.

Matthew peered over the edge of the planter, ready to drop back into cover. The driver lay in the middle of the road and for a moment Matthew thought he'd missed. Below the waist, the driver was untouched, but everything above that was just charred meat. His ears and broken nose had melted away. His hands raised, as if in surrender, were just stumps. Smoke poured off him and there was a smell like a burnt Sunday joint. The thought made Matthew's stomach roll.

Matthew watched him for a very long time to make absolutely sure he wasn't going to move then stood up and saw what he had made. The Porsche, and the shop it was embedded in, was an inferno and a line of flame, like a single tyre track from *Back to the Future*, led back to the convertible. He guessed that when he had thrown the burning sleeve into the petrol leaking from the convertible the fire hadn't climbed back into its fuel tank as he'd expected. Instead, the remaining petrol had boiled, forcing a jet of petrol vapour through the crack in its petrol tank. But it hadn't remained vapour for very long. He'd made the world's largest flamethrower and the driver had been right at the edge of it.

Matthew hobbled over to the man he had killed and tried to feel something. The films that had shown him the head-butt and the explosive power of petrol had said that this was the point for music – something poignant to tug at the heart strings. Until today the only dead people he had ever seen were his mum and dad, but he had known them before they went away. There had been a connection to the shells they had left behind. All he had seen of the driver was an angry psychopath who would have broken every bone in his body and laughed all the time. As much as he tried, he couldn't feel grief or even guilt. After everything that had happened today he just felt empty. Perhaps he'd dream about the man in the Porsche but right now he had a long way to get home. He limped away on feet that complained about each of the blocks he had scrambled over to get to the Porsche, and stopped and looked back at the driver. His mum had always said 'waste not want not'.

Chapter Seven
Ladbroke Road Station

The tube station entrance was a dark void between a mobile phone shop and a newsagent, and it looked completely normal. Matthew had run until his lungs seemed filled with razor blades and his new trainers circlets of pain around his ankles. Run until he could run no more. And then he had seen the tube station. He had watched from behind a dumpster that reeked of fish until his heartbeat was nearly normal and the first thing he noticed was how ordinary it looked. Commuters hurried home. Lost tourists gathered around the maps like flocking birds. The second thing he saw was the white on blue sign above the stairs leading down to the station. Ladbroke Road Station. He had run clear across the centre of the city. Perhaps he had run far enough to leave the epicentre of the madness behind.

A week ago, the streets around his office had been taken over by a protest against globalisation and Matthew had watched police battle anarchists from the safety of the second floor. Perhaps they had been disappointed by the lack of cultural change and had set off an LSD bomb outside the Bank of England, or an infiltrator had topped up the water coolers with ecstasy. But tomorrow they would be the subject of a countrywide manhunt and all the people he had seen making love in the streets would be feeling very foolish, and very sore. The police would have cleared the streets and the TV outside broadcast units would be settling like flies. He could get a train here and ride home in perfect safety in time to watch the rolling news reports on the search for the perpetrators.

Coming out from behind the dumpster was the single hardest thing he had ever done. After so long hiding and running, being out in the open felt vulnerable, exposed. As if he had stepped out on the stage and felt the pressure of thousands of eyes on him. He took two steps and realised that he could feel the magnetic attraction of the dumpster waiting to pull him back to safety. He waited for the surge in the crowd, as ordinary people became something monstrous, and realised that no one was paying him any attention. Across the street the businessman that could have been carrying a glass dagger folded away his copy of *The Times* and stepped into the entrance to the underground. A black cab dropped off a passenger and then failed to try to run him over as it pulled away. Everything was so normal, mundane even, and Matthew loved every boring minute.

Inside the station, turnstiles clattered as commuters swiped their Oyster cards and pushed their way through to the escalators. Lost tourists queued for advice and tickets. Matthew hung off to one side, apparently studying a map of Zone One, looking for confirmation that he wasn't about to step into the chaos he had seen outside his office.

Some of the people were oddly dressed; a dumpy woman wearing a bikini top with a knee-length skirt swiped through in front of a teenager wearing much too small Captain Kremmen pyjamas. At the ticket window a tattooed Rasta seemed unbothered by the fact that he was wearing only underpants below the waist.

Matthew watched the crowd and saw more strangeness, but everybody was quiet, nobody was fighting or fucking, and after all, didn't the magazines keep saying that conventional dress sense was dead?

He waited for a break in the stream of people, pressed his card to the reader and walked quickly to the escalators. The platform was surprisingly quiet for a Thursday night and he moved quickly away from the stairs. Normally, he would have waited for a train with toes ready on the yellow warning line, but that was before he had seen a businessman put a shard of glass into someone's throat for a sandwich.

The noticeboard lit up with a message. *Next train in five minutes.* Everything was so normal, so ordinary.

A gabble of overlapping voices from the escalators grew louder and together shouted, "WAAAHAAAYYYY!" The football cheer echoed down the platform and Matthew pushed himself back into the curved wall and snapped his head around so quickly that tendons at the base of his neck twinged. A pack of teenage boys flooded onto the platform and moved to the opposite end. They all looked as if they had been in the pub and had drunk just enough to be happy, which was perfectly normal for a night out in London. One of the first things Matthew had learnt in London was the importance of looking out for pools of vomit any night after nine.

Like most people under the age of nineteen, the group could only communicate by shouting at each other and Matthew soon learnt who Staci was seeing and why Mick was a tosser. The sheer normality of their chatter was relaxing and Matthew let himself look away.

The message on the board changed to *Next train in two minutes* and he waited for the piston of air pushed along by the train's arrival. It was still fairly quiet, there should be plenty of free seats, but after what he had seen today he would feel a lot happier standing by the door. Just in case.

"Tobie, Tobie, TOBIE!" The chant from the other end of the platform made him look idly around. For a moment all he could see was a tight cluster of teenagers. Then one of them stepped back, arm raised, camera in hand, and Matthew saw the focus of their attention. He was dressed in the uniform of youth, low-slung baggy jeans, tank top, and was standing with only his heels on the platform, urinating down onto the tracks.

"Higher, higher, HIGHER!"

Tobie stuck his tongue at the cameras around him, but lifted his stream higher, the arc of fluid reaching out to the third rail live with 400 volts. There was a loud crack of an invisible whip, Tobie flew away from the tracks, bounced back from the wall and landed on his back. Smoke billowed up from his charred groin and the air was thick with the smell of burning flesh. His friends seemed confused by his sudden disappearance. Looking down at the spot where he had been standing, looking each way down the tunnel and only then behind them. They watched the small flames begin to take hold around Tobie's crotch and then burst into laughter.

"Wimp!"

And then every member of the group took their position at the edge of the platform, unzipped their flies and began to lift their own streams towards the third rail.

Matthew sprang away from the platform wall as if ejected from a moving vehicle, pushed past the open-mouthed statues watching the teenagers and out towards the escalators. Loud snaps followed him as he ran up the stairs. The smell of burning flesh was thick like a blanket.

At the line of turnstiles he put a hand down on a card reader and clumsily pivoted over the barrier. Behind him someone shouted. He didn't stop. The cool air outside was blissfully clean. He paused briefly to be sick and then set off running.

***

Matthew unlocked his front door and fell through it. He lay there passively watching the pattern of shadow that grew and shrank in time to the sound of cars driven far too fast. He was bone tired even though he had spent as much time hiding as running. He had lost his jacket halfway down Praed Street when a man had snuck up behind him, slashed the back of it from hem to collar, held each sleeve and ran away laughing hysterically. His shoes were covered with indescribable filth, or at least filth he didn't want to describe, from the crazies that used the street as their toilet without breaking step. But the damage outside was purely superficial; the jacket was a cheap thing from Primark and the shoes had, after all, been free. The real damage was inside. He had walked through a city tearing itself apart. A city populated only by the mad.

Learning to distinguish between two very different types of insanity had been a very sharp learning curve. The dangerous ones were very quick and, like the Porsche driver, did terrible things without a second thought. Ready to hug one moment and kill the next, but they were easily distracted and lost interest in anything that took more than a few minutes. But the disturbing ones were the ones like Philip. They moved very slowly as if underwater. They stopped at pedestrian crossings, smiled and nodded but whatever they smiled and nodded at was only visible to them.

He had wondered briefly if they were really two separate groups or did one become the other? Which the chicken and which the egg? He gave up wondering when a hysterically cackling woman dropped a TV on him from a second-storey window. After that, he had run and hid, run and hid, scuttling from one concealment to another, waiting all the time for a sudden noise and a sharp pain as a knife sliced into his liver.

A grinding crash from outside brought him up to his knees, then to his feet. He found the light switch that would fill the room with comforting light. Light that could be seen from outside. He imagined the blank-faced ones looking up at his windows and the others banging on his door. He took his hand away from the switch and felt along the wall. The brass bookends had been a present from Kirsten with LO on one half and VE on the other. At the time he had thought them rather twee, now they were satisfyingly heavy.

Moving from room to room in the half-light, familiar things became traps for his feet and the sharp edges of the bookends gouged tracks into the walls as he stopped himself falling. In the kitchen he groped in a drawer until he found the disposable torch that had been free with twenty gallons of petrol and, after a moment's internal debate, swapped one of the bookends with its smooth shape. The narrow beam turned the clutter of the flat into disconnected images: a chair, a table, a reflection of his shocked, staring face.

He checked every room, every corner until he was sure, and then he did it again. He was alone in the flat and for the first time since lunchtime he felt safe.

The roar of big V8 engines and shrill screams from outside was very loud. He stood well back from the window and looked down into the street. It was thick with crowds of people all moving and surging like some human tide. Every hand carried a knife, a bar or a brick, and they were all being used. Matthew watched as a laughing teenager dashed across the pavement to a man, naked to the waist, and smashed the pole he carried onto the man's head. Blood sprayed like water over the pavement, but only for a moment before a dumpy housewife turned like a snake and buried a carving knife in the teenager's back. The three struggled for a moment then both the housewife and teenager turned on the man, still clutching his head, and began slashing and battering at his naked chest. The teenager threw the pole like a javelin and dashed into the road where a sports car hit him with a wet sound that threw him a hundred feet down the road. The car growled like a cat and darted forward, hitting the teenager again. Then it backed over him and forward, over and over, until the shape lying in the road didn't looked human anymore. The sports car paused to examine what it had done, and an articulated lorry smashed into its side, pushing into the crowds on the pavement.

Matthew stepped back from the window and held the TV remote, ready to turn the TV on and then turn the volume right up. But the TV would light up the room just as effectively as turning on the light, with the same effect. Instead, he reached for the headphones with their comfortably padded cups and clamped them to his ears. He wanted to press the brushed steel button that would fill the headphones with music, but the same button would light up the display – and the room.

Without noticing, he pulled a cushion to him and held it tight. Using it as a barrier, he pushed himself into the space behind the IKEA sofa and watched the sweep of headlights on the ceiling. He could still hear the happy laughter of children at play outside. Except their toys were razor sharp and the result blood red. He wondered where Kirsten was now and hoped that she was safe. It didn't matter who she was safe with, he had loved her and right now that was all that mattered. The screams from outside grew louder and Matthew thought he could hear Kirsten call out as the crowd took her away from him, her flame-red hair merging with the sunset as she became just another dot in a picture of chaos. And then at the limits of observability, she stopped, looked back and Matthew knew she wanted him.

He raced down the street, bare feet grinding over the pavement, past the madmen as they cut at each other and blood ran like water down the gutters. A fire engine-red Porsche, thick with the smell of flowers, screeched to a halt in front of him and its door flew open. Behind its wheel, Philip was horribly burnt from the waist up. Charred flesh sloughed off like falling leaves as he turned to Matthew and screamed. Matthew clapped his hands to his head, but the scream was a wall of noise that filled the world.

He woke up and the floor was vibrating under him. Pictures walked off the walls and glasses off a shelf. All caution forgotten, he dragged himself to the window, looked down into the street and then followed the focus of each upturned face. There was the briefest possible glimpse of a huge shape above and a wheel gliding past at roof height. Matthew pushed himself against the window, head cricked to one side, and watched the dark bat shape of a 747 moving very low over London. Its lowered landing gear touched a tower block and the plane skewed to one side and down towards the ground. A splash of flame grew into a dome that filled the sky. Bright sparks showered the street and a car began to burn. After-images painted globes of yellow across the room. From the street below there was laughter – and then more screams. Matthew held his hands to his ears and waited for the angry night to fall away.

Chapter Eight
Friends in High Places I

M'reth closed his eyes and pushed his hand into the bowl full of stones. He held it there for a very long time before slowly pulling it out. He held a white stone and his gasp of relief was very loud. He passed the bowl to Stroer, who looked as if he might pass out at any moment. But he too pulled out a white stone. The bowl made its way around the table with its picture of the blue planet below them. They had agreed that they would keep taking turns until one of them was chosen, but as the bowl made its way to Cheilith, the sinking feeling low down in his stomach grew heavier with each turn. Cheilith took the bowl from Teir and, without hesitation, pushed his hand into the pile of stones. His fingers seemed to have a life of their own, pushing, searching, and when they found a stone he knew it was the one. Cheilith pulled his hand from the bowl very slowly and showed everyone the stone he had selected. It was as dark as midnight, as black as coal.

The room broke out in wild applause. Everyone crowded around him and held him briefly as a mark of respect. But he saw the look they all shared and didn't fight at all when they held him very tightly and carried him to the table. Some held his legs down so he couldn't kick. Some held his arms to stop him fighting his way free. But for his head there was a broad strap to hold it completely motionless.

Rielk asked if he was comfortable and the moment Cheilith opened his mouth Rielk shoved a piece of flexible pipe in to muffle his screams. The Masters only believed in pain as a motivator; there were no anaesthetics available to them.

Zesh and Cheug hung the picture of the blue planet directly above Cheilith to give him something to look at while they worked. He told himself that this was their only chance, that only the people of the blue planet would be able to do what they could not.

It didn't help when the drill began to cut into his skull.

Chapter Nine
Such an Ordinary Day

Matthew woke to the repeated blaring of a car horn. Three quick stabs at the horn, a pause and three more stabs. The pause in the middle was nearly long enough to drift back to sleep. Matthew told himself it was just an impatient driver, but that would mean everything was normal outside. It would also mean that he hadn't seen a teenager electrocute himself, and he could still smell burning flesh.

Getting up from the space between sofa and wall was a series of sharp pains as he clambered to his feet and straightened out limbs that had been contorted into strange positions overnight. He wasn't sure what time he had gone to sleep or if he had been asleep at all. He had drifted all night on the dividing line between dreams and anxiety, never sure if the screams were happening outside or in his head.

Standing was agony on feet that were ripped and torn from running barefoot on London's streets. Moving was torture as overstressed muscles took their revenge. His face in the bathroom mirror looked very old. He washed it until his skin burnt and he tasted soap. It didn't look any better.

The three quick stabs at the horn, pause and repeat came again and Matthew's legs merely complained bitterly as he staggered to the window and looked out. After a long time he decided if this was indeed the apocalypse then it was a very British apocalypse. Everything looked so normal, so well ordered. Across the road people were queuing for the bus to town. The corner shop was doing a brisk trade with people buying milk and bread. A day just like any other – until he looked closer and saw that the people waiting for the bus were wearing underwear over pyjamas, shorts with suit jackets, or nothing at all. Matthew told himself that the man at the back of the queue was just wearing a wrinkled, pink top with matching trousers, but then he dropped his paper, bent down and Matthew looked away. No one else did. All of them were standing as still as display dummies dragged out into the street. The queue at the corner shop snaked out of the doorway but the store had burnt overnight and the counter they waited at was blackened and charred.

When Kirsten had left he'd thought about just getting out – sell the flat, max out his credit cards and travel, see the world; walk on golden beaches and feel the sun on his skin; just drop out of the rat race; get his head together and work out who he really was. He'd never done any of that, because he knew it would only be a matter of time before he realised that he was still the same person, only with no money, no job and no future. And when that happened he'd fill his pockets with stones, walk into a wine-dark sea and wait for the pain to go away.

He'd never travelled, but while he had not been looking, the world had slid away from him. And what it had left behind was something that looked like the city he thought he knew, but completely different in every possible way.

The impatient motorist sounded his horn again and Matthew found him in the middle of the queue of traffic that blocked the road. He looked relaxed, tapping his fingers on the steering wheel,

61

occasionally trying to peer around the car in front and never noticed that every car was empty. All down the column of traffic doors hung open and convertibles had been opened like clams. Matthew guessed that the only way this queue could be cleared was with a tow truck, but the traffic at each end of the road was equally static. First you'd have to recover the cars to get to the recovery truck to recover the cars. Suddenly, the old joke, 'How does the snow plough driver get to work?' didn't seem so funny anymore.

Matthew pulled the curtains tight and turned on the TV, thumb ready on the volume control. BBC1 showed an empty studio, BBC2 just static and ITV an advert for toilet cleaner that just looped over and over. All the satellite channels, the repeat channels, the infomercial channels were blank. Matthew watched the new miracle toilet cleaner blast away cartoon germs until he could repeat each excited voiceover. Then he turned the TV off.

The impatient motorist sounded his horn again.

Matthew felt he was the only sane person in a citywide asylum, but it was more than insane – it didn't make any sense. The woman masturbating next to him in the theatre. The teenagers electrocuting themselves on the underground. The dull-eyed robot that had been Philip. There was no thread that could draw everything together. He knew there were neutron bombs that could kill people but leave cities standing, but even the most paranoid ramblings of the internet had not suggested a weapon that could make someone masturbate in public. It was just madness and Matthew realised that that explained everything. He'd been under a lot of stress since Kirsten had left him, spent hours awake wondering what had happened to his life, and at some point it had all been too much. He wondered when he had lost his grip on sanity. Was it in the theatre when he had seen the shocked look on people's faces? Or was it before that, perhaps some minor incident at work that had tipped him off the sharp edge of sanity? Seen from this new perspective, everything made sense. The woman in the theatre was a distorted reflection of the hours he had spent wondering what exactly Kirsten and Janice did together. The businessman with his glass knife was a manifestation of the anger he had felt towards her. He wasn't sure where the teenagers in the tube station or the Porsche driver fit into that, but why should they? Madness had no rules. Some small part of his mind had obviously been trying to signal what was really happening when it had suggested an LSD bomb as a metaphor for the more exotic drugs he was no doubt receiving as part of his therapy. He just hoped he hadn't hurt anybody and they wouldn't bring him back to sanity just to be arrested for murder. He'd certainly thought about it, visualised in exquisite detail how to punish Kirsten for leaving him. Perhaps he'd carried out one of his less elaborate plans.

Matthew's stomach made a low growling sound and he realised he was starving. As far as he remembered the last thing he'd had to eat was over twenty-four hours ago. Perhaps that was part of his complex web of delusions. But right now he believed that he was starving.

His legs and feet didn't seem to hurt so much as he made his way to the kitchen. Knowing that none of this was real made everything so easy for him.

Matthew popped two slices of bread into the toaster while eating a big bowl of cornflakes with so much milk that it slopped over the sides. The minute the toast popped up, he slathered both slices with butter and marmalade. It tasted of lazy Sunday mornings, head aching slightly from the night before, and it was the most delicious thing he had ever eaten. He remembered that someone once had a hit single just singing about a little bit of toast. When he was better, he would find out its name, buy a copy and play it over and over. It was the food of the gods, a perfect balance of sweet and crunchy.

The moment he finished the second piece he dropped two fresh slices of bread into the toaster, reached for the lever to drop them down and then pulled one slice out and examined it carefully. It was spotted with dots of green mould. The few remaining slices in the pack were even worse. Matthew scraped at the mould with a fingernail then looked thoughtfully at the kitchen cabinets and quickly pulled out every food item and arranged them in a neat line on the counter. And because he was young, single, male and without a current girlfriend, every food item meant a packet of pasta, three cans of beans, a bottle of coke and a very small bottle of nuclear-hot chilli sauce. Matthew rolled the bottle from hand to hand and realised that this was what some gameshow had called the 'make your mind up time'. If he really believed that this was all psychosis then he'd be strapped down with an intravenous drip stuck in his arm and he could stay here until they cured him. But if that was all some bullshit that he wanted to believe, because the reality was unbelievable, then he could either stay here and starve or go shopping. He rolled the bottle from hand to hand a few more times and then began to lace up his shoes.

Chapter Ten
Alone

It was cold outside and Matthew hugged his jacket around him. The wind was blowing from the direction of the crashed plane and the air was thick with the smell of kerosene with an undercurrent of burnt meat. There were only a few people on the pavement, all moving very slowly, very precisely. As long as he didn't look too closely it might have been any normal day with people out enjoying the weak sunshine and window shopping. But not looking was like the guaranteed cure for warts – just drink a glass of water without thinking about pink elephants. The more he thought he mustn't the more he had to and he saw how slowly everyone moved and that every face was wooden, empty and completely expressionless. He watched a housewife wearing only a dressing gown take five minutes to cover the width of the small shop across the road. As she reached the dividing line between shops the dressing gown caught on something on the pavement and it slipped off one shoulder and then off completely. She walked very slowly towards the end of the street, completely naked, and her face never changed from bland emptiness.

Matthew walked along the frozen river of crashed cars until he found the one with the impatient motorist at its wheel. He was middle aged with neatly clipped, thinning hair. He wore a tie with the logo of some very minor public school over a white shirt dappled with blood. Matthew tapped on the window but he didn't look around. He pulled at the car door but it was locked. The driver stabbed at the horn again without ever looking at Matthew. No one looked at Matthew, even when he walked in front of them. Not once did a head turn in his direction. He tried standing directly in the path of a long-haired goth wearing a T-shirt with a picture of two kissing skeletons.

"Excuse me, sir, but can you tell me the time?"

The goth came to a halt nearly nose to nose with Matthew. He didn't say anything and his eyes never lost their thousand-yard stare.

"The time, sir? I've lost my watch."

The goth's face twitched unpleasantly. His mouth dropped open and just for a second Matthew thought he was going to say something. Then he pushed past him and carried on his way.

Matthew watched him go. It was like the time when he was four and had put a toy soldier on the tracks of his Hornby train set. The train had hit the obstruction and juddered and squirmed until it had pushed the toy out of the way. He'd tried the same thing later on with a book and the train had derailed, taking a chunk out of a skirting board. He wondered what the goth would have done if he had not been able to get away from him.

The window of the local Costa coffee was covered in starburst cracks but people were sat inside lifting empty cups. No one looked around when he hammered on the window. He ran down the road, feet tangling in clothes strewn outside the J.D. Sports, called out, but there was no answer. He looked up but there was only the tower blocks like gravestones. A word started to blink in red-hot neon in his mind and the word had razor edges that cut deep – alone. He had been subtracted from the world. He had become a pale shade of a person.

And then, amongst the blank-faced robots, there was just one person stumbling along, clutching at the pedestrian rail to stay upright, his mouth moving as he talked to himself. He was oddly dressed, jeans with a tweed jacket, red bowtie with a paisley shirt, but as he pressed his hands to his head Matthew saw something that identified him as surely as a fingerprint. He had leather patches on his elbows. A week ago Matthew would have casually dismissed him as a history teacher so deeply traumatised by trying to drill the Plantagenets into class 6a that he had dived into a bottle of scotch. But he was the most human person Matthew had seen in the last twenty-four hours. He found a way through the frozen traffic jam blocking the road until he could hear what the maybe-teacher was saying.

"I'll show them! Think they're so clever! Know what I'm doing! Teach them!"

Matthew stopped a safe distance away. "Are you all right? Can I help?"

The maybe-teacher looked up and saw Matthew for the first time. His eyes were red-rimmed as if he had been crying. His chin was slicked with drool.

"You what? You being fucking smart with me?" He released his hold on the rail and stood up, and Matthew realised that he was a lot taller than his five foot eight. A lot broader, too. "You're taking the piss too, aren't you? Having a laugh at the poor old cripple."

Matthew started to back away. "No, no, I just wanted to help."

"Show you if I want any help." He took a step closer to Matthew. "Reports of young girls banging inside Vatican. You see! All the colours! Still got it!"

He grabbed hold of Matthew's jacket and pulled. Matthew pushed hard with both hands. It wasn't exactly a punch, but it was enough for the maybe-teacher to lose his grip and Matthew ran. He weaved in and out of the blank-faced robots as if they were standing still, expecting any moment a hand on his collar pulling him back. At the top of the road, he looked back down the street. He could still see the maybe-teacher, but he seemed to have forgotten him already. Matthew then realised that if he'd thought more about what was happening outside and less about his stomach he might have wondered where all the manic ones had gone. All he had seen was that it was nice and quiet and he'd set off shopping as if today were like any other day. Well now he had an answer to the question he'd never asked. They had been hiding and were just starting to emerge from their holes. Perhaps like the bad guys in that Will Smith movie, they only came out at night, or they were just tired after yesterday's exertions. In just a few minutes the streets would be filled with more of the maniacs that would find it really amusing to slit his throat.

Matthew tried the door behind him and when that didn't work, wondered how long it would take to get home. A clock tower sounded the half hour in dull, booming tones as he tried the door of a mobile phone shop. It had been looted overnight and display model shells littered the floor. But the space behind the counter was big enough to hide him and he folded himself into its shelter. He wondered what would happen when night came. Would they flood the shop ready to play amusing games with sharp knives or drag him out to the street and use him as a target for the cars he had heard too much of last night?

A slit between two panels of the counter gave him a very restricted view of the street. All he could see was people walking past, but that was all they were doing. No one was running or fighting. It looked so orderly. No one had even looked into the shop.

The clock tower sounded the quarter hour and Matthew very cautiously backed out of his hiding space. His back clicked audibly as he stood up. He carefully placed his steps between smashed displays and looked out into the street. There was the permanent traffic jam, there was the blank-faced robots, but no wild-eyed figures racing down the street with knives in their hands. On the bridge were only more figures moving too slowly to be normal. There was no sign of the maybe-teacher.

Very slowly, Matthew saw that he might have been wrong. Even if something as unlikely as vampires existed, it was still several hours before dark when they could emerge from their coffins and roam the streets. But much more than that, the man on the bridge had been nothing like the maniacs he had seen last night. They had been bright-eyed with life, laughing hysterically, running as if they could never stop. But the man on the bridge had been belligerent, angry and ranting insanities. Matthew had seen the same thing most afternoons. There were always a few middle-aged men who thought they could still drink like they had at nineteen, finally emerging into the unforgiving daylight knowing that everyone was looking down on them. The man on the bridge had even shared their decisive declaration. *I'll show you!* What came after that didn't really matter. *I'll show you that I can still hold my own/fight/drive.* It usually meant hospital, jail or, in extreme cases, death. It didn't make any difference that all the man on the bridge had wanted to tell him was some dirty limerick. He had been a perfect example of loud-mouthed drunk, except for one thing – he hadn't smelt of alcohol. Matthew had been a lot closer to him than he wanted and had smelt nothing more than the need for more mouthwash. He had been clean, well-dressed and completely sober.

Matthew looked up and down the street carefully. Perhaps this was the lull before the storm of a new wave of insanity. First the hyperactive maniacs, then the dull-eyed robots and finally the angry sober-but-drunk? More than anything, he wanted to get back home, lock the door behind him and pretend that none of this was happening. He could worry about tomorrow when it arrived and stale pasta and beans would be perfectly fine as a meal tonight. He looked longingly back towards his flat and then towards the supermarket and made a deal with himself. He would go just far enough to prove that the supermarket was a burnt-out ruin or had been comprehensively looted. Then he could go home safe in the knowledge that he had done his best and it was such a shame that the trip hadn't worked out.

Matthew walked in the direction of the supermarket so quickly that it was nearly a run. A short time later, it was certainly a run.

Chapter Eleven
Shopping

The supermarket was a long, concrete and glass box surrounded by neat rows of parked cars. Some of the cars had smashed windows and a thick layer of litter had been blown into corners by the stiff breeze. But inside the supermarket, lights were on and each of its floor-to-ceiling windows glowed like huge rectangular diamonds. And behind each of the diamonds Matthew could see people shopping as if the end of the world had never happened. He watched the moving figures very carefully, ready to run the moment he saw quick, urgent motion or a spray of blood against the window. But all the shoppers moved with the slow, dreamlike motion of the blank-faced robots he had seen on the street.

He crouched and sprinted though the lines of cars. When he reached the lane that separated the car park from the building he dropped to one knee, looking under the cars for someone creeping up. Only when he was absolutely sure that he was safe, or alone, perhaps the two things were the same, he sprinted across into the cover of a coin-operated kiddie ride.

Some of the litter the wind had pushed into the interior of the big red bus looked very familiar and Matthew pulled out a rectangular piece of paper and studied it carefully. It was a £20 note. He looked down at the blueish-coloured litter blowing around his feet, at the shapes captured by the scrub brush around the car park. It was all money. Five- and twenty-pound notes scattered like leaves in autumn. He pulled a handful of notes out from the kiddie ride, then another and another. The most folding money he had ever held before was fifty quid he had won on the office sweepstake, but now there was hundreds blowing around his feet, thousands in the bus in front of him. He shoved handfuls of notes in his pockets, more inside his jacket, and then he stopped and looked at the blank-faced robots in the shop, at the plume of smoke still rising from where the plane had gone down, and emptied his pockets, giving the notes back to the wind. If he wanted money then he could walk into the Bank of England and help himself. If he needed a car to get there then there was a nice Jaguar parked just a few steps away. He could have anything he wanted, except all of it was worthless now. He was the richest man in a world that didn't use money anymore.

Inside the supermarket was almost shockingly normal. A display of free magazines had been spilled over the floor in a mess of glossy pages and the piped music silenced. But Matthew considered that a plus. He moved further inside the store, using the publicity displays as cover like an excerpt from some advertising executive's nightmare. There were only a few of the blank-faced robots pushing trollies – and that made no sense at all.

On the way here he had passed others like them, eating food that had been spilled from broken shop windows and licking water from the pavement, and here was a building full of food that they had never approached.

Matthew's original plan had been to run around the store as quickly as possible, scoop a few cans into his backpack and get the hell out of here. But the sheer normality of the store was almost seductive, and he took a trolley and set off as if today really was just another day.

He soon saw all the things that were not normal. A little old lady finished filling her basket with cat food, carefully unloaded everything at an empty till, stood there for a few minutes and then took her basket back. She filled it with more cat food and took it to another till. Nearly every till had a neat pile of cat food waiting to be scanned. In the frozen food aisle a teenager fumbled at the childproof catches they'd added to stop the kiddies helping themselves to a lolly while Mum pretended not to notice. At the end of the row he moved back to the cabinet he had just tried and started working his way back up the row. Matthew knew that he'd never get anything frozen home before it became a mass of slush and moved briskly past that aisle. Then he stopped, backed up and looked at the cabinet next to him. The catch was a pair of non-slip grips with a helpful sign showing how to squeeze them to slide the lid back. A bright three-year-old could operate them, but the teenager could not. Matthew watched the teenager try another cabinet and thought about the kids on the underground. They had seen their mate do something incredibly stupid and then done the same thing. There were people a few hundred yards away that were literally starving and had never thought to come here and help themselves. Philip had watched a simple screensaver until he had wet himself.

Matthew looked around, at the little old lady filling her basket with cat food, at the teenager trying the catches on freezer cabinets, and saw habit without intelligence. The little old lady was just doing her weekly shopping, but when no one took her money she couldn't see that she could just take her items and repeated her shopping over and over until she got the expected response. Or starved to death. The teenager was just helping himself to a lolly, but couldn't open the catches, or quit while he was behind. Something had drastically reduced their intelligence to much less than a bright three-year-old. All there was left of the person they used to be was the ingrained habits of a lifetime that they would repeat over and over like a computer stuck in a loop. He had called them stupid without realising how right he had been. They were as brainless as bottom-feeding fish, without even the drive to look for food.

Matthew wondered if the process would continue until the electrical activity of the brain had dropped to a level that would no longer tell the heart to keep beating, or was this the model for the rest of his life? In the Kingdom of the Stupid he would be God.

Matthew backed away from the teenager, testing his idea. It explained a lot of things, but it didn't explain the businessman slashing someone's throat for a dirty sandwich, and it certainly didn't explain group sex in the street. But just being able to explain some of what he had seen made him feel somehow in control. It was no longer 'X the unknown'. Names had power and just being able to explain what had happened to everyone meant that he could understand why they did things. It also meant that 99% of them would be dead in a week.

He looked across at the man licking spilled yogurt from a shelf, completely ignoring the spilled packets of biscuits he had walked over to get to it, then at the smartly dressed woman obsessively clawing at a tin of beans with her fingernails. Most of them would starve to death in a matter of days and the streets would be carpeted with the dead. Disease and infection would kill just as many, and the few that were left would be at the mercy of the uncontrolled fires that would sweep the city. This time next week he might be the only living person for miles, the great heart of the city stilled forever and grass would grow in the streets as nature reclaimed its own. The horror of never seeing another face gripped him as the room closed in around him, choking him with the knowledge that he would be forever alone, and how long would it be before he decided that death was a better choice?

In desperation, he picked up the least trampled packet of biscuits, ripped it open and poured Hobnobs onto the shelf directly in front of the man licking yogurt from his fingers. He didn't even look at them. Matthew edged closer, dropped a handful of biscuits into his hands and crumbs sprayed as he took a mouthful. His expression never changed from complete blankness.

When he had finished one mouthful, Matthew added more biscuits and then some more. If he could keep just one person alive then he would not be alone. He could come here once a day, twice a day, to feed him. Perhaps he could rig a hose to keep him watered. Wash and shave him to keep him nice and neat. He couldn't keep calling him 'the man'; he'd have to give him a name. Something like Bill or George. Perhaps he'd be able to teach him some tricks. He would make a nice companion.

Suddenly horrified by the idea of keeping a person like a pet, Matthew backed away, feeling very sad for them. It was two aisles later before he started to feel sad for himself. He'd escaped the effects of whatever had happened by some fluke of genetics or diet. But for how much longer? For the others the drop in intelligence had come so quickly that they hadn't had time to understand what was happening. But if his immunity was just a temporary slowing down of the process he would have time to know what he was losing.

He wondered what it would feel like to forget everything – how to read, how to take his trousers down before using the toilet, to even find the toilet. Would it be like school when he had forgotten his PE kit and everybody had laughed at him or his first job when they had sent him to the shops for a long weight and taken bets on just how long he would wait? He imagined everyone he had ever known looking down at him as he scrabbled for food in the gutter and his ears burnt with embarrassment. He wanted to lash out at whatever had caused this. He wanted someone to blame.

Just like the man on the bridge.

He had been unaccountably angry. He had called himself a cripple even though there had been nothing wrong with the way he moved. He had ranted about others being clever and smart. Matthew had thought him a teacher, but he had worn a bright red bowtie that no teacher could have worn into a classroom and made it out alive. He'd been a lecturer or professor of something obscure. Perhaps once the smartest man in the room, now just smart enough to know what he had lost.

Matthew felt guilty that he had not tried harder to help him, but he should have tried to tell him what he had lost rather than spouting dirty limericks about young girls in the Vatican. Matthew collected another two can of beans absently. Because there hadn't been a 'the'. What he'd said was 'Reports of young girls banging inside Vatican'. Even at the time the grammatical inconsistency had grated, but he'd pronounced each word so carefully. So clearly.

Matthew stopped abruptly in the middle of the aisle. At school they'd taught him 'Richard Of York Gave Battle In Vain', but it all came down to the same thing: a simple mnemonic to remember the colours of the rainbow – Red, Orange, Yellow, Green, Blue, Indigo and Violet. Perhaps the man on the bridge didn't remember what the simple rhyme represented, but he had tried to show Matthew that there was still a small part left of the person he had used to be, and Matthew had pushed him away.

Matthew pushed his trolley away and sprinted towards the entrance and then thought about how long it had taken to get here from the bridge and skidded to a halt. By the time he had got to the end of the street he had already lost sight of the lecturer. The chances of finding him again were slim to none. And even if he did find him, would he be just another of the Stupid by then?

Matthew hoped that when it was his turn to sink into idiocy, someone with a little more understanding might find him.

Chapter Twelve
An Object Full of Colours

The shopping trolley wheels were tough, resistant plastic that grated against the pavement's hard concrete. The noise as Matthew made his way down the street seemed to feedback on itself, growing louder with each step until he was sure that heads all over London were turning towards him. Only, the streets were eerily empty. None of the blank-faced Stupid were to be seen. He covered the first hundred yards in a sweat of anxiety, the second in a near run until the breath burnt in his lungs. At the end of the street the trolley dropped off the kerb in a shower of tins and he never noticed.

Matthew's original idea had been to fill the backpack he had bought to carry his work clothes as he cycled to work (before he discovered that cyclists were basically invisible to London traffic) and get home as quickly as possible. But that was before he thought that perhaps tomorrow the supermarket would be a burnt-out ruin. Or the manic ones might strip its shelves in the night. And besides, the more he took today, the longer before he would have to go out again.

Setting foot outside the air-conditioned shelter of the supermarket was the second hardest thing he had ever done. Everything outside was too big, too empty. He saw figures hiding behind every car. Every shadow concealed a wild-eyed maniac with a glass knife. The wheels of the trolley that had glided so silently across the perfectly smooth floor of the supermarket caught in every crevice of the pavement in a clatter that reverberated down the empty streets.

At each corner he stopped and peered carefully around the junction before moving on. But, little by little, 'carefully' became 'briefly', became 'not at all'. So it was a complete surprise when Matthew strode confidently around a corner and pushed the trolley straight into a group of people. He swallowed his automatic apology, turned and raced back to the corner with a lithe grace he no longer knew he possessed, feet moving so quickly he barely seemed to touch the ground, feet moving so quickly he never saw the discarded newspaper that wrapped itself around both ankles. There was the briefest sensation of flying, then knees, elbows and finally face hit the cold hard pavement with an electric jolt of pain that took his breath away. Even above the blood rushing in his ears he could hear the footsteps of the crowd as they surrounded him. He tried to crawl further away on hand and knees that barely seemed to belong to him. But as the footsteps grew closer his limbs collapsed under him and he rolled over to see the sky for the last time. He lay in the middle of the pavement like a stranded starfish, waiting for the hands that would hold him, the glitter of knives that would cut him. He waited some more before looking back down the street.

The trolley was canted over at an angle into the gutter, but beyond it was a wall of people. And every one of them was looking away from him. Climbing to his feet was a series of sharp pains as muscle pulled against bruised flesh, his hands hot and throbbing against the wall as it supported him. None of the crowd showed the slightest sign of movement. Except for the lifelike skin tones, they might have been tailor's dummies doing a new, initiative street campaign for urban fashion.

Matthew edged away from the silent crowd. The supermarket was only a few minutes away. He still had plenty of time to stock up again and make it home via another route before nightfall. There was no reason to go anywhere near the close-packed figures at the end of the street. But it was very strange how still they were. There had not even been the faintest flicker of attention when he rammed the trolley into them.

Matthew stood on tip-toes for the extra height it gave him. There was a brief glimpse of ranks of other figures beyond the ones he could see, all looking up at something above them. He edged slowly back towards the crowd, constantly judging the distance from the crowd to him and the distance from him to the open end of the road. A few feet in front of him a bus stop was surrounded by drifts of broken safety glass from its smashed screen, but the seats inside were metal and undamaged. Matthew placed his feet as carefully as if stepping through a minefield. His knees cracked like small gunshots as he stood up on the seat, but the additional height let him see over the crowd.

His first thought was that the bright thing hanging above the crowd was a child's helium balloon caught by the wind, but it stayed perfectly still as if nailed to the sky. It glowed with a cold light that washed all the colour out of each upturned face. He told himself that it was an American predator drone diverted from the war on terror to investigate the sudden radio silence of the British and he should jump up and wave at some remote operator. But the more he tried to convince himself, the more he remembered that the principal feature of a drone was that it moved, and the object above the crowd certainly didn't.

Matthew looked from the ranks of empty faces to the object hanging above them and crouched down very low until all he could see was a faint nimbus of light above the crowd. Very slowly its pure white glow became red, then yellow, then ink blue. Matthew wondered if the man from the bridge was in the crowd, silently repeating his mnemonic with each change. The colours began changing faster and faster, green bleeding into orange into indigo, leaving Matthew with after-images painted across the sky. He squatted lower until all he could see was a halo of light above the crowd, wondering if he should run or see what happened next. He was still trying to decide when the light went out. He had the slightest impression of something rising very quickly back up to the clouds and then the object was gone.

Matthew stood up very carefully until he could see out over the crowd. A few of the tightly packed faces were looking around. A much smaller number reached up as if calling the object back. He looked at the trolley he had so carefully packed at the supermarket and then at the crowd as it began to spread out. In a moment they would reach the trolley and then he could either starve or go through the whole tortuous trip back to the supermarket. Before he could reconsider, he jumped down from the seat, grabbed the trolley's handle and towed it behind him. At the corner of the street he looked back at the thinning crowd and ran.

***

Matthew unloaded the shopping trolley in his kitchen very slowly. If Kirsten had been here she would have pulled her face at the gouges he'd left dragging the trolley up the stairs. But she had probably been one of the crowd watching the object with complete and total fascination.

He'd jogged home as fast as the trolley would allow and spent most of that time thinking about the constant churn of the internet, offering up the wilder conspiracy theories to a mainstream audience for amusement, and finally ridicule when presented with inconvenient facts. The bunkers under Denver Airport were always good for a few column inches, as was Project HAARP or the internment camps ready across North America for political dissidents. But the big trade was in blurry images of flying saucers and other improbable craft based on the firmly held belief that Area 51 was literally hip deep in crashed alien ships. A single photo of the thing he had seen would have lit up the internet like a Christmas tree. But if anyone had the thing he'd seen then thousands of them would have been on patrol over Afghanistan – or Washington D.C. The fact that none of those things had happened meant that no one had the thing he'd seen.

And that was a problem.

Maybe a virus that made everyone into brainless drones might be theoretically possible. But that no one had something he'd seen with his own eyes wasn't. And the only way to make sense of everything was to qualify 'no one had' with 'on Earth'. If the object hadn't come from here, it had come from somewhere else. Somewhere not-Earth, which didn't make any sense. If the mysterious 'they' had come from another planet, and even if they had magical wrap drives that could turn light years into a quick afternoon drive, they must have steered straight past thousands of empty planets just to mess up one insignificant world.

According to the old black and white sci-fi films he'd loved as a child, the only reason that aliens would come to earth was to warn them that humanity's warlike intentions would one day threaten the other planets. He was almost sure he'd seen the scene in some classic film.

An impossibly vast room decorated only in shades of grey. A mountainous desk looking down on a sole human selected as an example of humanity. Behind the desk one of the panel of strangely human aliens raised his gavel. "It is agreed. Humanity is too hostile to be allowed to coexist in our peaceful universe, and that reversion to a simpler state will give them the chance to learn better ways. Deploy the IQ inhibiting ray!" Matthew thought that the President of the Galactic Council would sound exactly like James Mason. The only problem with that idea was that most of the Stupid would be dead in a week. And while dead men told no tales, they were also very resistant to learning.

The only other alternative to Galactic social workers was invasion. But that meant in a galaxy of millions of empty planets, only Earth had some mysterious mineral valuable enough to make them want to move in and take over. Only that didn't explain why they had turned most of the population into morons too stupid to even dig their mines. If they wanted the planet, then an asteroid dropped into the sun would cause a flare that would sterilise it first.

The only thing that did make sense was what he was already doing, collecting enough supplies to give him time to think. Stay in the city or leave for the open countryside? Find the offices of Capital Radio and shout for help or stay quiet and hide?

Matthew finished unloading his supplies and began to make himself his favourite pasta and chicken, only with extra garlic and chilli. Kirsten would probably have made wafting motions with her hand every time he spoke, but that wasn't a problem anymore.

Putting the meal together kept his hands busy, but left him plenty of time to think, and the only thing he could think about was the graffiti he had seen scrawled on a toilet wall – *Tragedy is when something bad happens to someone else, but when it happens to you it's a disaster* – because the question he had managed not to think about since the supermarket would not go away. Would his immunity to whatever had happened wear off? Would he wake up in the morning unable to read and by lunchtime unable to find the door?

He swallowed a handful of the Brain Smart memory supplement and Active Mind and Memory enhancer he'd found in the supermarket's vitamins aisle with a glass of wheatgrass extract that smelt like dirty socks. Tasted like that, too. Maybe they would just be a placebo, but it made him feel like he was doing something. He ate his meal with a copy of the Bumper Book of Word puzzles balanced on his knee. According to the book he'd found in the self-help section, the key to retaining an active mind was mental exercise. He'd brought a copy of Word Searches for Clever Kids – just in case.

Chapter Thirteen
Friends in High Places II

Cheilith woke to pain and darkness. He tried to claw at his face but his hands didn't move. He tried to scream but there was nothing. He was blind and paralysed, trapped in a tube ready for disposal. The operation had failed and they had thrown him away like a bad experiment. Soon he would feel the push as he was ejected and then the air would grow thin as the absolute cold of space began to bite. They would try again with another candidate, and another, refining the operation each time until they got it right. But none of that would concern him because by then he would be dead and forgotten.

Cheilith tried to make his peace with his ancestors. Between the pain of the Masters he had seen beauty. He had walked on strange new worlds, seen triple sunrises. He had been allowed to choose a mate, twice. Gone, all gone now.

And then the sun did rise in a blinding crescent. All Cheilith could see was light and colour, but he blinked his eyes and slowly the crescent grew larger, became a patch of colour that coalesced into a face that smiled at him. He knew it had to be Rielk but all he saw now was a collection of features that he no longer recognised.

Cheilith saw Rielk's lips move. He knew he was saying something but all he heard was sound without meaning. Cheilith made a tentative 'all is well' sign and there was scattered applause. Rielk said something again and held up a picture. Cheilith knew that it was a Master. He could describe its shape, colour and even its mood. But that was all it was, just a picture. There wasn't even a flicker of the instinctive need to obey. He made another 'all is well' sign and there was louder applause. Cheilith knew what the sound signified, how it was made, how it was used. He looked around the room and counted everyone there. He still had basic skills; what he had lost was the part of his brain that held labels and their learned responses. He was free. The operation had been a success.

He made another, more positive 'all is well' sign and unseen hands released their hold on him. Sitting up made the room spin around him and the same hands supported him until he could stand up.

Faces he no longer had names for smiled at him and made signs of respect. But he recognised the look of relief that each of them wore when they looked away. They had done their job and soon they would have what they had all worked for, for so long.

Rielk slipped the communicator from his hiding place. His lips made word shapes that Cheilith no longer understood but they had all practised the order of events.

"The operation was a success. Begin your escape."

Rielk would monitor the responses until all had confirmed and then everyone here would escape. And Cheilith alone would be left to talk to the people of the blue planet.

Chapter Fourteen
Paddington Green

The police station appeared completely untouched by events. The surrounding streets were littered with broken glass and thick with crashed cars, but the station looked as if the day shift could emerge at any moment to dispense British justice with British sarcasm. Matthew kept a small flame of hope burning as he made his way down the street. Perhaps this was a small island of normality and a small remnant of the Government was inside, planning how to bring the rule of law back to the British Isles. The hope lasted until he got closer and saw that its front door was wide open.

He found himself a space between a burnt-out car and an overturned rubbish bin where he could watch the station's open door. It was pitch dark inside, but the power was still on in the shops around him. So either a circuit breaker had tripped – or someone had deliberately turned off the lights. He checked up and down the street very carefully, examining each patch of shadow or doorway for someone waiting to see what would be drawn to the honey pot they had set out.

There were very few of the Stupid on the street, all of them dressed in the bizarre combination of clothes that came from vaguely remembering that getting dressed was something they did – but they were now unable to tell the difference between what to wear for bed and what to wear outside. There had been even fewer of them on the streets when Matthew had been jerked from a nightmare of blank faces and crashing planes by the sudden realisation that he needed a weapon. If this had all been caused by aliens they might want to look inside the skull of any survivors – without an anaesthetic. Or perhaps the Stupid would realise that there was plenty of food – as long as they didn't mind the taste of human flesh.

The most dangerous things he found in the flat were a carving knife and a hammer with a broken handle. Then he had sat looking out over a silent London wondering where he could find a gun. According to the press, every street in London bristled with homeboyz waving converted starting pistols and sawn-off shotguns, but the only guns he had ever seen were in films. Matthew thought about that for a long time. After the Dunblane tragedy, England had one of the most robust firearms licensing systems in the world. Even their Olympic shooting team had to train in France. But there was one organisation that was guaranteed to be based in England. And even the slick adverts showing that in the army you could see the world, sometimes had to show that you saw the world carrying a rifle.

If the internet had been working he could have found precise walking directions to the nearest army base, but the wonderful iPad that Kirsten had bought him would only respond to every search with 'failure to connect'. In the end, his only reference material was the free newspaper that got shoved through his door every week, whether he wanted it or not. Once it had been only good for mopping up spills, now it might be the last newspaper ever printed. He turned every page, looking for any reference to an army base in the area. Then he read every page again, looking for the more subtle clues of anything army: a car accident reported as being near a barracks or a fight in a pub with a soldier. He did that twice before reluctantly conceding that there wasn't even the smallest military presence in the paper's catchment area. After that, he stared at the paper for a long time before actually seeing its front page. Under an eight-point headline, *Terrorist Arrests*, two burly policemen bundled a pixilated figure into a police station. But it wasn't the article under the picture that interested him; it was the policemen. They were carrying guns. The sight of armed police had become so common after the 7/7 underground bombs that they had become almost invisible, but now he remembered every time he had walked past a policeman who had been transformed, seemly overnight, from genial neighbourhood cop into armed paramilitary.

Matthew picked up the paper with shaking hands and speed read to the part that had acquired a new importance.

The suspect was transported to London's high-security Paddington Green Police Station. The building, which was completed in 1971, is the most important high-security station in the UK for those who are held on suspicion of terrorism and is under permanent, twenty-four hour guard by armed officers.

And just to reinforce the point, under the article was a photo of a grim-looking seventies tower block, with an equally grim-faced officer guarding its door.

Matthew lowered the paper very slowly. Even on foot Paddington was just an hour away. Thanks to the paper he already knew what the station looked like. All he had to do was get into the station and he could arm himself to the teeth. He imagined grey-skinned aliens with huge black eyes striding down the street, and he could actually see their surprise when he stepped out from a doorway, a rifle in each hand, screaming defiance. "You can take our planet when you prise it from my cold dead hands!"

A little later, he picked up the paper again and reread the article. Security was there to stop people getting out, but it also meant that getting in would be equally difficult. Even after the police had forgotten their job and wandered off, there would still be some very secure locked doors. He would need a lot more than a hammer with a broken handle to break into a maximum security installation.

***

He found a hardware shop less than a mile from his flat. Its windows had been smashed and glass and sun-bleached displays had spilled into the road. But inside the shop looked almost untouched. He checked it very carefully from the safety of the road before slipping through its doorway. Inside it was far more crowded than any shop had the right to be, with shelves of dusty tools reaching floor to ceiling. But none held what he wanted. The space under the counter was filled with cryptically labelled drawers. Matthew tried one at random and a few minutes later found a pair of bolt cutters nearly as long as his arm. The cutters made a thin hissing sound as he swung them like a bat. He enjoyed the feeling of power they gave him and he did it again and again. He wondered if this was how the cavemen had felt when they had first picked up the long bone of an animal and realised the weapon it was.

On the counter was a display model padlock that looked large enough to hold a motorbike. Matthew placed the jaws of the cutters around its shackle, took a deep breath and pulled the handles together. The centimetre-thick bar parted as if it were just cheap plastic. Matthew picked up the heavy fragment of case-hardened steel and tapped it thoughtfully on the counter. A rat-like scrabbling sound made him look through the broken window at a flurry of litter whipped up by wind. This time it wasn't rats – but soon they would have unlimited food supplies and they would breed. He tried to push away the idea of the streets filled with carpets of grey, furry bodies and carried on searching. A few minutes later, he found a sledgehammer in a drawer tersely labelled 'hamr'. It was enormously heavy. Just lifting it was an effort. Swinging it made Matthew painfully rediscover all the small muscles in his arms. He scooped up both tools and instantly the cutters slid one way from his arms while the hammer went the other. Matthew stepped back smartly and said some choice swear words. If he had to carry the tools all the way to Paddington then he'd need a bag, something with a strap to sling over his shoulder, but strong enough to carry the tools. He tried all the drawers under the counter and came up empty. The only other possibility was the shop's back room, and the sliding door to that jammed after just an inch of travel.

Matthew stood back and studied it. It was a simple wooden rectangle, hung from two wheels that rode on a track above the entrance. All he'd have to do to clear whatever was in the way was lift it off the track and set it to one side. He gripped the door handle in one hand, the edge in the other and lifted. His first surprised thought was that the door was a lot heavier than it looked. Then it was pushed back into his face, and he went down with it covering him like a shield. He pushed the door away from him and it was slammed back into his face so hard that he saw stars. The door handle ground his fingers against the floor. The weight holding him down shifted from bottom to top, disappeared and there was the crunch of broken glass.

Matthew waited until he was sure the room was silent again before he slid out from under the door. His right hand throbbed as if he had pushed it into a wasps' nest. His lip was wet and when he wiped it his hand came away bloody. He looked from the boiler-suited man standing on the pavement to the spider web of scratches on the inside of the door and finally to the wedge jammed in the door's track. The poor bastard must have panicked when things started to fall apart and sealing himself into the back room had probably seemed a good idea. But then he had become too dumb to know how to open the door and he had robotically clawed at it until Matthew had so kindly opened it for him. Then he had walked straight over him and through the broken window to get outside. Matthew watched him to see what he would do next, but the answer seemed to be nothing at all. He had blindly followed his last thought before the light of intellect had gone out, and now he was outside he had no more idea what to do than a caveman at the controls of a 747.

Matthew shook his head sadly and walked into the shop's back room, and just as rapidly backed out. The stench in the room made his eyes water and his stomach did a slow roll. The store owner had been stuck in there for three, maybe four, days and while he couldn't find his way out of an unlocked room, all of his biological process worked just fine.

Matthew looked down. He'd stepped in some of the biological process.

***

Matthew soon discovered that if he wore the hammer and cutters slung from either shoulder the weight pulled him over to one side. If he wore them across his back every step became a jab to the ribs, and across the front a repeated punch that took his breath away. And in every position the sling he'd improvised from a length of rope sawed at his neck like an incompetent hang man. The only thing that stopped him dumping the ungainly tools and turning back home was the idea of seeing whoever had caused this through the sights of a high-powered rifle. In the last forty-eight hours he'd been abused, humiliated and chased across London. Everything he knew had been taken away from him, and somebody had to pay. He wanted to do something. He wanted to strike back.

Finding the police station had been a lot more difficult than he had thought, and only a chance sighting of the multi-storey building from the Marylebone Flyover had given him a clue to its location. And when he reached it, he realised that its front door was wide open. Matthew told himself that the door meant nothing. The world had been falling apart. It was too much to expect that that the police would remember every small detail. Except, it did matter; it meant that the station was not some small island of normality. Whatever had happened out here had happened in there. The only question was who was waiting inside.

He looked up and down the road. There were very few of the Stupid on the street. Most were almost normally dressed with just one by the entrance wearing a long fur jacket with a top hat badly sprayed silver. But there was no sign of a police uniform that might mean he wouldn't have to go into the pitch dark of the police station.

He ran across the road to the station, tools held tight against him to stop them making any sound. When he was hard against the station's grey, concrete walls he looked up the stairs to its entrance, trying to crane his neck to see inside. If he climbed just a few steps he'd be able to shine his torch inside without committing himself to actually going inside.

"You won't find anything in there you know." The words were slightly too loud and said directly into his ear.

Matthew twisted around and went sprawling on the steps up to the station. Standing over him was the Stupid with the fur jacket and silver hat. Except, he wasn't that at all. He was looking directly down at Matthew with an amused expression.

Matthew used the handrail to help him to his feet. "You're normal?" he said

The not-Stupid spread his arms out wide like a hell-fire preacher. "Normal is as normal does." He sounded slightly drunk.

Matthew held out his hand in a tentative handshake – "Matthew Rowe." – and was surprised and disconcerted when the not-Stupid converted his hallelujah pose into a hug that lifted him off his feet.

"Jeremy Eaton." He stank of booze.

Matthew hugged him back, briefly, before pulling away. "I thought I was the only one."

"First Normal I've seen since everything went to hell." Jeremy pronounced the capital N very clearly. He was both younger and taller than Matthew with an electric puffball of hair that the silver hat floated on. His face was all angles and lines as if skin had been too tightly stretched over bone. His eyes were very old as if they had seen everything, knew everything. "I saw somebody yesterday at the top of Basil Street that seemed more normal than these guys, but when I tried to talk to him he was just angry and incoherent."

Matthew nodded, backing away from the stink of booze around Jeremy. "Everyone has suffered a dramatic drop in intelligence. For everyone else it all happened too quickly, but he was smart enough to know what was happening to him. I saw someone just like that yesterday and realised what was going on."

"It took you that long to figure it out? What was your first clue? The manic ones literally slowing down? Their inability to dress themselves, even feed themselves? You didn't notice habit replacing intellect as their IQ dropped away? And wasn't their virtual catatonia a bit of a clue? Because all of those things reek of suddenly imposed low intelligence."

Matthew thought that perhaps he didn't like Jeremy very much.

Jeremy leant back against the wall and wasn't looking at Matthew anymore. "Human beings are very delicate flowers. Lots of things can adversely affect intelligence. Alzheimer's, brain tumours and of course the misfolded prions behind mad cow disease. But all of those things take time, and what happened here took place virtually overnight. That means an airborne infectious agent with a very low latency period capable of crossing the brain-blood barrier. My guess is someone's bio-warfare research proved a bit more successful than they thought. Could have been America, but just as easily Russia. Perhaps they were experimenting with mental retardation in place of all of those nasty nuclear bombs. Somebody was moving a test tube and they … tripped."

"But haven't you seen anything strange in the sky? I have and that must have something to do with what's happened."

Jeremy looked cautiously at him. "Are you saying you've seen a UFO? That all of this was caused by aliens?" he took a slow step back.

"I'm saying I saw something that makes a lot more sense than an imaginary virus that turns people into robots. Governments want things that kill people, not something that just makes them into a handicap when they move in."

"What exactly did you see?"

"A bright object about the size of a football. It hovered a few feet above a crowd of Stupid. It didn't make any sound, but it changed colour all the time. After five minutes it went dark and moved straight up as if dragged on a line."

"You saw a child's helium balloon. Thermal inversion caused by decreased car exhaust levels kept it spinning slowly in place. Distorted reflections of the sun and advertising displays made it look like it was glowing. When the wind popped it free of the inversion layer it rose so quickly it looked like it was going straight up. No mystery. No aliens. Just a cheap child's toy."

Jeremy sounded so confident that Matthew almost started to reconsider what he had seen. "No, I was there, you weren't. It didn't reflect, it glowed, and when it went up it didn't float – it was like it had been yanked up."

"Aliens," Jeremy said thoughtfully and hummed a few bars from *The Twilight Zone* theme. "Doo de do do! Doo de do do! They came from a dying world to take our women. Their mighty ships hovered above every city, ready to rain down atomic fire." He looked up theatrically. "Except they are not."

Great, thought Matthew. There are exactly two normal people in London and one of them is a small-minded dickhead.

"But it's not just the low IQ is it? What about the riots and sex in the streets? I was reviewing a play and the woman sat next to me started playing with herself. And at work my friend tried to kill me. That's more than somebody's bio-warfare project."

"Your friend attacked you?"

Matthew nodded.

"Friend implies a relationship over an extended period, and in all that time you've never had a cross word, mild disagreement or an argument over whose turn it was to make the coffee?"

"Well I got a pay rise, a very small pay rise, that he didn't and he was a bit miffed about that. But that was ages ago. I'd nearly forgotten all about it."

"But I'm sure he didn't, and normal social mores and natural restraint meant that he'd never say anything about it. Unless he was very drunk of course. And what happens when you are drunk? Depressed dorsolateral cortex function, but you've probably seen all those America dramas where they call it poor impulse control. There's a few CC of brain cells just above your eyes that's the little voice of Jiminy Cricket. It regulates behaviour and suppresses wild swings of emotion and once that's stopped working there's no self-control anymore."

"But it was such a minor disagreement! Barely worth thinking about. I bought him a beer and it was all forgotten."

"You've never been in a pub on a Saturday night and seen someone get punched just for wearing the wrong team's shirt? But alcohol just causes a minor impairment of the cortex. What happened here was a complete shutdown of that area and then there's no such thing as 'minor' anymore. Someone giving you the wrong change is the same as trying to kill you. You're hungry, so you steal food. Too hot? You strip off in the middle of the High Street. And thus the woman in the theatre. Let me guess. The play was the appallingly named *The Eternal Banker*?"

"Yes! But how did you know?"

"Because it's the only play that's opened recently that has a nude scene in it. She saw a bit of skin and was instantly horny." Jeremy looked at Matthew and made a sound like a horse. "Perhaps she didn't like the look of the available men and decided to enjoy her own company. As it were."

"Well that's where you are wrong; right play, but everything happened before that part of the play."

"Ah! The most powerful force in the universe. Antici ..." He waited until Matthew looked up at him. "... pation." He thought this was very funny. He was the only one. "Everything started because for some that area of the brain was affected first and until the rest of the brain reached the same depressed level they were driven hither, thither, downward, upward, by an infernal hurricane of impulses that never rested. No hope doth comfort them evermore, as Dante should have said."

Matthew eyed him carefully. He smelt like a drunk who took a shower once a year, whether or not he needed it, but he sounded like someone that could only ever use three words in place of one.

"But if it was an impulse, why didn't it just pass as quickly as it arrived?"

"You fought back."

"Of course I fought back, I was defending myself!"

"You misunderstand. That wasn't a question it was a reason. *You fought back.* If you'd just stayed perfectly calm then your assailant would have been overcome with guilt and probably thrown himself out of a window. There are snowdrifts of bodies around most high buildings because people became suicidal over much less important matters. Instead, you made your dear friend angry and then there was no way back."

Matthew looked away from Jeremy's smug expression and replayed those few moments in his office. Had there been a moment when the killing grip around his throat had weakened, just before he had brought both elbows back? He replayed the scene over and over with the 20/20 vision of hindsight. He saw the look on Carl's face as the filing cabinet came down. He felt sick; there were too many things he didn't want to think about.

"What happened for you? Where were you when it all fell apart?"

"Felda House. It's a student building in Wembley. It's a pretty rowdy place so I always keep my door locked." He looked sideways at Matthew. "Sometimes uni can be a bit intense."

Matthew nodded. He guessed that that university had not been much fun for someone that liked to bludgeon people into submission with long words while looking down on them from the height of their imagined intellectual superiority. In the pressure cooker of a university, he must have been blood in the water for anyone that liked the more extreme practical jokes. Locking himself in had probably been a basic survival skill. Matthew wondered how many times he had woken up taped to his bed before he had learnt that.

"At first it was just more noise in the corridors, but that was all perfectly normal. It wasn't until I looked outside that I realised something was very wrong. They'd used fire hoses to turn the street into a waterpark. Someone set a light to a car just so they could have a barbeque." Jeremy dropped his voice and leant towards Matthew. "There were people having sex – in public!"

"It was much the same for me," Matthew said. "I was working for *The Bulletin* and ...!"

Jeremy nodded briefly and carried on talking. "The madness went on all day and all night. But little by little I could see there was less running around like lunatics and more just doing nothing at all. I had a fridge and enough food for a few days so I stayed where I was until things got really quiet. Then I went downstairs, but the only people I could find didn't talk to me, didn't respond when I waved my hand in front of their faces. Most were completely static, with just a few repeating a ritual of their daily life over and over. I didn't know what came next, but I figured I'd need some sort of weapon so I came here and found bugger all."

Matthew looked up towards the police station and the offices he could see inside. "Certainly looks like there's plenty of stuff in there."

"Oh, there's probably plenty of stuff in there, but nothing you could ever get to. Certainly not with your Mickey Mouse set of tools."

Matthew decided that he really didn't like Jeremy.

"I knew that the police station was going to be tough to get into so I got a set of those claw things that they use to get into crashed cars from a fire engine on Baker Street."

"The jaws of life?"

Jeremy waved one hand as if swatting a fly. "Whatever. Its petrol engine made a hell of a racket, but when I put the jaws into a door jamb they popped it open with no fuss. I got through three doors like that, but the fourth had a warning sign *Authorised personnel only*, an eight digit punch lock and when I used the jaws nothing happened. Some of the trim came off the door and it was steel underneath with bolts on all four sides into a steel frame. There was no way I was going to get through that with the tools I had."

"How did you manage all that with the lights out?"

"Oh the lights work just fine. I just turned them off when I left to make the place look less inviting." He looked Matthew up and down slowly. "Looks like it worked."

"But what if any other survivors thought about coming here?"

"Then they could bugger off and find their own place. I had some idea about hotwiring a JCB and using it to rip open the building. I didn't want to go to all that trouble just to find out that some rapscallion had got here first."

Matthew smiled noncommittally, as if shutting out other desperate survivors from help was a good idea, and looked Jeremy up and down equally slowly. "Nice outfit," he said, and was rewarded with a blush of embarrassment.

Jeremy shrugged off the fur coat and dropped the top hat on top of a puddle of animal pelts that had probably looked a lot better on their original owners. Under a T-shirt with a picture of Albert Einstein and his puffball of hair, Jeremy was stick thin arms and legs. His jeans were mud-splattered to the knees and when he walked there was only the suggestion of broom handles inside. His arms were fish-belly white skin with no trace of muscle.

"I found the jacket in Harrods. I don't really remember where I got the hat. It probably seemed a good idea at the time. Things got a bit crazy when I realised what had happened. It was the silence that got to me. There was nobody to talk to. You grow up expecting an audience, that there would always be someone there to listen and suddenly there was only silence. Perhaps I went a little mad, I could do anything, and I did everything. I ate and drank and drank some more. I did things that perhaps I shouldn't. I did things I know I shouldn't. Alone is such a simple word, so clean, so harmless until you really understand what it means."

"But now there's two of us. Perhaps there are more, but we need to find some weapons. If we can't get them from here then we need to find them somewhere else. There must be a bookshop near here with a detailed map of the area. We'll find the nearest military base and have a crack at it together." Matthew heard an undercurrent of whine in his voice that he could not hide. Even if Jeremy didn't understand what was going on, he did, and more than anything he wanted to be able to fight.

"I see. Perhaps it would be prudent to acquiesce to your proposal. Even if we are divided on the subject of little green men, strength though greater firepower has always been a good idea," Jeremy said. "And where do you live?"

"Brent Park."

"I think we can do a little better than that. I have a place just a mile or so from here. I'll make you my world famous focaccia di recco with shrimp fra diavolo ecco fatto and we'll plan our next move."

Perhaps Matthew didn't look too excited by that idea because Jeremy added, "It's a very nice place. It's got a radio."

Behind them the wind took the litter and carried it away in waves.

Chapter Fifteen
A Very Nice Apartment.

Jeremy led Matthew back to his place by a route that seemed to include an unusual number of turns that added nothing to the route, except the time it took to get there. Matthew wondered if Jeremy was trying to conceal where he lived. Perhaps he had paranoid visions of the last two men in London fighting over one empty house amongst thousands. He needn't have bothered. The moment Matthew saw the green open space directly across from their destination he knew exactly where they were. It had only been a few minutes since they left Paddington, nowhere near long enough to reach Regent Park, so the green space in front of them had to be Hyde Park. In the distance, he could see an expanse of muddy blue that could only be the Serpentine, the largest lake in London. That meant this had to be the Bayswater Road and the familiar red and blue underground sign down the road was Lancaster Gate Station. He thought he could find Jeremy's lair blindfold, in the dark. But even without the geographical clues there was no way he could forget the building Jeremy was leading him to. Set back a little from the four lanes of the road, it was a gleaming, ten-storey building separated from its neighbours by the thinnest possible gap. All of its floors had tall windows overlooking the park, but only the top floor had delicate-looking balconies of squat columns supporting white stone rails. Its entrance was a flight of marble steps leading to a double-width door framed between rows of classical-looking columns.

"Come on in, let me show you all the attractions of life done right." Jeremy threw open the door and ushered Matthew into a long hall. The floor was alternating black and white marble slabs like a game of chess for giants. Light came from very discrete brass and frosted glass wall lights that looked more suited to the sepia-toned days of gas lamps than anything as common as electricity. Directly in front of them was a wide, sweeping staircase that only needed Fred Astaire and Ginger Rogers to star in a Hollywood film.

"I've got the penthouse suite," Jeremy said. "There's a lift, but it wouldn't be good to get trapped if the power goes off."

"That's okay," Matthew said, but suddenly the staircase didn't look so inviting. "How long do you think the power will stay on for?"

"Well thanks to all that crap about climate change, a sizably percentage of electricity comes from renewables, wind farms and solar panels. They could last for a hundred years, but it's the infrastructure that will fail. Power lines will come down in a storm, junction boxes will flood, and one day the lights will go out."

They started on the first flight of steps and, much to Matthew's satisfaction, Jeremy seemed to find them even harder work than he did. They climbed in silence.

The door at the top of the stairs was black and mirror-smooth. Jeremy shielded his hands very carefully as he unlocked it. Matthew decided that Jeremy really was that paranoid.

The door opened into a room easily as big as a double-width tennis court. The wall directly opposite was filled with gothic, arched windows that showed not only the full depth of the park, but the sprawl of Knightsbridge beyond that and the distant glitter of the Thames. The remaining walls were covered with antique panelling that had very carefully sanded saw marks along the bottom as if it had been stripped from some decaying mansion just before the bulldozers rolled in. Laid across the centre of the room was an ancient, gnarled tree that looked as if it had just fallen, except every branch and root had been trimmed off at exactly the right point to carry the glass top of a coffee table that must have been an inch thick. The carpet was pure white with trails of dirty footprints leading to three doors. Matthew guessed he already knew where the kitchen, bathroom and bedroom were. There were leather sofas scattered all around the edge of the room and that was where Matthew stopped looking at the room, because sat on one of the sofas was one of the most beautiful women he had ever seen.

"This is Gretchen." Jeremy's voice became louder as if he were barking out orders across a parade ground. "Gretchen, stand up."

She very slowly came to her feet.

"Smile, Gretchen, this is a happy occasion."

Her mouth crawled into a smile that showed perfect white teeth and then froze into a rictus grin. She was very slim and doll-like. Her silver dress was several sizes too large, but still short enough to display a generous expanse of finely toned leg. Her hair was pure flaxen blonde that flowed in waves around a heart-shaped face. High, chiselled cheekbones framed hypnotic green eyes that were completely blank. As far as she was concerned Matthew never existed.

Matthew's mouth dropped open. "You can talk to her? She's not like the rest of them?"

Jeremy looked at him with a surprised expression. "She's exactly like the rest of them. You're not very observant are you? All of them are very docile and obedient, although that's subject to change without notice. You tell them to do something and they just do it. I found out just by accident when it looked like three of them were trying to corner me in a supermarket. I shouted at them to go away, and they did. I tried a few more with the same results. Only simple instructions though. You can't, for example, say" – He raised his voice again – "Gretchen, shake Matthew's hand."

She didn't move.

"Because that's far too complicated an order. You have to break it down into very discrete steps. Gretchen, take two steps forward."

She flowed towards Matthew like liquid wax rolling downhill.

"Gretchen, lift your right hand."

Her arm drifted up.

"Gretchen, open your hand."

Her hand came open and she just stopped like a beautiful mannequin that some bored employee had posed for a joke.

"Go on, Matthew, trust me, she doesn't bite."

Matthew looked at Jeremy with disgust. He had ordered Gretchen as if she was nothing more than a machine. The fact that she was a person didn't seem to bother him at all. The fact that she was a stunningly beautiful woman wasn't even a factor in his worldview. Jeremy had no inconvenient empathy that would let him see people as anything other than cogs in a machine that provided service. As far as he was concerned, the only difference between now and a week ago was that people were easier to manage. He looked at Gretchen. She hadn't moved.

"She'll stay like that for hours. But put the poor girl out of her misery and shake her hand." Jeremy sounded amused.

Matthew touched her hand. It was pleasantly warm, smooth and she never reacted at all.

"Well, wasn't that nice. Sit down, Gretchen."

The beautiful mannequin started to sit down on nothing but air, her hand still outstretched.

"No! Take two steps back. Sit on the sofa." Jeremy watched her fold back onto the sofa with very slow, precise movements and then turned to Matthew. "It seems to help if you give them orders in a firm, clear voice. Perhaps it reminds them of authority figures they used to know."

Matthew looked from the stunningly beautiful woman on the sofa to Jeremy with his Einstein T-shirt, untamed hair and mud-splattered jeans.

"How did you get to meet her?"

"I found her in Harrods lingerie department yesterday. She was a bit worse for wear, but she's scrubbed up well."

"How do you know her name is Gretchen?"

"I don't, and it's probably not, but Gretchen is such a nice name." Jeremy gave him a very cool look. "You're not going to get all moralistic about this are you? In a week she'd starve to death, in a

112

month we may all be dead. This is it! The end of the whole damn thing. Just two normal people left in London, perhaps less than a hundred in the whole world. Just how long do you think we have until some routine medical thing carries us off? We have to make the most of the time we have left. Party like it's the end of the world, because it *is* the end of the world! Nobody is being hurt here. I'm just helping some of those that cannot help themselves and all I want is a little comfort in return." He lowered his voice and spoke very quietly. "Just think; there is a city full of people out there. Anyone you'd ever loved is out there and they need your help. But everyone is out there: the woman that looked at you like dirt just because you wanted to buy her a drink, the women that laughed in your face. They're not laughing now. But you can help them, you could look after them and who knows how grateful they really would be?"

Jeremy pulled Gretchen's knee towards him, opening up a shadowy space between her thighs.

"What do you think?"

Matthew thought that he'd punch Jeremy square between the eyes and storm out. He thought that first he'd kick him between the legs so hard that it would permanently make sex a theoretical concept. He was a pervert, a rapist. He was dangerous to be near. He was a monster.

But he was also right.

They might be the last two men in London. They had a duty to look after their fellow man – or woman. They could do anything and no one would know. They could do everything he'd ever imagined. There would be no restraint, no one to

113

say no. He knew where Kirsten lived, where she worked. He could find her in the morning, find her friend and then they could 'play' together.

Then he imagined Kirsten's face blank and empty. Whatever he found would not be the woman he'd known, with her quick humour and sharp observations on life. She would be just a shell and no matter what had happened between them he could not bear to see her like that.

Matthew eyed the distance to the door. He could be out of this teenager's wet dream in a moment, at home in a little while more. He told himself that he would only stay to look after Gretchen, that he would be her protector, but he knew that he lied. He had so easily rejected Jeremy's idea, but the idea was still there like a maggot festering in warm meat.

"Well, not right now," Matthew said.

Jeremy's face dropped. "Your loss, but I wouldn't take too long making up your mind. It's a very interesting phenomenon, but I don't think it's going to last. In a few days, a week at most, they're not going to be so malleable. Language comprehension is provided by Wernicke's area of the brain and either because of its location or complexity that's still working nearly normally. So they can understand everything we say, but Freud's tripartite structure of id, ego and super-ego has gone along with the other high-level brain functions. Then you have a situation where there is no filter between external verbal commands and the motor control systems." He must have seen Matthew staring at him open-mouthed because he added. "Three years of Cognitive Psychology. Once you've written a few essays on the biological substrates of behaviour you soon pick up the vocabulary." He gave Matthew a very superior smile. "Perhaps you might want to consider the time-limited nature of my offer while I make us something to eat."

Matthew sat down next to Gretchen and the moment Jeremy disappeared into the kitchen changed seats. Sitting close to someone that lacked all the small signs of life was deeply unsettling. Gretchen never changed her thousand-yard stare, never fidgeted, crossed her legs or looked bored. Except for the regular rise and fall of her chest, she might have been a corpse that had not had time to rot. If Jeremy planned to take her to bed tonight, then not only was he a pervert, but he lacked imagination. Lying next to her would be a scene from a late-night horror film, just waiting for the moment her eyes would shutter open to reveal inhuman silvery orbs. Then it would just be running and screaming.

"There you go." Jeremy dropped a loaded plate in front of Matthew and never noticed when he jumped.

Matthew wasn't sure what he had expected from Jeremy's grandiose posturing, but it certainly wasn't a microwaved pizza with boil in the bag noodles.

"Thank you, it looks lovely," he said, and tried to sound sincere.

Jeremy put a plate on Gretchen's lap. Her pizza had been carefully sliced into coin-sized bites.

He saw Matthew looking. "They don't feed very well. Sometimes they forget to chew and start choking. Baby food is perfect, but it takes ten of those tiny jars to make a decent meal for an adult, and then a bit later the, erm, solid waste produced isn't so solid." He pushed Gretchen's plate towards her. "Take one piece of food, chew and swallow." And the beautiful, blank-faced automation raised one perfectly manicured hand from plate to mouth. "Don't wait for her, she'll be ages yet, dig in! Enjoy!"

The pizza was soggy, the noodles tasted of ketchup. But it was Matthew's first shared meal since things fell apart and that made it perfect.

"Drink?" Jeremy produced a bottle and without waiting filled a tall glass to the brim and pushed it across the table. "Food of the Gods, the best cooking, the best comforts." He began massaging Gretchen's thigh with greasy fingers. "And unsurpassed personnel services."

Matthew took a drink as an excuse to look away and immediately began coughing.

"Only the best brandy for my friends. Heavy with the passage of time. Sweet with the dark, rich flavours of hillsides dreaming in the sun, and it's fifty percent proof." Jeremy took a long drink like it was coke. He didn't cough, but his face went very red.

They ate in silence, except for Jeremy's open-mouthed chewing and the drain-clearing sounds as he drank. From time to time Matthew picked up his glass and made a great show of drinking, and Jeremy never noticed that the level in his glass didn't change very much. Jeremy finished the bottle by himself.

Jeremy pushed his empty plate away from him. "Well that was nice, but now we've got to start planning."

"Plan what for? I thought it was all over."

"There's everything to plan for. You think we are the only Normals left in London? Even if the survival rate was a fraction of a percent that means there could be hundreds, perhaps thousands, of us scattered all over London. Hiding in basements. Behind closed blinds. And every one of them is looking for deliverance. Someone to lead them to a better tomorrow."

Matthew thought about saying that just an hour ago Jeremy had been very emphatic that they were the only two left in London. But he saw now that words had a very plastic meaning to Jeremy. He could make them fit whatever argument he was spinning. He would have made an excellent politician.

"Our mission is to find all those people, bring them together in a common cause and build a better tomorrow under enlightened leadership that will build on the successes of the past and avoid its mistakes."

Matthew wondered what role Jeremy saw for himself in his bright new future. President for life or dear leader? "But if these people are scattered all over London, how are we going to find them?"

Jeremy waved a finger at Matthew as if he had just said something very profound. "And that's exactly the sort of small-minded thinking that's always made progress so difficult. You need blue-sky thinking at times like these. Literally, blue sky. Heathrow Airport is only fifteen miles from here.

They'll have helicopters and stuff so we can cover London in an afternoon!"

"Can you fly a helicopter?"

"There'll be books and things. We'll read up on it. How hard can it be?"

Matthew knew exactly how hard it could be. For his eighteenth birthday, in place of the motorbike he wanted, his parents had bought him a helicopter experience session at a local airfield. The session had lasted just thirty minutes, but he had staggered out of the cockpit as if he had just run a marathon. He'd learnt very quickly that flying a helicopter was like roller skating, while patting your head and rubbing your stomach. There were levers for both left and right hands that made the helicopter move up, down and sideways. And if that wasn't enough then there were pedals that made the aircraft rotate. The instructor later told him that the longest continuous time he'd spent actually in control of the helicopter was just thirty seconds, when he'd managed the difficult feat of having it sliding sideways at fifty miles per hour. Matthew thought that their chances of flying a helicopter were only slightly less than getting to Heathrow in the first place. Jeremy had said fifteen miles as if the streets weren't a permanent frozen traffic jam and they could just hail a black cab to get there.

"In the morning, we'll find a printers and run off some leaflets to drop from the air. We'll direct everyone to Hyde Park, setup a few tables and offer them a hot drink and a sandwich when they arrive!"

Matthew guessed the printers might be the only part of Jeremy's brilliant plan that he would attempt. After that, everything else would either be too difficult or somebodies else's problem.

Jeremy reminded him of his manager in his first job. He had been very big on what he called broad-stroke planning: wild-assed plans that would completely transform the company into a world leader. Any requests for the detail that would make up his broad stokes was treated with contempt and the ideas that had dominated a whole day's meeting vanished like summer mist.

Matthew opened his mouth to ask where they would find the tables and a sharp ammonia smell caught the back of his throat and made him gag. He coughed, more of the pungent smell hit him and he coughed again.

"You alright?" Jeremy said. He lowered his glass and looked across at Gretchen, and then down. Matthew followed his gaze to the growing puddle on the carpet between Gretchen's toned legs.

"Gretchen!"

She didn't react.

"Stand up!"

She came slowly to her feet and Matthew saw the wet stain on the back of her mini dress. It was the worst thing he had ever seen. Worse than civilisation falling apart. Much worse than Jeremy's pawing at the unaware woman. She had wet herself.

Matthew's parents had been devout Catholics and every Sunday morning had been spent in church singing about God's bountiful love, although, as far as he was concerned, the central tenant of their faith had been that the body was dirty. His brother had been delivered by the stork after a mysterious stopover in hospital. Nobody went to the toilet or used the bathroom; they just popped out of the room for a moment. Baths were the briefest possible dip in tepid water in case anyone thought about what you were doing. Even years later, the memory of the time the flush had broken after using the toilet made him want to vomit. He had thought he had left all those feelings behind when he left home, but seeing the yellow threads of urine tracing down Gretchen's legs instantly recalled the disgust and revulsion he had been so carefully trained to feel. It didn't matter that Gretchen didn't know what was happening. He did, and he felt all the shame and humiliation she would have felt. Perhaps, somewhere deep inside, there was still a part of her crying with embarrassment.

"Bugger!" Jeremy said. "I tried to make sure she used the toilet at least once every two hours. Looks like I forgot. Come on, Gretchen, let's get you cleaned up." He tried to lever himself out of his seat and dropped back with an audible whomp. "Oops, that stuff goes straight to your legs." His voice took on the commanding tone he had used before. "Gretchen, go to the bathroom."

She trudged past Matthew to something behind him.

"No, not that door, the other door. Open the door."

Clunk of something opening.

"There's a big silver knob on the wall. Turn it all the way to the right." Jeremy waited until he heard the sound of a shower running. "Step under the water, hold the soap, rub it all over." Turning back to Matthew, he added, "You have to do everything for them. There's no way they can even tell you anything is wrong."

"Why are they completely silent? Shouldn't they at least have a few words?"

"Conduction aphasia caused by differing levels of impairment in the brain," Jeremy said confidently. "Language production comes from Broca's area and that is completely inactive. So that's all the linguistic labels gone but comprehension comes from Wernicke's area, which is nearly normal. The unequal cooling of the brain has knocked everyone right back to the pre-linguistic systems of our primate ancestors."

"So shouldn't they be able to growl or something?"

"Growling is a fear response. Fear implies recognition of a threat, and there's no hazard database to call on anymore. I could stand Gretchen in front of a speeding car and she wouldn't even blink. She's like a computer that's been wiped. It's only reflex arcs that allow her to breathe at all. Everything else is gone."

"So what happens now? How long before they starve to death?"

"We'll sort something out." But perhaps Jeremy didn't like that topic of conversation because he looked past Matthew towards the sound of running water. "That's long enough, Gretchen. Step out from the water. Use a towel to dry yourself off." Turning back to Matthew, he continued, "She's probably left everything in a mess, but there's another three bathrooms on this floor before we need to think about moving."

"Move? I'll give you a hand to sort things out in the morning."

"Why? It's like the old joke. When all the ashtrays in your car are full it's time to change it. We've got more to worry about than a few dirty floors. Your little green men for instance." He looked past Matthew again. "That's enough drying off, Gretchen. Come out and give us a twirl." To Matthew, he added, "She's got great …" He stopped mid-sentence and began to giggle. Then he laughed in a shrill, yapping sound. Matthew twisted to look behind him. Gretchen was standing in the bathroom door, soaking wet, covered with soap and fully dressed. "I didn't tell her to get undressed," Jeremy said between laughs. He levered himself out of his seat, using the table to help him stand. "If you want something doing, then you have to do it yourself." He looked down at Matthew and smirked. "You can help if you want. I'm sure she could be very … accommodating."

"Erm, no thanks. In fact I better go if I want to get home before dark."

Jeremy shrugged. "Why go? There are four bedrooms here you can choose from. Try the rose room. It's got a great view of the park and in the morning we can have a greasy fry-up and work out how to fight your invvvaddders from sssspace." Jeremy rolled his eyes, but his sneer looked forced, as if he really didn't want Matthew to go. Perhaps his new lifestyle was nothing without an audience.

Matthew forced a yawn and then realised it was only too real. "Well, okay then." He'd walked for miles through an empty city carrying a sledgehammer and a pair of bolt cutters. He'd met the only other normal person in London and discovered that he was a degenerate pervert. It had been a busy day. "I'll see you in the morning."

"I'll see you at some point. It might be a busy night." He winked at Matthew. "I hope."

Matthew made it to the door before he heard the sound of wet clothes being removed. And laughter.

The rose room had rose-patterned wallpaper, a shockingly pink carpet and vases of real roses on nightstands either side of a huge double bed. The roses had died several days ago and blackened petals covered the tables and floor. Matthew swept as much of the corruption as he could back into the vases, and then both vases into the bin. The roses on the bathroom wallpaper had cruelly barbed thorns with a tiny drop of blood on each point, which made him think about the apartment's real owners. He wondered where they were now, how the end came for them. Perhaps it had been merciful and between one breath and the next the light had gone out of their eyes. He hoped so.

There were men's pyjamas under the pillows on both sides of the bed, but nothing could have made Matthew wear them. He undressed as if about to be surprised at any second and slipped under rose-patterned sheets as quickly as possible. The bed was very comfortable and after some brief experimentation Matthew found the right switch to turn out the lights.

He lay in the darkness for an hour, watching the faint glow of the alarm clock on the ceiling as the silence gathered around him. He felt more alone than he had ever been before. Finding Jeremy had been the proof that everything really had changed. He closed his eyes and tried to remember pushing through the crowds on Oxford Street, the wall of people around any bar – gone, all gone. Very slowly, the city flowed away from him and he hung weightlessly, suspended between sleep and consciousness. The creaks and groans as the building cooled jarred him from sleep and he found himself burrowing further under the sheets like a child hiding from the bogey man.

Chapter Sixteen
Friends in High Places III

M'reth drew the knife across his throat, but his hand was slick with blood and the knife fell to the floor with a bright tinkling sound. He looked up at Cheilith and silently begged him for help.

Cheilith pressed a finger against M'reth's forehead as a mark of respect and then knelt down for the knife. He wiped its handle with a part of his shirt that wasn't already soaked in blood, held the blade to M'reth's throat and slashed it from ear to ear.

Cheilith stepped back from the arterial spurt of blood. But he knew that what they had done here today had soaked his very essence and he would never sleep well again until he could join the dead.

He looked around the room, listening for any sign of life. Some had taken poison rather than use the knife and their mouths dribbled foam, others had placed an explosive bolt cutter to their head and parts of their skull were missing. But most had cut their throats or slashed their wrists and the floor was pooled with blood. Some died easy, other died hard and Cheilith was always there to help. When he was done he looked as if he had stood under a shower of blood. He looked at the keen edge of the knife, pricked his finger with its point. More than anything, he wanted the freedom that the knife would give him. But the logic was remorseless. The surgery worked, but would be instantly noticed. The only sure way to escape the Masters' control was death, but some needed to survive to tell the inhabitants of this strange blue planet of the room in the pyramid that would let them turn the Masters' home to ash. They had worked the probability for a long time, and they were very good with numbers. Each slave left alive was a risk, and the safest number was one. Just one survivor and the black stone had chosen him.

The ceiling flashed blue and Cheilith realised that it was nearly time for the Masters to call on them again. He dragged the stolen welding kit from its hiding place and ran a rough bead around the edge of the door. It wouldn't stop them for long, but maybe long enough.

Cheilith pushed the welding kit back into hiding and kicked the communicator they had used into scrap. Then he stood quietly checking off a final item on a mental checklist, making sure everything was ready, because it had to be ready.

It had taken generations to get to this point, each year lying to the Masters just a little more, letting them know how safe their slaves were, how trustworthy they were. They had wasted a lot of that time trying to find a way to disable the source of the Masters' power, but there were too many interlocks, too many manual checks. But then they had realised that the defence's strength was also its weakness. There was no way to turn the power off without being noticed, but there also was no way to see that the power had been turned on prematurely during an invasion cycle. Then the Immunes would have the power of the Masters and could use it to wipe them from history.

The Masters had owned them, body and mind, especially mind. They had suffered until there were no words to describe their pain, but soon the bill

126

would come for everything they had done. And that day would be sweet beyond measure

Cheilith looked around the room they had lived in one last time. But it was also the room where the Masters had ordered them to rut like animals until there were enough pregnancies to provide them with a new generation of slaves. And that had nearly undone them. The Masters had thought the stillbirths and mutations were some protest and began a search that very nearly uncovered the real plan. Until they had managed to explain Minimum Genetic Population and the effects of long-term inbreeding to the Masters they had lived every day in fear.

Cheilith pulled the grate from the ventilation shaft that had been so easy to add to the construction. No one had questioned why a ventilation shaft needed to be large enough to admit a slave. He slid inside on clothes slick with blood and pulled the grate shut behind him. He inched along the shaft, around a corner and down into the bowels of the ship where he would be safe until it was time.

Chapter Seventeen
Communication

In the morning, Matthew felt newly dead. He seemed to have been awake more than he had slept. The only consolation was that Jeremy looked even worse. Despite his aim of being late up, he had already been in the living room when Matthew got up at seven. For a horrified moment he thought that Jeremy's immunity had worn off and that he was just another Stupid. His eyes were red-rimmed, his face slack, but then he had looked up and said, "Morning."

Gretchen wasn't with him.

Perhaps having his own living doll hadn't been quite the playboy fantasy he had expected. Perhaps there had been a brief moment of empathy when he had seen Gretchen as a person and himself as a monster.

"Good morning," Matthew said, unnecessarily brightly. "You look tired."

"And you look like crap," Jeremy said, without an attempt at a smile.

Matthew wondered for a moment if that had been some attempt at a joke or if Jeremy was always that rude and then decided that it didn't really matter. When he'd decided to stay he knew that Jeremy was the least awful choice. Perhaps in a week or two he might change his mind.

"Sorry," Jeremy said, massaging his head. "Not really with it yet. Give me a few minutes to come round and I'll get you that breakfast I promised you."

"That's okay, you did dinner last night. The least I can do is make breakfast."

"Sure?"

"Absolutely." Matthew thought that if what Jeremy had done to that pizza last night was any guide he was going to be doing a lot more of the cooking. Especially breakfast. Matthew's degree at university had been Multimedia Journalism, but the most important thing he had learnt was that a good greasy fry-up was the perfect cure for everything from a hangover to a bad grade. Discussions on the perfect breakfast had taken on an almost evangelical fervour. He had been one of the few standouts to maintain that a breakfast could only approach perfection if it included black pudding. Fried not grilled.

"Where's the kitchen?"

"The door behind me," Jeremy said with a backwards jerk of his thumb. "There's some stuff in the fridge. Thanks."

He might almost have meant it.

In complete contrast to the living room, the kitchen was an ultra-modern expanse of stark white units surgically lit by a grid of tiny spotlights hung from chrome rods. The fridge was a double-width American model and when Matthew opened it, it was nearly empty. A small packet of bacon lay in solitary splendour on one shelf, above it was a box of eggs and an unopened pack of eight sausages. There was no black pudding. He checked the fridge, twice.

As he took each package from the fridge, he carefully checked its best before date. He hated the idea of throwing out something just a few days older than its suggested date, but hated even more the idea of spending what might be his last days throwing up. He was pleasantly surprised to find that even the sausages had several more days before they could be considered suspicious. Everything must have been delivered just as things were falling apart. Matthew wondered what the owner had thought when he placed the shopping in the fridge. Had he been dimly aware that something was wrong? Had he – like the policeman – peered at the printing and wondered why he was having trouble reading?

The saucepans were heavy cast iron and Matthew put two to heat while he found the bread. It was a bit hard, but he was only going to fry it anyway. The sausages were some expensive brand that he had never heard of, but they browned nicely under the grill. At the precise point that the eggs were white with a perfect yellow centre, he served everything up on two plates and presented one to Jeremy with a flourish. "Your breakfast, sir."

"Wow, that looks amazing. Just one thing to make it perfect." Jeremy dodged back into the kitchen, came back with a bottle of ketchup and poured most of it over his carefully prepared breakfast. "Lovely."

He never saw Matthew flinch.

Jeremy tore into his mutilated meal as if it had been a while since he had seen real food. Perhaps it was, Matthew thought. When he had finished, Jeremy pushed his plate away with a sigh of contentment. "That was the best thing I've had to eat since everything turned to shit."

130

"No problem. It seemed only fair." And the best way to get something decent to eat, Matthew thought. A few minutes later he finished eating and since Jeremy's plate was precariously balanced on the edge of the sofa, Matthew picked that up as well.

"Thanks," Jeremy said, absently. "Two sugars in my tea please."

Matthew looked down on Jeremy, who in turn was fiddling with a TV remote, and resisted the urge to drop both plates in his lap from a great height. Jeremy obviously saw himself as the great tribal leader and Matthew as the kitchen skivvy. He decided that this time he'd let it slide, but if Jeremy tried it again then they would have what his mother described as 'a word' – a very pointed exchange of views on how things should be done, with most of the information flowing just one way.

Matthew loaded the plates and pans into the Swedish dishwasher while the kettle boiled. The more he saw of Jeremy, the more he resembled a twelve-year-old child, with a sixty-year-old brain. He was probably very smart, but he had never had the chance for his rough edges to be smoothed away – and that meant anyone who spent any time with him was in for a bruising experience. And Jeremy seemed to be the only other normal person in London.

The milk was just a day past its best before date and still smelled like something that had involved a cow. Matthew added just enough to get the correct colour then the two sugars that Jeremy had ordered and turned to leave. At the swing door into the living room he stopped to switch both cups into one hand and heard Jeremy talking and another male voice replying. He froze in place, one hand resting on the door, the other dribbling tea on the floor. The thickness of the door meant that he couldn't make out what either person was saying, but he knew exactly what was going on. Jeremy's story that they were the last two men in London had been just that. A story. There were probably hundreds, perhaps thousands, of normal people in London. Probably every room in this building was crammed with survivors. The only question was if Jeremy's story had been some sort of newbie hazing or an ethics test. Perhaps if he had gone along with Jeremy's suggestion and gone prowling for women, he would have been ejected from whatever the survivors were building.

Matthew pushed the door open, barged into the living room and stopped dead, trying to work out what he was seeing. Jeremy was talking into the TV remote he had been fiddling with and the answering voice seemed to come from everywhere.

Jeremy looked up and took a cup from Matthew's unresisting hand. "Thanks for that." He took a sip. "Nice cup of tea."

The omnipresent voice said something in a sing-song accent and Jeremy grimaced. "Great isn't it. The only person I could reach is Swedish and doesn't have any English."

"It's Norwegian," Matthew said. "He's asking you your name and where you are."

"You speak Norwegian! That's great."

"My girlfriend, my ex-girlfriend, was Norwegian. I only have a few words." Some of the words he had learnt after their breakup. He didn't

132

think 'bitch', 'lesbian' and 'slag' would be much use in polite conversation.

"Well, go on then, tell him who I am."

"How? Do I just talk and he can hear me?"

Jeremy looked at him as if he had just suggested flapping his arms to fly. "No, you'll need the remote. The top is a microphone for the shortwave radio in there." He jerked his head in a way that could have indicated any of the four doors to his left. "Press 'send' to speak." Jeremy's hands had left the remote warm and sweaty.

"*Hei jeg heter Matthew*," Hello, my name is Matthew, he said slowly.

The reply was a gable of Norwegian he couldn't follow. But he could hear that it was coming from the speakers optimally placed all over the room so that the sofa was their focus.

"*Sakte vennligst*," Slowly please, he said.

The disembodied voice repeated what it had just said, but very slowly and carefully as if speaking to a child.

"I think he's saying that his name is Arvid Gundersen and he's from somewhere called Lakselv."

"Ask him how things are there? Are there normal people?"

The best word Matthew knew for normal was okay, but Arvid seemed to understand what he meant. "He says that everyone else is *langsom*, slow. He tried an expedition, drive I guess, to the nearest city, but the road was blocked."

"Has he managed to talk to anyone else?"

"He says someone from Canada answered, but they had no Norwegian and the only word he managed to make out was stupid. It's the same in both languages."

"So it sounds like whatever has happened is worldwide. Has he seen any flying saucers or little green men?" Jeremy said with no inflection at all.

Matthew gave him a very cool look. "He says no, nothing at all." Matthew opened his mouth to say something and the voice from the speakers drowned him out.

"He's low on power and he'll talk to us tomorrow. I think Lakselv is right at the furthest edge of Norway, further north than Iceland. I guess the electricity can be a bit intermittent there."

The hiss of a carrier wave stopped abruptly and silence seemed to rush back into the room.

"I didn't know this place had a shortwave radio," Matthew said.

"Well, I did say."

"Yes you did, didn't you," and Matthew was sure the confusion had been deliberate. Jeremy used secrets like a bored child using a laser pointer to torment a cat, dropping hints and suggestions to tease his audience until they begged for the answer. He had probably been disappointed when there had been no reaction to his casual 'It's a very nice place. It's got a radio' and his second attempt had been to make sure that Matthew saw him playing with the remote to set him up for the big reveal. Jeremy liked playing games. He'd have to remember that.

"It was the shortwave that brought me here. After everything turned to shit I thought a transmitter would let me contact other survivors. I had no idea how to find one, so I walked around the edge of Hyde Park looking for a building with extra aerials. The first one I found was somebody's foreign embassy, and that was locked up tight. Then I saw the mast on top of this building. I started with the top apartment because it would have the required roof access and found the radio straight away. Have a look later if you want. It's got more dials and knobs than a 747, but the owner mustn't have wanted to be shut away when he talked to his friends because he had this fancy microphone/remote control. I spent ages yesterday scanning up and down each of the bands and all I found was that Swedish guy."

"Norwegian."

"Whatever. And he was a fat lot of good. I guessed that whatever happened was all over; being able to talk to Arvid just confirmed that."

"Well until we can talk to him again one thing we have to do is get some more food. The fridge is nearly empty and the only food items in the cabinets are pasta and a few cans of crushed tomatoes. I think the owners must have eaten out a lot. I've got several days' supplies back at my place. We can make a trip to get them and on the way back find a map or something so we can find the nearest army base and get some weapons."

"To fight the invaders from Mars?"

"Something like that."

Jeremy tapped his fingers thoughtfully. "You raided a supermarket for your supplies?"

Matthew nodded.

"Okay, well I've got my own department store just across the park. We'll take a backpack each and load up with as much tinned food as we can carry. There's a tourist information point on the ground

135

floor, so there'll be an A to Z and maps. We get the food today and tomorrow find some bikes to get to the nearest army base."

There was no upwards inflection at the end of Jeremy's little speech. It wasn't a question; it was a flat statement of how things would be. Matthew wondered if this was the time for a pointed exchange of views, but the plan made sense. Objecting to it would just be cutting off his nose to spite his face.

"Sounds like a plan," he said grudgingly.

"Okay, I'll get a quick shower and we'll make a start before it gets any later."

"What about Gretchen?"

Jeremy's face dropped and suddenly he didn't look so happy.

"I'll let her sleep in. It's probably better that way."

Chapter Eighteen
A Grand Hall

Harrods is the biggest department store in England, and arguably the most famous in the world. It started out as a small fruit and veg shop in London's East End before moving to Knightsbridge. In the sepia-toned days of the telex, its address – Everything, London – was used to order Rolls Royces for Maharajas and rich tea biscuits for ex-pats. The store covers over five acres and its Edwardian terracotta facade is a major landmark for lost tourists.

Matthew saw the burnt orange building the moment they turned into the Brompton Road and the static traffic jam that had overflowed to brush up against the building itself. Then he saw that cars had been driven across the wide London pavements to butt up against each entrance into the building. Because it was Knightsbridge, one of the richest places in London, if not the world, the nearest entrance had a gleaming red Ferrari parked across its doors.

"You sealed off the building?" Matthew said, incredulously.

"Yup! It was the only way to stop the Stupid from just carrying on ingrained habits and carrying things out of the store." Jeremy pointed at a flock of birds fighting over something on the pavement. "You see the mess on the pavement? I watched a very elegant lady carry a basket of shopping out of the store, dump it on the pavement and repeat. I guess that was where a car would have been to pick her up but she was just following a pattern and never noticed."

"How long did it take to close off the building?"

"Surprisingly enough, not long. The cars were just sat on the road, so all I had to do was pull one out of the queue and over the pavement. The worst part was driving that Ferrari. It's an automatic and I've never driven one of those before."

Matthew had already noticed the front end of the Ferrari was dented where it touched the building.

"Nice parking. But what about all the people inside?"

"That was easy. I found a microphone that was patched into the store's public announcement system. Then all I had to say was 'Leave the building' and most of them did. There were a few too far gone to understand the order and a few more that just wandered back into the store, but the whole thing only took a couple of hours. There's a service entrance on Basil Street that we can use. The door's not locked. I couldn't find any keys, otherwise I wouldn't have had to use the cars, but that's not a problem these days. None of these guys know how to use anything that complicated now."

"So we have all the food and they just starve?"

"And what's the alternative? That we let them all just wander in, pick up something that they have no idea how to use and then dump it on the pavement? If we let them in the only things getting fed are the rats and birds. They don't win and we don't win. Times have moved on since help thy neighbour was a good idea. The rules have changed and the sooner you learn that the better." Jeremy turned left into a side road. A hundred yards later, he stopped and pointed at the wall next to him. "Voila!"

Set almost invisibly into the wall was a sturdy wooden door reinforced with metal strips. Matthew guessed that even exclusive Knightsbridge must have its fair share of opportunistic thieves looking for an easy way in. Jeremy gestured him into a short length of industrial-green corridor and closed the street door behind them before pushing past him to the door at the other end of the corridor. He smelt of sweat overlaid with too much aftershave and Matthew's smile became very fixed as they came into contact.

Jeremy threw open the inner door and swept his hand down a bank of switches. "Welcome to my store."

Banks of lights lit up in sequence showing a grand hall bigger than a football ground. Light sparkled from gilt-encrusted, ornate pillars that reached up to a ceiling heavy with Art Deco mouldings. Shining glass counters waiting only for earnest young assistants were set in a very precise grid like a sieve to separate the unwary from their money. The honey-coloured floor was crunchy with smashed bottles and the air was thick with the cloying aroma of scent that made Matthew cough. One complete side of the great hall was windows looking out at the street and the slow underwater motion of the Stupid there. The opposite wall was lined by glass shelves, sparsely populated by kid leather handbags with jewelled handles and gaudy necklaces. Nothing had a price tag.

139

"This way," Jeremy said and walked briskly away, assuming that Matthew would follow. He didn't want to, he'd rather have been anywhere but here with him, but as Jeremy left him behind he reluctantly followed.

The worst thing about the store was its emptiness. Everywhere Matthew looked was designed for hordes of well-heeled shoppers and their absence created an almost physical pressure. Every small motion of designer fabric in the breeze from air conditioner vents held his eye as he dragged his head first left then right with the expectation of seeing a waiting assistant.

Jeremy stopped at a counter with a very discreet sign: *Visitor Information Centre*. "Hang on. Let me get a map and an A to Z," he said and ducked into a back room.

Matthew looked around the exclusive store and decided that the absolute worst thing was the shop-floor mannequins. They were just too lifelike, too like the Stupid outside. He found himself looking into the face of every mannequin around him, checking to see if their eyes were flesh and blood or just plaster.

Jeremy reappeared with a well-thumbed, thick book and a much smaller volume with a glossy picture of Buckingham Palace on its cover.

"The best I could find was a Yellow Pages and a guidebook with a central area map. It will have to do. The food department is just through here." Jeremy pushed open a fire door and Matthew knew with complete certainly that the worst possible thing was the sickly, rotting smell that poured out.

"Sorry about this. Some of the fresh food isn't anymore." Jeremy passed him a small jar of Vicks VapoRub. "Rub some of this around your nostrils; it blocks the smell."

Matthew pushed his finger through the jar's creamy gel and then under his nose. The decongestant tingled as if it were ice cold, but almost immediately all he could smell was menthol. As he handed back the jar he noticed that it was more than part used, and Jeremy already had a gel moustache in place. He must have applied it while looking for the guidebook, but he had waited until opening the door into the food department before offering the same thing to Matthew.

"I thought about throwing out all the perishable stuff. But didn't quite get around to it,"

I bet you didn't, thought Matthew. Because that would mean doing some real work, not just something flashy like blocking the doors with cars when a doorstop would have worked just as well.

Jeremy dropped his empty backpack on top of a display cabinet. "Drop your bag here and we'll fill them both up with what we need. Tinned stuff only, even if any of the fresh stuff looks all right we can't take the risk of coming down with food poisoning. Try for a mixture of sweet and savoury."

Matthew resisted the temptation to snap off a smart salute and put his bag next to Jeremy's on the display cabinet. Then he made the mistake of looking *into* the display cabinet. His first horrified thought was that the things there were somehow alive. A vague shape under a label seethed and boiled. The curved glass screen under his hands was flecked with pale dots. It was only when he saw that the dots were moving that he realised – it was meat boiling with maggots. It had lain here for five days and the flies had laid their eggs in what the rats had left behind. By tomorrow the great hall would be alive with black clouds of flies.

Matthew recoiled from the display cabinet and moved into the rows of shelves behind him, trying to keep his hands busy so his mind would stop replaying the crawling life under the glass. After he had an armful of cans he carried them back to the two open packs and dropped them in, making sure not to look at what was happening under the glass the backpacks were sitting on. He repeated the cycle two more times before he saw what Jeremy was doing.

Matthew looked up from a tin of nicoise olives (with zucchini and burrata) as Jeremy approached the backpacks with a handful of tins. But then instead of just packing them away, he carefully checked around him, did something quick with both backpacks before heading back to the shelves. Matthew watched as he disappeared behind a soup display. Because it had been such a furtive gesture, as if he were hiding something. And that made no sense at all. Pocketing something for himself would be like taking another mouthful at an all-you-can-eat buffet. They were surrounded by shops, cafes and supermarkets. They could eat until they threw up and never run out of food. But Jeremy had done something with both backpacks and Matthew studied them both carefully. Black Kevlar fabric, both nearly full. Completely identical.

Matthew made sure Jeremy was not in sight before he headed back to the counter. He placed each tin very carefully and realised that he had been wrong. The two backpacks were not identical. The one on the left was filled with everything lightweight: fibre bars, crisps and biscuits. The one on the right held all the tins, bottles of wine and long life milk. He hefted the leftmost one thoughtfully. It weighed virtually nothing, the other he could barely lift. Matthew guessed that when it was time to go Jeremy would casually take the lightweight bag, leaving him to do the heavy lifting while he skipped happily along.

"Nearly done," Jeremy said, very close behind him. "This lot should keep us going for a few days."

"It will. By the way, did you see any tinned prunes?"

Jeremy looked over his left shoulder. "Back there somewhere I think."

"Great, you get some of those and I'll get some orange juice. My old mum always said you have to be regular to be happy." Matthew's mum had never said any such thing, could never say any such thing. But Jeremy grunted and walked back into the rows of shelving while Matthew headed the other way. And the moment Jeremy was out of sight he did a U-turn and lifted the lightweight bag over the heavy bag so their positions were reversed. He moved a few tins into the lightweight bag for appearance and replaced them with a handful of cereal bars.

"There you go." Jeremy showed him two tins of prunes and placed them casually in the right-hand bag. Matthew held his breath in case he noticed that there were only a few tins on a bed of cereal bars and biscuits, but Jeremy just zipped up that bag, then the one he had so carefully filled with everything heavy, and lifted it on his shoulders. His smug expression instantly disappeared as he pulled up on the straps cutting into his shoulders. "But this isn't–"

"Isn't what?" Matthew said, but he said it as he pushed his arms through the straps of the other bag and lifted it into position. It was so light it was difficult to know it was there.

"Nothing," Jeremy said with a carefully neutral expression and turned towards the exit. His backpack was pulled into a teardrop shape by the weight of its contents. Matthew hoped that he had acquired them from a shop that believed in a quality product where seams were double stitched.

Before they had reached the doors leading from the food hall, Jeremy's confident walk had slowed and widened into a waddle like a child with a full nappy. Matthew choked off a laugh. The end of the world had come and gone and they were living it up in posh apartments and playing silly games. Jeremy barged through the door, letting it swing back in Matthew's face. But perhaps this was the time to play silly games because this was the easy bit. Soon the Stupid would starve to death and the city would stink like a charnel pit. Then they would have to leave their comfortable apartment and life without a fully stocked department store might not be so funny.

Jeremy leaned forward as if closely examining the floor to stop the weight of the backpack pulling him back. Now his centre of gravity was easier to manage, but soon all the small muscles low down in his back would be screaming in agony. Would he ask for help then, or soldier on, hating each footstep, and then find some way to pay Matthew back? Perhaps he would short sheet his bed or over-salt his food. Either sounded about right for the teen drama they seemed to be living in.

Jeremy looked back at him. "What's so funny?"

"I was just thinking that once they might not have allowed people like us into Harrods at all, but now we can just take whatever we want."

"We might be the last men. The least we can do is enjoy it," Jeremy said shortly.

When they reached the door to the street he turned off the lights and let Matthew grope along the last few feet of corridor in complete darkness. When Jeremy opened the door, the daylight outside was blinding.

Chapter Nineteen
Progress Test

After the crowded food hall, the outside seemed incomprehensibly open. The modern steel and glass building across the permanent traffic jam that filled the Brompton Road seemed more distant than ever before, the sky more vividly blue than anything they had seen before.

The Stupid that filled the pavement looked to be in very bad condition compared with the immaculate display mannequins inside. Some of them had trouble walking. One or two were slumped in doorways.

"How much longer do you think they have?" Matthew said.

"Before they die you mean?"

Matthew nodded.

"Two or three weeks I'd guess. Most of them haven't had anything to eat for four days but that's not what's going to kill them. According to the Discovery Channel, you can live for a surprisingly long time without food. It's not very pleasant, but I don't imagine any of them complaining. What's going to kill them is fluid intake, or rather the lack of it. They are not drinking anywhere near enough to keep things running. Soon their kidneys will shut down and that's game over."

"How are they drinking anything at all? I've never seen them do that. They just don't know how."

"Rain. Have you never seen them when it rains? And it's rained at least once a day since things fell apart. They just stand with their mouth open. Like plants I guess. They don't get a lot of water that way, but just enough to really stretch out the dying process." Jeremy stopped and pointed at a middle-aged man with olive skin and an enormously fat belly. "Look at this guy. That's not a tan, it's jaundice. Judging by his beer belly, he must have been quite a drinker so his kidneys were already in a bad state. The dehydration is just the last straw. In a day, maybe less, he'll just fall over and the rats will get busy. Children and babies will last just a little longer, but the bulk of the population could last for weeks."

They carried on walking until they reached Knightsbridge tube station and then turned left to cross the road into Hyde Park. Without even realising, they both checked left and right before threading their way through the static traffic jam.

"So what do we do then?" Matthew said. He had his own, fairly detailed plans on what should happen next, but he wanted to see if Jeremy was on the same page. Despite all his fancy words, he didn't think Jeremy was really all that good at planning ahead.

"We move. The cities will be unliveable for years," Jeremy said. "The question is where and how, and the how limits the where. I don't suppose you know how to ride a motorbike?" he said hopefully.

Matthew shook his head. "Sorry, never tried it."

"Blast! Oh well, it wasn't much of an idea anyway. The roads will be blocked by abandoned cars and the pavements by warm obstacles like these." Jeremy nodded at the Stupid scattered across the park. "That means we walk, and that way would

147

take a day just to reach the M25, and that would still put us right in the centre of the most populated area in England. To get to Devon or Cornwall, where the population density is significantly less, would take weeks."

"What about pedal bikes or even electric bikes? Quicker than walking but slow enough to avoid any obstructions."

"Possible, but it would still be a very long trip." Jeremy's already slow pace became even slower, and he suddenly looked simultaneously proud and embarrassed. "The only other option is the railways."

"We've no idea how to drive a train."

"No, not a train, a link trolley, maybe a scaffold, but if we're really lucky a draisine!"

"What?"

"Railway utility vehicles. When they are doing repair or maintenance work on the track they use a link trolley to carry equipment along the track to a site. It's just a flat platform running on 9.65-inch flanged wheels. There's no motor, so we'd have to take it in turns to push, but it only weighs fifty-seven kilos, and if we can find one of the new aluminium ones they're only thirty kilos. Load up a few supplies and punt and coast our way out of the city. A scaffold is much the same thing, except in place of a platform it's got an upright frame with two lifting points for heavier equipment. We'd have to rig up two hanging seats, but on the plus side it only weighs twenty kilos so it would be easier to carry around obstructions. But the real prize would be a draisine! The simple ones are just a small diesel engine to drive the wheels of a link trolley, but Network Rail has several of the new Kubota RRV vehicles, and that's a proper small, off-road four by four. A bit like a ride-on mower with street tyres but with drop-down flanged wheels that locate to the track. Nine hundred cc, three cylinder diesel engine, twenty mph on rail, twenty-eight on the road. We could cruise down the track and just drive around any obstructions. They'll be several at the main depot for London, but that's Wembley where they've got the forty-four-chain lifting jack and that's on the Midlands track, so we'd have to go all the way out to the Watford interchange before we could switch to the South West main line. Our best bet is the satellite depot at Royal Oak where they've been upgrading the co-acting trap points. They probably have at least one Kubota for the heavy lifting."

Matthew stared at Jeremy with the same unbelieving look he'd given Kirsten when she came out to him. You thought you knew someone pretty well and then they suddenly reveal a whole new side to their personality that changes the way you look at them. Because Jeremy hadn't just spoken knowledgably about trains; he'd been almost evangelical about the smallest detail of rolling stock. He'd spoken with a passion and intensity that Matthew had never seen before.

Even when he'd been pawing Gretchen.

His hand had kneaded Gretchen's thigh, but his expression had been grimly determined, like a small child gritting his teeth before swallowing bitter medicine. Matthew decided that there was a lot more to Jeremy's story than he had thought. He wondered how much of it Jeremy knew.

"So the most important thing is to get out of the city?"

"Eventually, but not immediately. You're right to suggest getting some weapons. If not for the 'aliens'" – Jeremy hooked two fingers on each hand to sketch quotation marks around the word – "then we're going need them at some point anyway. The West Country is the obvious place to head, and so obvious that we cannot be the only ones to think of it. If any other survivors are not on their way already – they soon will be. So either we'll get there and discover all the good places have been snapped up or we'll find somewhere nice and then some ragged survivors will show up and try to take it away from us. We're going to need something more than strong words then."

"So what do we do when we get to the West Country? Learn to fish?"

"We find a small farm. From Okehampton there's the old South Western Railway spur to Plymouth that runs right across Dartmoor. We follow the track until we see something that looks good, settle down, raise some cows and stuff, learn to drive a tractor …" He broke off and looked up and over Matthew's shoulder. "Jesus Christ!"

Matthew spun around. Behind a small screen of trees was a statue of a man hanging onto a rearing horse, and above the statue a small bright object was dropping smoothly from the clouds. Matthew grabbed Jeremy's jacket and towed him to the nearest tree until they were both hidden from the object. Matthew peered carefully around the tree. The bright object hung directly above the statue, seemingly pinned in place.

"Bloody hell! You were right." Jeremy's voice was shockingly loud and Matthew waved frantically at him. Jeremy brought his head back and looked at Matthew around the width of the tree. He looked stunned, but his eyes were wide and gleaming. "I'd never have believed it, but I saw it with my own eyes. It dropped down like it was on a wire but there's nothing there. That's nothing we've built; it really is alien." He finally saw Matthew waving at him. "What are you doing? They're not going to see us back here."

"No, but they might be able to hear us."

"Oh!" Jeremy said, and he said it very quietly.

They looked at each other and by unspoken agreement ducked to opposite sides of the tree to watch the bright object.

Matthew watched it carefully, as if at any moment it might send out death rays or explode in a ball of flame that would wipe the park clean of life. Jeremy watched it hopefully, as if will power alone could make it float lazily away like the child's balloon he had claimed it to be. The bright object did neither of these things. It remained almost insultingly still and unchanging, as if to say, 'Look how ordinary and harmless I am.' They watched for another few minutes before Jeremy scooted around until he could whisper directly in Matthew's ear.

"Is this what you saw?"

"Pretty much."

"It's not changing colour or anything."

Matthew looked around the edge of the tree. "It is now."

Jeremy looked over his head, steadying himself with one hand on Matthew's shoulder. The inner

151

glow of the object was tinged with red that became deeper every second until the neatly maintained grass looked like a sea of blood. Jeremy shifted position back to his side of the tree as red became blue, became green. Motion in the corner of Matthew's eye brought his head around. Moving with underwater slowness, waves of Stupid were closing in from every direction, every face upturned to watch the object. Matthew examined each face as it passed. There was no sign of curiosity or even a simple desire to watch the pretty thing. They were being drawn in like moths to a flame.

Matthew thought about the destructive power of flame. He watched the wash of colour on Jeremy's stunned expression and brought his head back around the tree until he could see only the faintest glow of light from the object. The colours changed faster and faster until each colour was only a stroboscopic pulse on the grass. And then with a suddenness that was shocking, the light went out. Matthew looked fully around the tree at the object and the crowd that had gathered under it. He guessed that there were three, maybe four, hundred people looking up at the dark object. The most people he had seen in one place since things fell apart.

The object jerked left and every face in the crowd tracked it as if following a game of tennis. Very slowly, the object slid back to its original position. Then, in very quick succession, it shot right, forwards, left and backwards like a pool table trick shot. The object hung motionless for thirty breaths and then jumped straight up a hundred feet, left a hundred feet and then straight up another hundred feet before repeating its staircase climb until it had disappeared into the clouds.

Matthew stared at the point where it had disappeared until he was sure it had really gone and then looked around at Jeremy. He too was looking up at the clouds, but he looked completely dumbfounded. His mouth hung open and a thread of drool reached slowly down to the ground. Matthew shook his shoulder and then grabbed it and physically hauled him away from the tree. "Come on, we should go."

For the first few yards Jeremy was a dead weight that would freeze in place the moment Matthew released him, but slowly he began to move under his own power.

"What …? What ….?" Jeremy took a deep breath and almost visibly pulled himself together. "What was that? What do you think it was doing?"

"I don't know," Matthew said. "But I think we ought to get out of here."

Jeremy looked behind them, at the crowd that was slowly thinning out across the park, and began to walk a little faster. "Do you think they are dangerous?"

"Not really, but do you really want to find out?"

Jeremy didn't say anything, but walked even faster, which was an answer in itself.

"You didn't say anything about that little dance it did at the end."

"Because the one I saw didn't do that. It just shot straight up like it was on a line."

They jogged, almost ran, until the breath caught in their throats and their lungs burnt. Matthew checked behind them. The crowd was little more than distant shapes and, without saying a word, they both slowed to a walk. Matthew watched Jeremy's face while they both took deep, cleansing breaths. He looked normal enough.

"Say," Matthew said, "how many tins of those fancy beans in adobo sauce did you pick up?"

"Beans?" Jeremy said incredulously. "We're about to star in a remake of *Independence Day* and you're worried about beans?"

"We might be living off what we got today for some time. I just thought it would be a good idea to know what we have."

"I suppose so. I think I picked up three cans."

"And I got another four. So that's six altogether."

"Seven," Jeremy said and managed to make the word a sneer.

"Of course. Hey, looking around Harrods reminded me of that old Audrey Hepburn film where she eats her lunch walking around some posh jewellers."

"*Breakfast at Tiffany's*," Jeremy said promptly. "Very loosely based on the book by Truman Capote. The book was better. In the film she was some sort of romantic heroine but in the book she's basically a slut."

"Capote! That's a hell of a name. How would you even spell something like that?"

Jeremy stopped and looked at Matthew suspiciously. "You're being really weird. Beans, old films and now this sudden interest in dead authors? C-A-P-O-T-E, born 1924. Used to live next door to the lady that wrote *To Kill a Mockingbird*. Anything else you want to know? Height, weight, sexual preference? Jesus! What is this? Some sort of alfresco quiz show?" And then he suddenly became very still and watched Matthew warily. "You're testing me to see if I've started to become stupid like everyone else. You're a bit late; whatever happened was days ago. I think we'd have noticed any delayed effect by now."

"Not necessary. It's too much to believe that thing just happened to turn up exactly as everything fell apart."

"Obviously."

"So there's some link between them. And, on the one hand, we've got an effect which is everyone dumb and, on the other …?"

"A cause? You think that thing made all of this happen?"

Matthew shrugged. "It's the most obvious link, but I've seen two of these things and you one, and neither of us have forgotten how to tie our shoelaces. And once you discard the object as a cause you're left with something much worse. That that thing is monitoring what's happening here. Perhaps it was measuring just how dumb people had become. Either it was packed full of sophisticated sensors, or maybe it was something as simple as how many people that pretty light show would attract in five minutes."

"What's so bad about measuring?"

"Because you measure something to see if it's ready. And when it's ready you do something."

"But they've done everything already; what more can they do?"

"I don't know, but Stephen King once described a crowd as human wheat."

Jeremy stared at Matthew with wide eyes. "You think they are going to harvest us? Collect up all the dummies? That doesn't make any sense at all. None of them are even smart enough to work as slaves. They're not going to eat us because we've been soaked in antibiotics and pollution for years. We probably taste like crap. So what else is left?"

"I don't know, but we have a choice to make. Either we get out of here right now or we hole up with as much food and weapons as we can gather and wait things out. And since whatever is happening here seems to be happening all over, I vote to stay and stock up."

Jeremy looked thoughtful and did something unexpected. He stepped forward and held out his arm to shake Matthew's hand. "Nice work."

Matthew stepped forward and Jeremy brought his hand up and punched him in the mouth. As punches went, it was more of a slap. It was the shock that sent him reeling back. His foot caught in a fallen branch and he went down with a thump that knocked all the breath out of him. Jeremy stood over him and Matthew waited for his face to become something monstrous. He waited some more before climbing shakily to his feet, watching Jeremy all the time.

"What the hell was that for?"

"For using me as your lab rat. You've never seen that thing twice. I saw how you hid behind the tree so you didn't have to look directly at it. I just didn't know what I was seeing. I bet you've never even seen it once. You already had an idea what it might be doing and made sure you didn't look at it then. But you were quite happy for me to take in the light show and then quiz me afterwards."

"But it didn't do anything."

"No thanks to you. I took you in, made my home your home and this is how you reward me?"

"And you would have done exactly the same."

Jeremy flapped his mouth soundlessly for a moment. "Maybe."

"Maybe shaybe. If you'd have thought of it first you'd have thrown me under the bus without a second thought. But now we know that there's another stage to whatever is happening, and when it arrives we had better be ready."

"Suppose so."

"You know so. Let's get these supplies back home and then we can check out the maps we got and work out how to get our hands on some weapons."

The mention of weapons made Jeremy look a lot happier and they headed towards the apartment in silence. Matthew made a mental note to lock his door at night. The idea of a vengeful, socially inept Jeremy with a gun made him nervous.

***

Jeremy opened the apartment door into the smell of shit.

"Gretchen," he said wearily. "I didn't take care of her before we went out. If you pack the shopping away, I'll sort everything out. Just as well I brought in some extra air fresheners."

Matthew took both backpacks and headed towards the kitchen while Jeremy snapped on a pair of rubber gloves, a disposable apron and a grimace.

The kitchen was cool and, more importantly, fresh. Matthew let go of the breath he'd been holding and started unpacking what they had brought back with them. From time to time he heard the toilet flush and the shower run. He waited until it had been quiet for some time before he went back into the living room.

Jeremy had used enough apple-scented air freshener to leave behind a thin haze that hid the ceiling. But Matthew preferred the smell of chemically reproduced apple blossom to the smell it hid and sat down facing Jeremy, who pushed a glass full of smoky liquid towards him.

"A toast to the human race. It was nice while it lasted."

"I thought we were going to have a look at the map and phonebook?"

"In a minute. It's been quite a day. We've discovered that not only was Carl Sagan right when he said we are not alone, but H.G. Wells when he said they are going to make us extinct. They're going to roll right over us. We don't stand a chance. So raise a toast to the amphibians that first thought it was a good idea to leave the sea. You were wasting your time, guys."

"It's not that bad. We don't know what's happening, but while there's life there's hope."

"You think? Have you opened your eyes recently? Something powerful enough to turn everyone on the planet into morons is about to drop on us, and all we have is a set of steak knives, a

158

meat tenderiser and a nice bottle of scotch." Jeremy drained his glass and topped up Matthew's, which instantly overflowed, but neither of them noticed.

"So we get some guns. We can shoot back."

"That's a great plan! And while we're there we can pick up some surface to air missiles and a couple of tactical nukes. Of course I'm sure the operating manuals and launch codes will be nice and handy. The two of us will have no problem fighting off a planetary invasion. Drink up! While we still can."

Matthew took a small sip and Jeremy filled up his glass the moment it left his lips.

"A toast to all those who set sail to conquer some primitive tribe. Well, now it's our turn. Cheers!"

Matthew took a longer drink and Jeremy refilled.

"And on the sixth day God gave man dominion over the fish of the sea and over the birds of the sky and over the cattle and over all the earth, and over everything that creeps on the earth." Jeremy emptied his glass and overfilled both glasses. "Shame it turns out that creation took seven days and something was given dominion over us."

Matthew emptied his glass and very slowly the day came apart into disconnected scenes. He remembered explaining why an invasion made no sense, but not if that came before or after Jeremy sobbing helplessly. He remembered telling Jeremy about the good times with Kirsten, but not how that linked to Jeremy's dad dancing to something loud and electronic. At some point, Matthew realised just how drunk he was. Time had ceased to have any meaning and anything beyond his glass was vague and indistinct. After the third attempt, he managed to stand up and only managed to keep standing up by hanging onto every item of furniture on his way back to his room. The only thing that kept him moving was the certain knowledge that if he fell asleep in his chair he'd wake at 3.00 a.m. with his chin glued to his chest with drool. And if he fell asleep on the floor he'd need the services of an expert chiropractor to ever move again.

Choosing one of the multitude of doors that swam in front of him was a matter of luck and he sprawled onto his bed without any attempt at pulling the sheets over him. There were thumps and slurred swear words as Jeremy stumbled to his bedroom, a heavy crash as something went over and then it was silent.

And the silence pressed down like a heavy hand. Suddenly, Matthew was wide awake. His blood was caffeine and each heartbeat a truck engine turning over. All the small sounds of the city that he had grown up with were missing. The sewing machine burr of a motorbike, the wailing of a siren taking someone to hospital. Everything was gone. More than anything he wanted someone to be with him. Not to hold him and say that everything was all right, because nothing would ever be all right again, but just to be with him. Everyone he had ever loved had gone away as certainly as dust spread before the wind. Kirsten was with Janice and even that didn't hurt anymore. He had a brother somewhere, but based on his infrequent postcards, somewhere could be anywhere from Edinburgh or Dublin to Atlantic City. Even his parents had gone.

Both of them had died three years ago. His father just a month after his mother, and no one that knew him had been surprised by that. After his mother had gone he became almost insubstantial, as if the best part of him had been left behind in the cold church.

While Matthew waited for the room to stop tumbling, he wrapped himself in the memory of his parents. Once he had hated them for their absurd beliefs that had poisoned his childhood, now he just missed them. They had tried to love him in their own way and he dropped into sleep thinking of the remote controlled car they had bought him for his tenth Christmas. His sleeping face smiled at the memory of his dad as he tried to steer the little toy, sending it careering wildly around the room, under the table, across the room.

Chapter Twenty
Landing I

Matthew woke to the sound of waves breaking on a shore. His head throbbed in time with each thunderous impact. His stomach curled and rolled, pulling him into a foetal ball. Pulling the pillow over his head, he tried to drift back into dreams of how things used to be: two hundred channels of rubbish on the TV; lying next to Kirsten; the look on Jeremy's face when he saw the bright object. He opened his eyes and pushed the bedclothes off with a single convulsive kick. He staggered to the window and looked out – and then up. The bedroom floor tilted wildly with each step as he lurched towards the door. In the living room his stomach clenched like a strong hand around a rotten apple and he dropped to his knees in front of a wastepaper bin. The taste of expensive brandy filled his mouth again but now he was drowning in it. He was choking in it. He held the bin and panted like a dog and then threw up last night's brandy, his breakfast. He threw up everything that he had ever eaten. When he was done he stood up and let the wall support him until he could fumble his way to Jeremy's bedroom and push the door open.

The wallpaper in the room Jeremy had chosen was hyper-vivid poppies sprouting from green vines the size of fire hoses. The curtains were drawn, but the light through their join turned the room into a box of light. On the bed, a long thin shape tightly wrapped in a duvet snored with a deep nasal rasping. Matthew grasped the nearest point of the mummy shape and shook it violently. The snoring stopped, but only for a moment before resuming its deep reverberation. Matthew tried again, unwinding some of the shroud, until he could see Jeremy's face.

"Wake up!"

Jeremy twitched as if dreaming and sank back into sleep. Matthew swore and fumbled his way into the attached bathroom, ran the cold tap until the water was icy and then some more until his fingers were numb. He splashed his face to finish waking up and then worked a pink towel in the bowl until it was completely soaked in freezing cold water.

Jeremy had pulled the duvet back over his face and Matthew carefully peeled it back and dropped the wringing wet towel on his face. Jeremy thrashed and twisted, trying to escape the bedding wrapped around him.

"You git! What the hell do you think you are doing? You evil-minded little shit!" He thrashed around some more until he had his arms free. Matthew waited until he had both feet on the ground before he reached forward, held Jeremy's upper arm and towed him towards the window. He swept back both curtains and held him close to the glass.

"Look!"

Jeremy looked down at the Stupid wandering aimlessly across the park, saw the shadows flitting over the green lawns and looked up. Above them, three neat lines of dark silhouettes were moving swiftly left to right. He clung onto the window ledge, pulled himself closer to the glass, craned his neck up and saw more moving shapes.

A cloud broke apart and something moving very fast burst through. Just as it seemed it would smash into the ground, it stopped with the crash of a breaking wave. Jeremy had the briefest possible sight of an oblong the size of Big Ben before it rose to join the procession above them.

Jeremy looked at Matthew, dashed into the bathroom and a moment later Matthew heard him being violently sick. When he came back into the room his face was very pale.

"They're spaceships? It's an invasion?"

"That's what it looks like. They must have liked whatever they measured yesterday and decided to collect."

Jeremy made a whimpering sound and looked like he was going to be sick again.

"How many are there? They just keep on coming."

"I think they are circling. See the one shaped like a rugby football? After it disappears off to the right, wait long enough and it slides in again from the left."

Jeremy barged Matthew away from the window and watched until he saw that the three lines above them were just part of a huge circular path with its axis directly above them.

"You're right, but why?"

"Why are they here? Why are they circling? But it doesn't matter. We don't have any answers."

"If we make a run for it we can get to Lancaster Gate tube station. At least we'd be undercover there."

"But first we'd be right under their flight path. We might as well hold up a big neon sign saying, 'Here we are'."

"So we stay here and wait for them to walk all over us?"

"Do we have a choice? But we might as well do what we can. Does this place have a pair of binoculars?"

"In the living room." Jeremy didn't move.

"Well if we can find them at least we can have a closer look at what's up there."

"Do we really want to?"

"Do we have a choice?"

**

Jeremy found the binoculars in a slim drawer unit and immediately took charge of them. Ignoring Matthew waiting patiently by the window, he made himself comfortable with a few cushions on the floor and took a good long look at the sky above. And to Matthew's surprise, less than a minute later, he handed the glasses over.

"I'm done."

Matthew looked suspiciously at him, raised the glasses and immediately saw why Jeremy had seen more than enough. The binoculars were German, no bigger than a pair of opera glasses, and looked very expensive. Even on their lowest power a single ship filled their field of view. Every ship seemed unbroken by doors or windows. They seemed almost to have been grown rather than constructed. Matthew made his own viewing spot on the floor and tracked a ship shaped like the star on top of the Christmas tree as it appeared from the left until it disappeared on the right. Then he flicked back to track a doughnut-shaped ship follow the same arc, then back to follow a triangular ship. Every circling ship was different. There was no common design shared between any of them. The only thing that was the same was that they were all different. Matthew wondered what the significance of the designs was; was it simply different generations of build or was there some cultural implication? Perhaps it was something as simple as a circular ship was ranked higher than a triangular ship.

The regular crashing sound as another ship arrived was almost restful and soon a dull rasping sound filled the apartment. Matthew looked around at Jeremy. His head lolled to one side and his chin was slick with drool. A short time ago he had been hyperventilating with panic and now he had fallen asleep again. Matthew suddenly felt very old. Jeremy was only a few years younger than him, but he seemed to live in another world.

Matthew looked back at the window as a distinctive cylinder-shaped ship on the outermost ring slid into view and he began counting each ship that followed. When he saw the same ship he would stop counting. Then all he would have to do was multiply the count by three for each ring and he would know just how many ships were in the armada above them. He knew that the total would be as useless as a swimmer counting the number of piranha closing in, but it made him feel that he was more than just an observer. He reached a count of fifty before a cylinder shape appeared. But this was a short, stubby barrel and his starting point had been a long, thin noodle shape. He carried on counting. The eightieth ship was a long cylinder, but not thin enough to be his marker. He carried on counting until he saw cylinder shapes simultaneously across all three rings and realised that they had reused the same basic shapes, but subtly different over and over.

Matthew stopped counting and just watched the procession of ships. Jeremy's snoring suddenly seemed very loud and he threw a cushion to shut him up. Silence filled the room like a dark cloud and Matthew wondered if the same circling procession was happening all over the world or had London been specially selected? But the only thing special about London was the two people there that were still normal. Suddenly, the circling procession looked a lot like a bullseye.

Matthew sat bolt upright and checked the clock, head cocked to one side, and began to count. He checked the clock again and climbed shakily to his feet. Jeremy was still fast asleep. He reached down, his back protesting angrily, and dragged him to his feet.

"What? I wasn't asleep."

"Doesn't matter. Ships have stopped arriving."

"What?"

"A new ship was arriving every three minutes but the last one was over five minutes ago."

"They've got enough for whatever comes next?"

"Guess so."

Jeremy knelt down, with only his eyes above the level of the window, and scanned slowly from left to right and back again. "Nothing seems to have changed. Are you sure you didn't …? Jesus! Jesus! Jesus!" His face was paper white, his eyes wide. Matthew followed his gaze to the eastern edge of

Hyde Park. In the distance, he could see London's jagged skyline, but in front of the row of the multimillion-pound mansions, a featureless cube was dropping smoothly to the ground, legs unfolding with a complicated origami motion. The cube landed a few metres from Speakers' Corner. If any of the orators that used the public area to set the world to rights were still there, it would have been as if a ten-storey building had been dropped next to them. None of the Stupid even looked up.

Jeremy tugged at Matthew's arm. "It's just one isn't it? Only one. The rest will go somewhere else. Let them deal with it. We've had enough. No more! Cannot take any more! Shit!"

Less than a hundred metres from their window, a sphere the size of the dome on St Paul's Cathedral was dropping smoothly to the ground. The room suddenly stank like a public toilet and the crotch of Jeremy's trousers grew dark. He dropped to his knees with a solid thud, clasped his hands together and began to pray in a rushed monotone. "Hail Mary, Mother of God, pray for us now. Forgive my sins and lead me to mercy. Give me the joy that comes from your salvation."

The sphere continued to drop without any unfolding of legs, its shadow sweeping across the manicured lawns towards a park bench. The sphere landed directly on top of the bench with a grinding crash. The floor shook as if from a minor earthquake and something in the kitchen smashed. The sphere rested on the remains of the bench for a heartbeat and then leapt fifty feet in the air as if it weighed nothing at all. The base of the sphere flowed like liquid metal into four extended legs. It dropped again and landed straddling the crushed remains of the bench. Jeremy began to laugh.

"We've been invaded by amateurs! They've never even passed their driving test. Left a bit, right a bit, land here. Woops, forgot to drop the landing gear. Never mind, it's only a scratch; it'll buff out. Other planets get professional invaders who really know what they are doing, but we get the also-rans who don't even know what button to press. Earth? It's a minor blue planet way off in the unfashionable arm of the galaxy. We'll send in the B-Team." Jeremy continued to laugh, his voice high and hysterical.

Matthew shook Jeremy's shoulder, which had no effect at all. He thought it worked in the movies. He then slapped Jeremy hard on the face. He stopped laughing and looked at Matthew like a dog that had just been kicked.

"What did you do that for?"

"To calm you down. This is no time to lose control."

"But it's all a big joke. An alien invasion as directed by Mel Brooks. They thunder across thousands of light years in their mighty spaceships, and then forget how to park." Jeremy started to laugh again, saw Matthew's unimpressed expression and stopped. "Sorry."

"I've not seen any other ships land. Perhaps this is just an advance party."

"And that's good?"

Matthew found a spot off to one side from the window where he could watch the cube at Speakers' Corner, the sphere that dominated the view and Jeremy. He watched the cube and sphere for the moment they would stop being enigmatic and start being dangerous. He watched Jeremy for the moment he would slip away to the toilets to slit his wrists. But both shapes remained completely static and Jeremy seemed oddly calm. Perhaps he had been stressed beyond anything he had ever known and had arrived in the still eye of the storm.

Matthew guessed that close by things beyond his comprehension were running complex tests on Earth's air, getting the ships' occupants ready to emerge. But from the outside all that added up to nothing at all, and watching three things do nothing at all got very boring very quickly. Matthew's feet began to go numb and he stood up, feeling and hearing his back click into a new configuration. He took one step back from the window and was in the perfect position to see when the sphere changed. There was the faintest impression of metal flowing like water at the rightmost point of the sphere and then a paper-thin ramp connected sphere to ground.

"And lo, our new masters emerge." Jeremy's voice was perfectly calm without even the slightest tremor of fear.

Matthew stood very still, barely breathing, watching the point where ramp met sphere until two cone shapes appeared. His first thought was that they were just land-going versions of the object they had seen yesterday. Then he saw the sinuous, muscular way they moved and realised that they were alive. Each cone was twice the height of a man and narrowed from a wide base to a domed head. There was no sign of eyes or mouth, but below the head a circle of stubbly tentacles was in constant motion like underwater plants. The tip of each tentacle had bright chips that might have been eyes and a circular, puckered mouth inset with rows of needle teeth. Both cones were grey and wrinkled; the only difference between them was that the nearest one had a slight green tint to its body. The muscular base of both cones extended and contracted as they inched down the ramp.

"Just like giant snails," Jeremy said, without noticing he had moved around and was standing directly behind Matthew.

He nodded fractionally. All his attention focused on the slow movement of both cones down the ramp. At the base of the ramp they both paused and waved tentacles at each other. Then they moved onto the grass.

"That's one small ooze for cones, one giant fuck up for us." Jeremy didn't sound quite so calm anymore.

The two cones immediately turned in opposite directions. The green cone turned left, towards the distant glitter of the Serpentine, while the grey cone turned right, directly towards them. Behind him he heard Jeremy's sharp intake of breath. Matthew tried to remain very still and discovered that the more he tried to remain still, the more he had to move. His legs shook and a spot on his chin began to itch insanely. He had to move, he had to scratch that itch. When the cone reached the cast-iron railings around the park, it reached down and ran one leathery looking tentacle over them for a minute, and then ripped off a foot-long piece and tossed it casually to one side. The cone moved right and out of sight, and they both let out an explosive gasp of air and sat down. There were no chairs under them, but they sat down anyway.

"That was entirely too close for comfort," Jeremy said.

"What do you think they would do if they realised there were still normal people?"

"I don't know, and I don't want to find out."

Matthew sneaked a look back to the cube near Speakers' Corner. There was no ramp there. The grey cone reappeared much further back into the park, heading away from them. None of the Stupid took any notice of the invaders, and yet they moved out of the way when either cone came close and flowed back behind them. Watching the cones move was like watching a soap bubble moving across dusty water.

"They are surrounded by some sort of force field in place of a spacesuit?" Matthew said.

Jeremy didn't answer for a long time and Matthew was just about to repeat the question when Jeremy said, "No," very slowly. "See the cone heading towards the flowerbeds? Watch as it goes under that row of trees."

Matthew watched the cone as it reached the trees and continued to ooze its way down a path that Henry VIII might have used. "Nothing happened."

"Exactly! Some of those branches are just a few feet above that cone, but they're not being pushed out of the way. I think each of those things is surrounded by some sort of exclusion zone that only acts on people, like an invisible electric fence."

The two cones met on the wide strip of Carriage Drive. There was more tentacle waving and then both headed directly towards the sphere much faster than before.

"They've had a look around and are off to report to the others," Jeremy said.

Matthew checked the cube by Speakers' Corner and the slow stately precession of the ships above. "Well nothing seems to be happening over at the other ships. Perhaps these two drew the short straw and got the job of checking out whatever it was they did."

On their way back to the ship, a young woman in a blue dress was caught exactly at the midpoint between the two cones and instead of being brushed aside like all the others, she was pushed forward.

"Those things are far enough apart so their exclusion zones only just touch. She's been caught in the V-shaped gap between two touching circles."

The sun came out from behind a cloud and Matthew saw that the woman's dress was a very specific shade of blue and she wore a bright necklace made up of two L-shaped pieces. She was a nurse, still wearing her uniform and stethoscope. A week ago she might have been pretty, smiling at her charges as she dispensed medication and pastoral care. Now her carefully styled hair was tangled and her dress stained. She didn't look happy at being pushed along. She didn't look anything at all. But she twitched and convulsed whenever she tried to stop. Matthew didn't think that touching the cone's invisible, electric fence was much fun.

The procession of two cones, apparently led by a young woman, covered another fifty feet. Matthew looked around at Jeremy.

"She's obviously in their way. Why don't they just move around her?"

"Why should we make sure we're not treading on any ants? It might be the same thing."

The woman's face suddenly grimaced as if she had tasted something bad and tried to break left. But she did it with the slow underwater speed of the Stupid and the leftmost cone only had to move a little to block her.

"They're not trying to get around her; they're herding her!"

Jeremy nudged Matthew and pointed at the ship. Each side of the ramp had sprouted two wire-thin, six-foot-high fences. The end of each fence flared into a wide outwards curve. The young woman reached the base of the ramp and hesitated until the two cones came close and forced her up and into the ship. The two cones followed, much closer now, and the moment all three had disappeared from sight the ramp flowed like liquid being sucked up a straw and the sphere was featureless again.

Jeremy looked from cube to sphere to Matthew. "Well, that tells us everything we need to know. They'll load all the Stupid into the ship and whatever happens next won't be good."

"Not necessarily. The cube ship didn't do anything. The fleet above didn't do anything. All they did was just take one person."

"Testing if the harvest is good."

"What?"

"It was your analogy: human wheat, remember? They had a look via the probe we saw yesterday. They liked what they saw and moved in. But before

174

they go full production they want to test a sample and make sure it's what they want. All those ships up there are waiting for these guys to say, 'Yes it's good. Come on in and fill your boots.'" Jeremy stood up and turned away in one complicated motion. "I'll just use the bathroom."

The bathroom door closed behind him while Matthew watched the sphere and tried to put another spin on what they had just seen. Perhaps they had taken the young woman as a representative and were trying to make contact. Perhaps they were just categorising the flora and fauna of a new planet. But he kept seeing the way they had herded the woman into the ship and how the ends of the fences had made a wide funnel shape ready to guide in large numbers of dumb animals. The memory of all the horror films he had ever seen turned on him. He could actually see the young woman strapped to a gleaming operating table, hear saws spin as they cut into vulnerable flesh, smell blood as it sprayed on the walls. The only question was if they would stun her before taking whatever they needed.

A door clicked open and he spun around. In place of his wet trousers Jeremy was wearing a bright pink pair of pyjama trousers.

"Very fetching."

Jeremy ignored him and waved at the window. "Anything happened?"

"Not yet."

"I suppose how long their testing will take depends on ..." Jeremy suddenly crouched down low. Matthew looked around at the window and crouched down himself. The ramp was back in place and two cones were already halfway down it.

This time there was no hesitation before they moved onto the grass. Both cones moved swiftly towards a tall, silver-haired man wearing what used to be a smart suit. The two cones briefly separated to pass him by on either side, closed together and then headed back to the sphere with him pushed before them. This time Matthew saw the fence appear at the edges of the ramp. Its smooth surface boiled and, like watching a backwards video of a glass of water being poured, the ramp leapt up into the fence they had seen before. The two cones herded the man up the ramp and into the ship at a near run and the ramp flowed back into the main body of the ship. The whole thing had taken less than five minutes.

Jeremy waited until he was sure that the ramp would not suddenly reappear before he stood up. "What do you think that was all about?" he said, thoughtfully.

"They were taking another subject for testing."

Jeremy gave Matthew a very cool look. "Thank you, Captain Obvious, for providing such a succinct summery of what we just saw. But the question was an attempt to derive the motivation behind the simple mechanics we both so clearly saw. They certainly took another subject, but why? If they wanted multiple subjects why not take them all at once? Instead, they took the young lady, buttoned up the ship and then had to do it all over again. I don't think they were expecting to need another subject, but the first one gave the wrong result. And I know it's wrong to try to read body language from something that hasn't actually got a body as we understand it, but the way those two came out at a run and back into the ship didn't suggest everything

176

working nicely." Jeremy face twitched into a smile. "I think it's a bad harvest. Something has gone wrong."

"Does that really make any difference? Whatever's done is done. Maybe it's not quite what they wanted, but they've fucked up the whole planet and we've got to live with that."

"True, so all we can do is wait. Maybe they'll take more test subjects. But at some point they've got to make up their minds what to do next, and right now I think there's a good chance they'll just bugger off and leave us alone."

"Or maybe they'll settle for what's here and we get to see just how many people they can push up that ramp at once."

"That's another possibility."

They both took a seat where they could see the sphere and waited.

***

The patch of light from the window had moved noticeably across the room when a line of shadow slid across it. Matthew took a deep breath and sat forward until he could see straight up. Very quietly, and with no fuss at all, a small gold pyramid was landing at the extreme right of their view. Compared to the cube and sphere, the new ship was very small, not much bigger than a large detached house. Each of the pyramid's four sides was stepped like the stone pyramids the Aztecs had built five hundred years ago. It didn't make Matthew happy that he remembered the Aztecs had used theirs to perform human sacrifices.

Matthew pointed at the stepped pyramid and said, "Looks like I was wrong. They've decided that whatever is here is good enough and they've moved in."

Jeremy sat forward until he could see the new ship. Then he looked straight up. "Not necessarily. Unless they are doing it very slowly, I don't see any more ships leaving the procession above us. Perhaps this is something to do with the testing they are doing in the sphere."

"The testing we think they are doing."

"Whatever. But if things aren't going too well then it makes sense that they've called in some help."

They watched the new ship very carefully, ready for the moment it would do something. Except, it didn't. After what seemed like an hour, but the clock said was only twenty minutes, Matthew said, "It's not doing very much, is it?"

Jeremy shrugged. "Just because we can't see anything happening, doesn't mean that it isn't. For all we know that ship is packed full of sophisticated sensors that are telling them much more than they could find out from either of the people they took."

"Sensors powerful enough to detect us?"

Jeremy didn't say anything, but he shrank back from the window and remained very still.

Chapter Twenty-One
Loading

The shadow under the sphere began to lengthen as the sun dropped and Matthew began to think what it might be like to have an enigmatic alien ship parked just a few metres from their window when it was dark outside. A few minutes later, he realised that neither the sphere or Aztec pyramid was what he had to worry about, as small shadows began to flit across the park. The circular procession above them was breaking up with ships arcing down like the ribs of an umbrella. In a few minutes the sky was empty.

Jeremy nodded thoughtfully. "It seems I may have been mistaken. They've made their minds up. It's harvest time."

The sphere just outside their window produced its ramp again. Matthew checked the cube to their left and the Aztec pyramid to their right. Both had ramps of their own. Two cones, perhaps the same two they had seen before, started down the ramp. But this time they were followed by a wall of cones that filled the ramp. The ramp on the pyramid was still empty. Three cones lined up neatly where the left side of the ramp touched the ground. Another three mirrored their position on the right. Their two lines formed a wide funnel shape that extended the lines of the ramp.

"Very organised aren't they."

"I think they've done this before. They've had a lot of practise."

The rest of the cones pushed their way across the park, letting the Stupid flow around them. When the cones were a hundred metres from the ship they stopped moving away, shuffled sideways until they made a perfectly straight line at right angles to the ramp and moved back to the ship. But this time the Stupid didn't flow around them; they were pushed back towards the ship. And with every foot the line moved, more Stupid were caught and forced inexorably to the ship.

"They're collecting people!"

Matthew nodded curtly. He'd seen the same thing before, only then he'd been eight and listlessly sweeping up a dusting of snow on his parents' drive. At first the broom had just collected a thin band of snow, but then the trapped snow had trapped more snow of its own until he was pushing a pie-shaped wedge of snow across the drive. He was seeing the same thing now, only it was a line of cones and hundreds of people being herded towards the ship. The people in the wedge didn't show any emotion at all. But the thin layer of people at the base of the wedge looked in agony when they were forced against the cones' exclusion fields. Some of them went limp and didn't move again. As the wedge moved across the park, some people simply fell off the edge of the line, but like the nurse, they were slow and the line only had to stretch just a little to scoop them back up.

"And suddenly everything that has happened makes sense," Jeremy said. "The people down there are completely defenceless. They can't run, they can't hide. They are just the human wheat you said they are and the cones are the scythe cutting them down."

Matthew pointed at the Aztec pyramid. "There's nothing happening over there. Maybe they're just taking more samples."

Jeremy took his hand and turned it until he was pointing at the cube and the same, almost military manoeuvring taking place there. "There's plenty happening over there. Perhaps the pyramid is just next on the list."

When the point of the human wedge was just a few metres from the ramp, both ends of the line of cones began to curl around until they joined up with the funnel shape. Then, like a strong hand squeezing a plastic cup, the cones closed up and forced the people they had collected into the ship. In just a few minutes, the strip of ground in front of the ramp had been swept clear of people.

"Well they did a very neat job there, but what happens now?" Jeremy sounded very calm, as if what had happened was just very interesting.

What happened next was that the cones moved up through the Stupid to the left of the ramp, formed the same straight line and herded everyone between them and the ship down to the ramp. The cones making up the funnel flowed into a backwards L-shape and helped drive the people caught by the line into the ship. Then they did it again with the Stupid below the ramp.

"Now this is going to be interesting," Jeremy said. "They've got all the easy targets, but now all they can do is sweep around the other side of the sphere. And bringing the Stupid all the way around would be like herding cats." He sounded far too calm.

"They could just put the ramp on the other side of the ship? The whole thing seems to be liquid metal."

"If they could do that, they would have already done it. Maybe only the outside skin is malleable."

The cones that had done the pushing moved away from the ramp and then just stopped. None of them changed position, moved their tentacles or showed any sign of life. For all intents and purposes, they seemed to be dead.

"Did we get it wrong and they're just robots?"

"Certainly didn't look it from the way they moved. I think they're just waiting for more Stupid to wander into the area. But that could take days or even weeks, and most of them don't have that long left." Jeremy stood back from the window. His eyes were shining. "They've screwed up!" His face lit up red as if he were standing by a stop light. But almost instantly red became blue, became yellow. Matthew looked out of the window and back at Jeremy.

"They didn't screw up."

Jeremy looked at Matthew, his face painted a bilious green by an unseen source, and stepped up to the window. The ramp from the sphere was lit up with bands of colour that rolled from the ground up into the ship. Each band started out half the length of the ramp and shrank as it ascended. By the time it reached the ship it was a sliver, barely an inch deep. The motion was almost hypnotic. The bands of light trapped the eye, drawing them up into the ship. 'Come up,' they said. 'Will you step into my parlour,' said the spider to the fly.

"It's not going to take weeks or even days to restock their catchment area now." Jeremy pointed off to the right.

Matthew covered the sphere with his open hand and followed Jeremy's direction. Across the nearly immaculate Hyde Park lawns a slow trickle of Stupid was heading towards the sphere.

Jeremy nodded thoughtfully. "We were nearly right when we said the thing we saw yesterday was some sort of progress test. Because it was all of that and also a dry run for this. Whoever they are, they must have spent a long time studying our physiology to come up with something so hypnotic it would attract even the brain-dead Stupid."

Matthew knelt down and watched as more Stupid flowed into the space between ramp and cones. Some even followed the bands of colour into the dark opening of the ship. When the ground was as crowded as it had been before, the cones suddenly came back to life. They shifted position into the same perfectly straight line they used before and swept the Stupid into the ship.

Jeremy nudged Matthew in the ribs to attract his attention and pointed down to the cube at Speakers' Corner. The cones there were also clustered around a ramp rolling with colour.

"Looks like perfectly synchronised sweeps in both places. Makes you wonder if those cone things are just very well trained or all controlled from the same place." Jeremy just sounded mildly interested as if he were watching something fascinating on the Discovery Channel.

The cones below their window returned to their waiting positions while more Stupid moved towards the moving lights. When the ground was thick with people the cones swept them into the ship. And then did it again. And again.

The place where Matthew's knees rested on the floor began to ache and then burn. The long muscles in his back cramped up and he arched his back to try to relieve them. Behind him, Jeremy wandered around the room, apparently unconcerned by what was happening outside. Matthew knew he should do the same, but as much as he tried, he just couldn't look away.

Like the pulse of some remorseless machine, the cones swept forward then backward and waited. Matthew tried to tell himself that the Stupid were just empty shells. They felt nothing, knew nothing. But as the cones pushed them into the ship, he could see faces twist in pain.

"They're getting fewer people in each sweep." Jeremy sounded almost bored and Matthew's back twanged as he looked around. At some point, Jeremy had made himself a cup of tea and he gestured at the advancing line of cones with a delicate china cup. "To begin with, their catchment area was wall to wall before they started sweeping them into the ship. Now they're lucky if there's fifty people in there." He took a long sip of tea. "Nice stuff this Earl Grey. It's a bit tart for me, but I'm sure I can get used to it. I guess the cones are running into the law of diminishing returns. They've over-fished this area and even their pretty lights cannot attract anyone that cannot see them. Between the cube and sphere they've just about emptied Hyde Park, but anyone just a few streets away is completely unaware of what's happening here. Although, truth be told, they're pretty much unaware of anything anyway. The interesting thing is that no one has been swept into the pyramid. Its ramp is down but the cones have ignored it completely. That supports the idea that it's some sort of technical support vessel. The big ships are transports for the livestock. The smaller ship is command and control."

Matthew looked at Jeremy, appalled. "Livestock! They are people!"

"You say people, they say livestock, but I don't think anyone is going to call the whole thing off."

"But maybe that's where they've made a mistake! Livestock don't fight back, but we can. That ship is less than a hundred metres from our window. Once we have some guns, the place where those things are working becomes a shooting range. We know their exclusion fields only stop the Stupid. We'll be able to pick them off one at a time. We can contact Arvid and send the word out! We can fight back."

Jeremy raised his hand like a small boy wanting permission to leave the room. But all Matthew could see was the cross hairs of a sniper scope moving across the park, the sudden jolt of recoil as the rifle spoke its single word, a splash of colour as a cone exploded, the shattering impact of mortars spraying earth like water as they zeroed in, the cones retreating in confusion, their ships harried by jet fighters as they tried to escape.

"We can set up a forward base on each side of the park! A few shots from one and then move to another. Keep them confused – off balance. They won't know how many we are or where we are. We can send them a message. Hell no, we won't go!"

He finally saw Jeremy's raised hand and the light went out from his eyes. "Yes?"

"Just one question before we go all Rambo and charge in there spraying hot lead from our twin chromium-plated magnums. Why?"

"What?"

"No, why? A three-letter interrogative pertaining to or conveying a question. But to expand the context, why should we do anything at all?"

"But those are people down there."

"Well I'll agree with you that they are indeed members of Homo Sapiens, although I've always suspected that most are in fact Homo Dickhead. But that doesn't change anything. There is no one down there that we know. There is no one down there that we care about. Your parents are dead and you haven't heard from your brother in years."

Matthew didn't remember telling Jeremy any of that, but there were large gaps in last night.

"Look at them all. They are the people in front of you at the cinema. They are the traffic jam making you late. We have as little to do with them as we do with the dogs that crap on the pavement. They are lemmings killing themselves in their thousands every day with cigarettes, booze and cars. So, unless you agree with John Donne and every man really is a piece of the continent, we - just - don't - care."

"But we can't just let them take them away like cattle."

Jeremy sighed. "Okay, try this. Don't think about what they are doing *to* us. Think about what they are doing *for* us. In a week, most of the Stupid will be dead. Imagine how things will be then. Mmmmm! Smell that stench of rotting meat. Watch out that the rats don't start gnawing at your toes. Whoops a daisy! This water tastes of bubonic plague. Oh dear, looks like I'm dead. But the cones are taking all that away from us. They are going to leave us empty cities, plentiful food and the perfect conditions to start over. They are the garbage men taking away the rubbish. They get what they want. We get what we want. It's win-win."

"But … but."

"But hold that thought. They've changed what they are doing."

Matthew looked down into the park. The cones were waiting in their corpse-like state, clustered around the ramp. He glanced up at the cube at Speakers' Corner. There was no sign of cones there and its ramp had vanished.

"Looks like they're getting ready to go?"

"But in that case why are they just standing there?" Jeremy looked thoughtful. "Although the English language doesn't really have the verbs we need right now. Are they standing, reposing or just plain lurking?"

Matthew gave him a dirty look. Jeremy almost seemed to be enjoying what was happening. Perhaps he saw himself riding down empty streets in one of his fleet of cars, eating in only the best restaurants. He was probably much more concerned about who would be maintaining those cars or cooking in those fine restaurants than what was happening below. As far as he was concerned, the people being herded into the ships were as alien as those that took them. Matthew tapped his fingers thoughtfully on the windowsill. Perhaps Jeremy hadn't thought through all the ways that cause could become effect.

"That's what they are doing," Jeremy said. "They're sweeping towards the pyramid."

Matthew looked down and realised that he was right. A line of cones was sweeping a last few stragglers towards the pyramid. Its ramp wasn't rolling colours as the sphere and cube had done, but this didn't seem to slow the cones down any as they pushed the crowd up and into the pyramid.

"Looks like you were wrong. The pyramid isn't anything special after all. It's just another transport."

"Not quite. The ramp on the pyramid has just disappeared and our strobiloid friends are heading back into the sphere. They must have taken thousands into the sphere, but less than a hundred into the pyramid. That sort of volume suggests they do something special there. Perhaps it's quality control so they know they have a superior product."

Matthew looked disbelievingly at Jeremy. He had said 'quality control' and 'superior product' as if he were talking about cheese.

The last cone disappeared into the sphere and the ramp quietly flowed back into the main body of the ship. Jeremy looked up and down the park. The cube, sphere and pyramid were just simple geometric shapes dotted over Hyde Park like a child's building set.

"I think they're getting ready to go," Matthew said. "The question is: will they be back?"

"Of course they will. The sphere probably only took a thousand or so. Much the same for the cube, I guess. Even with all those ships we saw in the holding pattern, the most they could have taken all together was half, maybe a whole, million. That's just a fraction of the world's population. They made the Stupid, came for the Stupid, and why go to all that trouble and then just return with a very small amount of it."

The sphere's four extended landing legs reversed their liquid metal motion and now it rested on nothing at all. Matthew glanced left, then right. Both the cube and pyramid hung motionless just a few feet above the ground as if they were nothing more than helium balloons. Then, with no sound at all, all three ships accelerated upwards.

Matthew shrank back from the window as the sphere passed by, but much less than a second later it was hundreds of feet above them. A second after that, it was just a tiny blemish on the clouds. Around it, more shapes rose to join it in long arching paths. The cloud directly above them churned like boiling milk and then the sky was empty again.

"Well that looks fairly decisive. They've gone."

The window behind Matthew flickered as if one of London's ubiquitous tourists had just taken a photograph with a flashgun. He whipped his head around and then up.

"But they've left us a present."

High above the park, a small, bright point glowed like a trapped fragment of the sun. Very slowly, it grew brighter and the flash gun fired again.

Jeremy nodded thoughtfully as if that made sense. "I think that's a fishing lure. It's not as good as the lights on the ramp. Not even as good as the probe thing we saw yesterday. But it's enough to attract the Stupid. In a few hours' time the park will be as crowed as a Rolling Stones concert. The cones will just be able to sweep them up without all that tedious effort of hunting them first. I guess the same thing is happening all over the world. Either each ship has so many square miles to cover, or maybe they are just targeting the major population centres. Same thing really I guess." He moved away from the window, sat down and smiled very patently. "So where were we before we were so rudely interrupted? Ah yes, you were trying to get me to join a new Charge of the Light Brigade, or perhaps re-enact The Battle for Chosin Reservoir. I'm sure you've had plenty of time to rehearse some rousing speeches exhorting me to close up the breech with our English dead. Although there is neither a wall, hole nor any actual dead. Or perhaps the speech from *Independence Day*. As long as you are not planning to save us all by learning how to programme a virus. But this is your moment, so have it!" He crossed his legs and smiled very patiently at Matthew.

"No speeches because you're right; the last thing we want is rotting corpses on every corner. Getting rid of them before they start to stink is the best possible outcome."

Jeremy looked disappointed, as if he'd carefully planned only the best sarcastic phrases to use. "Well, I'm glad to see we are all on the same page."

He raised a celebratory fist. "It's another triumph for rational thought!"

"Of course we've been lucky. It could so easily have been us down there. I wonder what went wrong."

"They screwed up. Judging by their landing prowess, even evil space aliens have an off day. When they were mixing up whatever they dropped into the atmosphere, they got a quantity wrong or forgot a process."

"Of course, that's probably what happened. Because the only alternative is that they wanted to leave some people unaffected."

Jeremy eyed him warily. "Why would they want to do that?"

"To breed. As you said, there could be thousands of normal people just in London, enough to start over again. The human race has driven enough species into extinction that we've learnt to leave enough breeding pairs behind to repopulate. We call it sustainable development. I wonder if the cones have learnt that lesson. Because if they have, then in twenty years' time we'll be relaxing in our apartments in Buckingham Palace, the world's population has crawled up to tens of millions, then one day we forget how to read, next we find a flashing light endlessly fascinating and then the ships land again and we discover what happens inside from personal experience."

A narrow V of concentration appeared on Jeremy's brow. His eyes were steady and unblinking. After a moment, he nodded very slowly as if he had just solved a difficult equation. "You are right," he said very slowly. "I wasn't thinking of the big picture. They are us as we are them. We're not saving them, we are saving ourselves. You did well to see it that way. I didn't know you were that smart."

Matthew's smile became lopsided. "Thanks for that."

"Anytime."

"The first thing we need to do is find a gun. We've got the guide and phonebook we took from Harrods. If we check for gun ranges or gun shops we should be able to find something less well protected than that police station."

"There's a TA centre in Shepherd's Bush. That's only a couple of miles away." Jeremy's reply was instant and completely mystifying.

"TA?"

"Territorial Army. It's a volunteer reserve for the Army. They spend a few weekends a month firing guns and blowing things up. Then they get the big prize of being called up when the army discovers there aren't enough real soldiers to go round. The TA centre in Shepherd's Bush has its own firing range in the basement. There should be all manner of things that go bang there." Jeremy looked suddenly wistful. "I used to be friends with someone that served there. But we lost contact, you know."

"Why didn't you say something before?"

Jeremy gave him a sly look. "I forgot."

Of course, Matthew thought, knowledge was power, and Jeremy wanted everyone to dance when he called the tune.

"Shepherd's Bush is quite a big place to search."

"It's on the Uxbridge road, just past the market. I've never been there but it should be easy enough to find."

"Even on foot that's only an hour straight down the Bayswater Road. If we leave now we can be back long before the ships return."

"Well I suppose that might be construed as a plan. But with two minor amendments: one, we don't use the Bayswater Road and, two, we wait until it's dark."

"Why? That just makes things more difficult."

The window behind Jeremy flickered as the bright point flashed again. "That's why. How hard do you think it would be for that to be both a lure and an eye? They want to attract the Stupid, but they also want to see when it's worth harvesting. And I don't think we want anyone, or anything, seeing any anomalous behaviour and swooping down to have a closer look."

"That's ... that's a really good idea."

"I know. That's why I said it. There's a service staircase that opens onto the back of this building. Then we can use the minor roads just off the Bayswater Road. Even if that thing has night vision and fancy detectors, I doubt it will be able to see us through several storeys of London architecture."

Matthew lifted the shortwave radio microphone from its stand. "In the meantime, we can try talking to Arvid. Things might be very different in Norway."

"If you feel you have to," Jeremy said, dismissively.

Matthew looked side-eyes at Jeremy and pressed the 'ready' button. Arvid's voice came in almost immediately.

"He says he's been trying to reach us ever since the *kjegle* left. I think that means cone."

"Well that tells us everything we want to know. Whatever is going on is worldwide. Ask him if they've been sweeping people like they have here."

Matthew didn't know the word for sweep and had to describe what they had seen as wiping people into the ship.

Arvid spoke quickly and excitedly, repeating himself several times.

"I think he said just one egg-shaped ship landed, and the *kjegle* steered people into it."

Arvid said something very quickly.

"He says we'll talk tomorrow." He pressed the off button and the room was very quiet. "I think he was saying that they'd left an *utstilling*, a display, behind. I guess that's the same thing they left for us. Which just goes to show that they are very efficient."

"But not so good at landings."

"Yes. That doesn't really make sense does it? Some things are done very efficiently and others very badly."

"But that's just on par with everything that's happened here. Turning everyone into morons makes no sense. They are no good to anyone like that."

"It makes sense to them I guess. Let's see, it's four now, it should be dark by six, so we'll leave then and see what the army reserve has got for us."

"And until then we wait." Jeremy settled back in a chair. Matthew sat down where he could see both the clock and the square of light from the window and watched them both move as the sun set. After just an hour, it suddenly occurred to Matthew that there was something missing.

"What's happened to Gretchen? I've not seen her today."

"I decided that maybe you were right for once and I've put her in the spare bedroom."

Jeremy looked away in a definite sign that that topic of conversation was over. The silence in the room became almost tangible and they both waited some more.

At five thirty, Jeremy said he was going to the toilet and the moment the bathroom door closed behind him Matthew was out of his chair and across to the spare bedroom. The wallpaper there was impossibly bright daffodils, the carpet screaming yellow and the room completely empty. There was no bed, dressing table or Gretchen.

A door clicked behind Matthew and he hurried back to his seat. Jeremy gave him a thoughtful look as he crossed the room, but didn't say anything, and after a long pause neither did Matthew. The clock ticked off the seconds and the patch of sunlight tracked across the carpet.

Chapter Twenty-Two
Jeremy's Story

They left the apartment at eight. It was dark at six, but neither of them showed any sign of wanting to leave. In the end it was Matthew that stood up and said, "If we don't go now, then we risk being caught outside when they come back."

Jeremy grudgingly agreed with him and led them to a much smaller staircase than the grand thing they had used before. The stairs were bare concrete and no matter how carefully they moved, the echoes of their steps echoed and multiplied, conjuring up an army of people marching towards them. There was a light at each landing, but it was a poor dim thing and the shadows between landings were veils of darkness that they rushed through. By the time they got to the bottom they were both covered in sweat.

The fire door to the street opened with a heavy clunk. Matthew pushed it fully open and stepped out to the back of the building. The street was lined on both sides by expensive cars, the pavement covered with litter and both were completely deserted. The right-hand end of the street was utterly dark as if tented with a fabric that was not merely black but actually absorbed light. Matthew told himself that it was just a broken streetlight. He wasn't sure if he believed that.

They both headed towards the other end of the road as if they were walking into a strong wind. Every footstep seemed an effort and the further away from the door the slower they moved. Behind them the fire door swung shut with a long shushing sound. Only, the sound never stopped. Matthew stopped and looked back. It was perfectly still and flush with its door frame. He listened carefully. The sound seemed to come from everywhere and nowhere. One moment it was no louder than the singing of the blood in his ears, the next it was louder than a thousand voices calling out.

"What's that sound?"

"The wind?" But Jeremy didn't look particularly convinced about that.

Without prompting, they both stopped at the corner of the street and looked back, much as a drowning man might look at a life belt. All it would take was just a few steps, a flight of stairs and they would be safe and comfortable again. Matthew looked at Jeremy and he in turn looked at Matthew. If either of them had said anything then they would have instantly turned back. But saying something would have been an admission of fear. Neither of them said anything.

Matthew squared his shoulders, turned the corner and walked straight into another person. He pushed back and used his body weight to pull free before he realised that there was nothing to pull free from. He took a step back and looked at the person he had collided with. He was young, male, and their face was completely blank and expressionless. Matthew looked past him. The street was full of more Stupid, all shuffling along with the hushing sound they had been hearing. All of them seemed to be looking straight at him. He took a step back, bumped into Jeremy and then they both moved as one back around the corner.

Matthew pressed himself into the wall while Jeremy looked around him. The stream of Stupid they had walked into passed the end of the street without ever looking in their direction. A flicker of light on the brickwork by Jeremy's face caught his attention, and he looked in the direction the Stupid were facing. The bright point the cones had left above Hyde Park was no brighter than a small torch, but in the darkness above the park it shone like a small sun.

"That's a very efficient fishing lure they've left us. I wonder if there are some subliminal wavelengths we don't recognise." Jeremy tried to sound detached and failed completely.

"At this rate, Hyde Park will be packed out in a few hours."

"And that's when they will start collecting again."

Pushing across the flood of Stupid heading towards the bright point was like swimming in rough water. They were jostled and bumped, but it was all completely silent, and each small collision was like being pelted with pillows. There was no attempt to react or to push them away. After a short time, Matthew just put his head down and shoved. He only knew when he had left the stream of Stupid because it was fractionally easier to move. Jeremy appeared a moment later and they both stood a short distance away from the stream of people heading towards Hyde Park.

"That was easier than I thought," Matthew said.

Jeremy pointed in the direction they were heading. The road was completely empty, but the cross street was crowded with more Stupid. "Good, because the next junction looks much the same."

Matthew slumped a little, but followed Jeremy up the road.

After a while their route developed its own rhythm. The streets were closed shops and broken windows. The junctions were pushing through a soundless crowd. But, little by little, the cross streets became less crowded until they were as empty as the streets.

Matthew looked behind them and stood on tiptoes until he was sure. "We can't see the light anymore."

"They can't see the light anymore. There's nothing to attract them now."

The air tasted hot and metallic. Matthew coughed. "Something's burning."

"We're lucky this isn't all burning. There'll be crashed cars all over London but if they were going to catch fire they'll have done that days ago. It will be the small things that start fires now. Hairdryers left on, cookers and gas rings left burning. Every apartment block is a bomb waiting to go off."

"So that's another reason to hurry."

The road began to slope downhill as the buildings changed from expensive houses to pizza takeaways, mobile phone shops and off-licenses. At the same time, the parked cars stopped being expensive and became just nice. A little later they became just roadworthy. The smell of smoke grew stronger all the time and without any discussion they left the pavement and walked down the centre of the road. Just as garishly decorated bars began to outnumber mobile phone shops, Jeremy stopped and pointed at a pub across the road.

"We must be nearly there. That's the Hobgoblin pub. Sometimes I used to meet Anton there when he'd finished with the TA. I wasn't really old enough to be going in pubs, but nobody seemed to care. It was that sort of place. Anton looked so handsome in his uniform. So perfect. We'd sit for hours over a coke and a half of bitter and talk about everything. Sometimes, if the pub was quiet, he'd put his arm around me." He stopped and looked back at Matthew. "Don't try to look so surprised. I've seen you watching me, trying to decide what I am. And if you find out the answer to that please let me know because I've no idea." In the muted glare from the streetlights, Jeremy's face looked tortured, as if he were vomiting up something from deep inside. "I thought I'd put all these memories away from me. Put them in an airtight box and sealed it shut so I could be the person I was expected to be. But memories are like acid; they never sleep, they never stop gnawing away. And just being here has opened that box and suddenly I'm fourteen again. Anton came to our school to talk about the Territorial Army and we got talking after his presentation. It turned out he liked trains too, and took me to the Neasden depot on his motorbike. It was an underground marshalling yard, but it was a nice thought. He told me all about his career in the TA, the places he'd been and the things he'd done. The ones he was security cleared to tell me, of course. Sometimes we … messed around together. But nothing serious. Nothing proper. But that wasn't what our relationship was about. Anton liked me. He made me feel special. He made me feel as if I existed for the first time and not just as a parental accessory. He took me to the Imperial War Museum, bought me things. For three months I saw him every day. The time I spent with Anton was the most wonderful time of my life. And then it stopped."

"What happened?" Matthew didn't want to know, he didn't even want to be here, but the silence demanded a response.

"My mother happened. It sounds absurd doesn't it, like something from a bad novel. A hectoring mother putting her foot down with a firm hand and forbidding something pure and innocent. It's only absurd if you had never met my mother. The polite description is that she was a strong-willed person. Certainly strong enough to put my father in an early grave."

They turned a corner and the smell of smoke was overpowering.

"I don't know if someone told her or it was just an accident. But one day when she should have been at bingo she came home and Anton and I were together. Not doing anything, just sat watching TV. But she looked at Anton, looked at me and just knew. She told Anton to get out and he never looked back. She locked the door after him and told me that unless I stopped all contact with him she would never talk to me again. Not talking was the nuclear weapon in her armoury and she knew it worked. When I was six I broke a plate. I don't think it was anything special, but my dad had died just the week before and my mother just thought I was looking for attention. She very calmly cleared up the broken pieces and told me that she would not speak to me for a week. And she kept her word. I can still remember crying myself to sleep, the silence in the house like a suffocating sheet. At the end of the week we sat down and watched the clock, and the moment it clicked over a week she starting talking again as if nothing had happened."

The wind blew a fine spray of ash into their faces and Jeremy broke off, coughing.

"That was the last time I ever saw Anton. I did try to disobey her, but when I phoned the local TA centre my mother had got there first and they just said there wasn't anyone of that name. And after that I was hers. You know how they make bonsai trees? They take a regular tree and cut off any bits that don't fit their plan. I was the tree. She literally took over my life. She told me what to wear, who I could see and when I was allowed out. Sometimes she arranged dates for me that I knew nothing about until she sat me in the car, told me the name of the girl and gave me a box of chocolates or a bunch of flowers to give her. Nothing really changed when I went to university. She had a key cut for my room so she could wake me up in the morning with a cup of tea from a thermos. She'd be waiting for me outside a lecture theatre and most evenings she'd watch the TV very quietly while I studied."

"I'm sorry."

Jeremy shrugged. "Why? You never met her. If you had then you might have had something to be sorry about. She wasn't a person; she was a force of nature. Something that would always exist, like the sun or rain, and when she wasn't there anymore I think I went a little crazy. I know it's not much of an excuse, but I did what I did with Gretchen because all my mother ever wanted was proof that I was normal, and I stopped because that was something only she wanted. And you were looking in the wrong bedroom; Gretchen is in the one by the kitchen."

Matthew pretended to wipe his face to hide his look of surprise at being caught peeking. "I'm sure your mother only wanted the best for you."

"You don't understand my mother at all do you? Let me try to explain. It was the week before I left for university and I think my mother was becoming desperate. There were more arranged dates, more catalogues left open at the lingerie pages. I just gritted my teeth and ignored it all. I still thought that university would change everything. And then I came home one day and found my mother had another date waiting for me. Only this time it was different. Her name was Crystal, and I should have guessed right there. She was very pretty, stunningly pretty; she made Gretchen look dull. My mother said she'd be back in two hours, looked me straight in the eyes and told me to have a good time. The moment she was out of the door Crystal was all over me, kissing me, hands running up my thigh, rubbing … me. I'd never been with a woman and I must have said something because Crystal said those immortal words that I will always remember: 'It's okay, just lie back and I'll take good care of you.' And I realised that my mother, the woman that had owned and operated me for years, was so worried about what I was that she'd bought me a prostitute so I could prove myself. I'd say imagine how humiliated and degraded I felt, but

I don't think it's possible. So remember all those dreams of being naked in front of the class? Now put them on the big screen, with cameras giving close up of your genitals and a running commentary on their size, the whole place packed out with woman laughing and pointing. And if you can imagine that then you're a tenth of the way to feeling what I felt. Crystal was very apologetic and 'did I want to try again?' She left very quickly after that. I'd say she was embarrassed, but I think she was more concerned about having to offer a refund. My mother came back exactly two hours later looking disappointed and went to bed early. A week later, I moved into rooms at university."

"I'm sorry."

"Sorry and fifty pence will buy you a cup of coffee. What's done is done. Except it isn't, because the most important part of her will always be here." Jeremy pressed one finger to his forehead. "And the only way to prise her out would be through therapy. And I don't know if you've noticed but right now there's a distinct shortage of good Jungian therapists that can even spell their own name." Jeremy turned away and carried on walking. The sound of his footsteps on broken glass was very loud.

Matthew followed reluctantly. "I don't know how long she's been gone, but they say that time is a great healer."

Jeremy's face twisted through several unreadable expressions. "Gone? You mean dead? She's not dead! Certainly wasn't the day before everything fell apart. We had fish and chips together in my room. I've been looking for her ever since so

I could give her the care and attention she deserves."

Jeremy turned the corner and stopped dead. Matthew caught up with him and then looked past him. Across the road, a row of shops had burnt and charred window displays filled the pavement. Behind the shops, ranks of buildings had collapsed leaving piles of rubble between walls without floors or roofs. Everything was bright with pinpoints of glowing embers that grew and waned with the wind. Matthew looked left and right and there were only more buildings that had burnt.

Jeremy looked back at Matthew. "And we've been wasting our time! This all burnt days ago! We've more chance of finding rocking horse shit than a gun. Anything that was in the TA centre is either charcoal or buried under tons of rubble. We'd have been more useful sitting at home."

"Which is where we should be right now before they come again. Sit down and have a think about what to do now."

"Retrench, regroup and respond. The three R's of any good plan."

"First we have to get back home."

They followed the same route back that they had used on the way in. Jeremy walked very slowly past the Hobgoblin pub.

Chapter Twenty-Three
Friends in High Places IV

Cheilith pulled himself through the junction of two sections and sealed the iris behind him. Very carefully, he pulled the oxygen mask away against its elastic strap, ready to let it snap back into place at the slightest hint of the bitter almond smell of cyanide gas. The air seemed good and he pulled the mask away completely. The Masters would let the section he had just left bathe in the fatal gas for five minutes, then they would flush it out for another five minutes before they dared enter. The Masters were slow, but very methodical. They had chased him across a complete level of the ship with the same painstaking detail and they would follow him to the very last concealment on the ship and then they would kill him.

He had a supply of the brown pellets the Masters used to feed their slaves, but he wasn't hungry. What he wanted more than anything else was to see what had gone wrong.

Working carefully in the cramped space of the ventilation shaft, he slid the viewer from his bag and cycled through the remote feeds. And they were all wrong. By now all the Masters should have been dead. The battle should have been over, but instead it had not even begun. Their great sacrifice, that had cost them so much, had been no more than a small blip on the Masters' plans.

He pushed the viewer away from him and considered it possible that they had been wrong. The people of the blue planet had seemed perfect. So cunning. So adaptable. They had watched the recordings of a tribe of small brown humans armed only with primitive projectile weapons fight a much larger tribe armed with enough airships to darken the sky. The very jungle had burnt with the liquid fire they called napalm, and yet the brown people had won. They had progressed from those crude airplanes to space flight in less than fifty years. And yet all of them had failed to see what the slaves had died to give them.

He held onto the faint hope that the few desperate survivors were so traumatised by the social breakdown the Masters engineered, that they were too busy living to think clearly about what was happening.

He checked the time. He had another six minutes before he had to move again. Time enough to make a decision. There were enough sections of the ship to keep him moving for tens of days. But the Masters would have picked this world clean in a fraction of that time. Would the Immunes have seen the gift they had been given before it was too late?

Four minutes left. And then Cheilith saw the answer. He had recordings of the humans' insane babble of languages. They would need minimal editing and then he could use the ship's transmitters to talk to the whole planet, telling them what they needed to do. It was so clear, so perfect, that he hugged himself. Then he saw the problem and stopped hugging himself. Then he saw the big problem and screamed.

The first problem was one of simple logistics. There was a tap point in each section of the shaft to access the ship's transmitters. But the moment he made that connection the Masters would know exactly where he was and their slow, painstaking search would become a swift point response. They had built enough twists and turns into the ventilation system to keep him one step ahead, but the number of possibilities would narrow exponentially. He would have less than three turns of the blue planet before they would find him. Just seventy of their hours before he was dead.

And that was the big problem. There was nothing on the recordings about the room in the pyramids. That had been his job, to explain complex concepts in simple words until the humans understood. If he died before he could talk to the humans a simple victory here would become a race against time.

Cheilith had never seen his home world. His people had been taken from there long before he was born. But he had heard the old stories, and one in particular of a bird that built nests in an area infested by venomous snakes. From the moment an egg was laid it was a race between snake and egg. If a snake found an egg before it hatched then it would suck it dry. But if the egg hatched first then the snake would be food. The Masters were the snake. Low, treacherous, cunning but shrewd. They must have crippled the Masters' home world when the slaves there had committed suicide. But they would rebuild. They already had a few remaining ships. They would reach out and take the humans as new slaves and they would never let themselves be fooled again. They would watch their slaves with an unblinking gaze and their empire of pain would go on forever. But the humans were the egg. A symbol of hope and life. Because, at the same time that the

Masters were rebuilding, the humans would be unlocking the promise of the pyramids.

He heard the scream of the cutters as they began to open the iris he had sealed behind him and pushed towards the next section, but as he moved he readied the connector he would need at the tap point. There really was no decision to be made at all. He would tell the world what they needed to do and when the bitter almond smell of cyanide gas filled his lungs he would die at peace with himself. And if the humans didn't understand the lesson of the pyramids then he hoped they would make good slaves.

Chapter Twenty-Four
Sixty-four Hours Remaining

Matthew woke to the sound of waves breaking on a shore. He pulled a pillow over his head, but that did nothing to block what the sound meant. He tried to lose himself in the memories of other days and watched his favourite TV show, felt the touch of Kirsten's face. But no matter how he tried, he kept being drawn back to how the cones had moved and the look on Jeremy's face when he spoke about Anton. In the end, he kicked off the bedsheets and padded over to the window. The clouds seemed lower than ever and pressed down on London like a firm hand. Matthew watched more ships drop through the dull, grey cotton candy before he went to wake Jeremy.

The living room curtains were already open and the washed-out morning light made the living room look like a student squat. It didn't need much help. The carpet was patterned with dirty footsteps like a dance diagram and littered with glasses and bottles left over from the night they had seen the probe. Piles of dirty plates were precariously stacked on a fake antique drawer unit and some of Jeremy's ketchup had dripped down its exquisitely inlaid front. Matthew wiped some off with a finger and realised that the fake antique was almost certainly a real antique.

"I see they are back again." Jeremy's voice behind him was hoarse and very quiet.

Matthew spun around, slipped on a tangle of underwear and went down with a thump that shook his teeth. As he climbed to his knees, he pushed the underwear away and looked back at the windows. Jeremy was propped up on a pile of cushions like the badly made scarecrow he resembled. He still wore the smoke-stained T-shirt and jeans he had worn last night. His eyes were dark panda circles around red-rimmed eyes and his hair was flat on one side. Matthew remembered a tramp he'd seen sleeping in the doorway of WHSmith. He had stunk of alcohol and looked like his last bath was a distant memory, and he had still looked better than Jeremy.

"I couldn't sleep," Jeremy said.

"I know what you mean. I lay awake till three, but then I must—"

Jeremy talked over him. "It's a shame we couldn't get a rifle. We'd have been perfectly placed here."

"Well, nothing has landed yet. They might not even—"

Jeremy carried on as if Matthew had said nothing at all. "All those miles we walked in the dark to get to Shepherd's Bush and we came back empty-handed."

Matthew looked at him suspiciously. It had only taken an hour each way, but Jeremy was making it sound like finding the source of the Nile. "Well, we can try again. Have a look at the map and—"

"It was really stressful. All that time waiting for either the cones or the Stupid to get us, and all for nothing."

Matthew realised that there were two completely separate conversations taking place here. He wondered if Jeremy would even notice if he left. In the end, he said nothing at all.

"By the time we got there I was so tired. The strain of the last few days, the shock of seeing those creatures, just got to me. I don't even remember much of what happened at Shepherd's Bush. I hope I didn't say anything silly." He stopped and looked at Matthew expectantly.

Matthew thought quickly and twisted his face into the same exasperated expression he used for lost tourists.

"Yeah, well, I had better things to do than listen to you ramble on. The evening wasn't exactly a walk in the park for me either. You wittering on was just dull background noise."

Jeremy held eye contact for entirely too long and then nodded curtly. He turned back to look out of the window and after a long minute, Matthew stood next to him. Physically, they were inches apart but for all practical considerations there was a huge gulf between them. When he had first met Jeremy he had thought him weird and standoffish. But circumstances had pushed them together as surely as coal became diamonds. And last night that had all changed. Jeremy's relationship to Anton had obviously been something very private, until he had dragged it kicking and screaming into the light. Matthew wasn't sure what Jeremy was so afraid of. That he would be disgusted and revolted? That he would harangue him with the more judgemental parts of the Bible? Or perhaps he was just afraid of a traditional gay bashing with a baseball bat.

After they had said a very stilted goodnight and retreated to their bedrooms, he had spent a long time thinking how he really felt about Jeremy. And he had come to a conclusion that surprised him. He didn't care. After Kirsten had come out as a lesbian and left him, he had boiled with anger and hate. Homosexuals were the abomination the Bible said they were. They were against nature, against everything that was good. Everywhere he went he saw 'them', flaunting their degenerate lifestyle choice, holding hands in public where children could see them. Sometimes he deliberately pushed between them as hard as possible, excusing the contact with a half-hearted apology. Online, he raged and swore at the perverts, the freaks. His accounts were blocked and reopened under new aliases many times. And then one day the wallpaper that Kirsten had chosen, and they had put up during one wonderful weekend, started to peel and he stopped at the local DIY giant for a tube of glue. Only, he had to walk through the Home Decorating section to get it. The moment he turned into the aisle he saw two men bickering over wallpaper. Matching, tight, faded jeans, red T-shirt versus green T-shirt, equally stupid haircuts. Matthew knew the type: nights in the gay bars epileptically dancing to eighties pop music; days sneering at the breeders with their boring, conventional lifestyle. They were everything he hated. He slowed down and led with one shoulder, ready to accidentally barge into them. And then they smiled at each other and Matthew realised something very important. They were happy. He had been miserable for so long that he could barely remember what happiness looked like, but he was seeing it now. And with that he saw they were just another couple that had found each other and, for a second, he would have done anything to have a fraction of what they had

213

together. After that moment of revelation, the thought that Jeremy might be gay or bisexual had all the emotional weight of choosing between tea and coffee. If they could talk about what had happened then they could have put it behind them. But Jeremy had just declared it 'The Secret That Must Never Be Spoken'. And Matthew knew from bitter experience that secrets were like raw meat on a hot day. Soon they began to rot and fester. Then they would fill the air with poison that could only push them further apart.

"Now they're landing." Jeremy pointed at the ships arching down.

Matthew nodded and followed three of the descending shapes rapidly growing bigger. To their left, the cube shape settled into place with an unhurried unfolding of landing legs. In front of them the Stupid flowed away from a circular patch like blown dust. He had the briefest possible glimpse of the marks where the sphere had landed yesterday before its legs filled them.

"The sphere landed at exactly the same place it did yesterday. Even its landing legs dropped right into the depressions they left yesterday."

"Autopilot," Jeremy said, confidently. "They did all the hard work yesterday, finding a landing spot. Now they've probably got a button that just takes them right back here."

The rightmost point of the sphere shivered and the ramp flowed down to the ground.

"Not wasting any time are they," Matthew said.

"They did all the quality checks yesterday. Now it's just more of the same."

The very top of the ramp shivered and two wing-like strips slid out, left and right, making the ramp look like a giant letter T propped against the sphere.

"It didn't do that yesterday," Matthew said.

"And it doesn't make any sense. If they herd the Stupid like they did yesterday then some of them will spill down the side strips and off the ramp."

There was motion in the dark space where ramp met sphere and Matthew saw a familiar shape emerge. "And here come the cones."

The first of the cones moved onto the ramp, but instead of moving down the ramp it moved onto the wing-like strip on the left of it and down to its end. The next cone followed it onto the strip until they were touching. The next followed it like threading beads on a wire. When the leftmost wing was full, the next cone moved onto the right-hand wing.

"It's some sort of viewing platform so the senior things can keep an eye on the plebs?" Jeremy said.

"So why didn't they do that yesterday?"

Jeremy shrugged.

When both wings were full, cones stopped leaving the ship.

"Well, that rules it out as an observation point. The only cones are the ones on the wings, so there's nothing to watch."

Something moved at the top of the ramp.

"Hang on! There's more cones leaving the ship."

But what appeared on the ramp weren't cones; they were people. First there was the nurse the

215

cones had taken; next to her was the businessman. Behind them a double row of Stupid marched down the ramp. Each of them had a thick, gold, headphone-like band that stretched from ear to ear.

"Mind control! That's what they do," Jeremy stated, confidently. "That's what they've been doing to the people they took yesterday. They find some developing planet and dump something in the atmosphere that wipes high-level brain function."

At the bottom of the ramp the double column of headband wearers split into four columns, each column then split into four more until there was a spreading cloud of gold headbands moving through the crowd of Stupid.

"The band is just the surface of something that taps into the motor cortex and maybe the deep limbic systems for a little pleasure-pain feedback."

The ramp started rolling colours.

"If they do something wrong they get a jolt of pain and if they do something well then they get a little orgasm. There's your conditioning and control all in one nice little package." Jeremy pointed excitedly at the ramp. "And look how well it works! Yesterday, all the people on the ramp were slow, docile and completely harmless. Now they're like soldier ants. Perfectly disciplined, following orders without a second thought. All the cones have to do is sit back and watch."

The people wearing gold headbands reached a point a hundred metres from the ship, stopped moving and formed themselves into a rough curve centred on the ramp.

"Why aren't there more of them?" Matthew said. "They herded thousands of people into the ship, but there's only a handful here wearing those gold headbands."

Jeremy shrugged. "Still being processed? In cold storage waiting to be sent back to their home world to become butlers? Or maybe these are just a prototype and the cones are watching to see how well they perform."

The Stupid suddenly pulled away from the line of gold headbands, leaving an empty buffer zone between them.

"And I'd say they are doing quite well. Just like the cones, they have their own exclusion fields and they're using them perfectly."

The row of gold headbands began moving towards the ship and the Stupid caught in front of the line were pushed along in front of them.

"The more Stupid they sweep into the ship equals more headband-wearing drones," Jeremy said. "More drones equals more Stupid swept into the ship. It's a classic feedback loop. Tomorrow they'll have a hundred drones under their control. The day after, two hundred. They'll be able to sweep the whole park in an hour."

The last of the Stupid disappeared into the ship and the line of gold headbands broke up to repeat the whole process to the left of the ramp.

"Which all means, if we're going to do anything, we have to do it soon."

Matthew looked over to the right of the window. While they had been watching the sphere, the Aztec pyramid had landed and its ramp was open and waiting. A flicker of motion in the corner of the window caught his eye and he leant forward. A group of three gold-headband wearers were heading towards the row of houses between them and Lancaster Gate tube station. He looked sharp left. Another group of three was heading towards the houses there.

"There are drones heading towards the houses on either side of us."

Jeremy stepped up to the window and pushed him out of the way. "Where?"

"On the right, just by the phone box, and on the left, by the crashed double-decker bus." Matthew inserted himself at the window ledge next to Jeremy and breathed in his unlovely body odour as he pointed. His view of the street was blocked by Jeremy's puffball of hair, but around it he could see the three drones on their right vanish into a house just a short distance away.

"They can't be looking for more Stupid," Matthew said. "The park is pretty much packed. Perhaps they are looking for a few souvenirs to take back."

There was a solid thump behind them as if something heavy had fallen. Matthew looked around, but saw nothing out of place.

"That doesn't make any sense," Jeremy said slowly. "Compared to the civilisation that built those ships, anything we might have would be just crude trinkets." A muffled slamming noise echoed up the stairwell and they both looked around at the front door.

"Did we lock that last night?" Matthew whispered.

"I don't know. I mean, there was no need." Jeremy was whispering as well.

"Where are the keys?"

Jeremy pointed mutely at a desk on the left of the door. Matthew ran towards it and was right in front of the door when it clicked open. He threw himself towards the far side of the desk like a rugby player diving for the goal line. His elbow banged into the wall with an electric jolt of pain. He pushed himself into the desk's kneehole space until his back was pressed hard against the wall and his view of the room a truncated, waist-high slice.

Jeremy was frozen in place against the window, his mouth wide open. Matthew waved frantically at him and banged his elbow again. There was a hushing sound as the door swung open and Jeremy pushed himself against the furthest side of the grandfather clock. For a moment, the situation seemed almost funny, like two brothers hiding from an outraged wife in a hastily enacted French farce. Then someone walked into the room.

All Matthew could see from under the desk was a pair of mud-covered shoes and the bottom half of a pair of filthy trousers. The shoes looked handmade, the trousers expensive. Both now were only fit for the bin. The shoes took another step into the room and Matthew could see their owner. He was very tall, solidly built and his face was completely blank. Matthew looked past him to Jeremy. Pressed in tight against the clock, all he could see was one half of his face. Jeremy saw him looking and very slowly touched his eye and then the top of his head. Matthew nodded. He had already seen the bulge on top of the gold band and the glitter of a lens there. The drone was wearing a camera.

The drone looked left and right and took a step towards the door that led to the kitchen, but also towards Jeremy. The drone looked around very slowly and deliberately. Matthew immediately saw it as a panning shot for this fleshy robot. It took another step forward. Now Jeremy was just a foot to his right. Jeremy's hand reached up to the side of the clock. The drone stepped forward, looked left and started a slow turn that would finish with him face to face with Jeremy.

Jeremy brought his hand down on the top of the drone's head with a dull thud. The drone took two faltering steps. Jeremy stepped out from the cover of the grandfather clock, lifted his arm and brought it down again. This time the sound of the impact was much louder and the drone dropped face down on the carpet.

Matthew pulled himself out of the knee space of the desk and across the room. Jeremy dropped something heavy on the floor as he staggered back. His face was very pale.

"He nearly saw me! He was going to look right at me. I had no choice. I had to do it."

Matthew took his arm and sat him down before he could fall down. The drone made a sighing sound and Jeremy grabbed an ashtray, lifted it and then very slowly replaced it. Around the drone's head, the carpet had a spreading crimson halo and his short, dark hair was slick with blood. Next to his head, an L-shape as large as a paperback book was growing its own halo.

Jeremy grabbed Matthew's hand. "I had to do it. I had no choice," he repeated.

Matthew squeezed his hand and then discreetly let it go. "You did the only thing you could. What did you hit him with?"

"The winder thing for the clock. I think it's solid brass. It was the nearest thing to hand. Is he still alive?"

Matthew looked down at the drone. On the TV and movies they placed one hand on a patient's neck and confidently announced life or its absence. But he had no idea what he was meant to be looking for.

"I don't …"

The drone coughed.

"He's alive."

"Christ!"

Matthew wasn't sure if that was relief because he was alive, or disappointment that he wasn't.

"He's facedown to the floor, so the camera is just getting a close up of the carpet. But there might be some sort of tracker. We have to get rid of him."

Jeremy stopped shaking and looked up at Matthew.

"You mean …?"

"I mean get him out of here. When he comes round they'll see us. And once they see us they'll do something about us."

"There's a service lift by the fire exit. We can take him downstairs and dump him by the back entrance."

Matthew looked the drone up and down slowly. He was well over six-feet tall and solidly built. His shoulders were broad and his neck barely existed. Under his stained shirt his chest looked as big as a barrel.

"I don't think we'll be able to move him by ourselves. He must weigh sixteen stone easily." Matthew bent down and pulled at the drone's sleeve. "Is there a trolley or …" He stopped in mid-sentence and Jeremy watched him warily. Matthew brought his head down until his ear was nearly touching the drone's gold band and listened carefully.

"It's talking to him."

"What?"

"The band, it's talking to him. Get your head down here and listen."

Jeremy slid forward off the sofa and down to his knees. He looked at Matthew suspiciously and then very carefully brought his head close to the drone's until he could hear a small voice. He leant down some more until he could hear what it was saying.

"Look left. Look right. Lift your arms. Drop your arms. Step backwards. Step left. Step right." The voice was as bland as a lift announcing floor arrivals.

Jeremy touched the gold headband with an outstretched finger and it moved off one ear. He prodded it again and the band slipped completely off the drone's head. The bland voice was much louder now. The inside of the headband looked puffed up, as if badly stuffed. There was a small grill at each end of the U-shaped band.

"They're talking to him! There's no surgery, no brain implants. It's just a set of headphones."

"But the Stupid make the worst robots ever. Every instruction has to be broken down to the smallest detail."

Jeremy tapped the headband. "But that's exactly what they are doing. A computer uses the camera on the band to see what's in front of them. Bit of image processing and it issues some orders."

"It would have to be one hell of a computer. The camera is a 2D lens looking at a 3D London. So that's your depth perception gone. Stairs must be a nightmare. And the lens on that thing was tiny. Looking through it would be like watching one of those found footage horror movies – all wildly shifting points of view with no link between them."

"I think we can worry about that later on. There's a sort of trolley in the broom cupboard. I think it was used when the kitchen appliances were installed. We can just roll this guy onto it, secure him with a knotted bedsheet and then it's easy."

"Okay, you get that and I'll see how we are going to shift this guy."

Matthew watched Jeremy scuttle off to the kitchen. His abrupt change of subject had been very telling, and what it told was that he didn't believe what he had been saying either. Trying to operate a remotely controlled car on a perfectly flat floor was easy enough when you could stand over it. Trying to operate a drone via a head-mounted camera must be nearly impossible. Look down to see where you're stepping and you don't see what you are stepping towards.

"I've got the trolley."

Jeremy was towing an old-fashioned porters' trolley, a tall L-shape with handles at one end, two wheels and a small footplate at the other.

"That's nearly perfect. If we lie it down we can just roll this guy onto it."

Matthew knelt down next to the drone and studied the headband. If he just lifted it up and wrapped it in a tea towel then its operators would have a brief view of the room and perhaps their staring faces. If he dropped the tea towel over the headband and picked it up, its smooth surface might just as easily slip free.

All the sound drained out of the room. The small hairs on his arms stood up straight, small ant tracks ran over his hands and face. The headband shifted like a cut worm into a straight bar and carried on moving until its two ends touched and twisted past each other into a pretzel shape. Its gold colour tarnished and flaked off in leaf shapes as the band sagged into a pool of dull-coloured liquid.

The sound returned to the room. The hairs on Matthew's arm lay flat again.

"Well, that was something. They must have decided that they wouldn't be hearing from this drone again and hit the self-destruct button."

Jeremy reached out very gingerly and held his palm above the pool as if warming it on a cold night. "Or maybe released the compose button. This isn't hot at all. It looks like they can mould matter to any shape they like. Perhaps they told some to look like a headband and just stopped that instruction." Something outside the window caught his attention. "And here's this guy's replacement. The cones really are very efficient."

Matthew looked past him at the ramp. A tall man wearing a soiled tracksuit marched down the ramp. His gold headband was very bright against his bald head. He turned smartly right at the bottom of the ramp and walked quickly towards them. Both

224

Matthew and Jeremy moved to the sides of the window and watched through a single eye. The replacement drone stopped directly below them and a moment later, two more drones appeared from the entrance to their building.

"Not a lot of sentiment for their fallen comrade," Jeremy said. "Looks like there won't be a volley of fire or even a quick chorus of taps. They just discard and move on."

The three drones entered the building next door. Matthew checked in both directions and slid out from hiding. "Well, at least we don't have to worry about being seen while we move this guy."

"Why do anything at all? The most important part was the headband and that turned itself into a puddle. We wait until this guy comes round and then we just order him out of the room."

"Unless there's an embedded locator tag and later on his owners wonder what happened to their property."

Jeremy pushed the trolley forward and laid it down parallel to the drone.

"All we have to do now is just roll him across." He smiled helpfully. "I'll hold this in place while you pull."

Matthew placed a foot on the tubular upright of the trolley. "That's no problem. This way we can both pull."

Jeremy's smiled vanished. Very reluctantly, he reached forward and grabbed a lapel.

Matthew soon decided that Jeremy's use of the word 'just' had been a masterly piece of understatement. Trying to move the drone was exactly like trying to move a heavy chest freezer.

But only if the freezer had a jacket that ripped when pulled and limp arms and legs that flopped out, making rolling impossible.

Finally, they got him completely onto the trolley. Matthew fed a bedsheet under the arched back of the trolley and knotted it around the drone's chest.

"Ready?" he said, breathlessly.

Jeremy nodded and beads of sweat dropped into his eyes. They each held one of the trolley's non-slip handles and lifted. The back of the trolley came up until it was nearly upright.

"Easy!" Jeremy said, and the trolley's paired wheels shot forward. The handles pulled away from them and the trolley thumped back to the floor. "Bugger!" Jeremy said, and Matthew agreed with him.

"Okay, let's try it again, but this time I'll keep a foot on one of the wheels."

Jeremy looked at him with an expression of mute suffering as he reached down. This time the trolley came upright and Matthew towed it backwards to the door. The carpet in the corridor was much more basic than the expensive one in the living room and moving the trolley became nearly as easy as Jeremy had suggested. While the service lift climbed towards them, they both used the wall to prop them up. When the battered lift doors opened, they pushed the trolley together.

The lift doors closed automatically and opened just as automatically when they touched the drone's arm that had lolled over one side of the trolley. Matthew bent down to move it out of the way and suddenly everything was far too real. The hand was greasy and tried to slip away from him. But it was warm and alive and suddenly Matthew couldn't pretend anymore that he was touching something as anonymous as a Stupid or a drone. He was a person. A few days ago he had a life, perhaps a wife and children, and now he was just something to be shifted around like unwanted furniture.

"If you've quite finished bonding, we have things to do," Jeremy said.

Matthew straightened up and looked Jeremy in the eye. Neither said anything but Jeremy looked away first, pressed the button labelled G and the lift thrummed into life. The display above the button panel changed from six to five and Matthew stood back and looked thoughtfully at the lift's battered sheet-metal doors.

Jeremy smiled confidently. "Don't worry. If the power goes out we're not going to be stuck in here until we are reduced to gnawing on this guy's shinbones. There's a trapdoor in the ceiling; there must be a ladder or something in case of emergencies."

"I'm not worried about the power. I'm worried what might be waiting for us when these doors open."

Jeremy looked at the doors just as thoughtfully, and then moved into the furthest corners of the lift as the display counted down from one to G. The lift then stopped with a jerk, the doors slid open and outside it was completely deserted.

"Thought it would be okay," Jeremy said. "Why would their drones be hanging around a service area?" He smiled, but Matthew had seen the breath he released to say it.

Matthew stepped around Jeremy and pulled the street door open very slowly. "There's no one outside. We'll just leave him here and prop the door open. When he comes to he'll probably just wander out."

"And what if the cones see that nasty wound on his head?"

"They'll probably just think he tripped over something and knocked himself out. He was very hesitant moving around."

"He was, wasn't he," Jeremy said, thoughtfully. He was unusually quiet as they rode back up in the lift.

Chapter Twenty-Five
Sixty-one Hours Remaining

Back in the apartment, Matthew locked the front door and then tried the handle over and over like an absentminded housewife making sure the house was really locked this time.

"Should we drag the desk behind the door?"

"No, the door's pretty solid and if anything happens we'd want to get out of here in a hurry." Jeremy sounded distracted, not looking at the door at all but staring out of the window thoughtfully. He turned back to Matthew with a very strange smile. "Could you do me a favour and count how many drones there are down there operating under remote control?"

Matthew looked at Jeremy suspiciously. He just smiled back and looked very smug. Matthew stepped up to the window and looked down. A line of people wearing gold headbands was herding a much larger group towards the ramp leading into the sphere. He started at the furthest point of the line and counted each headband down towards him. Then he counted back up the line and arrived at the same number.

"Well, there's nineteen people with headbands in the line sweeping towards the ship." He looked down, left and right. "And there's three teams of three working house to house. So twenty-eight in all."

"Twenty-eight. Well isn't that interesting. Because that's exactly the same number I counted."

"Why? Because you can still count?"

"No, because you were counting drones with gold headbands while I was counting the number of cones on their viewing platforms. I started to think about how hesitantly our drone had moved in here – step, look, step, look – and I realised that you were right. The whole idea of computer control via that little head-mounted camera was rubbish. You did very well there." Jeremy made it sound like he was rewarding a puppy that had found the newspaper and not the carpet for the first time. "But I also remembered how smoothly all of them moved outside. That didn't make sense. But what really made me think was how quickly his replacement arrived. He walked out of that ship minutes after that." Jeremy gestured at the puddle that was all that was left of the headband. "That meant he was all ready to go, but there was some limiting factor that stopped them bringing him on. And I realised that the limiting factor was the number of cones. Each cone is operating just one person and they are perched up on that viewing platform to see what they are doing. The camera is only used when they are out of sight. The instructions we heard were being dictated by a cone based on what they were seeing."

"Which is what we've always said; the Stupid are useless as workers."

"No, you don't understand; they are worse than useless. Not only would you have to have one cone watching one Stupid all the time, telling them exactly what to do – lift this, press that – but you'd have to feed them, and that means factories making disgusting human food. If you don't want them stinking the place up then you need to remember to send them to the toilet and wash them down at regular intervals, have somewhere for them to sleep. That's a lot of overhead. Do you know where the expression white elephant comes from? The King of Siam used to give an albino elephant to anyone that had displeased him. Keeping the elephant was very expensive as the owner had to provide it with special food and build a temple for the people that came to worship it. They couldn't get rid of the elephant as that would be an insult to the king, so instead they slowly went broke. The Stupid are the ultimate white elephant. Any work they might do would be massively outweighed by the infrastructure required to maintain them."

"Maybe the plan is to use them as soldiers in some war. That would be something they would be perfect for. Fearless, completely obedient. The cones watch from orbit and just send in waves of drones to swamp any resistance."

Jeremy made a sound like a horse coughing. "You watch too many old war films. That sort of thing was good in World War One, but even when they rebooted it as WWII twenty-three years later it wasn't about thousands of people marching on a target. By then it was carpet bombing from fifty thousand feet and ballistic missiles. Any wars the cones might fight are probably decided by dropping planets into suns."

"So we've no idea what's happening or why."

"None whatsoever, and that doesn't change a thing. More than anything else we need to find a gun and do something before they come for us one day. We've still got the guidebook and Yellow Pages we got from Harrods. We need to look for gun shops, shooting ranges or anything military. I'll make a start with the map and check it area by area. You take the Yellow Pages and do the same."

Matthew thought about saying something cutting, but didn't know what, and took the well-thumbed phonebook with a noncommittal grunt that Jeremy never even noticed.

***

Matthew soon discovered that while the phonebook was perfect for finding an address it was less wonderful at finding a business. The most useful thing in the book was the small section at the back that listed only businesses, but not grouped into business type. The first entry was AAA Car Hire, and Matthew began to slip his forefinger down the page. Some of the businesses had names that gave no clue to their function. Did Balzac Sewer alter clothing or dig big holes in the road? Matthew stopped at the unfortunately named Canker Services and looked across at Jeremy wrestling the map into submission.

"Anything so far?"

"Not a thing. I would have hoped that anything touristy would have more to say about England's long and glorious military history than ..." Jeremy folded the map and read. "... *Changing of the Guard takes place daily at eleven a.m. (check schedules)*. But that seems to be the extent of the information here. If I don't find anything soon I think we'll have to find a real bookshop with proper maps. From the tone of your enquiry I suspect you're having the same lack of success?"

232

Matthew nodded and went back to the phonebook. The patch of daylight under the window had moved noticeably across the carpet before he looked up again. "There's a place in Muswell Hill called On Target. That might be a shooting gallery? That's only five or six miles away; it might be worth a look."

"I think I've found somewhere much closer, in fact practically under our noses. Because it was never the map we should have been looking at. It was its cover." Jeremy held up the guidebook with its bright glossy cover of Buckingham Palace and crumpled map hanging like a defeated flag. "See the chocolate-box soldiers with their wildly impractical red uniforms and bearskin caps guarding John Nash's monstrosity? Well, according to the inside cover, that's a detachment of the Household Cavalry based just three quarters of a mile away at Hyde Park Barracks, Knightsbridge." He waved Matthew over to the window. "You see the ugly seventies tower just across the park? That's Hyde Park Barracks. But what the guidebook doesn't say is that the weapons they are holding aren't antique blunderbusses to look good for the tourists. They are L85A2 light support automatic rifles. That's the Heckler and Koch updated version of the SA80. Gas-operated, magazine-fed, selective fire. Bullpup configuration with its action and magazine in the stock so it's only thirty inches long. Fires the five point five-six times forty-five mil NATO round from a thirty-round magazine. Effective range four hundred metres and a fire rate of six hundred rounds per minute." Jeremy smiled brightly as if he had just won first prize for reciting obscure facts. "Anton used to tell me things like that." He stopped smiling.

"But what if that's locked up as tightly as the police station?"

"What if your place in Muswell Hill is a dry cleaners? At least the barracks is only the other side of the park. We can be there and back in an hour and all we need is a convenient sign – 'This way to the armoury' – or just one Stupid still carrying a rifle."

"Well I guess so."

"I know so. If the ships leave at four then there's another two hours before it's dark. If they have left any sensors behind the darkness won't be much of a concealment but it's the best we have."

"Why four?"

"They left at four yesterday. On its own that's just one data point. But this morning they arrived at eight and yesterday you abruptly woke me at eight twenty. So I'd say there's a better than even chance that their window of activity is eight to four. It fits with the autopilot that positioned them at exactly the same point as yesterday. Everything is planned and organised down to the smallest detail."

Matthew stared at Jeremy and tried not to look impressed. "I hadn't noticed that."

"You surprise me. It's only ten now so the next significant event is when the ships leave. If we have something to eat now we can rest up after they've gone. I'll have a sandwich with some crisps." He looked hopefully at Matthew. "Do we have any cheese?"

Matthew was torn between telling him to fuck off and just punching him. In the end he stood up very stiffly, told Jeremy he'd see and left the room quickly.

***

The rest of the day developed its own rhythm. On the half hour, Matthew got up and checked the view from the window. On the hour, Jeremy repeated the process. Every time the view was the same. A line of gold headband wearers sweeping Stupid towards the sphere. Towards the end of the afternoon the size of the crowd in the park had shrunk from the low hundreds to just tens. At quarter to four, nothing was said but they both drifted to the window. At five to four, the ramps were still in place. The headband wearers still marched in formation. At four o'clock, Matthew held his breath and waited for something to change. At a minute past, he released that breath and knew that Jeremy had been wrong. He had made a wild guess and tried to back it up with some hastily cobbled together observations. Mr Know-it-all was not quite as perfect as he liked to think.

"The ramps have gone."

Matthew looked up and saw that Jeremy was right. The ramp leading to the sphere had vanished. He looked left and right; both the cube and Aztec pyramid were equally unmarked. He checked the time. It was just three minutes past four.

The sphere drifted upwards. As it drew level with the window its landing legs melted back into the body of the ship. The bottom of the ship became a diminishing half-moon shape against the top of the window and disappeared completely.

"Well that looks as if they are on ..."

The sphere dropped back into sight and carried on dropping until it hit the ground with a thump they felt as much as heard. The featureless surface of the sphere grew spikes that thrashed in waves and collapsed. Violet halo bands ran down the sphere. The base sprouted landing legs that were twisted and misshapen. The violet glow grew brighter until it was hard to look at and vanished with a snapping sound.

"I don't think any of that was meant to happen," Jeremy said slowly.

The sphere rolled a few degrees left until the landing legs were either trapped underneath or waved uselessly in the air. A jackhammer roar started up and the sphere lumbered into the air. Where it had floated gently, now it clawed for every inch of lift. Sometimes slipping back. Sometimes lurching up. When it reached the mid-point of the window, the jackhammer sound became a shrill dentist's drill and the sphere hit the ground with a thud that rattled glasses.

"Engine problems?"

The surface of the sphere twitched and slowly poured into a halo platform around the sphere's equator, making it look like a scale model of Jupiter and its rings. The rightmost point of the sphere peeled back to make an opening and a cone oozed out onto the platform. For a moment it didn't move. There was the suggestion of movement from inside and the cone moved along the platform to their left. Matthew thought it moved very slowly, perhaps afraid of the distance to the ground. When the cone reached the midpoint of the platform it stopped and the surface of the sphere opened a single enormous eye. Matthew and Jeremy backed away from its terrible gaze and then stopped, because the eye was a hollow socket and they could see into the sphere, and inside the sphere it was alive.

Grey, muscular-looking tubes linked head-sized masses that slowly pulsed as if breathing. A network of thumb-sized, blood-red veins swelled and contracted like a snake that had swallowed a football. Thin, clear mucus began to spill out from the eye.

"Is that alive? Did that used to be people?" Mathew said.

"I'm sure one or two doctors might have noticed if we had things like that inside us." Jeremy sounded relaxed. He certainly didn't look it. "I think that's the future. Imagine what Nano technology and DNA-sequencing might look like after a hundred years, after a thousand years. Machines begin to look like flesh because that's the most efficient design honed by millions of years of evolution."

The cone reached deep into the ship and pulled out a slowly beating egg shape. He held it against the resistance of the grey tube connecting it to the ship and examined it briefly then released it and let the grey tube snap it back into place. The cone moved a foot to its right, reached into the ship, pulled out a slim oblong and released it. Another foot and it repeated the sequence with a rounded cube.

"If he's looking for the problem then he seems quite casual about it," Matthew said.

"There's probably some sophisticated analysis equipment doing the real work. All he's doing is just showing it different modules."

Matthew nodded as if he agreed with him, but still thought that what he was seeing looked exactly like a drunk rummaging in a drawer for a set of car keys.

The cone reached the end of the eye-shaped opening, moved back to where he had started and pulled out the egg shape again.

"He's going to do it all again?"

"Hang on. He's got some help now." Jeremy pointed at the entrance into the ship where another cone had moved onto the platform around the ship. The new cone moved equally slowly around the platform until it was standing next to the one they had been watching. The new cone was a foot shorter and its body was a dull red colour to the other's black. The two cones waved tentacles at each other for a few minutes then Red reached into the sphere and pulled out the same egg-shape that Black had already checked twice. There was another bout of tentacle waving before Red thrust the egg at Black so enthusiastically that he staggered back. He immediately released it then let its grey tube pull it back into the ship before pulling out the oblong and showing it to Red.

Matthew leaned against the window to watch and the cool pressure on his forehead sparked a memory of long trips in the back of his parents' car, forehead pressed against the car window, watching the world slide past. Sometimes at the end of those trips were beaches or educational experiences, but always the long, empty miles. Tyres droning against

238

broken tarmac with only traffic jams and broken-down cars to break the monotony.

He stood up straight and saw the scene below with new eyes – broken-down cars.

Red swiped the oblong away from Black and moved up until they were touching. Both waved tentacles but now they were hitting each other with a noise like wet towels.

"I've seen this before," Matthew said, very slowly.

"You've seen two aliens trying to fix a spaceship? You must have a very rich fantasy life."

"No, you've seen it too, except it's any weekend on a motorway and there's a nice new car on the hard shoulder with a fat, middle-aged bloke rummaging around under the bonnet. You just know that he's absolutely no idea how to fix it, but he's doing something in the vain hope that the car will spring into life. Sometimes there's an equally fat wife offering helpful advice and even passing at seventy you can just feel the tension." Matthew pointed downwards. "Those two have no more idea how to fix that ship than we do. The first guy didn't want to be there anyway and the second is arguing with him."

"Well, they're the pilots; how should they know how to fix it? To use your analogy, they're waiting for the Automobile Association."

"Then why send them out there at all?"

Jeremy ignored that and craned his head right. "Well here's the recovery service. I hope their subscription is up to date."

To their right, the Aztec pyramid landed with no sound at all. The sphere shivered at its rightmost

239

point and the ramp flowed out to touch the ground. A second later and the pyramid had its own ramp. The two cones left the eye-shaped opening and moved towards and then down the ramp. A moment later, a single-file column of cones emerged from the ship and followed them.

"They're abandoning ship?"

The column of cones reached the ground and drew a straight line towards the pyramid.

"Certainly looks like it."

Jeremy counted as each cone entered the pyramid. "Twenty-eight. There's no one left behind."

The pyramid folded its landing legs and remained disconcertingly motionless. Then it drifted up and out of sight.

"They're not going to try fixing it and are just going to send for the galactic tow truck?"

Matthew shrugged, moved closer to the window to watch the pyramid disappear and felt heat on his face. Below them, the sphere was flickering like a shade around a windblown candle. Then it began to melt. The top of the sphere collapsed, making a donut shape. The ramp boiled and dropped away as the halo platform wilted and ran like candle wax. They both backed away from heat like standing in front of an open furnace. The donut spread out into a puddle surrounded by a border of charred and smoking grass.

"They're just going to destroy it? But what about all the people inside? Where did they go?"

The smell of a thousand burning barbecues filled the room and they realised that the people had not gone anywhere. They were still there. Trapped under molten metal.

Matthew made two steps before he was violently sick. Jeremy didn't manage that much. He threw up on himself.

Chapter Twenty-Six
Fifty-five Hours Remaining

They couldn't smell burnt flesh anymore. All they could smell was the Vicks VapoRub they had plastered around and in both nostrils. The sharp menthol taste separated them from the stench of ruined meat until they spoke and the smell reached the back of their throats. They didn't talk much.

Both of them pretended that the window didn't exist, that when their eyes moved across the room they reached the edge of the window and skipped across to the other side as if the space between were a blind spot the brain could not accept. Both of them had looked out only once and their minds, seeking order from chaos, had showed them skulls, pelvises and long bones under cooling metal.

They sat at opposite sides of the room, purposefully not making eye contact as if somehow complicit in the atrocity they had seen. Matthew kept thinking how it must have been for the people in the ship when the walls began to glow and the air burnt in their throats. Had they screamed as vulnerable flesh blistered and charred, or had they remained blissfully unaware as their brains boiled in their skulls?

"They threw the ship away." Jeremy's voice was a small thing, but each word dropped like a stone into the silence that filled the room. Matthew turned to look at him and the dying light made his face into a mosaic of shadow with one bright eye.

"If you mean they destroyed the ship and murdered hundreds of people, then I'd have to agree to that."

"Tisk! Tisk! Tisk!" Jeremy's head switched from profile to profile with each expulsion of air. "You'll have to learn to separate emotion from analysis otherwise you'll go crazy. They threw the ship away like a malfunctioning TV remote without even changing the batteries, and that's important. Even if they have thousands of ships, even if that ship came free with a box of cereal, they put time and effort into filling it with people and then binned the whole thing."

"So?"

"So that's not everything. When they landed they forgot to deploy the landing gear. When we saw the probe it didn't go straight back up, it bounced all over the sky like a pinball machine."

"It reminded me of my dad trying to drive my remote control car."

"Because he had no idea what he was doing?"

Matthew nodded.

"I think we were nearly right when we said the cones had no idea how to repair that ship. But it's much more than that. They've no idea how to use the technology we've been seeing. Forget the idea of the cones as multi-brained geniuses. They are idiots pressing buttons and hoping. The probe bouncing all over the sky? Imagine a toddler playing with Dad's Xbox. The landing gear? They were probably just happy to get the ship on the ground."

"But they got here and wherever they came from has to be a long way away."

"The autopilot? It didn't just do the last part of the trip, it did the whole trip. The cones were just along for the ride."

"So who programmed the autopilot and where did the ships come from?"

Jeremy drummed his fingers thoughtfully. "The cones are a very old civilisation. They've had perfect machines and a perfect society for thousands of years. But now the machines are breaking down and no one knows how to fix them anymore. So they're looking for simple, self-repairing machines that can reproduce with the help of a little internet porn. They've probably been watching our planet for years. First as academic interest and now as a warehouse they can raid. They scratched together the remnants of a mighty fleet for one last desperate raid. Only the machine that changed everyone went wrong and the rest we know."

Jeremy sat back and looked smug. It was almost a shame to burst his bubble.

"Well, for one thing, those ships don't look like the last remnants of anything. In fact they look brand new, straight off the production line, still with the new car smell. And if their society is falling apart, the last thing they'd need is thousands of Stupid to look after. It would be like pouring sand into a failing gearbox."

Jeremy stopped looking smug. "I suppose so," he said, grudgingly. "But at least we know one more thing about them now." He waited until he had Matthew's full attention. "That we mean less to them than the ants on the pavement. They threw away hundreds of people without any attempt to save any. When the slavers that raided the African Coast lost a boat they might try to save a few poor souls for their economic value, but they didn't even care that much." He glanced at the clock. "Another hour before we can leave for the barracks and do something more than just sit back and watch." His face looked hard and Matthew wondered how true that face was. Maybe this was the real Jeremy stripped of all his amusing mind games and sense of superiority, but it was equally possible that this was just another mask. Perhaps Travis Bickle from *Taxi Driver* or a young John Wayne before the world grew too old for cowboys.

Matthew dug around the back of the sofa until he found the remote. "We should try to contact Arvid before we go."

"In case we don't make it back."

Matthew pressed the 'ready' button and the room filled with the roar of static.

"Turn it down!"

"Already doing it." Matthew held the volume button until the static was just a distant white-noise hiss. "It didn't make all that noise yesterday."

Jeremy pointed out of the window. "A lot happened today. Perhaps the two are connected." He stood up very quickly. "I'll find the torch for later while you talk to your pen pal."

And while Matthew was still processing that sentence Jeremy had barged open the kitchen door and vanished, which was odd because the torch was standing in plain sight on a table, just a foot to the right of the door. The only way to not see it would be to not want to see it.

Matthew watched the door swing shut behind Jeremy, opened-mouthed. He had always seemed very casual about contacting other survivors, but he'd just made using the radio sound like passing notes in class. Nevertheless, Matthew found the microphone down the back of the sofa and waited for Jeremy to get over whatever had dragged him away so suddenly. In a few minutes, he heard sounds from the kitchen. But not searching. It was the distinctive click of the kettle then the rattle of spoon in cup and then Jeremy's opened-mouthed slurping at a cup of tea. Matthew realised that he wasn't coming back anytime soon.

Matthew tapped the remote with a fingernail in a slow metronome beat. He was starting to think that Jeremy was like one of those cheap 3D postcards that from one angle was Snow White but from another the Wicked Witch. The moment you thought you understood him he became something else. But Jeremy's sudden change seemed somehow connected to the remote. Matthew studied the slab of plastic carefully, trying to see why Jeremy seemed so dismissive of it. And if not the remote then the contact it permitted. Jeremy didn't understand the language Arvid spoke but he would be happy to teach him. And then he realised; Jeremy had run because teaching him anything was a threat. Any sense of self had been eroded by his mother, all he had left was his intelligence and he used it like a crutch. He had to be the smartest man in the room because otherwise he was nothing. He'd probably arranged some dispensation with himself to attend university at all. Perhaps he saw it as a meeting of minds or passing on the torch of knowledge. Certainly nothing as simple as teaching.

The slurping sounds from the kitchen were replaced by a rustling that sounded very like the stealthy unwrapping of a packet of biscuits. Jeremy, as Travis Bickle, hadn't changed at all.

246

Matthew held the volume button until he could hear Arvid over the static. The roar of white noise grew and subsided like some distant ocean. In the lull between peaks of incoherence, they swapped disjointed sentences. Some of the conversation went easy, most of it went hard. Matthew tried to explain what had happened after the ship crashed and what it meant, but the best he could manage was to call the cones *dåliga användare*, bad users. Arvid spent a long time repeating variations of 'Garden of Plants' before Matthew understood what he meant. But he understood 'Montana' perfectly. After that, the pulse of static picked up speed, slicing Arvid's voice into a free-form haiku.

"Static voices
Unlocked frequency drifts
Single broadcast."

And after that there was only individual words twisted and distorted with static.

Matthew turned off the radio and silence flooded back into the room. Jeremy sat down opposite him, holding up a torch.

"Sorry it took me so long to find it. Did I miss Arvid completely?"

Matthew replaced the remote in its charger and twisted his head just a little more to see the table by the kitchen door. The torch there was missing. Jeremy had taken a long time to find something in plain view just a few feet away. A very convenient amount of time.

Matthew pasted on a smile that didn't quite fit right. "Afraid so. But we had a very useful conversation. Seems that Arvid has made contact with some more shortwave operators and they in turn have contact with other operators. Everyone is on different frequencies with differing range so any messages have to be passed up and down the line."

"How many in all?"

"Not sure. Stations come and go as they drop offline for power or rest. The best Arvid could guess was a floating population in the low thousands."

"Is everybody seeing the same sort of thing we are?"

"Pretty much. The cones sweeping people into ships, the headbands and pyramid ships. I tried to explain to Arvid our idea that the cones have no idea how to use the technology we've seen."

"My idea."

"Of course, my apologies. But that idea made sense to Arvid because a ship landed in the Jardin des Plantes in Paris, only he kept calling it the Garden of Plants. But it landed at several hundred miles per hour and dug a hole a hundred feet deep. The sound of its impact broke windows all over the city."

Jeremy looked unimpressed. "Except for scale, that's just what we saw."

"But it's what happened next that's interesting. The ship seemed undamaged and put down its ramp and did the whole thing with the light show to attract the Stupid, even though there was nothing living within a half mile of that landing. At the end of the day, it went back empty and in the morning came back to exactly the same point and spent the day repeating the whole thing."

Jeremy's face lit up. "Fascinating! That handily distinguishes between unfamiliar technology and

248

raw intelligence." He paused and Matthew looked suitably blank. "It was always a possibility that the ships were something the cones had found. Perhaps a remnant of a much more advanced civilisation that they didn't fully understand."

Matthew continued to look blank.

"Think about an aboriginal tribesman finding a working jeep left behind by a mining company. They might be able to start it and perhaps use it for raiding other tribes; they'd have no idea how to fuel it or do a five-point service, but at least they'd know how to steer it around a tree. But in Paris the cones basically drove into a pit and it never occurred to them to do anything else. They're not very smart. They've got some flashy and very powerful technology but they literally cannot think themselves out of a hole."

"Perhaps whatever they did to us affected them as well? When they left home they were highly advanced, but by the time they got here they were only just a little smarter than the Stupid?"

"It would explain a lot, the blotched landing, the raiding parties for the things we have, but they must have a wildly different physiology. What are the chances that whatever they did could affect them?"

They looked at each other in silence for a moment.

"What else did Arvid have to say?"

"Two very interesting things. The first was Montana in the United States. An operator there was in contact with someone in Canada even before things fell apart. When the cones landed, he reported much the same things we saw. But then things changed. He became angry, belligerent. He kept talking about the New World Order and chemtrails and that he wasn't going to sit back and watch them take his country away from him. And because this was America he had a gun, lots of guns apparently. He told Canada that he was the first of a new generation of Minutemen and that he was going to strike a blow for freedom. That was thirty-six hours ago. Nobody has heard from him since."

"He stuck a blow and so did they. I think they won." Jeremy's gaze was suddenly empty and unfocused. "Okay, if we find a weapon at the barracks we fire it from the barracks. Two shots then we drop everything and run. If the sky doesn't fall on us we go back for two more shots." He met Matthew's eyes and whatever he saw there made him smile. "What? You expected me to cut and run? But that's just one thing. What else was there?"

"The static that we heard when we came online. It's been going on at least all day and everyone is being affected. Arvid has been doing shortwave for years and some of the people he's talking to have even more experience. They think that it's another transmission, but one that's drifting across the whole shortwave spectrum and clashing with the bands we use."

He stopped and looked expectantly at Jeremy.

"And that's it? There's a bad station out there? I'm surprised there's only one."

"But this one is special, because they've been doing some timings on the bursts of noise and they occur at effectively the same time all over the world. That means they are coming from just one station, but that means a station more powerful than

250

anything they've ever seen before. They think the transmissions are coming from one of those ships we saw and that there are different factions there that don't agree with what's happening here and are trying to reach out to us."

Jeremy's face remained completely still for a moment. Then his lip twitched and turned upwards. His mouth dropped open and he let out a strange coughing sound. "You think there's a rebel alliance? That's the stupidest thing I've ever heard." The coughing turned to laughter. "If they are so keen to help us how come they're not down here handing out the plasma rifles? What exactly are they trying to tell us that's so important? This isn't some Hollywood blockbuster where they release the self-destruct codes to make all the ships explode in the last five minutes because the writers were too lazy to think of a better ending. Thomas Carlyle said that it wasn't brute force but persuasion and faith that are the kings of this world. We can discount faith; that ship sailed a long time ago. So that leaves persuasion, and you'd have to be very good with words to stop the cones harvesting us." He pointed an accusing finger at Matthew. "Do you know what Pareidolia is? And it's not the name of a Spanish holiday resort. It's the name they give to seeing ships in clouds or our redeemer's face in a slice of toast. The mind wants to pick order out of chaos, and it's quite happy to see what's not there. There's lots of chaos right now and everyone wants to live happily ever after. You said the transmissions were all at effectively the same time? But what exactly does 'effectively' mean here? Probably some guy using a stopwatch to time radio waves traveling at the speed of light. Of course they're going to come up with the answer they want. They're probably picking up thunderstorms or some backwash from the ships themselves and have woven that into some fantasy that Luke Skywalker is going to descend in clouds of glory to save us all. Only no one is going to ride to our aid. We're on our own."

"But Arvid sounded so certain."

"Of course he did!" Jeremy exploded. "He's probably down on his knees right now, praying to a crucifix made from circuit boards with an LED Christ. He wants to believe and if you also believe then maybe faith will become flesh. But try this on for size. You don't invade planets overnight. It has to take months, years, of planning. So if there's someone up there trying to help us why did they wait until it's eleven fifty-nine and the cones are on the ground harvesting us like wheat? Why didn't they do something before? Because they don't exist!" He threw his arms up in the air. "Does nobody think clearly these days? Don't answer that; I already know the answer."

Matthew looked away from the intensity of Jeremy's glare. "I'll get some supplies together in case there isn't anything at the barracks."

"What an excellent idea."

Chapter Twenty-Seven
Fifty-two Hours Remaining

Seen from across the park, Hyde Park Barracks had been just a shape on the horizon. Seen from its entrance, it was a layer cake of alternating levels of blue-tinted windows and dull grey concrete. The first few floors showed distorted reflections of the frozen traffic jam that filled the streets, but above that there was only the vague impression of a deeper darkness against the night sky. Behind them, the streetlights carved tunnels in the darkness that pressed down like a thick blanket. Every ninety seconds the lure the cones had left behind flashed like a flash bulb. The light gave them a snapshot of what was beyond the road, but rather than reassuring, the light was somehow threatening and they had spent the whole trip counting down until the next flash and then starting at every half-seen thing the light showed them.

The hardest part of the trip from Jeremy's expensive apartment had been deciding which way to go. The barracks was diagonally across Hyde Park, so Matthew had suggested the obvious route – turn left and take Bayswater Road and then Park Lane – but Jeremy pointed out that by the time they had taken the less observable streets beyond those they might as well have turned right and taken Kensington Church Street and then down past the wedding cake tiers of the Albert Memorial. When argument failed to make the decision, they decided the traditional way. The coin came down heads and they turned right.

The streets were deathly quiet and the footsteps of the Stupid, as they headed towards the lure, sounded like a mother shushing a teething child. As soon as they turned into Kensington Church Street they heard a voice calling out to them. Pressing themselves into every inch of cover from crashed cars, they crept down the road until they could hear that the voice was coming from a very old-fashioned-looking pub, so covered in dying flower baskets that its name, The Churchill Arms, was almost hidden. Very slowly, they crept closer and saw that all its doors and windows were open, and somewhere deep inside a fifty-cigarettes-a-day voice was whispering about the look of love. Matthew looked at Jeremy as they crossed the road towards it. They stopped just as the thick malty scent of beer and stale food wrapped around them.

Matthew rested one hand on the wall and peered around the door jamb. Inside the pub was oddly neat, with half-empty drinks on tables and a congealing plate of something and chips on the bar, as if at any moment thirsty customers would return from the toilet or smoking area.

"Doesn't look as if anyone's home," he said.

Jeremy indicated the wet pavement and then the untouched dust on the floor inside. "I don't think anyone has been through this entrance for days. Someone just left a CD on repeat."

The singer ran out of ways to say how much they missed their unnamed lover and there was silence for a moment. Then a beat started up like someone kicking in a metal door, tortured guitars growled and an inhuman voice snapped out words like bullets trying to machine gun his audience.

"Is that even music?" Jeremy said. "It sounds like a special effect from a sci-fi movie."

"I don't know. I think I recognise it."

"What interesting tastes you have. Pornographic theatre and weird music." He walked away very quickly and nothing more was said until they reached the barracks and were simultaneously disappointed and encouraged.

Jeremy was disappointed that there were no armed soldiers standing vacantly around outside, ready for them to just slip a loaded rifle off their shoulders, wait a few hours, take a few shots and then maybe he'd wake up in his university bed with only his mother to fear.

Matthew was encouraged that a door was open into the barracks and the lights were still on inside. The idea of stumbling through a darkened maze of corridors with only the slim beam of the torch to guide them filled him with a crawling dread.

Walking there through the tunnels of light that the streetlights made had been okay, or at least passible. But they had spent the whole trip walking down the middle of the road, safely away from the darkness that seemed to grow ever closer. But inside there would be no space and no time to react.

Jeremy stepped up to the open door and threw it open. The room inside was no bigger than a small garage with a single closed door on the opposite wall. The room was brightly lit by banks of florescent panels and the light glinted off the network of bars that separated the room into two halves. Two turnstiles with revolving gates made from horizontal metal bars allowed access to the second half of the room. Except, it didn't when

255

Matthew tried the nearest gate. It moved just a little and stopped with a heavy thud. He tried the second gate with the same lack of success.

"Card reader," he said, pointing at a black frame with a thin slot on the edge of the gate. "You need a registered card to unlock this."

"I know the sort of thing," Jeremy said behind him. "Looks a bit like a credit card except it would be anonymous white without any badges or logos in case it was ever lost. There'd be a barcode in the top left corner for inventory."

Matthew looked around and Jeremy held up a white card marked only by a barcode. "It was on the floor. You stepped over it on your way in."

Matthew took the card and swiped it slowly through the reader. The gate unlocked with a solid clunk. He pushed the gate just enough to prove it was open and then stepped up to the bars and shuffled through as the gate rotated. He then passed the card back to Jeremy though the bars. "There you go."

Jeremy took the card with a very strange smile. "Well, I hope I go. Because it all depends if this gate is smart or dumb. If it's dumb then all it knows is that it's a good card and I could stand here all day and swipe in every member of the Millwall Football Club. But if it's smart, then a computer somewhere has just logged this card as entering the building and if the same card tries to enter again then the computer will know that someone is trying to cheat the system and will lock the card. That means no one will be using it to get in." He tugged at the bars between them. "Or out. Perhaps there's a pair of bolt cutters the size of a telegraph pole inside."

Jeremy held the smile for an uncomfortably long time and then swiped the card through the reader.

The gate shivered very slightly as it unlocked.

"Well what do you know! I thought Her Majesty's Armed Forces would have better security. Cutbacks, I expect." He pushed his way through the revolving gate and as he emerged there was a snapshot of time where his head was perfectly positioned for a hard downwards blow.

Matthew gripped the torch very firmly and began to lift his hand. Jeremy turned, saw Matthew and what he saw in his face made him take a hurried step back.

"Perhaps we should have tried the card before we used it," Jeremy said.

"Perhaps we should." Matthew swung the torch into his cupped palm with a slap that made Jeremy twitch. "Perhaps we should."

Jeremy took another step backwards, felt for the door handle and pulled the door open as a shield between them. "After you!"

***

The corridor on the other side of the door ran left and right with a door at each end almost close enough to touch. Both doors were unmarked by any label or designation. But neither of them noticed this because directly in front of them was a board filled with left and right arrows. The first entry was *Human Resources*, pointing left, but the last entry was *Armoury*, pointing right.

Matthew looked at Jeremy, who flinched only a little, and wordlessly they turned right.

There was no card reader by the door at the end of the corridor and Matthew pushed it open without slowing down. The board in front of them now had a new list of military acronyms, but the last one was still *Armoury* and they followed it right.

Each corridor seemed identical to the last, with its dull green carpet and institution grey walls. Some of the overhead fluorescent tubes had begun to flicker and they moved through those sections in stop-motion animation.

All the doors they passed were closed. Some of them had wire reinforced windows that showed empty offices and meeting rooms. One of the offices wasn't empty and the man sat behind a desk smiled at them with an impossibly wide smile where his throat had been cut from ear to ear. They didn't look through any more windows after that.

A bank of lights began to flicker more rapidly and Matthew knew that when the lights went out they could spend days or even weeks fumbling around this maze of corridors. He felt the weight of the building above them. The very air was thin and difficult to breathe. The walls seemed closer, were closer. They were being squeezed like a tube of toothpaste. He began to walk faster, nearly running now. He saw Jeremy looking at him from the corner of his eye as he picked up speed to stay with him. But he didn't say anything. Perhaps he wasn't a big fan of the situation either.

At the end of the corridor, another sign, another corner, another length of institutional grey walls. Matthew remembered some old computer game he'd found in one of the internet's dusty corners. The game had advertised itself as a thrilling interactive puzzle hunt. But all it had seemed to do was repeat, 'You are in a maze of twisty little passages, all alike.' He'd closed the webpage after only a few minutes. He was starting to regret that.

When they turned yet another corner and saw the door at the end of the corridor with its label, *Armoury*, Matthew had never been more grateful. He tugged at the door, but it was locked. Jeremy reached past him and produced the access card like a magic trick.

"Let me," he said and slid the card down the reader slot and pulled at the door. He moved; the door didn't. He then stood back and examined the door carefully and tried the card again, with the same result. He tried sliding the card very slowly and precisely through the reader. Then a little faster until the card seemed to be a continuous loop through the reader.

Matthew reached past Jeremy and stopped his hand. It was hot and sweaty. "Watch this as you swipe the card." He pointed to a dark spot at the bottom of the reader.

Jeremy didn't say anything, but he ran the card through the reader one more time. The spot lit up red.

"We don't have access," Matthew said. "This card doesn't have access."

Jeremy said something softly under his breath. Matthew was sure it had probably been very rude. Then Jeremy surprised him by gripping the door handle with both hands, first pushing, then bracing himself with one foot on the door jamb and pulling until he was red in the face. Matthew heard sinews creak and Jeremy's breath coming fast. But the door didn't move.

"Well that's that. We're locked out and this was all a wasted trip." Jeremy slumped against the wall and managed to look both dejected and irritated.

"Not necessarily," Matthew said hopefully. "This building must have housed hundreds of officers with at least as many weapons. All we need is just one gun left behind or just a better access card."

"So your cunning plan is to search all thirty-three storeys for something you could step over in a dim room? Of course that's just weapons. If we start looking for an access card then we get to check every pocket on every jacket and pair of trousers. I hope military neatness isn't a myth, otherwise we'll be here all week."

"There's always the place I found in the phonebook. That could be a shooting range."

Jeremy looked unimpressed. "On the other hand, it's a laundrette and we walk for several hours to discover if they've got any specials on dry cleaning." He tapped the wall proprietarily. "As much as I hate to admit it, this is probably as good as it's going to get."

He turned back and stalked back to and around the corner. He didn't look back to see if Matthew followed him, but after a second he did.

The corridors unwound with the same helpful signs that had guided them in. Except, each corridor seemed a little longer, the light a little dimmer. Jeremy walked quickly, as if trying to leave Matthew behind, and when he stopped abruptly Matthew walked right into him. Jeremy stepped to one side and pointed at the door they had just passed. "We were so busy searching we forgot to look."

Matthew read the sign – *Proving Ranges* – and looked at Jeremy, who looked back at him with the same expression of strained patience that Mrs Bradley had when he'd spelled CAT with a K.

"Don't you see?" Jeremy said. "You prove something to show it's true, consistent or plain works. If this were a university then the indefinite pronoun could refer to Goodstein's theorem or the mass of a quark. But the addition of ranges implies testing something that acts at a distance. Guns! These are gun ranges where they try out new weapons before they are released to other units. There's no card reader on the door so they are open access, and we don't care if we find the latest prototype with go faster stripes just as long it goes bang." Jeremy smiled confidently, grasped the door handle and pushed. The door didn't open. He stepped back and examined the full length of the door frame. Then he rested both palms on the door and pushed. It opened with a whooshing sound. He held the door open and ran his fingers down its edge. "Rubber gaskets for sound isolation. The doors are probably packed with steel wool. Just the sort of thing you'd need for a gun range."

A small click punctuated the end of his sentence.

Matthew followed him through the door to a short-length corridor with close set doors labelled *One*, *Three* and *Five* on the left and *Two*, *Four*, *Six* and *Eight* on the right. A tube had burnt out and the cold florescent light didn't reach all the way to the end of the corridor. Jeremy stepped up to the door labelled *One* and looked through its wired window.

"Definitely a gun range," he said, waving Matthew to look.

Jeremy smelt of unwashed armpits and too much aftershave. Matthew breathed through his mouth and looked through the window. The range was a long, thin room with the silhouettes of charging soldiers at the far end. But between door and targets was a table. The only time he'd seen machine guns before was in the movies being wielded by Arnold Schwarzenegger or Sylvester Stallone but that was more than enough to recognise two of them on a table just a few feet away.

"All the weapons we need in one handy stop." Jeremy reached for the door handle and Matthew indicated the card reader on the door frame.

Jeremy swore, and not under his breath. "Might as well try," he said and ran the access card through the reader. Neither of them was surprised when the light flashed red.

"Well that's it," Jeremy said. "Back to plan B. We do a room-to-room search through all thirty-three storeys." He kicked the door in disgust as he turned away.

Matthew started to follow him and a small motion trapped his eye. He cocked his head towards the shadow at the end of the corridor, took a step towards it and nearly laughed. What he had so casually written off as shadow was an open doorway. After all the time they wasted trying to get into a locked room, the door into range number seven had been open all the time.

"Hey, Jeremy, remember what you said about not looking?" he turned back to point at the open door and saw that it was closing. He had half a second to realise that the piston of air as they opened the soundproof door had in turn pushed the door to range seven fully open. He had heard the click as it bounced back from its doorstop and never realised what he had heard. He pushed himself away from the wall and towards the rapidly closing door. Behind him, he heard Jeremy say something that was cut off before it was fully formed as he saw what was happening. As he passed range three, Matthew thought the door might have as much as four more inches of travel before it closed and permanently locked them out. As he passed range five, something clicked in his ankle with the sound of a distant firecracker and his run became a drunkard's confusion of limbs. He reached range seven just as his ankle became a bolt of pain and he dived forwards. Above the siren call of his agony, he heard a small click as the latch on the closing door touched the frame's strike plate. He pushed his hand blindly forwards and was rewarded with a small increment of pain as the door crushed his fingers into the frame. Matthew felt the door wanting to latch itself shut. The breadth of a hair would let the two parts of the lock engage and he tried to force his screaming fingers further into the gap between door and frame. Behind him, he heard a steam engine wheezing and the thump of feet. Jeremy hit the door and there was a moment when it seemed the lock had passed the point of no return. Then it sprang open.

"Well spotted," Jeremy said.

Matthew rolled over and raised his sole good hand. And Jeremy stepped over him and into the range. Matthew dropped his arm and watched the ceiling and wondered just how good it would feel to punch Jeremy just once, but very hard. Somewhere above him he heard Jeremy laugh.

"Well, at least someone is glad to see us."

Matthew started to clamber to his feet without putting weight on his ankle or pushing with his mashed hand. Amazingly enough, after a few minutes, Jeremy came back and helped him up. Matthew limped into the range with Jeremy as support and understood why he had laughed. Just a few feet inside the room a partition borrowed from an office cube farm blocked their view down the range. From corner to corner a banner was strung with brightly printed letters a foot high that spelled out *WELCOME*. It looked like the sort of thing normally only found at a three-year-old's birthday party.

Jeremy shrugged his shoulders and walked around the partition, and a moment later Matthew followed.

The range itself was the same long, thin room as range number one. There was only one target at the end of the room, but there was an identical table by the partition. And on the table was something that Matthew called a gun because he didn't know what else to call it. Most of it was a tube the width of a drainpipe, but ventilated with thumb-sized slots that showed a much smaller tube inside. A few inches of the smaller tube extended beyond the drainpipe and was tipped with a box the size of a Rubik's cube cut with angled vents. The other end of the maybe-gun barely existed. In place of a moulded stock designed to nuzzle up to the shooter's shoulder there was just the skeleton outline of a stock. On top of the gun was what looked like three penlight torches bound together by silver duct tape and stuck on top of the gun to light up whatever the gun was aimed at. But whatever it was, it made the gun look top heavy, as if the whole thing would fall over except for its tripod stand.

Matthew looked around at Jeremy. "Is that one of your light support weapons?"

"I don't know what that is! It looks like something from Star Trek. It's nothing I've ever seen before."

On the table next to the maybe-gun were three vertical rows of switches and before Matthew could come up with a good reason not to, Jeremy had clicked the nearest switch. A low mummer gradually built up speed until it was a whooshing sound. They both looked over the edge of the table and saw an upwards pointing block of industrial blowers under the gun's barrel.

"To get the shooters used to desert conditions?" Matthew said.

Jeremy held out his hand in the air flow from the fan. "Doesn't seem to be hot."

Matthew followed a rat's nest of power cables from the blowers to where they plugged into a squat block the size of a suitcase. "Perhaps there's another power setting on this thing?"

"Maybe," Jeremy said, disinterestedly as he knelt down to examine the gun. "There doesn't seem to be a viewfinder on this thing. There's no way to see what you are aiming at." He stood up a little to examine the three torch shapes on top of the gun and prodded several parts of it. Something clicked and a wash of colour lit up his cheek. "There's a little TV set, probably for low light conditions and so on." He pressed his eye against a rubber ring and the wash of colour disappeared. "Nice clear view." He moved the gun on its tripod stand. "No image blur when moving." He sounded as if he were checking out a second-hand car. "Hang on!" He moved the gun a little more and then looked up at Matthew. "It's broken. The dot thing isn't in the middle and it's bouncing around." He stood up with a small cracking of knees. "Have a look."

Matthew peered through the viewfinder and saw what Jeremy meant. The meeting point of two crosshairs was positioned exactly over the X's bullseye of the target. But above and slightly to the left of the X, a bright dot was shifting position like a distant star seen through a heat haze.

"Perhaps it's broken? Maybe that's why it's here," Matthew said.

"What?"

"I said maybe it's … Can you turn that blower off? It doesn't seem to be doing anything useful."

Matthew heard a click and the whir of the fan stopped. And the bright dot in the viewfinder moved smoothly back to the intersection of the two crosshairs. He pulled his eye back from the viewfinder and looked up at Jeremy.

"What did you just do?"

"I turned off the fan." Jeremy took a defensive step back. "You told me to."

Matthew looked back into the viewfinder and the bright dot was completely motionless where the crosshairs met.

"I did, didn't I. Could you just turn it back on?"

Jeremy looked at him suspiciously, didn't say anything and pressed one of the bank of switches, and the bright dot moved straight up.

"Let me guess," Matthew said. "You pressed a different switch, one of the centre row this time?"

"Yes, does it make a difference?"

"I think it does. Could you press one of the right-hand row switches?"

As the fan spooled up, the dot moved further up and to the right.

"And another switch, any switch."

The dot moved straight up.

Matthew stood up and matched Jeremy's confused expression with a knowing smile. "It's compensating."

"What?" Jeremy said, over the howl of the fans.

Matthew reached past him and turned off all three fans. "Have a look though through the viewfinder now. The dot is right in the middle?"

Jeremy looked through the viewfinder and then up at Matthew. "Yes."

"Okay, I'll turn on a switch from the right-hand row."

The fan's murmur built up speed and Jeremy pressed himself closer to the viewfinder and Matthew knew that he was right.

"Here's another right-hand switch. And another." After that he didn't bother to announce each switch. He watched Jeremy instead. When he had run out of switches the noise in the room was deafening. He swept his hand across the three rows of switches, turning them off with one motion. The silence in the room seemed to sing like something distant.

Matthew touched the top of the gun. "I think what's happening is that the wind must affect a bullet just as much as a car on the motorway. If there's a stiff breeze from the left then by the time the bullet reaches its target the wind has shoved it to the right. This thing must be measuring wind speed somehow, probably lasers – most things are – and shows the shooter where the bullet will really hit."

"All The Priests Hide When Sleeping Deeply," Jeremy said.

"What?"

"It's an acronym that Anton used to remember all the things that can affect the trajectory of a bullet. Altitude, Temperature, Pressure, Humidity, Wind Speed and Distance. At six hundred yards, a standard range distance, a stiff breeze will drift a bullet's impact by four to five inches. They've had gadgets for years to measure all of those things so the shooter can dial a compensation into their scope. But this thing is doing it automatically and in real time, and if it is using a laser designator then it knows the wind speed at every point between gun and target, not just around the shooter."

"You know about this stuff? Did Anton show you how to shoot?"

Jeremy shook his head. "No, the whole time I knew him, Anton was on light duties after a covert mission with the SAS went wrong."

And Matthew, who could still smell mainly menthol, detected the pungent aroma of bullshit.

Seemingly, unlike Jeremy, he actually knew something about the SAS from too many comics that tried to be educational. And he knew that the chances of a weekend soldier being part of an operational mission with the best trained soldiers in the world was only slightly better than the chances of winning the lottery when you hadn't actually bought a ticket. But even if that were true, then Anton had somehow sustained an injury bad enough to keep him behind a desk for a whole summer, but not quite bad enough to stop him going on day trips with a fourteen-year-old boy. Other things that Jeremy had said slotted together like the parts of an ugly jigsaw. Anton had enjoyed the same unlikely interest in trains as Jeremy, even though he didn't know a tube station from a railway station. Jeremy had phoned the TA, only they'd never heard of him. He'd never taken Jeremy to where he worked and instead had travelled halfway across London to the war museum. And all of that meant that Anton had almost certainly never been part of the TA, and there was only a passing chance that his name had been Anton. Almost certainly he'd been a pervert who had bought himself a uniform and found a school whose head hadn't done enough background checks. He'd probably been ready to disappear back into the anonymity of his real name if anyone had asked any difficult questions, but instead he found a naïve young boy who thought he'd found a father figure. Instead, a paedophile had found him. 'Anton' had groomed him just as efficiently as a child making new friends on the internet who just wanted to talk about kids' stuff that boring old parents wouldn't understand. Perhaps the next step would have been for 'Anton' to introduce young Jeremy to some friends, perhaps groups of friends, maybe some travel and the starring role in some very specialised films. Instead, Jeremy's mother had stepped in. Matthew wondered how much she had known, or had she suspected anything at all? Perhaps she had seen the whole thing in one moment of terrible clarity, or seen only an unsettling friendship. But either way she had sailed in with all maternal guns blazing and poor Jeremy had traded one abuser for another.

Matthew suddenly realised that Jeremy was looking at him thoughtfully.

"You okay? You looked miles away."

"Sorry, I was just thinking we need to see if we can find some bullets for this."

"You mean like these I found in a drawer?" Jeremy held up a stubby cylinder as thick as a fat crayon. "I did tell you. Sure you're okay?"

"Yes, sorry, just wool-gathering."

"Well, feel free to daydream anytime you find we're not in the middle of an alien invasion. Give me a hand and we'll see if we can load this magazine and get it into the gun."

Matthew looked at the back of Jeremy's head as he bent towards the gun. He knew he should say something. He should tell him what he had seen in his few casual words. Perhaps he was wrong and Jeremy would just laugh at him. But there was always the possibility that he would be kicking away one of the foundations of Jeremy's life. And after that there would be nothing left for him, except waiting to use the gun to blow his brains out, leaving Matthew completely alone.

Jeremy held out a long, slim box that looked like an industrial-quality pencil case. "If you're not too busy?" He didn't look around; Matthew was very glad of that.

While Matthew held the box Jeremy managed to push just five stubby carriages into it against an unseen spring. "Well, that was easy enough," he said, although the sweat on his forehead disagreed with him. "Now let's see how we get this into the gun."

There was a rectangular slot on the underside of the gun. And with both of them pushing, shoving and twisting, the magazine slid into the gun and locked into place.

"Well, all we've got to do is remember what we did when we need to reload," Jeremy said as he inserted himself between Matthew and the gun. "But in the meantime, let's give it a try."

Matthew stepped back from the table and put his fingers in his ears as Jeremy brought his face down to the gun's outline of a stock. He watched as Jeremy made repeated back/forward, up/down adjustments. He became very still and Matthew saw the two-inch gap he had left between shoulder and gun.

"Shouldn't you be—"

The gun fired and its sound was a physical thing that clapped at Matthew's ears. Its stock punched back into Jeremy's shoulder with a wet slapping sound. He jerked away from the gun, holding his right shoulder with his left hand.

"Jesus Christ! It broke my arm! It broke my bloody arm!"

"I'm sure it's not that bad. Let me have a look."

Matthew very carefully pulled Jeremy's T-shirt away from his shoulder. His skin was the pallid white of something that lived under a stone and had never seen the sun. A red patch, the exact shape of the gun's stock, stood out like a branding mark. Matthew gently touched the centre of the patch, but not gently enough because Jeremy swore for a whole minute without ever repeating himself.

"Okay, I don't think it's broken." Matthew didn't know any such thing, but he did know that the level of medical aid he would be able to offer (two pain killers, a cup of strong tea and a sticking plaster) could never be enough for a serious break. "Try lifting your arm slowly."

"Slowly? Is that the full extent of your in-depth analysis, Dr Kildare?" Jeremy said through gritted teeth. But he lifted his arm very slowly as if tethered to a balloon. Matthew watched for the tell-tale signs of jagged broken bones moving under snow-white skin. Jeremy's arm reached parallel to the floor and he dropped it equally slowly.

"I think that's okay," Matthew said, and he meant it this time. "Probably just bruised."

Jeremy tried his arm again, reaching out in front of him, then lifting it up to point at the ceiling. "Suppose it's okay," he said grudgingly. "What happened anyway?"

"You didn't have your shoulder flush up against the gun's stock and the recoil kicked it back into your shoulder."

"When did you get so knowledgeable about guns?"

Matthew shrugged to avoid having to say from every cowboy film he'd ever seen and looked away to the target at the other end of the range. At first glance he thought Jeremy had missed completely. Then he saw that the large number seven marking the outermost ring had almost been completely obliterated.

"Made a mess out of the target."

"And just one target. It would have been an excellent sales pitch." Jeremy looked up from massaging his shoulder. "Don't you get it? The gun all set up ready to fire? The welcome banner? This was a product demonstrator. They probably had the leaders of several unstable countries all ready to wheel in here and show off their latest toy. The effective range of a rifle bullet is typically around two miles, for this monster it's probably five. Normally, it's wildly inaccurate at that distance, but not anymore, not for a weapon that's sampling all the factors that can affect a bullet's accuracy hundreds of times a second. How much do you think the President for Life of a small struggling country would be prepared to pay for a weapon that could let him reach out and touch a rebel leader five miles away with an ounce of lead traveling at eight hundred miles per hour?"

"A lot," Matthew said, weakly.

"Sell a few hundred units and somebody gets a knighthood for services to the empire. Okay, so we know the gun goes bang. All we need to do now is get it up high enough so we have a good view of the cube at Speakers' Corner when it lands in the morning. That's less than a mile away; for this gun that's probably like scratching your ear."

"Well shouldn't I try a shot first? Both of us should be able to operate the gun."

"What's to operate? It's like a video game; you point and shoot. But if you want to indulge your sense of machismo by dominating a paper target, have at it."

Jeremy leaned against the wall and looked away with apparent disgust, as if he hadn't been the first to use the gun, like a small boy wanting the first go with a new ball.

Matthew pressed his eye to the gun's scope and realised that Jeremy had been right. It was exactly like playing a video game. Seen through the scope, the target looked almost cartoonish. With all the fine detail removed by image processing software, what was left looked like a still from a *Tom and Jerry* cartoon. Matthew wondered what would happen if you pointed the scope at a person. Would you see a living, breathing human who might look down the tunnel of the scope at the wrong point, or only a bland, generic target, stripped of all its humanity, so there could be no inconvenient empathy as the shooter squeezed the trigger? Perhaps this was the future of warfare. Human beings rendered as anonymous targets to be shot based on computer models fed from satellites, drones and radio chatter. Matthew wondered where the humanity was in that system and realised that its absence was probably a design goal.

Matthew sighed and walked the crosshairs slowly across the target to the X at its centre. He pulled the stock close into his shoulder and squeezed the trigger. The sound of the shot was still a huge thing that overwhelmed his ears, but he was expecting it this time and he avoided blinking automatically as the centre of the target vanished.

"Nice shooting," Jeremy said. "You must have been a grand master at *Call of Duty*. But while you were playing I found the case for the gun so we can pack it away to get it upstairs."

Matthew straightened up from the gun and gave Jeremy a weary look, which he never noticed. Propped under his arm, like an absurdly bulky crutch, was a long slim case made from dull grey plastic. He lifted the case onto the table, clicked open two catches and threw the lid open. The inside of the case was preformed into a series of shaped depressions, like a series of dried-out concrete ditches, for each part of the gun. The whole thing looked impossibly complicated, but at the centre of each depression was a small pictogram showing the right way to pack the gun with a big tick, and the wrong way crossed out with a bold X. Matthew thought it looked like IKEA assembly instructions, only simpler, and they had the gun packed away in a few minutes.

Jeremy stepped back from the case and the arm he had been using perfectly well suddenly hung uselessly at his side. "All we need to do now is get it upstairs. I'd like to help but, you know, my arm."

Matthew understood exactly about his arm. Jeremy wanted to make him carry the gun because he could. For Jeremy, life was a zero-sum game. For him to gain a point someone else had to lose that point. It was his way of knowing that he was better than anyone else.

Using only his undamaged hand, Matthew slid the case to the edge of the table, dropped one end to the floor and discovered that it had a suitcase-like set of wheels at two corners.

"They must have been expecting a very high unit price." Jeremy looked at the door with a smug expression and after a second Matthew dropped to one knee as if a wheel had become lodged in something. It hadn't and he took the time to see the world through Jeremy's eyes. When he was sure he had it all, he stood up and gave the case an experimental pull.

"Well that's obvious really – the childishly simple packing instructions, the easy portable storage. This was designed as a highly mobile unit to maximise effectiveness and that means it was never seen as one gun per soldier or even one gun per hundred soldiers, and low sales means a high unit price to recover R and D costs. Self-evident really." Jeremy gave him a look that in a sci-fi film would have set him alight, and pulled the door open. As it closed behind him, Matthew coughed, only it sounded a lot like 'Smartarse'.

Matthew soon discovered that not only were the wheels on the case like the ones on a suitcase, they also had all of their disadvantages. Left to its own devices, the case would wander off-track until it hit a wall and would have to be manhandled back into position. At corners, it would try very hard not to follow that corner and hit another wall. He tried pushing it for a while, but that only made it more unstable. By the time they found a lift, Matthew was thoroughly disenchanted with the case. While he shoved it to the back of the lift, Jeremy studied the bank of floor buttons.

"Top floor?" he said, but it obviously wasn't a question because he pressed the button anyway.

The lift bleeped at him. He pressed the button again and then several of the buttons under it. The lift bleeped like a supermarket checkout, but didn't move.

Matthew pointed at a thin slot surrounded by black plastic, just above the buttons Jeremy had been so enthusiastically pressing.

"Do you think the lift might be card controlled as well?"

Jeremy was turned away from him so he couldn't see his face, but Jeremy scrabbled in his pocket and forced the card into the slot as if it had personally offended him. He pressed the button for the top floor again and the lift bleeped again.

"Good idea, but wrong idea."

He played a tune by randomly pressing some more buttons to show just how wrong Matthew was.

"Probably the lift was locked as part of a building-wide shut-down when things started to fall apart. There's no way we can ever shift this."

Matthew looked around Jeremy's shoulder. The bank of floor buttons was a tall, thin grid divided into two halves by a thick horizontal line. Matthew pressed the first button *under* the line and the lift jerked into life. "It's just like the doors to the armoury and proving ranges," he said, helpfully. "This card must have a fairly low access level, so it's not going to give access to secure areas, and that includes the top floors where the high-ranking officers lived. But it's fine to give us access to floors up to and including floor fifteen." He pointed at the lift display and Jeremy became very still and his neck flushed red.

There was a lot of silence in the lift after that and when the doors slid open, it flooded out, carrying Jeremy along like a fish from a broken aquarium. Matthew followed more slowly, navigating the gun case over the gap between lift and floor.

The corridor was brightly lit and seemed empty of either Stupid or Jeremy. Closed doors marked only by an incrementing number marched away to the right. To the left was only a closed fire door.

Matthew turned right.

Except for the eerie emptiness, he could have been towing a suitcase down the corridor of any mid-range hotel. The carpet was the same dull green, the walls institution grey that they had seen before. All the doors he passed were closed. Except for a broken bottle in a doorway, there was no sign that civilisation was a fad that had come and gone.

He peered carefully around another corner and a voice from behind made him jump.

"There you are. Been looking all over for you. I went back to the lift, but I took the long way around the building to check it out, so we must have been chasing each other around."

Jeremy bounded up the corridor until he was standing next to Matthew. He smiled happily and Matthew thought it was the most genuine expression he had ever seen there.

"As far as I can see, the whole floor is empty. I guess when things started falling apart everyone was ordered out to try to maintain order. I've found us two rooms either side of a kitchen unit so we can get some breakfast in the morning. They both look east so we should have amazing views of the city. Here, let me take that."

Jeremy took the case's towing handle from Matthew's unresisting hand and pointed down the corridor.

"There's a meeting room there with windows that should look over the park. We'll have to smash a window so the gun's super-duper scope can lock onto the target, but I'm sure we can figure that one out in the morning."

Jeremy bounded ahead so quickly that the case began to rock from wheel to wheel as small imperfections in the carpet were translated into increasing sideways motion.

"We'll leave the case in here overnight. I don't think we need to worry about sneak thieves." Jeremy let the case run ahead of him and turned it so he could push it through an open door. Matthew had a quick glimpse of an empty meeting room, complete with whiteboard and projector.

Jeremy let the door swing shut on its automatic closer and turned back to Matthew. "I've put you in room one-five-five-six, just across the corridor. I've had a look around and it seems okay. En-suite bathroom and a bookcase full of military history that look so dull they could be packaged as a cure for insomnia. Now I don't know about you but I'm exhausted so I'll turn in now. Tomorrow could be the first day of the rest of our lives. It might get busy."

Jeremy flashed him another smile, swung the door open to 1558, stepped though and pushed it shut behind him like a reverse jack-in-the-box.

Matthew looked at the closed door with amazement. In the few minutes between Jeremy leaving the lift and finding him again he had been completely transformed. The spiky, arrogant person that used words as weapons had been replaced by somebody, well, nice. Perhaps he had seen himself as others saw him and didn't like what he had seen.

Matthew moved down the corridor and opened the door to 1556. It was an almost square room with a single bed made up with military precision, a small bookcase filled with identically bound, thick volumes and a single easy chair that didn't look easy at all. Matthew was immediately pleased that the room was unused. There were no photographs of friends or relations whose absence would haunt the room. The bathroom was a few square feet of green carpet hemmed in by the usual apparatuses. He tried the shower and sink just to make sure they worked and then used the toilet for real.

According to the windup alarm clock, it was nearly midnight but he didn't feel tired. There had been too much adrenaline, too much tension for too long to just switch off. The only thing to read was in the bookcase, so he selected a volume at random, settled back in the easy chair and began to read about the Battle for Galveston. After a few minutes, he moved to the bed; it was more comfortable. Either Jeremy had been more right than he knew or Matthew was more tired than he had thought and the names of the ships competing for ownership of the city began to blur and multiply.

Matthew dropped the book on the floor and undressed slowly and haltingly. The bedsheets were cool and crisp and he pulled them up around him like a long drink of water. He fumbled at a switch near his head and the lights went out. And were replaced by a dim, yellow glow. Matthew stared at the light on the ceiling and down to the window framed in sodium yellow. He'd forgotten to pull the curtains before he went to bed. The glow from the streetlights below was dim; it would be so easy to close his eyes and drift off to sleep. But while the glow was dim, the sun rising at too early in the morning would be certain to wake him, and then he'd never get back to sleep again. Climbing out of bed was like swimming against sand but he managed it somehow. He staggered across the room and only banged his toe once. He held a curtain in each hand and saw the city. Large sections of London were dark where the power had failed. But even the lit parts looked dead. There were no moving cars on the streets, no moving people. When something did move it held his eye and he watched the traffic lights at Hyde Park corner change to red and, a moment later, lights on Park Lane to green. The veneer of normality only emphasised how the city had changed. Now it was a place only for machines, and relays would click and transistors change state until the power failed.

Matthew tapped his fingers on the windowsill to the rhythm of the song at the pub. And then its title came to him and it was so very nearly perfect. 'Saturday night in the city of the dead' by Ultravox – before they went all New Romantic. But it was only nearly perfect because now every night belonged to the dead. London's mighty heart would be forever still. It was over, they had lost. Whatever they achieved tomorrow would be like throwing a dart at a whale. The cones might not even notice them and if they did then they would step on them. They would be better off finding the nearest pub, working their way through its stock and waiting to see if it would be alcohol poisoning or cirrhosis of the liver that would give them peace.

But what the cones had done, what they were still doing, was unfair. It was plain wrong. They were picking the planet clean like a fat man at an all-you-can-eat buffet. They had killed thousands of years of progress and someone had to let them know that it was not going to be easy. Perhaps tomorrow might just be a dart, but it might be a harpoon. It might be enough to say, 'No more!'

Matthew closed the curtains with one swift movement and got back into bed. He closed his eyes and this time sleep took him as suddenly as a swimmer being pulled down to the cold depths where dreams never reach.

Chapter Twenty-Eight
Forty Hours Remaining

Matthew looked at the back of Jeremy's head and saw how he would kill him. The windows in front of them looked over Hyde Park and a pollution-free sky the colour of new denim. A stiff breeze scudded cotton-ball clouds across their view as if they were being chased. Below the beautiful sky the frozen face of the city had the sterile beauty of a perfectly painted death mask covering the disease-ridden features of an old whore. But Matthew saw only the exact spot on the back of Jeremy's head where he would hit him with the fire extinguisher. However, just smashing him over the head would be too easy. Too quick. It needed to be personal; he needed to see Jeremy's eyes as he realised what was happening.

Matthew walked his gaze down to Jeremy's neck. He bet he could fit his whole hand around it. If he used both hands he could place his thumbs firmly in Jeremy's Adam's apple and squeeze. He could almost see the small veins in Jeremy's eyes rupture as he struggled for breath, feel his hands failing uselessly. He flexed his hand under its bandage and a bolt of pain made him wince.

Matthew had woken to distant metallic sounds and a strangely familiar smell. He had lain in the bed for a long time, knitting strands of memory into a picture of yesterday. When he realised that the smell was coffee and the sounds were of a working kitchen, he got up. He tried to spring out of bed with the easy grace he had once used, but he was stiff from walking and he clambered out of bed like one of Dr Frankenstein's less successful creations.

His face in the mirror looked creased where he had slept on it and his hair was pushed into a strange pyramid shape. He knew he should shower before anything else, but while cleanliness might be next to godliness, right now coffee was an act of grace.

Matthew padded out to the corridor on bare feet. He was still trying to decide left or right when he heard Jeremy call out to him.

"Morning! Good to see you."

The kitchen was on Matthew's left and Jeremy was sitting right at the back looking pleased with himself. Matthew realised later that he looked far too pleased, but by then it was too late.

"I've made you a cup of coffee. It's black I'm afraid, unless you like lumpy milk. I think that went over days ago. There's cereal for breakfast, but only if you like the aforementioned rancid milk. I've settled for toast. The bread was dry and hard, but that only means it's halfway to being toast anyway. They don't seem to have a toaster, cutbacks I expect, so I used the grill." He pointed at the open drawer-like space in the middle of the old-fashioned gas cooker with the chrome handle of a grill tray sticking out. "In a bit of a disappointment, there's no butter, only margarine, which I personally think is the spawn of the devil."

Matthew thanked him between sips of coffee as he pulled two slices from a loaf of thick sliced bread and gripped the metal handle of the grill tray. An electric bolt of pain shot up his arm and he jerked his hand away. The tray came with it and clattered to the floor. He put his hand between his knees and tried to squeeze the pain out of it.

"What's wrong?" Jeremy said and reached down for the grill tray. "Jesus! It's red hot. It must have picked up the heat from the grill. Appalling design. We need to get your hand in some cold water."

Jeremy ran the cold tap so Matthew could bath his hand under the cool stream. He raided the freezer and found an ice pack and made a crude bandage so Matthew could hold it when needed. He even made him another cup of coffee with three sugars for the shock. He was very helpful. So helpful in fact that there was absolutely no reason to suspect that what had happened was anything but a nasty accident.

And yet there was.

For one thing, Jeremy was too helpful. The Jeremy he had come to know would have looked down at Matthew writhing in pain and been casually dismissive. Instead, he had been helpful and supportive. All the things he wasn't. And for a second thing, while Jeremy was taking a much needed shower, Matthew examined the grill tray. It was a simple metal tray with a chrome lift-out rack and of course the handle. Jeremy had called it an appalling design, but judging by its numerous dents and scratches it had been used many times before. All without incident, otherwise the lawsuits would have dropped like summer rain. And yet Jeremy had used it just once and the next person had been burnt. He ran a finger along the handle to where it joined the tray and back again. In normal use, it might get a bit warm, perhaps hot enough to need to use the tea towel decorated with a picture of the Queen. But not hot enough to burn, unless the handle, and not the tray, had been put under the searing heat of the gas burners and only reversed a few seconds before he had walked in.

Matthew examined his palm. As burns went, it wasn't bad; it wasn't even as bad as the time he was four and had picked up the drill his father had just used to drill through a wall and temporarily branded the 'dr' of drill into the tip of his little finger. There would be no long-term damage, no scarring, just a few days feeling like he was holding a hot wire. A few more days with a board-like hand and then it would all be over and forgotten.

Except it wouldn't. The memory would linger. The betrayal would always rankle. He didn't know why Jeremy had set up a nasty practical joke. Perhaps he saw himself with the starring role in a film entitled *How we drove back the invaders and saved the world.* Perhaps it was just because Jeremy had briefly lost his position as smartest man in the room. But the reason didn't matter. What mattered was that Jeremy was a chromium-plated, razor-edged psychopath.

The shower sounds stopped and Matthew quietly replaced the grill tray in the cooker. When Jeremy stuck his head in the kitchen he was apparently engrossed in a dog-eared copy of *Horse & Hound.*

"How's the hand?" Jeremy said, brightly.

Matthew looked up as if startled. "Not too bad."

"Excellent. I'll just get dressed then we can set up the gun ready to give the cones a big surprise."

Matthew watched the kitchen door slowly close behind him on its automatic closer. In three to five days his hand would be good enough so that he could punch Jeremy very hard in the mouth and hopefully break his jaw. And then his thin smile disappeared. Three to five days was not a period of time. It was a destination. Depending on what happened in the next few hours, they would either strike a valiant blow for freedom or they would find out why Montana went silent after trying something very similar.

Matthew didn't look so happy when he left the kitchen.

***

Reassembling the gun was very nearly as easy as taking it apart. If there was the slightest doubt about which way things went together then there was a small pictogram to avoid confusion. Jeremy had cleared the whole meeting room table to give them room to work and, even with Matthew's bandaged hand, they had the whole thing back together in just a few minutes.

Jeremy wheeled the storage case away and just for a moment the gun stood alone in the middle of the meeting room table like the fantasy of anyone that had spent too long in a meeting that was nothing to do with them. When he pulled the gun towards him its non-slip tripod legs left great gouges in the table's highly polished top. He spent the next few minutes adjusting the position of the gun. Matthew thought he looked surprisingly competent and then he spoilt the whole thing by pursing his lips together and making a brrr brrr brrr noise like a boy with a toy machine gun.

"Die alien scum! Die!" He looked up at Matthew. "Just kidding." He walked around the desk and tapped the centre of the window in the gun's line of fire. "We'll need to smash this so the gun's smart scope can lock onto the target." He looked around hopefully.

"I know just the thing," Matthew said and left before Jeremy could ask what the thing was. When he came back in the room he kept one arm behind him.

"Did you find something?" Jeremy said, and Matthew showed what he had hidden behind his back. It was an axe with a long pine handle and a head painted red. Matthew held its razor sharp edge entirely too close to Jeremy's face, turning it so the carbon steel glittered in the light.

"Fire axe, I saw it in the fire point by the lift last night."

Jeremy backed up a little and Matthew followed, maintaining the distance between soft, vulnerable flesh and cold-edged metal. When Jeremy ran out of room, Matthew grasped the handle in both hands and swung. Glass rained down into the street and Jeremy flinched. Holding the axe made Matthew's hand hurt, but the look on Jeremy's face was worth it.

While Matthew ran the axe around the edge of the window frame, Jeremy scuttled away and put the width of the table between then. When the frame was completely empty, he turned to Jeremy.

"There you go! That's how to deal with problems."

"That's a good idea." And Jeremy's voice changed key partway through.

The wind that might have been a gentle breeze at ground level was an ice-cold blast on the fifteenth floor with an empty window frame. Matthew moved into the shelter of the remaining windows on the right of the room and, to no surprise at all, Jeremy moved to the opposite corner. The wind picked up the minutes of vitally important meetings and chased them around the room like oversized snowflakes. Sometimes a sheet of A4 hung in the centre of the room and Matthew would see Jeremy looking at him. He wondered how much Jeremy understood of what was happening right now. Did he see any connection between what he had done and his reaction? Or was he simply adrift on a sea of social interactions with no map to guide him home? A small part of Matthew knew that he should feel sorry for Jeremy, and an echo of a forgotten church service said that he should forgive them for they do not know what they do. But Jeremy had known exactly what he was doing and was intelligent enough to know that it was A Very Bad Thing. Matthew saw Jeremy looking at him again from across the room and he looked away quickly. It was almost a relief when the ships landed.

The cube-shaped ship settled into its position at Speakers' Corner and Matthew craned his head left until he could see the pyramid ship touch down. There was no third ship.

"Interesting," Jeremy said. "There's no replacement for the ship they destroyed yesterday. Everything they've got must be fully committed across the world." With the diversion of the ships landing, he sounded confident again.

They both watched from the shelter of the remaining windows as the cube unfolded its ramp with its T-shaped viewing platform. From Jeremy's expensive apartment on the Bayswater Road they had seen the cube at an angle, but from Knightsbridge they saw the cube with its ramp pointing right at them. When the cones took up their places on the viewing platform there was something strangely familiar about the scene. Matthew watched the last of the cones take their place and then the Stupid, with their remote control and completely blank faces, marched down the ramp. The Stupid spread out across the park in the same patterns they had seen before. But Matthew watched the cones trying to see what was so familiar about the long platform with its tall, regular shapes above. And then he smelt frying onions and diesel fuel, heard over-amplified music and girlish screams and knew.

"It's a shooting gallery," Matthew said.

"What?"

"You never went to the fair and tried to win a goldfish at the shooting galleries? The target was usually a line of tin soldiers that you had to knock down with a single shot. You've got the same thing here, only I expect that gun will be much more accurate than an air rifle with a wonky sight."

"We never went to the fair. My mother didn't believe in them. But if you've quite finished playing nostalgia perhaps we can get on with the job in hand."

Jeremy took his position behind the gun and nuzzled up to its stock. Matthew stood behind him and alternately watched the back of his head and the line of cones. Jeremy seemed to take a very long time minutely adjusting the gun's aim. Then the gun fired and two things happened – one of them unexpected.

The sound of the shot was a hand clap to the ears, as expected. But what wasn't expected was the pink haze that sprang up around the cones, hiding them from sight. The interval between shot and haze was so short that it seemed the same trigger had activated both.

Jeremy looked over the scope. "What the hell is that?"

"Some sort of protective screen? I can't see anything moving under it and nothing else is going on. Hang on."

The nearest corner of the cube boiled like molten tar and extruded a pencil-slim aerial. Matthew wondered if the cones were calling for help, but only for a second before the aerial became a cylinder as fat and long as a telegraph pole. A second after that and the cylinder had pulled away from the ship and jumped a hundred feet in the air.

"I don't know what that is but I don't like it."

"They're probably phoning for help, but you won't get anything here," Jeremy said and pulled the trigger again.

The cylinder flipped over until it was parallel to the ground and began to spin. Soon it was only visible as a disk, like the flying saucers aliens were meant to arrive in.

"I think we should back off and wait to see what's happening here."

"Bugger that! We've got them pinned down. Under that pink comfort blanket they're probably shitting themselves." And Jeremy fired again.

The spinning cylinder slowed and now each rotation was visible like a roulette wheel ready to stop at double zero and everyone loses.

"I really think we should go, leave the gun here and come back in half an hour."

"You leave if you want. This is the chance we've been waiting for. Our moment to show them what the human race is made of."

The cylinder stopped spinning and swung lazily. Matthew watched the nearest end track left then right of them. He realised he had been wrong. The object the ship had sent out wasn't an aerial, telegraph pole or any of those things. It was a compass needle and they were magnetic north.

Matthew reached down and shook Jeremy's shoulder. He looked up and saw a new moon hanging in the sky and then realised that it was just the end of the cylinder, because it was pointing straight at them. After that, everything happened very quickly. Jeremy looked up and saved his eyes when the windows blew in. Something sharp touched Matthew's lip and his hand came away bloody. Jeremy lifted his hand and his eyes bulged as he saw the shallow cuts that ran from wrist to elbow. Matthew rested his hand on the table to steady himself and bright shards of glass tore at his palm. Shreds of the A4 pages that had flown so easily across the room rained down like confetti. Jeremy tried to say something but got no further than a 'huh' sound that he repeated like a hiccup. Matthew grabbed his shoulder and hauled him towards the door.

"Run!"

Jeremy lunged through the door and turned right. Matthew caught his shirt and pulled him back. "Not the lift! The stairs!"

As they reached the end of the corridor, the floor jumped and Matthew looked back to see every door on the park side of the corridor burst open and fill the air with a shower of broken glass and shredded ceiling tiles. He turned back to Jeremy, but he was already halfway down the first flight of steps, barely touching each tread. The stairwell was thick with dust and small lumps of concrete rained down on them.

The stairs jumped like a rollercoaster and Matthew's feet slid out from under him. His head crunched down on a concrete step and he saw stars. Then, beyond the constellation, he saw the rapidly spreading web of cracks on the ceiling and pulled himself to his feet. Taking steps two at a time, three at a time, he barrelled wildly down the stairs. Jeremy had stopped at a landing to catch his breath and Matthew raced past leaving only the fragment of a sentence behind. ".... ceiling ..."

Jeremy looked up and saw the tube of the stairwell twisting and folding like a straw being tied in a knot. The floor lurched again and now they were running down a puzzle-house stairway twisted to one side, using their arms as much as their legs to keep moving. The rain of rubble became a flood and head-sized lumps of concrete raced them down the stairway with dull thudding sounds.

The ground floor was already thick with shattered concrete with more crashing down every second. The top half of a door with its warning, *Alarm will sound if opened*, was just visible through the dust.

Jeremy arrived next to Matthew, sweat running down from his hairline, cutting tracks in the dust that caked his face. "What do we do?" he screamed over the sound of the building collapsing above them.

"The door. We have to get to the door."

Jeremy looked at the mounds of rubble that half-filled the ground floor. In some places it was piled ten feet tall. In other places it was only knee-high, but all of it turned like the gears of a city-sized machine as the building shook. A slab of concrete the size of a small car slammed down and machine gunned them with shards of rubble.

"No way! We'll be crushed."

"We don't have a choice," Matthew said and, before he could reconsider, stepped out onto the broken concrete. A lump of rubble under his foot twisted away from him and he stepped forward to stay upright. His foot caught under a block and he sprawled forward. The concrete under his hands moved and his arm dropped between two refrigerator-sized boulders. He tried to pull his arm out, but the concrete moved again, trapping it in place. Jeremy linked his hands around Matthew's armpit and pulled him free. Together they stumbled to the slab of concrete riding above smaller rubble. The doorway was nearly close enough to touch now and they held onto each other as the slab tilted, spilling them forward. Matthew clawed at the wall to stay upright and the wall was hot. He slid down the slope the slab had made and his feet crashed into the door with a hollow sound. Jeremy hauled at Matthew until he was upright and both looked around the edge of the slab they were standing on for the quick-release bar that would pop the door open. They saw it a foot below them, locked in the closed position by the concrete beam under it.

"Kick!" Matthew yelled, and swung his foot at the door. His shoes were fashionable trainers with whisper-soft soles. The door was hardwood with an internal aluminium composite frame. The door didn't move. He held onto the edge of the slab under him and kicked again. And again.

Jeremy stared at Matthew for a second and then came up on his tiptoes and jiggled up and down like a fat man testing the ice underfoot. "No! jump! The slab's unstable. We have to guide it towards the door." And he jumped into the air as high as possible and landed with a thud that made the slab underfoot shiver.

Matthew looked at him, looked at the gap between the tip of the slab they were standing on and the door, and sprang into the air. More debris rained down from above. Mixed in with the broken concrete were pieces of office furniture, and a flat screen monitor exploded like a bomb behind them. With every jump the slab shivered, but it tilted a little more towards the door. Part of the staircase landed on the far edge of the slab and it lifted back up to its original position. The staircase balanced for a second and fell away from them. The slab tilted back to the position they had jolted it into and kept moving. The door resisted the multi-tonne weight of the slab for only a second before it popped open and they fell into the street in a cloud of dust and rubble. A shower of broken concrete followed and tried to bury them. Matthew came up onto his knees and saw a building flow into the street in a slow motion avalanche of bricks and glass. Something behind them groaned and he whipped his head around to see the open door outlined by a growing web of cracks.

Jeremy was a dead weight as Matthew hauled him to his feet. He twisted Jeremy around to see the wall around the door bulging towards them like an expanding balloon.

"It's all collapsing. We have to get to under cover." And he took his own advice and sprinted away. He slowed after the first hundred yards to look behind him and Jeremy bulleted past him. His face grimly determined, he was a machine dedicated to only running.

A wall of superheated air nearly knocked them off their feet as something behind them exploded. Matthew held onto a lamppost to stay upright and looked back. A car at the end of the street was burning so brightly it was hard to look at. The next car exploded into flames and then the next in a necklace of fire rushing towards them. Matthew ran until the breath burnt in his throat, ran until the back of his legs ached so much he couldn't run anymore. Jeremy had stopped at the end of the street, not so much leaning on as draped over a bin. Matthew slumped to a halt next to him, hands on knees, gasping for breath.

"Which way to a station?" Jeremy's voice was a very small thing over the jet engine roar of the firestorm behind them.

Matthew looked around and realised that he had no idea where they were. He had walked through Knightsbridge hundreds of times, on his way to the park with Kirsten, to watch the tourists and sometimes even to shop when the prices became briefly sane. But that Knightsbridge had been bright sunny streets crowded with people. This Knightsbridge was rubble-filled streets lit by a shifting lattice of fire. All the landmarks he relied on had been erased the moment the object from the ship had begun firing. A rooftop penthouse exploded with a flashbulb's glare and he saw a familiar sign at the end of the street. "There!" And he took off running. After only a few yards the ache in his legs became twin bolts of pain and the run became a hobbled walk. Jeremy passed him a moment later, but only just, because he was limping with both legs.

With every step, the red circle of the sign stood out just a little more against the dust like a target. Soon it was the only thing they could see. Everything else faded into insignificance as it pulled them in. When Matthew touched the metal sign he said thank you to a god he didn't normally believe in.

While Jeremy caught up, he looked down the stairs into the underground station. The air was thick with dust, but he could see the warm glow of electric light.

Jeremy leant on Matthew's shoulder. "Is it safe down there?"

He turned to Jeremy, saw the bus behind him sliding down the street, then threw him down the stairs and dived after him. He felt every one of the stairs as a sharp punch in his knees, chest and groin on the way down and sprawled on the station floor next to Jeremy. Glass showered over them like bright lethal rain.

Chapter Twenty-Nine
Thirty-seven Hours Remaining

They lay there for a long time before Matthew stood up and shook himself like a wet dog to get some of the glass off him. He hurt everywhere. His front felt as if it had been beaten with hammers. A cut over his left eye dripped blood that made him blink repeatedly. He looked back up the stairs and his view was completely blocked by a red London bus.

"Is there a way out?" Jeremy said, between coughs.

"Don't think so, but the last place we want to go is back out there." Matthew crouched down and rested his palm on the floor. There was a moment when he thought he was wrong and then the floor pulsed as if there were a great slow heart beating deep below them. He waited for another pulse and looked up at Jeremy. "They're not giving up; that thing is still firing."

"Urban clearance courtesy of the cones." Jeremy sounded on the ragged edge of hysteria, ready to break out in tears or insane laughter at any moment. The lights began to pulse in time with the great slow heartbeat below the floor. "If the lights go out we're screwed."

Matthew wondered what Jeremy would call their current situation, but the pulsing of the lights picked up speed until it was the epilepsy-inducing light show of a rave. The lights remained perfectly steady for one long breath. Matthew looked at Jeremy across the room and the lights went out. The darkness was unbroken by any chink of light from above or even an exit sign running on battery power. Matthew held his hand in front of his face, moving it closer until it touched his face, and there was no change in the depth of the darkness. Jeremy made a sound that was less a word and more a moan and Matthew called out to him.

"Stay where you are. Don't move and I'll come to you."

Matthew bent down to the thing he had seen just before the lights went out. He held the wooden pole in both hands until he found its end, put that end down on the floor, put his foot on that part and pulled till it parted company with the shaft.

"I've got a broomstick that I can use as a cane. Keep talking so I can find you."

"What do you want me to say?"

"Doesn't matter. Tell me more about your course in Psychology. Describe the last film you saw. Just make some noise so I can find you."

There was a pause where Jeremy did none of those things and then he started reciting as if he were standing on a stage. The empty ticket hall worked just as well as singing in the shower and Jeremy's suddenly deep, commanding voice rolled back from the walls like that of an angry God. Matthew stopped waving the broom in front of him as he made his way across the hall and the small hairs on the back of his neck stood up.

"The stars still move, time runs, the clock will strike, the Devil will come and we shall be dammed. See where Christ's blood streams in the firmament! One drop would save us – half a drop. If thou wilt not have mercy on my soul, impose some end to my incessant pain."

The broom touched something and Jeremy stopped reciting. Matthew kept the broom still and moved carefully forward until he touched him.

"Okay, I've got you."

Jeremy hugged him and Matthew surprised both of them by hugging him back. Rain began to drop on them, but when Matthew ran his hands through his hair it was dry and gritty. Soon, sharp objects began to drop on them.

"The roof's coming down."

"I thought you said we'd be safe here. Didn't they use the underground as bomb shelters during the war?" Jeremy said.

"That's the platforms way below us. The entrance would always be a weak point and that's just had a number nine bus shoved in it."

"Which way?"

"I think the escalators are over here." Matthew pointed, as if either of them could see anything, and held Jeremy's arm as they made their way across the ticket hall and discovered that the darkness held extra directions that no compass would show. Because *here* was a small window with a slot that Matthew thought was a ticket window. The escalators were *there*, a complete left turn from where he had thought.

Matthew found the endless rubber band of the escalator's handrail and slid his foot onto the first slotted metal step. "The escalators aren't moving. They must have gone with the lights." He felt for the next step and Jeremy walked straight into his back, nearly pushing him down.

"Hang on! Give me a minute."

Jeremy didn't say anything, but the familiar, over-the-shoulder pressure of an impatient commuter disappeared. Matthew took another step and discovered that the escalators that were so helpful during the day were a long series of tripwires in the dark. At the top of the frozen escalator the drop between steps was just shallow enough to be confusing. It wasn't until the midpoint of the escalator that the steps became nice and normal. Deceptively normal, as it turned out, when the steps became shallow again at the bottom and Matthew's downwards momentum abruptly became forward momentum and he left the stalled escalator at a near run.

Matthew slowed himself just enough to find his way in the pitch-dark tunnel when Jeremy bowled into him, pushing him further away from the escalator, which turned out to be a heavily disguised favour when there was a roar like multiple Titanics finding their own iceberg. The taste of concrete dust became so choking that Matthew suspected, even if it hadn't been perfectly dark, they wouldn't have been able to see their hands in front of their faces. A short time later, more small rubble rained down on them. But this time it rained sideways.

Matthew pulled Jeremy further away from the horizontal hail of debris. His mouth was full of fine dust and he spent five minutes coughing before he could talk.

"I think that was the ticket area collapsing. We're lucky that the rubble closed off the escalators before any big stuff could make its way down to us."

He coughed for a few minutes and then there was only the sound of more rubble compacting above them. And then, even though he couldn't see Jeremy's face, he could perfectly describe the expression that was forming there. First one, or both, eyebrows would lift quizzically then his lips would try for a thin smile and fail miserably into a confused expression, and finally he would say, "But if the escalators are blocked, how are we going to get back up?"

Matthew rested his hand on the floor until his racing heartbeat had slowed enough to let him feel the subterranean pulse. "I'm not sure there's an up to get back to. They've already demolished the barracks, the ticket office above us and probably everything between those two points. But they're not stopping and I don't think they're going to stop until they think we're dead."

"So they've won. We're stuck here until the whole station falls in. We might as well not have bothered leaving the barracks. At least that would have been quick."

"We're not stuck here. All we have to do is find a platform and follow the tracks to the next station. That's either Hyde Park Corner to the east or Gloucester Road to the west."

Jeremy let out a laugh that sounded uncomfortably like a sob. "All! *All* we have to do is find our way through a maze of pitch dark tunnels before they collapse. And when we find a platform we'll have no idea if we're going east or west, but it won't make any difference because both stations probably went at the same time as the roof above us."

Matthew shook his head, realised that Jeremy couldn't see that, and tried to sound confident instead. "The cones aren't going to burn the whole city. They went to a lot of trouble to get everything just right. They've got Hyde Park all programmed in so all they have to do is land and collect the harvest. So the thing that came from the ship will be centred on the barracks and both of those stations are far enough away to be safe."

Matthew crossed his fingers and dust made the contact feel like sandpaper.

"And of course you're right?" Jeremy sounded simultaneously contemptuous and disbelieving.

Matthew found Jeremy's arm in the darkness and used it to turn him until there were both facing the same direction.

"The escalators are directly behind us, so if we just walk forward the turn-offs for the platforms should be on the left and right when we reach the end of the tunnel. We'll choose one and follow it down to the platform." Matthew released Jeremy's arm and used the broom to feel his way forward before Jeremy could realise that he hadn't answered his question.

"That almost sounds like a plan. Lead on and I'll follow."

Matthew moved the end of the broom across the floor in front of him and stepped forward.

Jeremy's voice was a small thing behind him, but very clear. "And on the way we can discuss the question you didn't answer."

He had noticed.

Almost immediately, the sound of Jeremy's footsteps became imperceptibly quieter. When

Matthew stopped and asked the emptiness, "Where are you?" Jeremy's reply was very distant. Matthew reached for the wall and felt his way back up the tunnel – and then around the corner he hadn't known was there. "Why did you turn off the main tunnel?"

"I didn't. I went straight on. You were the one that turned off."

Matthew resisted the temptation to grasp Jeremy warmly by the throat. "Well perhaps it's for the best; this could lead to a platform."

"So you're saying I was right?"

Matthew rolled his eyes at the darkness. "Just try to stay next to me as we make our way along."

Jeremy didn't say anything this time and they set off again. Matthew soon realised that 'next to me' had become a very flexible concept. If Jeremy tried to follow him then their paths would diverge rapidly. If they held onto each other then there was not enough hands to navigate around obstructions, and it felt a little weird as well.

Matthew stopped and let go of Jeremy's hand. "This isn't working. Have your trousers got a belt?"

"Yes. So?"

"Take it off. Feed it back through just one loop on your trousers and buckle the two ends together to make one big hoop. I'll do the same, but I'll link it through your hoop. That gives us both hands free and we won't get separated again."

"So you won't get lost again."

Matthew tasted dust as he ground his teeth together and pulled his belt free with unnecessary force. Threading it back through just one loop and buckling it around the hoop that Jeremy held out silently was an exercise in patience that was already badly overdrawn.

"Right, let's give it a try."

Matthew stepped forward and Jeremy jerked him right.

"We have to move together."

This time, Jeremy pulled him forward before Matthew was ready. After a few more faltering steps Matthew was irresistibly reminded of his tenth-year sports day. The head teacher had smiled far too broadly as he announced that the next race would not be a test of speed and stamina, but of cooperation and trust. The other teachers' smiles had almost been smirks as they divided everyone into pairs and strapped right legs to their partners' left. The moment the starting whistle had been blown Matthew knew that any event called the three-legged race was really just a bad joke. Several pairs of runners had immediately fallen over at the start line and writhed around in the mud trying to get to their feet. Others stumbled on robotically with one half trying to overpower the other and drag them along as a dead weight at the same time as the other half was doing the same thing. Matthew's memories of that day were of the taste of mud and bruises like mismatched socks. And now he was doing much the same thing, a hundred feet under London's streets, in the pitch dark, with someone he'd rather punch than trust.

Matthew walked into a smooth, tiled wall and they both fell over. As they both got up he stood on Jeremy's foot. At the next corner, he went down first, but it was Jeremy that trod on Matthew's foot. After a few more minutes, Matthew started to feel like a rat in a maze. The tunnels seemed to go on forever and his fingers began to hurt where they trailed along the curving walls. He kept telling himself that all he had to do was keep his left hand touching the wall and, just like the apocryphal way of solving a maze, they would find their way to a platform. That was fine for the long stretches of smooth wall, but then there were the corners or rubbish underfoot, when the wall would slip away from them. Then the question became one of memory and kinaesthesia. Had they been walking in this direction or had they been twisted around and were retracing their footsteps? Sometimes they disagreed and argued like an old married couple linked together by a malicious god and sealed in a circular room.

The flood of adrenaline that had driven them on disappeared as quickly as it had arrived and, like Wile E. Coyote in his endless pursuit of the Road Runner, looking down and seeing that he had been running on air for the last few minutes, they realised just how desperately tired they were. Jeremy suggested a break first, but if he hadn't then Matthew certainly would have. The floor was cold and hard, the curvature of the wall exactly the right shape to be uncomfortable, but the constant wind that roared down from above was warm, almost hot. The darkness that had been both threatening and concealing was suddenly comforting. Matthew closed his eyes and began to dream.

Kirsten laughed as she swam through an ink-dark sea. Matthew swam clumsily after her, calling her name as she slipped away from him. Bright geometric shapes began to rain down from above and he pulled away from their taste of electricity. A flashbulb pop of light lit up a great cyclopean city below them and they both dived down. Thousands of people poured through the city's mile-deep streets and heads turned to track them as surely as any radar system. But every face was blank, each body smooth and sexless. Kirsten turned to laugh at him, but her mouth was a simple slit in a featureless face.

Matthew woke up with his scream still echoing in the tunnel. After that, moving was an exercise in pain as muscles that had been stressed beyond their limits protested their disapproval and joints that had been at rest wanted to stay that way. Matthew was still dragging Jeremy's dead weight when he felt his way around another corner and suddenly the echo of his probing stick sounded different. The claustrophobic feeling of being trapped in a tunnel no wider than two arm spans had been replaced by a great empty silence, as if they were standing in a cathedral. He held the broom above him as if summoning a taxi and there was still no contact with the ceiling.

"What's happened? Why have we stopped?" Jeremy sounded tired, more than tired, ready to drop.

"I think this is a platform." Matthew moved carefully forward and felt the end of the broom drop away from him. "I'm just going to unlink so I can check it out."

Jeremy didn't say anything, but Matthew thought he heard a sharp intake of breath, as if the only thing worse than being connected was not being connected.

Matthew undid his belt, bent down and walked his hand forward until he felt a rounded edge with only space beyond. He drew his hand back, fanning it left and right until he felt a smooth strip parallel to the edge. Holding the broom at arm's length, he let the end drop down over the edge until he heard a rattle. "Definitely a platform. I can feel the painted yellow strip they're always warning you to stay behind, the platform edge and the gravel around the rails."

"It's about time."

Matthew swivelled around to where Jeremy's voice had come from, because it had sounded like him and yet very different, as if some important component was missing.

"I'll jump down to the rail bed," Matthew said, "and then I can give you a hand down."

"Oh goody!" Jeremy's voice sounded no more human than a speak-your-weight machine.

Matthew sat down on the platform with his legs in front of him and walked forward on his hands until he felt his heels drop over the edge. And then he understood the fear of every primitive man when the sun was swallowed by the horizon at the end of the day. Even without the help of the broom, he knew that the drop from platform to rail bed was just a few feet. Sometimes, confused tourists jumped down to retrieve dropped selfie sticks, even if most of those were reported under headlines: *Tragic Incident on the Underground*. Matthew knew all these things, but as he sat on the edge of the platform, he learnt the gulf between knowledge and belief. A million years of evolution screamed that he was about to jump into a bottomless, dark pit and that he would fall forever; the rushing wind would tear at his face and he would reach out into the darkness and there would be nothing there.

"Problem?" Jeremy said from above him. His voice tipped the scales of indecision and Matthew jumped. His shoes slid out from under him as he landed and he sat down hard on a rail. He took a long, deep breath that seemed sweeter than anything he had tasted before and called up to Jeremy.

"I'm okay; the jump is nothing really."

And Jeremy jumped down – as if it were really nothing.

Matthew backed away from Jeremy's body odour and moved a little more, relishing the sudden freedom of not being attached to another person.

"At least we won't need to link up again. It's not like we're going to get separated in a tunnel."

"Unless there's a junction with another track, but there wouldn't be anything like that on one of the most complex underground systems in the world, would there?"

Matthew discovered that he could talk through gritted teeth. "Okay, but we'll have to attach on just one side so we can walk in single file. The third rail is just the other side of the tracks. It probably went out at the same time as the lights, but if it didn't then it's still live with six hundred volts."

"I'll be sure to remember that," Jeremy said, as they both threaded their belts through a new loop on their trousers and linked them together.

"It doesn't make any difference which way we turn now," Matthew said. "I think South Ken Station is a bit further from the edge of the park than Hyde Park Corner, but both of them are a mile directly left or right of a line drawn between us and the cube."

"So right it is."

"Why right?"

"Well I could make up some story about the Roman belief that the left hand was sinister, or quote Psalms 118:16 – The right hand of the lord doeth valiantly – but mainly because it seems we've both attached ourselves by our left sides so turning right will stop the link getting snagged in anything sticking out from the wall."

"Good plan," Matthew said, as he stepped forward, and Jeremy dragged him back. They tried again and managed six feet before colliding. After a while, they developed some coordination and managed at least five minutes before Jeremy stopped for no good reason and dragged Matthew back, or he walked too fast and bumped into Matthew. The tunnel seemed to go on forever and it was only the contact of a cable or switch box on their trailing hands that told them they were not just trapped on an endless treadmill. They walked in complete silence and when Jeremy screamed Matthew nearly wet himself.

"Something touched me. There's something else down here. On my shoe. I felt it."

Without thinking, Matthew bent down to touch the floor. Coarse hair brushed against his hand and before he could pull away, he felt small leathery feet scrabble against his palm.

"Rats. It's rats running away from Knightsbridge tube station as it collapses."

Matthew felt a tug at his waist and something flopped down against his leg. He reached down and found his belt still buckled into a loop.

"What are you doing? Why have you disconnected yourself?"

"I'm looking for something." Jeremy's voice was no longer just over Matthew's shoulder and the crunch of his footsteps on gravel was definitely moving away.

"Looking for something? This isn't the time to worry about losing your keys."

"It's exactly the right time."

There was another small sound of gravel shifting underfoot and then the smack of skin on metal.

"It's not working!"

The slapping sound came again and again.

"What's not working?" Although Matthew already knew.

"The third rail. You were wrong; it's not live at all."

"What? Why?"

"Because I'm tired, scared and I want it all to stop. What happened up there was as much of a fight as pouring boiling water on an ants nest. This is the end and even if we walk out of this, what do we have to look forward to? A few more years scrabbling around in a dead city waiting for them to come back and finish the job? I don't want to live through that. I suspect you don't either. But this is where I get off."

The roof groaned and small chunks of rubble began to rain down on them.

"Look, we can talk about this later. But we need to get out of here before the roof comes down."

Jeremy made a coughing sound that sounded almost like laughter "That's not a reason to go! It's a reason to stay. It's dark in here but it won't be any darker when the roof comes down, except I won't care."

"What about Arvid? All the shooting seemed to be this way so there's a good chance the apartment and its radio will survive. We have to let him know what happened here before someone else tries the same thing."

"Tell him I said goodbye." Jeremy's voice was very distant now. And there was a period, so brief that it barely existed, when it would have been so easy to consider himself well rid of Jeremy's dead weight and just walk away, free of his whining self-pity, body odour and spiky personality. Whatever was happening above ground had to stop at some point and there would be enough of the city left for him. He could find a new place to live and there would be enough food, booze and porn for him to live like a king. But he would be alone and the word wrapped itself around him like a noose. He could cover himself with diamonds and there would be nobody to tell him that he looked an idiot. He could do a handbrake turn in a Ferrari straight out of the showroom and nobody would laugh when he made a mess out of it. If he was wrong and the radio had been destroyed then he might never talk to another person ever again. The most desperate prisoner in the depths of a super-max prison knew that one day he would walk free, but Matthew knew that his sentence would be for life. And just how long would that life be in complete solitude? How long until he decided to test the crash protection of that Ferrari by driving it into a wall at 150 miles per hour? How long until he decided that a handful of sleeping tablets washed down with a bottle of vodka would be just right to sleep at night? And suddenly he realised that Jeremy was still a whining little shit, but was also a lifebelt. Together they would fight like an old married couple, but on his own he would be dead in a year.

Matthew tried to move stealthy back towards Jeremy and heard his footsteps scurry further away.

"If we don't make it out of here how can I punch you in the face for that nasty little joke with the grill pan?"

And the sound of Jeremy's footsteps stopped.

"You knew?"

"I do now." Matthew turned his head from side to side, trying to triangulate Jeremy's position. "Why did you do it?"

"Because I was jealous of you! You had a girlfriend, a mother that wasn't a monster and a life. You went places, did things. You had the perfect life and then you laughed at me. I'm sorry for what I did; it was wrong."

Matthew snorted and used the sound to mask a step forwards. "My perfect life? Shall I tell you how it really was in my perfect life? You know my girlfriend, the one that I loved and loved me sooooo much? After we'd been together for six months I phoned her pottery class and found out that not only wasn't she there, but she hadn't been there for months. She'd found somebody new and do you

314

know who the new love of her life was? Janice. Six months of being with me had turned Kirsten lesbian. Just how perfect do you think that made me feel?"

Jeremy's voice was a little closer now. "I ... I didn't know."

"Why should you? You were just more upfront with your problems."

Jeremy laughed and Matthew was sure he was only a few feet away from him now.

"What a pair of losers! The last men in London and we've both been fucked over by life. If we ever make it out of here we should launch a class action against the pottery class and the TA for deprivation of affection. We'll ask for ten million and settle for a small Greek Island."

Matthew was sure he could feel the small movements of air as Jeremy spoke. He might be just beyond arm's reach. "You're right! Sue the pottery class and the TA of course."

There was silence for a beat before Jeremy spoke again. And now it sounded uncomfortably as if he were crying. "You know there was the slightest pause before you said TA, almost as if they weren't involved. Almost as if you were trying to decide whether to tell me that Anton was nothing to do with them. The moment I said that line about covert missions I knew it was a step too far. Shame, it sounded really good in my head."

Matthew took a step back and almost tripped on an empty can.

"You knew that Anton lied to you about being in the TA?"

"I figured it out eventually. I had my suspicions when I couldn't contact him. Not even my mother was that persuasive. But I knew for certain six months later when I saw him at Paddington underground station. He was on the westbound platform and I was on the east, so there were two train tracks and twenty feet between us. But I knew it was him. He looked tired and was wearing a stained boiler suit. Judging by the way people moved away from him, I think he smelled. I think he was probably working on the bins or sweeping the streets. And then he looked up and knew me. I saw his lips move but then his train came into the station and he was gone. It was another twelve months before I used Paddington Station again. I used to change trains three times rather than go through there."

"But why didn't you–?"

"Do something? Tell the police? Stalk him on social media? Roam the tunnels under the station wearing a half mask for a climactic showdown? But instead I did what every good child is taught to do. I told my mother, and she instantly started talking about how long the grass was and should we buy a new lawnmower. How do you think I got so good at hiding inconvenient truths? I learnt everything from my mother. I'd like to think she was trying to save me from the trauma of an investigation, but I think she was more concerned about what her bridge partners would think."

More rubble began to rain down on them.

"I wanted to tell you everything that night. At last it was my chance to put down the heavy load I'd been carrying all these years. I walked right up to that line and then I chickened out and told you the lie, the one where I wasn't a stupid kid that some pervert had got their hooks into. But you saw straight through that and you'll never know just how thankful that made me. You opened a door and let me unload all of the guilt, the pain, the disgust I've carried for so long."

In the distance, part of the tunnel roof collapsed with a long roar. Matthew reached out to the darkness.

"But that's all gone. The past is dead and buried, but if you let it it will bury you as well. This is our chance to start over and be the people we want to be. But only if we get out of here."

There was silence and Matthew's arm began to grow heavy. And then Jeremy reached out and found Matthew's hand in the darkness. It stung as Jeremy pulled him forward. But it was a meeting between equals and besides that, the pain was nothing.

Chapter Thirty
Nineteen Hours Remaining

Five minutes later, Matthew fell over. One moment he was walking with his right hand trailing on the wall and the next the wall had disappeared and he fell sideways, catching his ribs on the top of a much lower wall.

"You okay?" Jeremy said in his ear.

"Yes." Matthew pulled himself upright. "The wall's changed. Now it's only a few feet high."

He reached out to the changed wall and felt his way up to the edge he'd fallen on. The top of the wall was smooth and very deep. He moved until his armpit was hard up against the edge of the wall and still he could only feel the same smooth surface. Matthew knew another word for a flat surface raised above ground level.

"I think this is a platform. We've found the next station."

"Certainly stinks in here. Maybe it's just a drain cover."

"It could be, so there's only one way to find out. Come over here and lace your fingers together to give me a boost up."

It took two attempts before Jeremy could hold Matthew's foot long enough to be useful, and he rose up and sprawled up onto the platform. Something scraped close by and a second later, the something jabbed Matthew in the side.

"I've passed you up the broomstick so you can find your way around."

Matthew knelt up and pulled the stick away from his painful ribs. "It found me."

318

He stood up very slowly, expecting every second the dull crunch of his skull on a low roof or that he would find a sheer drop inches from his foot. When he had avoided both of those things and was standing fully upright, he probed with the stick in all directions.

"Certainly feels like a platform. There's the same flat surface around me as far as the stick can reach and I can't touch the ceiling. I'll keep the edge at my back and feel my away across. If this is a platform I'll find a wall with displays, seats and so on. Then I can give you a hand up and we'll work our way down the platform until we find an exit."

"You make it sound so easy."

Matthew wished it was that easy. The tapping of the stick as he made his way across the maybe-platform echoed back in strange, unpredictable ways. Sometimes his foot touched something that he hoped was litter left by the last commuters wondering what was happening to them.

"Anything yet?"

"Nothing but more flat surface. Maybe this is only some sort of storage area."

Matthew swung the stick again and this time it hit something with a dull thud. He slashed the stick at waist height and again the same soft yet solid impact. He reached forward and felt the warmth of skin, the roughness of stubble. Eyelids itched against his palm and he recoiled in horror.

"Jesus, there's somebody down here with us!" Matthew backed away so quickly that he fell backwards and the darkness was briefly populated with stars.

"Who is it? Who's there?" Jeremy sounded very distant as if he were in another room. Matthew tried to listen above the sound of his panting as he walked backwards on his elbows, but there was only silence. He reached the side of the platform and balanced on the edge ready to drop down to the safety of the tracks.

"Clap your hands twice," Jeremy said.

Matthew twisted around to look in his direction. But before he could ask what Jeremy was talking about there was the double smack of flesh on flesh. The sound reverberated strangely, but it was definitely the sound of someone clapping.

Jeremy laughed. "It's a Stupid! Don't you get it? The smell in here, the way they didn't answer but did exactly as told. They must have been on one of the last trains before everything turned to shit. They probably only got off the train because that's what they always did, and after that there wasn't enough left to tell them what to do next. The cones' fishing lure wouldn't reach them down here so they've been standing here all the time."

"You sure?"

"No, but it fits the facts." And in a louder voice, he added, "Stamp your foot."

Matthew looked up quizzically. From his position on the platform floor it had certainly sounded like someone stamping their foot, but also wrong. The person he had touched, if it were a person at all, was a foot or so in front of him. But the thud of shoe on concrete had come from his left, or possibly his right. There was something very strange about the way sound echoed here.

"Well I think that's conclusive, but also an opportunity. There are fewer friends of cancer every year, but it's worth a try. If you have a cigarette lighter then light it now. Stop!" Jeremy's voice became slower and somehow patient as if he were talking to a very slow child. "If you have a lighter, take it out from your pocket. Hold it in front of you. Light the lighter."

There was a soft rustle, seemingly all around Matthew, and then a beautiful golden flame unfolded in mid-air a few feet in front of him and to his left and right. He sat bolt upright and looked around. As he'd expected, he was lying on the platform of a London underground station. Below a thin strip that repeated Green Park were posters for holidays that would never be taken and mobile phones that would never be sold. What he hadn't expected was that he was surrounded by a crowd of blank-faced people, all of them with one hand in front of them. Some were holding lighters.

"Bloody hell!" Jeremy said. "We were nearly right, but it wasn't one person stuck here; it was a whole train full. They must have been carried along when a wave of people fought their way off a train and then they were just left behind."

Matthew climbed slowly to his feet and looked into the face of the nearest person. Judging by her smart suit and tastefully understated necklace she had been somebody important, perhaps a feral lawyer or advertising shark. But now her mouth hung open and her face was completely relaxed. Matthew waved his hand and her eyes never tracked for a second.

"You're right," Matthew said, and to his amazement Jeremy didn't immediately agree with him. "All of them have just been standing here for days. There's an exit just a few feet away; they could have just walked out of here at any time. But they just didn't know how anymore."

He reached down to Jeremy and helped him up to the platform and he in turn looked around at the crowd on the platform. "They're just waiting aren't they," he said, "for the next train, for someone to tell them what to do or maybe for death to set them free. Whatever made them human has gone and left behind empty shells."

Jeremy sounded more shaken than Matthew expected. Perhaps he had used the goal of fighting back as a shelter from the reality of what had happened to the world, and now that protection had been stripped away, there was nothing to distract him from the truth.

"Just one question," Jeremy said. "How come this is Green Park tube station? That's not one of the stations you said we'd come to?"

"Because we're idiots. Underground trains have doors on both sides. There used to be websites that told you which side to stand for a given platform. But we were just feeling for a platform on the right. We walked right past Hyde Park Corner Station and never noticed."

"Idiots is right, because, has it occurred to you, while the platform here is full of stranded commuters we groped our way through Knightsbridge Station for roughly forever."

It hadn't occurred to Matthew, but now he realised that it should.

"So either Knightsbridge, one of the busiest stations on the network, was unaccountably empty when things stopped or we managed to walk through the whole thing without bumping into anyone. We spent all that time feeling our way along when we could have just shouted give us some light or *Lumos Maxima* for any fans of J.K. Rowling. I thought it smelt funny as we made our way through the station, but I never stopped to think why. But at least we'll have no problem finding our way to ground level. We'll have our own torchlight parade." Jeremy stopped as the smell of burning flesh filled the air.

"Shit! Everyone turn off your lighter," Jeremy said and darkness flooded back like a thick, oily liquid. "One of the lighters was running hot or somebody wasn't holding theirs properly. That was burning skin, only there's no way for them to tell us. Okay, we're going to have to be a bit smarter about this. Everyone light your lighter." The platform flooded with light, but only for a moment before Jeremy said, "And off," and the darkness poured back.

Matthew heard him whispering very quietly and then just one flame unfolded in front of him.

"We're going to have to do this as a relay race. Let this guy light the way until his lighter either runs out of fuel or gets too hot. And too hot means we smell burning flesh. Then we switch to another member of our entourage."

"So everybody comes with us?"

"It's a fair exchange. They light the way for us and we get them out of here."

Jeremy didn't wait for a reply and called for everyone to line up by the exit in double file. The hushing sound of shoe on concrete as everyone moved was both commonplace and yet strange. If Matthew didn't look too closely at what was happening it might have been any ordinary day with stressed commuters waiting impatiently for their train. But he did look closely and saw blank, empty faces and business suits that looked normal – but only above the waist. Because everything below the waist was a stained and foul-smelling mess. Matthew also saw the ones that didn't move. The crumpled heaps dotted across the platform, some with a desperate hand reaching out. He guessed they were the old or infirm and they had been the first to starve to death and fall where they stood.

"Ready?"

Jeremy had pulled the lighter holder from the queue he had created and was waiting by the exit sign. The single flame flickered and billowed, filling the platform with shadows that seemed more alive than the people there. The light glittered in the endlessly open eyes of a young man that had fallen along the warning yellow line, making it look as if he had got the punchline of a final joke. Matthew pulled himself away from his fixed gaze and joined Jeremy by the exit.

"Very ready," he said.

Jeremy raised his arm above his head and said, "Follow me," very clearly and, together with the lighter holder, took the first step up the stairs. Matthew followed them and all the people that had been patiently standing on the platform followed him.

Sometimes the flame from the lighter seemed worse than no light at all. Shifting shadows made the steps a moving target that Matthew missed as much as found. At each landing Jeremy paused to let the queue catch up and Matthew briefly became the filling in a people sandwich.

Matthew went over his arguments with every step, turning them over and viewing them from every angle until he was sure they were sound.

"Doesn't it strike you that there is something very strange about the Stupid?"

"Other than they have the IQ of a goldfish?"

"Yes, because down there they knew what a lighter was, how to read an exit sign and enough numbers to know what double meant. They didn't have the will power to just walk off the platform and yet they still had basic skills."

Jeremy thought about that for a complete flight of stairs and Matthew knew that it had been a good question. "Not strange at all," he said slowly. "One definition of intelligence is the ability to apply knowledge and skills. All of those things are still there, but what's missing is the drive to use them. They're still the same people they used to be, but now they are a library without an index, an engine stuck in neutral." He turned a corner and there was a dim glow in the distance. "At last!"

Jeremy sprinted down the corridor and into a long, low room. On their left, a smashed ticket machine was surrounded by a snowdrift of blank tickets. On the right, a row of ticket barriers all locked open. But in front of them a flight of stairs was lit by dull light from above. Jeremy threaded through the nearest open barrier and Matthew and the crowd they had collected from the platform followed. Jeremy took the steps to the outside two at a time.

The sun was very low and blades of dull sunlight shone through rents in the cloud like God's searchlights. It was bitterly cold and a stiff breeze blew rubbish down the street and pinned it to the railings around the park that gave the station its name. When the wind dropped, the tapestry of litter rustled and flapped as if applauding their arrival. Some of the stalled cars that blocked the road had leaked oil and the gutters were full of grey, scummy liquid that was overflowing onto the pavement. It was the most beautiful thing Matthew had ever seen.

He turned slowly like a music box marionette, feeling the air on his face and soaking in the incredible brightness of everything. The sun cast his shadow as an impossibly elongated stick figure that danced and capered. He watched it for some time before he realised that the sun was very low over Piccadilly Circus, and that meant it was low in the east. They had been underground all day and night.

Chapter Thirty-One
Seventeen Hours Remaining

They left the Stupid they had brought up from the platform, mechanically chewing two slices of bread to one mouthful of water, in a corner shop. The bread was days old and covered with green fur, but Jeremy said it was not only the best thing they'd had to eat for days, it was the only thing and since they had got them out of the station one good turn deserved another.

They left the shop feeling happy. After the crushing darkness of the underground, just being outside felt like floating. They walked down the street, gawking at the way broken glass shimmered like diamonds in the daylight, how impossibly green the grass of the park was. All the colours seemed deeper and richer than ever before, as if the world had been processed by an Instagram filter.

Jeremy said that Matthew probably needed a change of underwear after he had touched the Stupid's face and he replied that Jeremy's face was so filthy it was politically incorrect. They play punched each other, laughed and made jokes. They were having a good time. Then they turned a corner and saw the wasteland. The wide street and elegant townhouses stopped just a few feet ahead, beyond that there were only static waves of bricks and concrete that towered above them. A deep earthquake groan brought their heads around and Matthew saw a building that had been perfectly sliced in two, so they could see interior rooms, was slowly sagging into the wasteland. He looked beyond the building and saw a perfectly straight dividing line separating London-Normal from London-Wasteland as if a ruler had been placed across the map and everything to its left had been obliterated by God's eraser.

Matthew's feet carried him unwillingly to the crest of a wave of bricks and he saw that a strip of London had been demolished more efficiently than anything dreamed of by the Nazis. In front of him, undulating waves of brick, concrete and metal lapped up to the edges of a Hyde Park where every tree and shrub had been splintered away at roof height. Beyond the park, he could see where the same ruler-straight edge had ripped through fashionable Kensington leaving behind fractional buildings that were collapsing like dominos.

"Very … efficient weren't they."

Jeremy was standing to Matthew's left, looking at the destruction with the same stunned expression that Matthew was sure he wore. The left side of the strip was ragged and the buildings there were either untouched or missing like rotten teeth. At one point, Matthew thought he could see the muddy blue of the Thames, which had to be impossible. The river was miles away. He looked away and followed the ruler-straight edge behind them, to their right until it turned back in a sharp angle and became the far edge of the strip cutting through Kensington. Matthew followed it further until it joined the ragged left side and around to become the straight edge behind them. And he understood. It wasn't a strip; it was an arc, a pizza-shaped slice. Its point was where the cube had been and only at the very edge of the arc had the destruction been anything less than total. The cylinder the ship had ejected had spent all night turning back and forth in a tight arc centred on the barracks. It had fired and the buildings within range had been broken. It had kept firing and the buildings had fallen and it had not stopped until there was only rubble.

"They didn't need to do all … this." Matthew flapped his hand at the devastation. "We stopped, we ran away, but they just kept on."

"Don't you get it? They were sending us a message that whatever we did they were prepared to go massively beyond that. This slice of London? This was just a lesson in power."

"But it didn't work. We escaped."

"To do what? Try again and let them blow a slice out of Mayfair or Paddington? Perhaps, if we're really lucky and keep moving, then we can get London to look like a pretty flower seen from space. Only its petals would be like this, arcs of shredded brick and glass and metal. And do you know what all of that destruction would mean? Absolutely nothing. We never touched them. If yesterday had been a boxing match then we would have been out for the count the moment the first punch had been thrown. Only, they never stopped. They kept on punching and smashing and lashing out until there was nothing to hit anymore. Then they went home and had a nice rest as if nothing had happened, which is a fair summery of what did happen – to them."

"At least we can tell Arvid what happened, so no one else makes the same mistake. We were right; the flat and its radio were never in the line of fire. I can see it from here."

"And you can see it from here because all those inconvenient buildings that were in the way are dust. There'll be some amazing sunsets for years. We'll be able to watch them while we hide away so the cones can carry on without any annoying interruptions."

"At least we can do some good."

"By being good little vermin and not nibbling at our master's table?"

Matthew took Jeremy's arm and used it to turn him away from the wasteland.

"We have to go." He took an experimental step downhill and counted slowly to three before he heard Jeremy follow. The loosely packed rubble shifted underfoot like walking on ball bearings and he slid as much as walked to a section of untouched pavement. Jeremy stumbled to a halt next to him in a shower of brick dust.

"We'd best take an anti-clockwise route back to the apartment. This lot" – Matthew jerked his thumb over his shoulder at the sea of rubble – "reaches all the way to Chelsea."

"Oscar used to live there. Oscar Wilde, fountainhead of a thousand motivational posters. He said that the stupid have the best of it in this world. If they know nothing of victory, they are at least spared the knowledge of defeat." Jeremy pointed at a solitary Stupid standing in a doorway. He was covered in dust and a deep cut on his cheek pulled his mouth up in a permanent, sardonic smile. "You see? He has no idea what's going on, but he's happy. Perhaps we would be better off like them."

"In which case we'd be inside one of those ships by now wearing a fancy headset ready to take orders."

Jeremy thought about that for a second and pointed up the road. "The next left should take us up through Mayfair towards Oxford Street and Marble Arch. Then it's just a bit of the Bayswater Road and we're home."

***

The streets were completely empty and the low morning light trailed their shadows on exclusive shop windows and elegant houses. As they passed the concrete monstrosity of the US Embassy, a shadow swept overhead and they both looked up and saw the cube dropping down to Speakers' Corner. Matthew felt something hard pressing against his back and realised that he had retreated into a doorway without knowing it. Jeremy caught his eye from an adjoining doorway.

"We make excellent cockroaches don't we. The slightest hint of our masters and we run and hide."

The sun was high in the sky by the time they reached the back door into Jeremy's building. He opened the door cautiously, but there was only dust and a musty smell waiting for them inside. They climbed the stairs very slowly, as if the force of gravity had doubled in their absence, and they fell into the apartment. But even the apartment was not what it had been. They had left a large airy room with panoramic views over the park. The room they had come back to was just as big, but now it had invisible corridors that kept them tight against the walls where they could not be seen from outside.

Matthew found a spot in the furthest corner from the window and hooked two dining chairs towards them with his foot. Jeremy muttered something that might have been gratitude and they sat and watched the sundial sweep of light from the window walk across the floor.

Matthew soon discovered that while the chairs were probably excellent at looking good around a table, they were rubbish to sit on. The expertly hand-carved back prodded in places that anatomy resisted so subtly that the pain was almost a surprise.

After an hour, Matthew got up, slowly, and went to make some tea. He wasn't thirsty, he didn't think he could ever be thirsty again, but the kitchen faced away from the park and it was an opportunity to escape the window's unblinking gaze and move around freely.

If anyone had watched Matthew in the kitchen they would have thought they were watching some experimental ballet rather than anything as simple as making tea. He moved very slowly; plugging in the kettle became an exercise in controlled motion that would have made Nureyev cry. But no matter how slowly he moved the tea was ready and he became fascinated by a previously unremarkable feature of the kitchen. It had chairs, several of them. They could sit here, chillax, open a bottle of wine and wait for the cones to go away. He just stood for a few moments, impressed by his flash of genius, and then realised that while he couldn't see the park, he could still hear it, and the lack of context made the sounds into something dreadful. The creaks as the building cooled were the footsteps of the Stupid sent to get them. The wind through the trees was a not-telegraph pole zeroing in on them. He realised that he was caught between the comfort of the kitchen and not knowing what was happening outside, or the certainly of what was happening. He dithered for a moment then decided that on the whole he preferred certainly and sat down next to Jeremy and offered him a cup of tea. He took one mouthful and said it tasted like mud. Matthew tried a sip; he was right.

"We should contact Arvid," Matthew said.

Jeremy leaned forward the absolute minimum amount required to see the grandfather clock. "Not for another few hours; we don't want to upset our masters while they're busy."

Jeremy went back to watching the light from the window as it inched across the floor, and after a moment Matthew joined him.

***

The base of the pyramid disappeared off the top of the window and Matthew stood up with a theatrical series of groans. "Looks like we're clear now. I'll get the remote to contact Arvid."

"Before we're sure that they are really clear?" Jeremy said, without moving. "What if they are just waiting for any radios to be turned on so they can use them as targets? I think we should wait a little while."

Matthew briefly considered this and sat down again. A little while turned out to be an hour and a half. When he stood up again the groans were real. The remote turned out to have hidden itself down the side of the sofa and he spent five minutes fishing it out before he could turn it on.

The sound of the carrier wave filled the room and a short while later Arvid's voice joined it. Matthew began to explain everything that had happened and almost immediately the roar of static tore his words away. Matthew looked at Jeremy, waited for the noise to subside and tried again. He managed just a few more words before the static came back and made conversation impossible.

"That sounds different," Jeremy said. "Before it was just random noise, but now each pulse of noise has its own internal consistency. Listen."

Static filled the room, but this time Jeremy waved his hand like a conductor without an orchestra. "You see, or rather hear? There was a definite puh sound in there and a sibilant 's' sound. Perhaps it's possible that Arvid was right. But I don't think whoever is on the other end of this link is trying to find us – they've found us. All that's left is just fine tuning."

The static came again. Matthew turned the volume higher and heard that Jeremy was right. There were sounds under the waterfall of noise, word sounds.

"But to say what?"

Jeremy shrugged. "I don't know, but it seems they've been trying very hard to talk to us for a long time. They think they've something important to say and maybe we should listen. I don't think we'll have long to wait."

The pulse of static came again and this time the noise was a little less and the word sounds a little clearer. With the next, the noise was distant rain and the words almost close enough to understand. With the next, clearer still. And then there was just a thin reedy voice.

"Blod."

Matthew looked at Jeremy. "Blod? Is that a name? A place?"

Jeremy made shushing sounds and angled his head towards the speakers. There was a long pause before the voice came again and said something in a softy spitting accent.

"Is that Arabic or something?"

Jeremy shrugged.

The voice said some more liquid sounds and paused, said some more and paused.

"It sounds like someone's reading a shopping list. So much of this and a pause. Item and pause."

The voice stopped mid-word and there was another long silence before it spoke again, this time in a thick heavy accent with flowing 'r's and long drawn out 'e's.

"That's French! He just said, '*Sans voix*.' That's silent or voiceless," Matthew said.

"What else did you get?"

"That was it. I only have a few words from holidays."

The voice continued its slow delivery and after a few minutes, Matthew looked around at Jeremy. "If that's a list he's reading then there's a lot of repetition. He's said '*faible*' more than once."

"You repeat something to emphasise its importance. He's trying very hard to get us to understand something."

And the voice changed to the clipped tones of a 1950s newsreader.

"*Talk stupid.*"

Jeremy raised a quizzical eyebrow.

"*Order defective. Our benefaction to you. Vacuous are tool. Stupefied are instrument. Vacant are cudgel. Empty are weapon. Use torpid. Use insensible. Attack. Attack. Attack.*"

"That's the big important message?" Jeremy said. "*Empty are weapon.* He's got to be talking about the Stupid, which is a brilliant plan. There's lots of them, only they are slow and docile. An attack from them would be like being savaged by a dead sheep." Jeremy snorted and something about that sound reminded Matthew of the click of the lighters in the underground station.

"But didn't you say that they are still the people they used to be?"

"Yes, so what?" And then Jeremy's face dropped. "I've been stupid. We've been stupid. They are the people they used to be." Jeremy sat up and smiled. "I said that didn't I. I should listen to myself more often. We accepted them being physically slow because they are mentally slow. But they are just as strong, just as agile, only the drive to use those abilities has been taken away. But that's what we have, the ability to order them. But let's try a small experiment." He passed Matthew one of the cushions from the sofa, shot across the room and opened a door. "Gretchen, come here." A moment later, she was standing in the doorway. A moment later, the smell reached Matthew. If Gretchen were Jeremy's pet he'd certainly been feeding her, but he hadn't emptied her litter tray. Above the waist she was slightly shabby supermodel; below the waist ... Matthew tried very hard not to look down. He'd seen his parents' living room carpet after next door's cat had been locked in there over a long weekend. It was pretty much the same effect.

Jeremy pointed at Matthew. "Run to this man. Punch the cushion he's holding."

And Gretchen sprinted across the room like a doped-up racer exploding out of the gate, like a section spliced from a film. One moment she was across the room and the next her enigmatically blank face was inches from Matthew's.

Gretchen was small and delicate and Matthew barely felt her punch.

"Keep punching. Punch as fast as you can."

Her second punch moved Matthew back on his heels. Before he could recover his balance, the next punch pushed him back across the room. He held the cushion close and tried to brace himself, but each impact followed the last so closely it was like walking into a hurricane. His feet tangled in something and the cushion flew away from him as he fell. Gretchen dropped to her knees and brought her interlocked hands down.

"Stop!"

Gretchen froze with her hands crushing down on Matthew's chest.

"Shit! Sorry about that. She was a lot faster than I thought. Gretchen, stand up and back away."

The pressure against Matthew's chest disappeared. Jeremy reached down and held out a hand to help him up.

"Not so harmless are they? I could order her to punch that wall until she got to the other side, and she'd be there until her arms were bloody stumps. I could order her to run to John O'Groats. And she'd do it. She'd probably drop dead somewhere around Birmingham, but until then she'd never stop."

The newsreader voice from the speaker began to repeat its message.

"... *Our benefaction to you. Vacuous are tool* ..."

"Listen to him! He made this all happen! The Stupid are tools, and you can use a tool anyway you like! You can use a hammer to drive in a nail, or you can use it to hit someone over the head. We were so gung-ho about spraying the alien scum with hot lead that we didn't stop to think about what we'd been given."

"Okay, so they can run and punch, but the cones have still got their exclusion fields. So unless you plan to tell everyone down in the park to run away, that's not much help."

"Ah, the exclusion fields. Thank you for reminding me. A bit ago we called that an electric fence, so let's run with that metaphor. An electric fence is a naked strand of wire live with a hundred volts or so. A cow touches it, gets a shock and wanders off. But what if that cow charged at the fence? Eighty stone of angry ruminant doing twenty miles per hour versus a strand of wire? What about hundreds of dumb animals charging an electric

338

fence? Maybe thousands? What do you think would happen then?"

"I don't know."

"I don't either, but you couldn't pay me enough to be on the wrong side of that wire."

"If we're going to overwhelm them with numbers then some of the people will die. Until their shields collapse, people will fry."

"Yes, very sad, but one day their names shall be spoken of in Valhalla. Or possibly inscribed on a small monument, but the important thing is that we have a way."

The voice switched to something that sounded like Spanish and Matthew turned the volume down until it was a background murmur. "We might have a way, but we're going to need a lot more than that if we're going to achieve anything more than a little local difficulty."

"We're going to need the most difficult thing of all – planning and organisation."

Chapter Thirty-Two
Attack

"We should have realised something was wrong when the cones didn't talk to the Stupid," Jeremy said, as he teased a staple from the skirting board.

"They talked to them all the time. via those headset things." Matthew voice was muffled by the speaker he was carrying. It wasn't particularly heavy, but it was taller than him so he was carrying it with his face smushed into its fabric cover.

"But they only talked to them after they'd been in the ship overnight. They thought they were doing something so the Stupid would accept their commands. Otherwise, they wouldn't have bothered with that light show to get them into the ship. They could have just said 'Go into the ship' and stood back as they marched in." Jeremy pointed at the speaker Matthew had just moved. "But he'd already done something to make the Stupid obedient and the cones never noticed."

They both stopped what they were doing and looked at the speaker as if it would suddenly speak up and agree with them. But the speaker remained obstinately mute and they were sure they would never hear from it again.

The voice had recited its list of nouns and verbs in a continuous stream. Each language had been repeated until it was all just background noise. They had tried talking to it, asking it questions, but the flow of information remained strictly one way. And then, just after midnight, it had stopped. Matthew sat bolt upright from his doze and shook Jeremy's

340

arm until he too was awake. The sudden silence seemed somehow threatening and they watched the dark fabric cover of the speaker as if it would transform into a snarling mouth with ink-black teeth. Without ever knowing, they edged further away and then the speaker had a new voice. It was male, sounded elderly and spoke English with a strange accent, but only for part of a word before it broke off, coughing. When it spoke again it was with a strange rattling sound, as if they were talking through a mouthful of gravel.

"*Avenge us! Cheilith is all undone.*"

The voice coughed once more and never spoke again. A moment later, the hiss of the carrier wave stopped.

No one spoke on the shortwave for a long time after that, but then the debate about what they had heard started. And debate became disagreement, and disagreement became argument, competing points of view being swapped like marbles in the playground. Arvid, sitting in his web of communications, tried to give them a digest of the opinions, but that was like dipping a thimble into the sea and using it as an example of the weather in a country they had never heard of. At four in the morning, they took a vote on the most basic of plans. Do nothing or do something? Everything else was trivial ornamentation. At five past four, they made a decision and Jeremy said, "May God have mercy on us."

Moving the speakers in the apartment turned out to be one of those jobs casually dismissed in a few words that took much much longer than anyone thought. The largest speakers were the size of refrigerators, but there was also a bewildering array of woofers, subwoofers, midranges and tweeters, all of which had been screwed down and connected with yards of delicate cable tacked very low on the skirting board. They searched the whole flat, twice, and the nearest thing to a tool kit they found was a screwdriver for tightening spectacles and a pair of secateurs for trimming house plants. While Jeremy swore at the screws he was undoing with a butter knife, Matthew was inviting the staples he was removing to have sexual relations with themselves.

By the time they were finished and all the speakers were stacked in front of the windows, the sun had risen just above the horizon. Matthew lay back on the sofa and tried to rest, but he was simultaneously too tired to move and too wired on adrenaline not to move. He fidgeted, kneading the supple leather like dough, until the noise got on Jeremy's nerves and he told him to shut up.

"Sorry, just a bit nervous."

"You surprise me."

"Do you think it's going to work?"

"Yes," he said, but Matthew noted the delay between question and answer. "But only because Cheilith set everything up for us. He, they, whatever, made a trap and the cones oozed right into it. All we had to do was use the tool we had been given and he even had to tell us to do that."

Matthew went back to watching the clock while Jeremy brushed imaginary dust off the sofa. By the time the clock clicked over to eight, he was knitting and re-knitting his fingers together.

"Curtain up," Jeremy said, climbing to his feet. It took Matthew a little longer; his legs were stiff and unresponsive. The wall of speakers in front of the window cut their view of the park down to a glimpse of sky, but that was enough to see the pyramid settle into its expected position.

"Score one for our team," Jeremy said, and Matthew nodded in agreement. The possibility that the cones would realise that something was wrong and change how they worked had taken up half of the discussion last night.

Matthew handed Jeremy the microphone. "Good luck."

Jeremy's smile was very faint. Matthew thought he was regretting winning the toss.

The ticking of the clock became very slow, the motion of its minute hand glacial. Matthew took his time moving a subwoofer so he could see the ramp leading down from the pyramid. When he was done they both watched the clock as it became 08:30 Greenwich Mean Time, 04:30 Eastern Standard Time, 09:30 Central Africa Time. Matthew pressed his eye to the gap he had made in the wall of speakers and put his fingers in his ears. Jeremy's amplified voice was distant thunder.

"Run to cones! Attack cones! Punch cones! Kick cones! Rip cones! Gouge cones! Tear cones! Kill them! Kill them all!"

He managed to sound almost Churchillian to motivate the Stupid. In Australia, they used the voice of the Queen, in Moscow it was Vladimir Putin, but the results were all the same.

The slow shuffle of the Stupid into the ship suddenly became a pressure washer jet of people towards the cones on their viewing platform either side of the ramp. The first people to reach the cones were forced into the exclusion fields by the crowd behind them and there was an electric crackle and the smell of burning flesh. The crowd flowed over still-twitching corpses and more trod over them until the domed tops of the cones' fields were covered by a boiling mass of people, all kicking, gouging and clawing to reach the cones. And then, very slowly, the whole seething mass slipped off the viewing platform and splashed as it hit the ground. The surge of people that had been climbing over each other to get up the ramp changed direction and flowed like hot wax over the globe shapes of the exclusion fields. There was a series of small, unimportant popping sounds as the fields collapsed and the crowd dropped down onto the cones.

The cones' blood was blue and it sprayed up through the seething crowd like sand behind a dog digging on the beach. The head of a cone rose above the crowd, but only the head, held aloft by a woman, stained blue by the blood running down on her. Other hands reached up and the head dropped back into the crowd. Matthew saw teenagers tear at the head, housewives rip at it with their teeth, and in a moment there were only scraps of flesh. Soon, even that was gone and still the Stupid did not stop. They tore at anything blue, at anyone as tall as a cone, at each other.

Matthew looked away from the horror below and saw only more horror. The space in front of the cube was a boiling mass of people around blue smudges. As the mob surged forward, bodies were left behind, pressed into the mud. When Jeremy had ordered the Stupid to attack his smile had been wide and shark-like. Now he looked appalled at what he was seeing, disgusted by what he had done.

"I … I didn't know it was going to be like this."

A heavy, thickset man saw a splash of blue on a young woman's face and lunged at her, fists and teeth all smashing and ripping.

"We have to finish what we started. Tell them to move on. Otherwise this could all be wasted."

Jeremy nodded and swallowed several times before he raised the microphone to his lips. "Run into the ship! Find cones! Kill cones! Find cones! Kill cones!"

The knockdown fights in blue-stained mud stopped instantly and columns of Stupid poured into the ship. The ground they left behind looked nothing like the immaculate lawns that Henry VIII had laid down. The turf was ripped up, the earth stirred into mud and smeared with blue. But between the blue were the bodies. Some moved feebly, most didn't. Matthew started to count the number of dead that their magnificent attack had left and stopped almost instantly. He didn't want to know how many people they had killed, and he'd do anything rather than find out.

He turned away from the window. "How long have they been inside?"

Jeremy tore his gaze away from the horrors below them and looked at him with dull, shocked eyes. "Five minutes?"

"About what we decided. We should pull them back."

"Yes," Jeremy said dully and clicked the microphone. "Stop fighting! Come out! Leave the ship! Come out!" He repeated the message several times until the outward flow of Stupid had stopped.

"I guess that's most of them," Matthew said. "There might be some right down in the bowels of the ship where they can't hear us but I don't think there can be many."

"And now the difficult bit. We wait."

The debate on what might happen afterwards had taken up the other half of the night. Large numbers of people had pointed out that even one ship left untouched would be too many. Then their glorious victory would inevitably be followed by the sun expanding to fill the sky or thousands of not-telegraph poles dropping like snow. Nearly as many people had pointed out that the ships only landed in major cities where they already had a contact. In the end, they had decided to just wait and see. At the time it had sounded really simple.

The smell of burnt flesh seemed to grow thicker with each breath. Matthew found an aerosol air freshener, which did nothing except add the smell of flowers to charred meat. Sometimes there were sounds outside that Matthew told himself couldn't be more of the injured dying. It was a relief when the radio crackled into life.

Matthew translated for Jeremy. "Arvid says that there have been no reports of reprisals and no one has gone off the air unexpectedly."

"So we've won." Jeremy raised his fist very tiredly and dropped it. "Yay! Go us! We're free to be the smartest people on the planet until our appendices burst or we break a tooth on month-old bread. We won the battle but lost the war. King

Pyrrhus said that another such victory would utterly undo him. I think he would have been proud of us."

"But we won!"

The radio spoke again and Matthew listened carefully, sometimes asking Arvid to repeat words he didn't understand.

"He says none of the ships have moved or changed in any way."

Matthew was looking away from Jeremy and never saw his thoughtful expression.

"He says he's opened a bottle of Vodka to celebrate and thrown the top away because he won't be needing that again. He says he'll probably talk to us tomorrow. Perhaps we should do the same. There's four bottles of Champagne in the fridge, good Champagne at that. We've been through a lot to get here and now we can relax."

"We could," Jeremy said. "We could certainly quaff a few glasses of wine, strong, sparkling, bright and clear. Or we could go down and into those ships outside."

"Why?"

"Two reasons. One is that the people that were taken into the ships before we did what we did are still there. They might have heard us calling to them, but they're locked away, trapped in a room they can never leave, never again to feel the sun on their skin or feel the very breath of Mother Nature through their hair, trapped in the dark, slowly starving to death, and their pain is our pain. We are all part of the great community of Mankind and if you prick us do we not bleed?"

Matthew rolled his eyes. "And the second reason?"

"There are spaceships down there! Real live spaceships that have travelled thousands of light years to be here. Think what it would be like just to touch them and feel the weight of all the places they have been. Ever since I saw *Forbidden Planet* with Leslie Nielsen as the square-jawed captain I've always wondered what it would be like to walk through the mile-long machines of the Krells and peek at their thermonuclear reactors. And the next best thing is parked right outside. How can we turn down that opportunity?"

"I guess you've got a point. I'll take one of the pokers from the fireplace to use as a crowbar."

"I don't think anything that has travelled thousands of miles of absolute zero space is going to be much bothered by a small strip of wrought iron that was chosen just to look good."

Chapter Thirty-Three
Inside the Pyramid

The air outside smelt of the sickening, overpowering stench of death, so thick it could have been cut with a knife. The acrid odour of charred flesh reached Matthew first and his stomach lurched. Then the rich metallic smell of blood filled his nose and he clasped a hand over his mouth and nose. Tried to breath shallowly to stop being sick, and nearly made it when the heavy sulphur smell of burning hair reached him and he threw up into his hand.

He crossed over to the park still hiccupping wildly, looked back and saw that Jeremy hadn't crossed the road at all and was walking quickly away.

Jeremy saw him looking and called back to him. "We should start with the small pyramid."

"What's wrong with the cube?"

Jeremy stumbled over something on the pavement that Matthew never saw and it was a moment before he replied. "The pyramid is smaller, so less opportunity for us to get lost inside. Once we've found our way around that I expect the others will have the same internal layout."

Matthew looked at the pyramid and back at the cube and wondered just how similar they could be inside. But he guessed there must be some common features.

"I guess that makes sense," he said.

"Of course it makes sense. You just have to look at it the right way."

The lawn in front of the pyramid was torn up into a sea of mud and they stepped daintily around splashes of blue like an old lady visiting the countryside for the first time. Matthew thought that the ramp leading up to the pyramid looked much larger when you were standing right in front of it.

They moved from one edge of the ramp to the other, trying to see further inside, but all they could see was a few feet of brightly lit corridor.

. Jeremy placed one foot on the ramp with all the care of a man stepping into a minefield. He hunched his shoulders, held his arms close to his chest and brought his other foot up until he was standing on the ramp. Matthew watched his face as if at any moment he would sink into the ramp and be stripped into raw minerals and a few pints of water or that his face would suddenly be emptied of intelligence. Neither of these things happened and he looked back at Matthew.

"Come on in, the waters fine," he said and walked slowly up the ramp towards the entrance.

After a moment, Matthew followed.

The surface of the ramp looked as slick as glass, but walking on it was like wading through tar. Every footfall seemed to be quicker than it should have been, as if the ramp were sucking his foot down. Lifting his foot came with a momentary delay as if the ramp were reluctant to release him. Matthew wondered why the cones had made the surface like this and realised that the answer was obvious. Quality control. The cones had come a very long way to sweep up the Stupid; they didn't want any of their harvest falling over and hurting themselves. That would decrease their value.

Jeremy was standing at the top of the ramp with one arm on the outside of the ship and only his head inside it. Matthew looked past him and decided that he wasn't sure why Jeremy was standing like that, because he couldn't see any more than he could – because there wasn't any more to see. All that was there was a short length of corridor leading away from them, with the tantalising possibility of a doorway or recess a few feet on the right. The other end of the corridor was less than twenty feet in front of them and a central floor-to-ceiling seam suggested a pair of sliding doors. The ceiling, walls and floor all glowed with the same yellowy white. The only other colour was a splash of the cones' blue blood that stretched the full length of the corridor.

"No sign of anyone at home," Jeremy said. "The Stupid must have swept through here like a dose of salts."

"Assuming of course that those doors, if they even are doors, just opened to let the Stupid in. Otherwise, who knows what's waiting inside."

Jeremy looked around at Matthew. "Thanks for that."

"Any time."

"But, nevertheless, all we can do is go inside." And with that, Jeremy stepped inside.

Matthew watched him with something that was nearly respect. He'd spent a lot of time with Jeremy, far too much time in fact, and had come to see him as damaged, deeply hurt but also irritating, sarcastic and the last person to be first to volunteer for anything. But now he seemed completely transformed by events and had walked into an alien spaceship as enthusiastically as if they were handing out free chocolate bars inside.

Matthew put one foot forward and transferred his weight by tiny increments until he too was inside. There were no shadows in the corridor. The light that came from every side made it feel like they were walking through an industrial-sized fluorescent tube. Everything was a little too bright and Matthew screwed up his eyes to see clearly. Without the subtle clues of shadow to guide them, they found it difficult to judge distances and halfway to the maybe-door, Matthew tripped over his own feet and stumbled into the wall. He had a fraction of a second's expectation that the wall would be the burning hot of a light bulb before he touched it. He shook, as if already feeling its scorching heat, and then realised that the wall was in fact slightly cool to the touch. He visibly relaxed, pushed himself away from it and his handprints stayed behind. A perfect image of both hands was printed onto the wall in shades of blue that slowly faded until there was only an outline, and then even that was gone.

"Are you planning to be there all day?" Jeremy managed to sound both bored and exasperated. Matthew ignored him and touched the wall with one finger as if pressing a lift call button. This time the image left on the wall was very small and was quickly gone.

"What've you found?"

Matthew stood to one side and pressed his hand against the wall, fingers spread in a V for Victory sign. "Just this," he said and pulled his hand away.

Jeremy watched the symbol fade away, open-mouthed, and then pressed his own hand to the wall and saw the image he left behind.

"Some sort of reaction to the light emitting elements in the wall?" Jeremy pressed the tips of all five fingers to the wall and left a half moon of dots. He drew a smiley face, a stick figure and the message: *Jeza wos here*.

"Interesting, but not particularly useful."

He drew a triangle. The triangle shivered and then rotated, apex over base, base over apex, as if they were watching a wire-frame model on a computer monitor. The triangle got smaller with each rotation and soon was too small to see.

"That was different."

Jeremy drew a circle and it shrank as if he had dropped a ball into a void. He drew a square then quickly drew another one to its right and joined each corner to its partner. The shape rotated like a discarded Rubik's cube.

"There must be a computer somewhere," Jeremy said, slowly, "that's interpreting the things we draw as three-dimensional objects and showing how they would move. Perhaps this wall is some sort of scratch pad to show new designs." He began to talk faster as he elaborated on his idea. "That's it! This isn't a corridor at all; it's some sort of meeting area where the cones would gather to show each other their ideas." Jeremy smiled broadly, utterly convinced of his own genius.

"Or those are real objects that you're making."

Jeremy stopped smiling.

"The outside of this ship moves like Plasticine. Perhaps this is its control panel. Whatever you draw is being made somewhere. We draw simple geometric shapes and that's what we get. But maybe the cones knew more advanced designs, like the ramp, the halo walkway around the ship and the pole object that shot at us."

"If it were a control panel, it would be in the control room, not stuck out here in a corridor."

Matthew noticed that suddenly Jeremy's meeting room had reverted to being a corridor, but he didn't mention it.

"It's by the entrance where you'd need a ramp, but maybe there isn't a control room at all. Just because *Star Trek* shows us Captain Kirk in his throne surrounded by minions beavering away at mysterious displays, doesn't mean it has to be that way. Maybe this ship is fully distributed and it doesn't matter where anyone is to do their job. If every wall is a fully configurable control then why have just one room to control things?"

"I suppose that's possible," Jeremy said and suddenly became fully involved in drawing complex shapes on the wall."

Matthew watched him for a moment and then leant close. "Of course, if this is the control that made the ramp then it would be really quite bad if we accidently drew a command that made it disappear."

Jeremy stopped drawing in mid-stroke and lifted his hand away from the wall.

"Perhaps we should move on."

The door recess they had seen from the entrance turned out to be a panel set a little back in a silvery frame. Jeremy touched the centre of the panel with one outstretched finger and backed rapidly away like a child playing knock and run. His fingerprint didn't appear on the door, but it didn't open either. Matthew pressed on the door with one open hand and tried to push it open and then used both hands to slide it open. The door remained closed.

"Locked when the cones went away?" he said, doubtfully.

"I guess so. It certainly looks like a door but there doesn't seem to be any way to open it. It doesn't even respond to being touched like the wall." Jeremy drew his finger across the door, touched the silvery frame and the door slid open. They threw themselves back from the opening door and pressed into the wall.

Matthew watched the edge of the door, expecting to see a terrible, avenging cone ooze out to punish the half-evolved apes that had hurt them so badly. The moment passed, and then another, before he peered around the door frame. The room inside was the size of a double-car garage and was completely filled by a tree made of glass. A barrel-thick trunk in the centre of the room reached from floor to ceiling and branches covered with wide, flat leaves grew out sideways to touch each wall. Matthew touched the nearest leaf and a flurry of bright sparks ran back up the branch to the trunk, and the whole tree briefly sparkled as if lit with thousands of Christmas lights.

"Some sort of decoration?"

"That fills the whole room? Not likely. But for all we know it could be part of the main drive or an integral component of the waste disposal system." Jeremy touched the door frame and the door slid shut; he touched it again and the door opened. "Well, at least we know two things." He waited for Matthew to ask what and when he didn't, he carried on anyway. "For one thing we know how to open the doors and for a second we know that the Stupid must have been through every room. All they had to do was brush against the door frame and – et voilà! – the door opens."

Matthew looked thoughtfully at the door frame and tapped it several times, watching the door open and close.

"Enjoying yourself?"

"Not really. There's something strange about this door."

"There's something strange about an alien door in an alien spaceship? You do surprise me. I thought it would be just like the ones at Tesco."

Matthew looked nearly patiently at Jeremy and they moved on down the corridor to the closed door at its end. Jeremy reached it first and touched the door frame and the door slid open. He looked through and then back at Matthew. "You were wrong. There is a control room."

The room was nearly as Matthew had described it: large and hexagonal, a console in the middle surrounded by chairs facing angled control panels filled with displays, dials and switches. And every single panel was dark.

"No, no, no!" Jeremy ran to the nearest panel and pressed a switch and then another and another. When none of those lit up he moved to a panel across the room and repeated the process, only faster and with more force, as if that would be sufficient to bring the control panels back into life.

Matthew watched him as he idly spun the nearest chair on its swivel.

"None of these are working. It's all dead." Jeremy looked across at Matthew. "What are you doing?"

He spun the chair around to face Jeremy. "This is a chair."

Jeremy rolled his eyes. "Congratulations, you've successfully passed basic furniture recognition. Next week we'll start the advanced syllabus and learn the essential difference between an armoire and a wardrobe." He stood up straight and crossed his arms. "Of course it's a chair. Did you really need to point that out?"

Matthew brought the chair around and sat down. Using his feet, he turned back to face Jeremy. "This is a chair designed for humans, here in the control room of a cone spaceship."

Jeremy looked sharply around at the nearest chair and, after a moment, sat down. "You're right; this was made for people very like us." He jumped to his feet and pulled the seat until his face was red. "And it doesn't move."

"And that's important?"

"Yes! If you wanted to operate this panel then you'd have to sit here to do it. We could stand between chair and panel and still be able to operate it, but the cones were much too wide to do that. They were taller as well, and their hands, tentacles, whatever, were right at the top. So unless the cones were more flexible than they looked, they'd have to operate these panels at maximum reach. That would be like us typing on a keyboard stuck to the ceiling.

And all of that means that people were pretty much essential to controlling this ship."

"Like the doors. I thought something was strange about how we opened them. And you were nearly right when you said we expected them be like the ones at Tesco. Because that's exactly how we were opening them. Just like the doors with a touch pad, we were touching the frame at waist height. That's fine for us, but several feet too low for the cones. So, unless they bent right over to open every door, the frame works if touched at any point. This ship was built just as much for men as for cones."

Matthew had a sudden sinking feeling. "What did we kill? Were people and cones working together all the time, but we just saw evil space aliens and killed them? Was this a federation of different species working together?"

"Again with the federation. I'm sure you must have a posable Captain Kirk figure at home, but I don't think we need to worry that this was any sort of partnership. We'll skip over the cones' sterling history of interaction with humans, whatever they did to everyone's intelligence or the way they killed hundreds of people when they melted the sphere. Let's concentrate on what's new." Jeremy pointed around him. "This room. Doesn't it seem strangely unbalanced? All these seats for humans and just one cone here in the middle." He pointed at the console in the centre of the room. It was a thick horseshoe shape like a wraparound bar, but raised up on slim rods until its upper surface was at head height for a human – ideal height for a cone.

"Someone has to be in command. Perhaps it's different in the other ships."

"Command," Jeremy said, slowly. "That's a good word but perhaps an older, more fundamental word would be better. What do you make of these?" He kicked a thick loop, crudely welded to the base of each chair.

"A foot rest?"

"Not unless you have very strange feet." Jeremy sat down, put both feet on the loop and watched them slide off. "I think these have another function altogether." He jumped to his feet and started rummaging through a series of bins attached to the wall. "It's possible they kept them somewhere else, but there must be spares. Ah, here we go." He turned towards Matthew with a three-inch hoop in each hand, joined by a thick cable. "These are shackles. The people here were slaves. The cones kept them literally chained to their desks."

Matthew touched the cable, felt its weight. One of the hoops had a rough edge stained black, and he knew that it was dried blood. Suddenly the room felt much smaller around them. The doors seemed to shrink with every rapid breath. There was a sharp smell in the air, as if the very walls were releasing the stench of years of pain and fear.

"They're not chained to anything right now. They wouldn't have been affected by what we did to the cones. So the big question is where are they?"

"No, the big question is why did the cones, who already had a room full of people smart enough to fly this thing, want hundreds of Stupid who literally couldn't find their arses with both hands. But we're not going to find any answers in here.

359

Nothing works even though there's still power for the lights. The best thing to do is move on and see what we can find. There's four doors here; let's be original and call them North, South, East and West. We came in through South, so let's see what's behind the North door."

Jeremy stepped around the centre console, tapped the frame and the stench of rotted meat and shit poured out at them. The room inside was thick with blood, pooled on the floor, dry and black on the walls. Around the edges of the room dead humans were stacked like logs. Faces with dull, staring eyes looked through them. Mouths open in silent screams. Hands clawed at the air. Blood began to seep over the threshold and Jeremy frantically tapped the frame again to close the door.

Matthew fought the immediate need to be sick, found a spot under a ventilator and let it blow the smell of death away from him. "Jesus! Now we know where the people that were here went."

"They killed them all. They must have tried to fight back and the cones killed them all. It explains the mistakes we saw, the botched landing, the inability to fix their ship. All the people that actually did those things were dead by then." Jeremy cocked his head to one side and looked back at the door. "I'm going to have another look in there."

"You want to see in there again?"

"I *have* to see in there again."

The door slid open and Jeremy stood to one side to let the blood creep past him. He spent a long time looking at the piles of dead bodies before he waved Matthew over.

"See all these people on the left? Slashed wrists, cut throats. Some have dried gunk around their lips. Others have a single wound to their heads. Nobody killed them; they killed themselves." Jeremy pivoted and pointed at a single body dumped on the right that barely looked human. "But this guy is different. Multiple stab wounds, slash marks from head to foot. Some … parts are missing."

Matthew nodded, trying not to breathe. He'd already seen that both hands were missing several fingers and its open mouth showed a bloody mess where teeth had been ripped out.

Jeremy nodded as if the scene made sense. "He's been beaten, stabbed, mauled, attacked over and over, long past the point he was dead. Whoever did this didn't want to just kill him. They wanted to punish him more than anything else. I think this is Cheilith. The rest of them killed themselves to be free of the cones and this poor bastard stayed on just to tell us what we were too stupid to see. And when the cones finally caught up with him they punished him for every slave they lost."

Jeremy tapped the door closed. "They died that we might live. That was the tagline for the war to end all wars. Millions died, but each of them thought they had a chance of making it out alive. They were wrong, but at least they had a chance. The people here must have woken up one morning knowing what they were going to do, and they did it anyway! Thousands of people, perhaps millions of people, killed themselves so we could have the opportunity to drink ourselves to death."

"There's the rest of the ship yet. We should try to find the people the cones took before we stopped them."

Jeremy looked up from his minute examination of the floor. "Yes we should. Perhaps we can find something that will make it all worthwhile." Quickly, he tapped open both East and West doors to show equally long lengths of corridor with the possibility of doors at regular intervals.

"Okay, two directions. We'll take one each and meet outside in, say, thirty minutes. You've still got a watch? I'll take West and hope that Shakespeare wasn't right and that scarcely off a mile, in goodly form comes on the enemy."

The door closed behind him and Matthew watched it thoughtfully before taking the remaining door. He checked each room as he passed. There were completely empty rooms, rooms filled with things that were either plants or organic-looking machines, rooms with walls that swelled as if breathing, and then he saw the door at the end of the corridor. Or, more accurately, he saw the floor in front of the door and the brown stains that once he would have blamed on inconsiderate dog walkers. Tiptoeing past the mess, he touched the door frame and the door slid open on a wall of blank-faced Stupid. He stepped back and in something he didn't notice, then told everyone to follow him and walked slowly back to the control room, feeling like one of the tour guides leading a crocodile of tourists that only saw London through a viewfinder. From the control room to the ramp, the air was cleaner and a stiff breeze helped waft away the fetid stench of the unwashed and un-toileted people following him. At the end of the ramp, he stopped and wondered what to do next. Finding the people the cones had taken had sounded a great idea at the time, but now he realised that it was only the start of a good idea. The Stupid would starve to death just as well outside as inside. Perhaps Jeremy knew what came next. He'd been very keen to get them out in the first place.

After thirty minutes, Matthew looked expectantly up the ramp for Jeremy. At forty minutes, he told the Stupid to stay where they were and went back to the control room. At sixty minutes, he started down the West corridor – and walked right into Jeremy coming the other way.

"Found a ramp leading down to a lower level and got lost there," Jeremy said, unprompted.

"Anything interesting down there?"

"Oh no, nothing useful at all."

"I found a room full of the people they took and brought then down here. There might have been other rooms, but I think this is most of them. What do we do with them now?"

"Do?" Jeremy said, looking surprised. "Well, we need to, erm, find them some food I guess. I think there's a small shop by Lancaster Gate tube station, and that's just a few metres away."

"We'd best check the other ship first. Then we can take anyone we find over in one big group."

"Do we have to?" Jeremy said, with a thin undercurrent of whine. "Can't we just leave the Stupid in there? They won't know any difference."

"We would. We'd know that they would never feel the sun on their faces or feel the very breath of Mother Nature."

Jeremy gave him a very cool look. "Yes, very good, very clever. I did say that, didn't I." He told the larger group of Stupid to stay where they were and set off to the cube at a brisk walk. "If it were done at all then twere done quickly," he said, breathlessly, when Matthew caught up him. "We need to be in that ship, release the Stupid, get the hell out of there, then open a bottle of something alcoholic and pour ourselves into it."

Matthew watched Jeremy out of the corner of his eye as they made a wide loop around the burnt area where the sphere had been, towards the cube at Speakers' Corner. On the way out, he had been bright, happy and enthusiastic. Now he had reverted to normal – quiet, dour and dismal.

"I wonder why each ship is different from the next," Matthew said, trying for bright and cheerful but achieving telephone answering service.

"Unique is the word you're looking for. Different from the next implies only an even/odd variation, which means only two separate classes or phylum. Unique, on the other hand, means exclusive, solitary or distinct. Unique, from the Latin *unicus*, meaning single or alone."

There was a lot of silence after that as they made their way across the park.

Chapter Thirty-Four
Inside the Cube

Matthew knew that the cube was much bigger than the pyramid, but he had known this like a fact read from a book. *Texas is three times the size of England.* It was only when he was standing at the base of the ramp that he really understood just how big the cube was. Walking into the pyramid had been like walking into a large house. Walking into this would be like walking into St Paul's Cathedral.

Jeremy stopped with one foot on the ramp and looked back at Matthew. "Shall we?"

The ramp was the same slick-yet-sticky surface and the light inside slightly too bright. Everything else was different. The floor had non-slip dimples that only appeared when their feet touched the floor. Doors irised open like camera lenses. The control room was laid out like an old-fashioned classroom before the advent of cooperative learning, with a console looking out over rows of long bench seats.

"No shackles here," Matthew said. "Come to that, why is everything different here? Haven't they heard of economy of scale and modular technology? Everything seems to have been built from scratch."

"Perhaps each ship is a work of art and being different is the whole idea."

Jeremy stood on tiptoes until he could see the top of the horseshoe-shaped console that looked out over the benches. "Maybe no shackles, but there is this." He pulled something down. "I think it's a whip." Jeremy held out what looked like a baseball bat covered in short blue fir. He waved it experimentally a few times. The blue fur glistened as if it were wet.

"It doesn't look much like a whip." Matthew touched the blue fur and an electric shock of pain burnt through his hand. He tried to pull his hand back and the fur ripped at his flesh. "Get it off!"

"Calm down! Let me have a look." Jeremy leaned forward and studied Matthew's finger from a safe distance. "Okay, I see how to fix this. Have you got a tissue?"

"Yes! Why?"

Matthew saw Jeremy's wrist tighten a second before he pulled the bat away and an inch of skin came with it. Matthew dropped to his knees as if shot. Holding his finger in his clenched fist, he rocked back and forward.

"You could have warned me."

"Why? So you could anticipate the pain? There really wasn't any alternative." Jeremy held up the bat in front of his face and blew on the fur, watching the strands part and move. "The tip of each hair must be smaller than glass fibre and it just sinks into flesh. But when you try to pull away there's a barb that rips your skin. If you let the barbs stay in place they probably work their way further in. Just being brushed with this would be like crawling over broken glass."

"It bloody hurts."

"I'm sure it does. It was designed that way to keep the lower orders under control. But we should move on. There are six doors out from here; we'll choose one and see where it takes us."

As Matthew came out from behind the console, the wall behind him moved. He stopped and looked at it closely. It was the same steel grey as all the others, but in places it hung in folds. He reached out and felt coarse fabric. Finding the join between two pieces of the fabric proved to be as difficult as finding the join in any pair of curtains, but he finally located an edge and pulled. Under the fabric there was a bronze-looking plaque as large as a flat screen bought on credit with no deposit. Matthew looked at it for a long time until Jeremy realised he wasn't following.

"What's that?"

Matthew stood to one side so Jeremy could see the plaque. It showed a stylised naked man with his arm held out in a handshake, and touching his hand was the tentacle of a cone. Both the free hand of the man and another tentacle of the cone were up and appeared to be waving at the viewer. Under the image was a block of writing in characters made up of only straight lines.

Jeremy ran one finger over the picture. "It looks like something the old USSR used to put up, showing the strong courageous soviet man hard at work. I expect the text is much along the same lines. *Moving together into a new era of cooperation.* Or something shorter. *New friends tackling new challenges as one.*"

"You think they were working together?"

"They did." Jeremy pointed at the image of a half-constructed cube under the arch of the handshake. The figures around it were very small and Matthew leant forward until he could see cones handing tools to men, and men passing components to cones. "It doesn't matter what technical resources the cones had. You don't want someone building

367

something as complex as this ship under duress. Far too easy for them to overtighten this, or forget to connect that. Much better to have them build it because they thought it was going to be theirs."

"But how could they work with the cones? They must have seen the whip or at least the shackles, and unless every ship was built at the same time then there must have been stories about what happened to the people that built them."

Jeremy looked thoughtful and then smiled. "I think the cones said that they had seen the error of their ways and realised that they were wrong to treat people so badly. Perhaps they said they had turned over a new leaf or opened a fresh page, and that from here on they would work together in mutual support."

"You'd have to be pretty gullible to swallow that story."

"Nearly as gullible as the Stupid who do exactly as they are told." Jeremy looked side-eyes at Matthew. "Perhaps gullible is the wrong word. Would you prefer impressionable, compliant or obedient? The Americans used to have a saying: when you've got them by the balls, their hearts and minds will follow. How much more convenient would it be to just have their minds? You could tell them any half-arsed story and they would still believe it. That's the cones' superpower; the whole thing about low intelligence is just a diversion, or possibly a mistake. Probably they were aiming for nice, obedient slaves that would work with them out of respect. But something went wrong and they got robots."

"That's the most horrible thing I can think of."

"It is, isn't it," Jeremy said, brightly. "You could tell people they were building their own prison and they'd smile and lay another brick. You could ask them to design a single molecule thread, bind thousands of them to a cylinder and then tell them to bare their backs as you whipped them with something they had just made."

"No, sorry, that doesn't make any sense. If they had the absolute control you say they had then the whips and shackles make no sense at all. If you have one you don't need the other."

Jeremy snorted. "Need has nothing to do with it. The cones were just having fun. It was obvious really. Back in the pyramid's control room they shackled people to their chairs but left them sitting in front of a console that could have dropped the ship into a passing sun. And here there are twenty chairs; that's at least twenty people verses one cone with a whip. No one wins those sorts of odds unless you're Steven Segal. The cone should have been battered to a pulp before the ship even left the ground. The whip and shackles were toys just to keep the cones happy. They were sadists beyond anything the poor old Marquis thought of."

Matthew thought about that for a moment and then shook his head. "But torturing a Stupid would be like torturing a side of beef. No matter what they did there'd still be no reaction."

"But you can't deny that the cones were abusing the people here?"

"But I do deny. Because they weren't just ill-treating them, they were basically torturing people they already had absolute control over. That whip is an absurd weapon. Hit somebody with it and even if you don't break any bones then you'd rip their faces off. Chaining people to their desks is just needless humiliation. And what about Cheilith back in the pyramid? They just kept on attacking him long after it made any sense. I think the cones didn't just use people, they hated them so much that they wanted any possible excuse to cause them pain."

"Why? The cones had everything they wanted: servants that would build them a spaceship or sweep up after them."

"I don't know. But I do know that they were monsters. Not the sort you read about in books. All they do is rip off limbs and kill people. The cones were a whole new level of evil that got inside people's heads, into the place where you really live, and made you into someone else, someone that trusted the creatures that would whip and enslave you."

"And suddenly you don't feel so bad about what we did to the cones do you? In fact you'd like to reanimate a few just to kill them again. But you're right; Stalin just killed forty million people, Hitler only thirty million. Only the cones could have ordered each of those people to step up to a mincing machine and stick their heads in."

Matthew looked slowly around the room and suddenly the cold industrial walls seemed haunted by the horrors that must have taken place here. He could almost hear the crack of the whip, see smiling happy faces ripped open – and still the faces smiled. The very walls cried out with pain. The smell of blood was choking.

"Places like this should not exist. When we're done here we need to dynamite each ship, bury every piece and salt the earth so nothing will ever grow here again."

"This unblessed spot will sterile be and bare and look upon the wondering sky with unreproachful stare." Jeremy was very pale and he looked restlessly around as if the walls would reach out and hold him. "We need to get out of here."

The rest of the ship was the similar-yet-different, fairground mirror reflection of the pyramid. The room full of the dead was larger and there was no single mutilated corpse. There were no breathing walls but walls with slit mouths that opened and closed. They brushed past each room with a casual look until they found a room packed shoulder-to-shoulder with empty-faced Stupid. Jeremy ordered them to follow him and he led them out of the ship without pausing.

The air outside the ship seemed almost sweet and Jeremy marched his procession to the group they had brought out from the pyramid, and then the combined group to the shop by the tube station. As shops went, it was more of a kiosk selling papers (weather damaged), crisps and sweets (also weather damaged), but they distributed what there was and left as quickly as possible.

Chapter Thirty-Five
Bowtie Man

Matthew prised the cork from a bottle of champagne and scored a direct hit on the chandelier. He splashed the foaming stream over two glasses and some of it went in the glasses. The champagne was tart, ice-cold and tickled pleasantly as it went down. Matthew toasted world peace and Jeremy replied with, "Gentlemen, start your livers," which made Matthew laugh more than it should. Jeremy raised his glass, only it was empty and so was the bottle. He quickly cured both problems with a fresh bottle while Matthew loaded a CD with thick fingers. All the speakers were still pointing towards the park, but Jeremy fixed this by turned the volume up until the glasses on the table began to rattle in sympathy. They fixed this by keeping their glasses in their hands and moving constantly from bottle to mouth ... and repeat.

Jeremy kept the glasses topped up while he explained how he was going to travel. He laid out a shopping list of countries he would visit. He'd camp out in national parks, busily returning to nature, eat in only the best mouldering five-star restaurants.

Matthew asked him how he planned to reach all those places, and Jeremy waved his glass so enthusiastically that most of its contents spilled out, and said that he'd find a way and then he changed the subject by stumbling towards the kitchen for another bottle. He came back a few minutes later empty-handed.

"You said there were four bottles of champagne in the fridge?"

"Yes."

"No. Not anymore. There's no champagne, vodka or even beer. We've run out of booze."

Matthew sat up and then stood up, the former much easier than the latter. "There must be something. There was loads of stuff a few days ago."

"*Was*, past tense. We forgot the supply part of the consumer cycle. We've drunk everything."

Matthew staggered towards the kitchen, stared owlishly into the fridge and then dropped to his knees and literally poked his head into every cabinet before reluctantly agreeing with Jeremy. "It's all gone." He looked around sadly at the ruin they had made of the kitchen. "I guess it's late. We should go to bed and stock up again in the morning."

"Bed? But we have a magnificent victory to celebrate! We have won the world and we shall drink it dry. There's a posh wine shop just around the corner. We shall sally forth and return with enough booze to toast the apocalypse."

"Well, we could–"

"We shall!"

And Jeremy pulled Matthew to his feet and towards the door.

***

It was cold outside and Matthew instantly regretted not finding a jacket first. The pavement seemed flexible under their feet and directions difficult to maintain. The shop that had been 'just around the corner' turned out to be at the end of a confusing maze of crashed cars and unexpected walls. It was only the glitter of florescent light on broken glass that guided them in. Despite the broken windows, the inside of the shop was nearly untouched. Only a few bottles had been smashed, filling the air with a heady smell, and a young man wearing a bowtie was still standing behind the counter waiting for a last sale.

Matthew gathered up an armful of random bottles while Jeremy found an empty cardboard box and put it on the counter next to Bowtie Man. Matthew added bottles of champagne while Jeremy concentrated on the staple food groups – chocolate bars and crisps. When the box was full, Matthew lifted it and its bottom immediately pulled away, spilling bottles over the counter. While he tried to corral all the bottles back into one group, Jeremy searched for another box.

"Nothing," he said, almost instantly.

"There must be something. Bottles don't come in those plastic rings like cans of beer. What's under the counter?"

Jeremy slipped behind the chrome and glass counter and crouched down low. A moment later, his hand lifted a small wooden box into sight.

"Plenty of these, but too small to be useful. Where the hell do they keep the empty crates around here?"

"Antgtnun!"

Jeremy looked up, startled. "What?"

Matthew pointed back across the room, at Bowtie Man standing above Jeremy. He looked at Matthew and then very slowly turned his head to follow Matthew's pointing finger until he was looking directly up at the assistant's face. His lips were moving slightly like someone talking to themselves. His eyes were in constant motion, looking at everything, over everything without pause. Jeremy stood up and put the width of the counter between them. To Matthew, he said, "Did he say something?" And then to Bowtie Man, "What did you say?"

"Antgtnun!"

"You ain't got none? Is that what you said? But you said something, anything." Jeremy turned back to Matthew. "He's waking up, not normal yet – not even close to normal, but he's changed!" He leaned across the counter and machine-gunned questions at Bowtie Man "How do you feel? Can you tell me your name? Where you are? What year is it?" Jeremy waited expectantly while Bowtie Man's face twitched as if choosing an expression. Then he placed both hands on Jeremy's shoulders, looked him straight in the eyes and pushed, hard.

"Geroufher!"

Jeremy staggered back across the room, never once taking his eyes off Bowtie Man. "But we can help."

Bowtie man came around the counter and Jeremy hurriedly backed through the open door. Matthew followed a second later and the door slammed shut behind them.

"But we have to talk to him, find out how much he's progressed. Simple question-answer response was certainly present. Very restricted vocabulary but that might be a limitation of fine motor control. I'd say his IQ had to be in the high forties."

"He's not the only one." Matthew pointed up the street at a long-haired teenager shambling towards them, across the road at the middle-aged woman rooting through her purse, at the couple very slowly picking up spilled cans.

"They're all coming back to normal!"

"Yes they are. Isn't that strange," Matthew said in a very cool voice.

"Not strange at all, when the power went out in the ships it must have stopped them from pumping out whatever was causing the mental retardation."

Matthew looked slowly around at Jeremy. "I'm sure that's the case."

"We best get back and tell Arvid what we've seen. He can pass the word so everyone knows what to expect. In the morning everyone will be back to normal.

Chapter Thirty-Six
Control

In the morning, nothing had changed.

Matthew leant his head on the window, watching the confused wanderings of the people in the park. From time to time there would be something so normal that his breath would catch in his throat – two people stopping to talk or a man lighting a cigarette, but then the two people would walk past each other or there would be no lighter or no cigarette.

At three in the morning, Jeremy remembered Gretchen and opened her door with a wide smile and a list of simple tests. The smile vanished when he realised that the room was empty. While they had been out she had simply walked away.

The sun came up at six, and at half past they walked around the block. At eight, they did the same again and as much as they tried, there was still no sign of normality.

Matthew clicked the microphone off. "Arvid says that nothing has changed. He's not even seen the fractional improvement we have here. No one else has seen anything either. Things only seem to be different around here." Matthew replaced the microphone in its charger and very slowly looked round at Jeremy. "What did you find in the pyramid, Jeremy? What did you do?"

"But I ..."

"But you were very keen to get into the pyramid. Positively enthusiastic to go off on your own. When you finally came out I thought you were disappointed because you hadn't found the people they took. But you found something and, more importantly, you did something. What did you find?"

Jeremy pulled his mouth into a sulky smile. "There was a room on one of the lower levels. It was full of dead panels, just like the control room. But there was just one control still lit up. I twiddled with it a few times but it didn't do anything."

"You *twiddled* with it?"

"Yes, but it didn't do anything. It looked broken."

"And you never thought to mention this?"

"It didn't do anything. I only tried it because I thought if I could fly the ship then it would help us to rebuild things."

"Got it! You wanted to be the first person on the planet with their own spaceship. Perhaps the only person. But why the pyramid? Why were you so keen to look there?"

Jeremy's sulky smile became a real smile. "Isn't it obvious? There was something special about the pyramid from the start. It only landed when the cones seemed unhappy about what they found here. Arvid said that shape had been seen all over the world, so it was the only design they used more than once. The other ships could hold thousands of people but the pyramid only a few. So it wasn't just a bulk transport. My guess was that it was some sort of local control centre and it was only brought down to supervise operations. And if you're looking for something to control, then a control centre is the best place to start looking. But those were the subtle clues. Everyone, the whole planet, missed the big personalised message we were given." He looked expectantly at Matthew and then rolled his eyes. "What did Cheilith say to us before he so inconveniently died?"

"He said, 'Avenge us.'"

"But before that he said part of a word. He said, 'Pyr.' Now, he might have said 'Pyre' or 'Pyrite', but none of those make sense when combined with 'avenge us'. But pyramid does. In fact, it changes a desperate plea into an instruction – 'Pyramid to avenge us.' I thought he was just telling us that the pyramids were special. I didn't realise just how special."

"Isn't avenge an odd choice of word? You avenge someone by fighting and that makes the pyramid some sort of weapon."

"Except, there's no one left to fight! The cones are all dead. We won, remember? Cheilith just didn't have a very good grasp of English, that's all."

"I guess so. But it looks like whatever you did in the pyramid made people more normal. So we're going to have to go back and–"

"Yes, I got it. We should tell Arvid what we are doing, just in case we don't get back."

"Good idea."

***

The corridors of the pyramid still glowed with the same disquieting light that made them screw their eyes up. Matthew wondered just how long the power source would last. A year? Tens of years? Or would the corridors still be glowing when man was a discarded experiment of evolution?

Jeremy swept through the control room without slowing down. One corridor sloped down so gradually that it was only the angle of door and floor that said they were moving into a lower level of the ship. Jeremy didn't open any of the doors they passed.

"How will you know which room you went in before?"

Jeremy looked back towards Matthew. "You'll know it when you see it." He turned a corner, stopped and moved to one side to let Matthew see what was in front of them. "And this is it!"

In front of them a door buzzed like an angry insect as it opened and closed on the object holding it open.

"It's the one with the dead cone wedged in the door."

A cone lay on its side with its head inside the room. The base of the cone, the part they were looking directly at, had been ripped open, showing tough, leathery-looking muscles oozing blue blood. Matthew followed the pool of blood in front of the cones down towards them and stepped quickly to one side.

"As soon as I saw this I thought it had to be special." Jeremy edged up the side of the corridor and tapped the cone with a toe. "Whoever this guy was he wanted to be in this room in a hurry. That meant it was somewhere important."

"How come this is here at all? We've seen blood, but no bodies before. I thought the Stupid carried them all away."

Jeremy grinned, showing too many stained teeth. "And that is exactly the question I asked myself when I saw this. Why was just this one left behind?" He leant against the wall and tapped the cone again.

Matthew waited for him to continue and waited some more. When he realised that this was just another of Jeremy's little games he looked at the cone, at the door holding it in place and finally around the door. "There's no strip around the door to open it. The Stupid could open any of the other doors just by brushing against them. But here there was no way to open the door to get at the cone."

"And that is the right answer! No strip around the door, but there are these." Jeremy pointed at five small squares above the door. "I think these are the same sort of thing as the strip we've seen everywhere else. But I tried one and the door didn't open. There seems to be an equal amount of smudges around all five, so I think you have to touch all of them at the same time to open the door. A cone could just use some of its tentacles and it would be in, but a human would need at least two friends to do the same thing. And I think humans hanging around here would be noticed. It's not much of a security system, but that's not what it's for. If you wanted somewhere that a cone could get into in a hurry, but would hold back humans for just a few minutes then it's ideal."

"What's inside?"

Jeremy bent low from the waist and brought his arm around in an exaggerated wave towards the door. "After you."

Matthew looked from Jeremy to cone and back again. He stepped around the threads of cone blood, looked at Jeremy, who smiled blankly, and put one foot on the cone and stood up. It felt solid and yet yielding, like standing on a car tyre. The corpse shifted a little and Matthew had a moment of absolute conviction that the cone's tough skin would split open and swallow him whole. He shuffled further onto the corpse until he could jump down inside.

The room inside was the size of a toilet cubicle, only not as crowded. The walls were covered with empty picture frames, with just one, on the wall opposite the door, half-filled with a softly glowing egg shape. Below the frame was a dinner-plate sized wheel with stepped edges, like a cog wheel for a watch the size of a swimming pool. Matthew looked each wall up and down slowly. All the other frames were dead and empty. The egg shape glowed pinkish in the centre and was covered in dark blotches. There was nothing else.

Jeremy clambered over the corpse of the cone with a noise like walking on a leather sofa. "You see? There's just one display and that looks like it's broken. The screen's all messed up."

Matthew looked at the dark blotches on the screen. A dark oval halfway up on the left matched with a symmetrical partner on the right. In the centre of the screen an upwards-pointing, thin triangle hung above a jagged curve like a picket fence built across the bottom of a valley.

Matthew looked at the screen closely, from a distance, then screwed up his eyes until all he could see was a vague blur. "It's a face." He ran his finger around the edge of the egg shape, touched both ovals, the triangle and finally traced the curve at the bottom of the screen. "You see? Eyes, nose, mouth and skull."

"And the skull is only pink in the centre. In fact I'd say only forty percent of it is pink right now, and isn't it a big coincidence that Bowtie Man in the shop last night had an IQ around forty points? But only after I moved that wheel."

"What did the display look like before you changed anything?"

"I don't know? The pink might have been a bit smaller? I was in a bit of a hurry. But it did change and suddenly everyone is a little smarter, and that makes sense. The cones weren't taking the Stupid for what they were, but what they could be. They get everyone nice and dumb, scoop them up and keep them for a while until there're sure they are really domesticated. Then, little by little, they turn up the volume control on their intelligence until they make good servants. And all the time someone in this room watches them very carefully for any sign of discord. At the first sign of anyone believing in outmoded concepts, like free-will, liberty and the pursuit of happiness, that dial gets turned right down and they spend more time being housebroken."

"Discord? The Stupid are nice and docile unless you tell them not to be."

"Bowtie Man wasn't very docile, was he? And isn't that strange because, according to that plaque, the people that built this ship were very obedient at a much higher IQ. But Bowtie Man had only been dumb for a few days. Perhaps after a few months like that he'd be malleable at any IQ. And then everything that has happened looks a lot like the cones' business model. They get everyone nice and dumb, so not only are they defenceless but ready to be housebroken until they are really useful. Only, this time, Cheilith cut them off at the knees when all the other slaves killed themselves. Then he kicked them in the head by making everyone obedient so we could use them as a weapon." Jeremy smiled ruefully, like a man who had seen the puddle only after stepping in it. "And if I'd been less interested in giving glib answers we'd have known that. When we first met I said that it was an accident that Wernicke's area of the brain, the part that listens to commands, was still active, which sounds completely plausible, except that was also my explanation for why the dorsolateral cortex was suppressed first, turning everyone into maniacs. That's either a lot of accidents or part of a design. This room shows us that the cones had the ability to selectively control intelligence, then you only have to go another half step, add a little fine tuning, and then we have everything we've seen. They supress the cortex so we're too busy wondering what's going on to see what's going on. Then they damp down overall brain activity and they have dumb, defenceless sheep they can hoover up. And only then can they start the long, slow process of getting us housetrained by reducing the suppression on the language areas, and their commands are the voice of God."

Matthew wiped his hand where it had touched the cogwheel, as if suddenly aware that he had touched something soaked in blood and tears. "I guess that makes sense, but you have to ask yourself if it was worth all the effort. The cones must have lived on their nerves, all the time watching for the moment their slaves would rise up against them, sleeping with one eye open, waiting for the sudden noise in the night."

"Oh, I don't think the cones were losing much sleep over their chattels. In fact, I think they were quite comfortable, thank you very much. Maybe too comfortable because our friend here was not watching all these screens; he was outside having the equivalent of a cigarette or maybe chatting up the nice young blonde in the typing pool. If the cones had the slightest idea there was any possible threat then there'd be a room the size of the Albert Hall with a hundred cones watching monitors. What happened here must have been as much a surprise as a TV remote suddenly demanding equal rights."

"So all we have to do is just turn the cogwheel until the pink fills the skull shape and suddenly everybody is back to normal?"

"Either it changes nothing, and we had a free unguided tour inside one of their ships, or it changes everything and we get a university named after us. The Jeremy Eaton Institute of Advanced Learning. I like the sound of that."

"Before we get too excited, isn't all of this terribly convenient? The cones are dead, nothing else has power, and yet here they went to a lot of trouble to keep something alive that positively screams, 'Here is the magic control. Turn this and everybody lives happily ever after.' Unless of course this is a very elaborate piece of cheese designed to be found by any unruly slaves, and the moment they touch this wheel it gets very hot in here, like thousands of degrees hot."

"I moved the wheel and lived to talk about it."

"But you only moved it a little. Turning it all the way and making everyone normal certainly isn't part of normal business."

Jeremy looked at the cogwheel and back to Matthew, who was looking at Jeremy and back to the cogwheel.

"We should do it now."

"Yes, time is of the essence."

Jeremy touched the cogwheel and pulled his hand away quickly. "We have a duty of care to all the people outside."

"Thousands of people. Maybe millions of people."

It got very quiet in the room. Matthew could hear the blood singing in his ears and Jeremy's footsteps as he backed away from the display.

"We should do this together. One for all and all that crap."

Jeremy's hand was shaking like a leaf. Matthew reached out and guided it to the cogwheel. Jeremy tried for a smile and missed.

"When they make a film out of this I want to be played by Brad Pitt."

"You should be so lucky. I hear they're going to do you in CGI like Gollum from *Lord of the Rings*."

And together they turned the cogwheel.

It moved like pulling a spoon through treacle. Just a quarter turn made their arms ache, but the display's pink glow filled more than half the skull shape now. A drop of sweat ran down Jeremy's forehead, down the length of his nose and splashed on the floor. Matthew leaned into the wheel, letting his body weight pull it and another drop of sweat hit the floor. By the time they had completed a full turn, their faces were as wet as swimmers and the floor was slick and hard to push against. The skull shape now was nearly all pink now. There was only a paper-thin gap left to fill.

"Nearly there," Matthew said.

"Easy stuff," Jeremy said, but he had to pause for breath between words.

"Last turn."

They both pulled at the cogwheel and pink completely filled the skull.

"So that's it?" said Matthew. "Now we just pop outside and everyone is normal again?"

"I guess so. I moved it a bit and things improved a little, so moving it a lot–"

The screen flashed white and a piercing whistle drowned out Jeremy's voice. He recoiled away from the cogwheel as if electrocuted and sprawled over the cone's corpse with a wet slapping sound. Matthew reacted just a second later, tripped over Jeremy's feet and fell on top of him. Jeremy pushed Matthew off him and sat upright with his hands in front of his face, turning them back and forth, examining every inch of flesh as if expecting to see it rot and decay, exposing dull, white bone.

Matthew checked his own hands, arms and face, found them normal and then looked past his hands and saw the wall. The picture frame that had been half-filled with a skull shape now contained a much bigger outline of a skull. But in the centre of the screen was still the original skull, now completely filled with pink. He grabbed Jeremy's arm and held it until he looked up from his obsessive examination of his hands. "Look," he said, and pointed at the screen.

"It's bigger," Jeremy said. "No, the original skull image is still there with its eyes, mouth, et cetera, but now there's a bigger skull around it."

He stood up very slowly and stood very close to, but not touching, the new image and then turned to Matthew with a very strange smile. "So if the original image was a representation of a normal IQ, then the new larger image shows a better than normal IQ. They can damp down intelligence or turn it up on demand. The screen pyrotechnics and the sound effects were just to let whoever should be in this room know that they were about to boost intelligence."

"That doesn't make any sense. They reduce IQ and then increase it? Wouldn't that be like mugging someone and then giving them twice their money back?"

"It doesn't make any sense unless you think about how they built their ships."

"We know how they built their ships. We saw how they built their ships. They lied to the people they took."

"Okay, you're people, so if I asked you to make something simple, say one of these doors, you'd be able to do it? There must be something around here like a machine shop, we'll find it and off you go."

"What does that prove? That I still remember Mr Stamp and Thursday afternoon's Applied Technology? But if the plans are in English, I'll give it a go."

"Sorry! No plans. Everything here has been designed from scratch. So before you can start building tab A and slot B, you have to plan, model and test what you are about to build."

"Nobody could do that on their own; you'd have to be a bloody genius–" Matthew swallowed the rest of his words.

"Which isn't a problem if you can grow your own geniuses. It probably makes them bleed out through their ears after a while, but I doubt if the cones were too worried about that. When the cones wanted another ship all they had to do is take a handful of their most domesticated slaves away from general population, feed them some lies, *achieving progress together*, and then boost their IQs so they can build a vessel worthy enough to spread peace and happiness across the galaxy. The slaves build something different each time, because for them it's the only time. And when it's finished, any survivors whose heads haven't exploded get their IQ knocked right back down and installed as just another part of the ship."

"It's a good idea. It's a horrible idea. Suddenly there's no need to spend years learning about thrust ratios and payload weight; all they have to do is ask their good friends to do it for them."

"They were the ultimate lotus eaters, although the Bible said it best. They spin not neither do they toil. I wonder if we'll ever find out their backstory. Because once they probably went out into space with the best of intentions, but then they met their first humans and realised that some party trick of technology gave them the ability to manipulate IQ, and then, like Ernest Tubb said, that's all she wrote. All their striving to grow and develop stopped right there. And year after year they grew a little more stupid until they couldn't see what was happening right under their noses and wound up being ripped apart by the very people they enslaved."

"You almost sound sorry for them."

"Call me old fashioned, but I think it's possible to believe in two things at the same time. One of them is that the cones were a level of evil that would have made Hitler vomit. The other is that once the cones were probably just like us, but they were offered the ultimate temptation. They could have everything they wanted just as long as they didn't worry about who they had to tread on to get it. Do you really think we'd have done any better?"

"I wouldn't worry too much about the cones when you realise that their plans for us were to die along with them. This console still working makes sense now. They hated their slaves; they hated us because we had the possibility to be better than them. We had something they never could and if they died, they wanted all their slaves to stay at their posts until they starved to death."

Jeremy nodded solemnly. "You're right. They wanted everyone to go down with their ship. We should get out of here and see the world made new."

He left the room without looking back. But first he kicked the corpse of the cone as hard as possible.

***

The world outside the ship looked much as it had before: Individuals wandered aimlessly across Hyde Park's ankle-deep lawns; small groups sheltered from the chill wind behind trees and bushes. From the top of the ramp, they looked around for any sign of change and were still looking when they reached the bottom.

"Perhaps it takes some time for things to return to normal," Matthew said, hopefully. He stepped in the path of a middle-aged man wearing the remains of a smart suit and waved a hand in front of his eyes. He recoiled a little and then carried on walking. "No obvious change. We should get back to the apartment and tell Arvid what we've found. Maybe the other pyramids need to make the same change." He turned away just as the businessman reached out and grabbed his arm.

"You, where am I ...? I was in a meeting ... I'm very hungry. Food, I need some food." His voice was hoarse, little more than a whisper. But his eyes were alert and intelligent.

Matthew prised his fingers away and looked out across the park. Heads were turning in their direction. There was the low murmur of conversation.

Matthew turned to Jeremy. "We've won!"

Chapter Thirty-Seven
Pity

Matthew threw another stone at the empty beer can before the tide pulled it further from shore. The stone missed, but the brief splash of white foam against the leaden sea was closer than anything he'd achieved all morning and he rewarded himself with another long drink from the bottle of vodka. One drink became two, became the whole bottle. He threw the empty in the air and watched it smash on the rocks next to him then reached for another stone and stabbed the tip of his finger on something sharp. He lifted his hand with the exaggerated care of the very drunk and studied the shard of glass that protruded like a talon from his finger. He pulled it out and watched the blood drip slowly down his hand and then watched as the flesh zipped itself back together until there was only a thin white line where it had been. After a moment, even that was gone.

He found another stone, but the can had already been taken by the tide and was only a distant point of colour. He threw the stone anyway.

He reached up and down with both arms, as if trying to draw a rock angel on the beach, but he had already finished the six-pack and both bottles. Briefly, he considered returning for more supplies, but the distance between beach and mansion seemed more than just physical. He looked up and down the rock-littered strip of beach, made sure it was empty, and said very quietly, "Maybe this time."

He snuggled back against the rock and focused on the place where the sea joined with a greyscale sky. He breathed slowly and deeply in time with the white hiss of the tide, letting it pull his essence away from the crude meat of his body with only a fraying umbilical cord holding him back. The world fell away and he floated in the rhythm of the sea. All there could be was the sound of the tide drawing him further away, stretching the cord holding him prisoner to the thinnest thread. One breath would break it and he could fade away, like a single drop of ink in a great dark ocean, leaving his body behind until bone fused with rock and he was no more aware of the sun or the rain than the seagulls that wheeled and clawed above the beach.

"Hello? Matthew? Hello?"

And with no transition at all, he was back on the beach, bound into his prison of flesh.

"Yoo-hoo, Matthew!"

And even if he hadn't recognised the voice, there was only one person on the island that would use such an old-fashioned expression.

Matthew stuck his hand above the shelter of the rock and waved, and then reluctantly sat up and looked around. Jeremy waved back and changed direction towards him. He was wearing a T-shirt in an eye-hurting shade of yellow and a pair of jeans so old and battered-looking that they had to be brand new. But at least he was wearing something other than the dirty dressing gown he had been wearing for weeks. Matthew had tried to talk to him about it, and he had smiled and nodded – and carried on smiling and nodding long after Matthew had gone.

Jeremy walked oddly across the shifting pebbles of the beach, using only one arm for balance. Matthew wondered if he had hurt the other one doing something athletic – like opening another bottle.

"Hi! Been looking for you everywhere. Mind if I sit down?" He did anyway, narrowly avoiding the points of broken glass. "I've had an idea."

"I guessed there was something."

"Every night we sit around, talk about the old days and drink ourselves to a standstill. But we do that every night, every single night, so I thought how about something new!"

"It's worked so far."

"Yes! But it's time to move on, shake things up a bit. So I thought we could have a parade! Nothing fancy, just take the canvas top off the jeep – no one uses it anyway – and drive slowly down Main Street. Turn the radio up loud while people throw confetti. It wouldn't be much, but just for a little while we could pretend it was Oxford Street again and that thousands of people were calling our names while jet fighters did low passes. We could be 'The Men That Saved The World' again, even if only for a little time."

Matthew smiled like he meant it. "That's an excellent idea."

Jeremy sat back and smiled. "There's only one small snag. Who would cheer and throw the confetti?" Jeremy stopped smiling. "Everyone here is 'The Men, Or Women, That Saved The World'. We all had the parades down Sixth Avenue, Tiananmen Square or Via dei Fori Imperiali. We've got the medals and statues to prove it. So do we take it in turns? So many a night ride in the jeep? Of course our benefactors would be only too happy to make something to throw the confetti for us. In fact I'm sure they'd jump at the chance to repeat the original parades. We could have a World Salvation Day every month." Jeremy dropped his eyes and scratched at his left arm, the arm he had been so conspicuously not using as he walked across the beach.

"Never mind; it was a good idea," Matthew said, kindly.

"I just thought it would be nice to have people looking up to us for a change." Jeremy brought his left arm across his body to continue scratching it. Matthew guessed that he was meant to ask if there was something wrong with it, but instead of Jeremy's mind games, he said, "But they do admire us. They love us and they would do anything for us."

Jeremy opened his mouth to say something, but a low foghorn note took his words away. Matthew stood up and helped Jeremy to his feet. "There you are!" he said, brightly. "Proof of just how much they love us. We'll go along, see what's new and then have a party."

"A party. Just for a change," Jeremy said, flatly.

The island was very flat and as soon as they moved off the beach, the box shapes of the village rose up against the sky. Every mansion there had been designed exactly to the wishes of its owner. Matthew had been drunk when they asked him what he wanted and he had vaguely asked for something out of a Hollywood movie, the good ones of the forties and fifties. The result had twelve bedrooms, fourteen bathrooms, wide-sweeping staircases to all ten floors and a ballroom that could hold a hundred people without being crowded. And the outside of every mansion was an identical box-shape no bigger than a shipping container. To begin with, it had all been very funny and for a while the standard conversational opening had been "My God! It's bigger on the inside." Some places had witty name plates outside. *Welcome to TARDIS house* or *It's bigger than it looks* or even *It's a transistorised mansion.* But then people started to worry about where all those rooms really were, and how a single-storey building could have a view from two hundred feet up and what happened if the power went out. Their benefactors apologised for the inconvenience of such compressed accommodation and said that it was necessary to get so many people on such a small island. But if they wished to join them on Oclao-Two or Vaunov-Prime then they could have ten acres of prime beach-front property with stunning views of the dual sunset. No one took them up on their offer and most moved into a ground-floor room close to an exit. Matthew had been living in the entrance hall of his twelve-bedroom, fourteen-bathroom mansion for the last month.

The centrepiece of the village was an open square with benches surrounding a statue of a child on its knees with one hand raised for help. The message on the pedestal, in six-inch-high letters, was: *We owe you a debt that can never be repaid.* After the statue had been in place for just a month someone had painted *Stick this where the sun doesn't shine* on it in green paint. No one asked why

Matthew wore gloves for the next week. No one had to. Everyone knew.

The square was more crowded than it had been for a long time. Faces he'd almost forgotten waved hello as they made their way closer to the centre. The low murmur of voices ebbed and flowed like the tide. Matthew thought some of those conversations were particularly interesting.

The low foghorn note came again and the crowd fell silent. "That's our one-minute warning," Jeremy said. "Bet you it arrives from the south."

"It's going to be the north this time," Matthew said, confidently. "And besides which, you still owe me three gold bars."

Jeremy ignored this by checking in all directions, starting with away from Matthew. A minute later, they realised that they had both been wrong when all heads turned to the west.

The transport was a sky-blue disk the size of a Frisbee and it moved in eerie silence a hundred feet above them. It stopped in the exact centre of the square. For a moment, it looked like a child's toy suspended on a line, then it unfolded as if the disk had been only a placeholder for something much larger stored in another dimension.

The transport grew downwards like a developing picture of the 2001 monolith. There was a puff of displaced air as it reached the ground and then, in a change to the usual programming, a set of stairs unfolded.

Actually sending someone to talk to them was something that had never happened before. That they were doing it now sent a ripple of excitement through the crowd. Matthew guessed at an emissary with a new and exciting offer for them.

The man that came down the stairs looked both vaguely familiar and yet a complete stranger. Matthew guessed that their Netflix, email and Facebook accounts had been minutely examined for clues to their ideal authority figure. The emissary's eyes were Daniel Craig's cool blue, the cheekbones almost certainly Benedict Cumberbatch's, but the hairstyle was definitely late-career Bruce Willis. He was bald.

Matthew looked along the rows of faces watching in interest and it occurred to him that either a lot of people shared his taste in films or everybody was seeing something different.

The emissary paused at the last step and then stepped down to the ground with the same sort of expression Matthew thought Neil Armstrong must have had when he stepped onto the surface of the moon. He looked around the wall of faces watching him and smiled with too many teeth.

"Thank you for the privilege of being here today." The emissary's voice was low and pleasant, but it carried as if small speakers were spread through his audience. "My name is Jason, and this is the high point of my career and a moment that I shall remember forever. A million people entered the ballot to stand here, and when my name was selected I knew there could be no higher honour."

"Get on with it!" The yell came from behind Matthew and was accompanied with laughter.

"Of course. As you must have guessed, today is a special occasion. A short period ago our scouts found the home world of the cones." The ship was suddenly hidden by an IMAX-sized screen showing a satellite view of a planet that could have been Earth. Except the clouds were pale pink and the ground orange. Matthew looked sideways at the rapt faces apparently watching the edge of the screen and decided that everybody was indeed seeing something different.

"The planet was in chaos after their fleet failed to return. The whole basis of their society seemed to be the slaves that ran everything, and as far as we could see they all died at the same times as the martyrs on the ships. There was widespread starvation and some sort of civil war was in progress. They had tried to own not just our bodies but our minds, and this was our response."

The picture changed to a distant view of the planet and the edge of a bright yellow sun. A spark fell into the glare and the sun instantly collapsed into a needlepoint of light. A low murmur ran through the crowd, but only for a second before the sun exploded, filling the whole screen with mottled yellow.

Click.

The viewpoint pulled back until the exploding sun was just a yellow dot. The dot became a ball that reached out with angry plumes past the edge of the screen.

Click.

The viewpoint pulled back again, centred on a spreading cloud of light.

"And that, as they say, was that. Their planet is not even a cinder now; at best it's a cloud of elementary particles. In a thousand years you'll be able to see the supernova we created during the day, but we have already named it the Redemption Nova in your honour." He paused for a beat, as if expecting applause, then quickly carried on when there was none. "Of course there is always the possibility they had outposts on other planets and we promise you that we will search every planet in every solar system for the cones. And if we find them we will exterminate them." The emissary didn't sound pleasant anymore. He didn't even sound human.

A much close voice shouted, "There are hundreds of billions of planets in our galaxy alone. Are you really going to search all of them?"

Matthew thought the voice sounded familiar and then realised that it had been his.

The emissary showed even more teeth.

"And that is an excellent and perfectly timed question, sir."

The IMAX screen cleared and showed a dot heading towards a cartoon solar system. Little lightning bolts reached out from the dot to each planet. Then the smallest planet came apart into more dots that reached out to more solar systems that made more dots until the screen was nothing but swarming dots.

"This is our Punition Probe that we released today. It is already searching the nearest surviving solar system to the cones' home world and then it will disassemble the smallest planet there to make more probes that will enter more solar systems in a wave of exponential growth that will reach the limits of our galaxy."

The screen vanished and the emissary was holding a long tray in front of him.

"To commemorate this historic moment we have minted a special, solid gold medal showing a symbolic hand reaching out, as each of your hands reached out to the control that saved us all. And now, if you'd like to come forward in alphabetical order, it would be my singular honour to present each of you with your personised medal."

There was an awkward silence as nobody moved, and if the emissary's smile slipped at all it was only fractionally.

"Of course I understand that you will want to hold your own private ceremony, and I will leave these here for your later use." The emissary placed the tray on the ground, which is exactly where Matthew expected it would remain until somebody threw it in the sea. "And as part of your celebrations on this momentous occasion, please accept this gift." He gestured to his left, at a truck-sized block being extruded from the monolith. "The very last vintage Bollinger champagne in the world."

The crowd had begun to murmur at 'vintage' and everything after 'champagne' was lost in the wild cheers and whoops as the crowd flowed around the block like ants to sugar. The emissary's smile certainly slipped now. Matthew could actually see muscles twitching as he fought to stop it disappearing at all.

The monolith produced a much smaller case that made the emissary's smile reappear.

"We have also provided a few mementos of our explorations so that you can feel part of our great adventure: jewels from Apator that sing when you touch them, sand from Nedril that glows with a cold fire when you hold it and, most beautiful of all, a plant from Sorson that releases fist-sized crystal spores that shower coloured threads."

Matthew guessed that the case of mementos would remain untouched only slightly longer than the case of medals. And only because it would be more difficult to get rid of.

"But our invitation is always open. Come with us, be part of something amazing. Be the first man to set foot on strange new worlds. There are settlements on a thousand worlds and any of them would be proud to have you amongst them. You could live on Xiater where the gravity is so low that you can fly or Chonoe where triple suns eclipse each other at midday."

The emissary smiled hopefully at his audience, except they were busily unloading the truck-sized block of champagne.

"Well, thank you for your time and I hope that one day we can work together and carry forward the memory of this special day." He raised his hand in a half-hearted wave and turned to climb back up the stairs. But, just for a second, he looked back and Matthew saw the expression he had been waiting for.

Pity.

There had been a lot of pity since they saved the world. To begin with everything had been wonderful. Every day had been a whirl of interviews, photoshoots and meetings with people they had only seen in the papers. Books were ghost-written and docudramas hastily rushed into production. But all the time the pyramids were waiting all over the world and people started to think about what they represented. They chose a pyramid way up at the top of Canada, and a twenty-year naval man named Gabriel volunteered to turn the cog tooth wheel just the slightest amount; the average intelligence for a few thousand people became 110. And then they waited. Nobody bled out through their ears; people were just a little smarter. Then Gabriel turned the wheel some more, and then all the way to its end and the average intelligence around the pyramid was 160. There was a pause for evaluation before the same change was made to every pyramid around the world and the average IQ for everyone was 160. Except for the few that had been immune when the cones first arrived. They told themselves that it wasn't too bad being only 60% as smart as everyone else. They didn't really feel too marginalised. It wasn't too often that people talked down to them. It was okay. They could manage. Then someone whose IQ had already been 160, and was now close to 300, took one of the pyramids apart very carefully and said that the technology was childishly simple and made something that boosted the average to 200. A week later, Zheng Thàm in China made that 250. For a while, there was an arms race. 'We cannot allow our country to be disadvantaged.' 'There must be no IQ gap.' The average IQ increased a hundred points every month. And then every week.

Language was the first thing to change. English became a hyper-evolved syntactical nightmare that drew in elements of Mandarin, Pashto and Esperanto. But it didn't matter that none of the survivors could understand it. Everyone was so accommodating and switched back to Old English while they were around. And there was always someone around to read signs for them. They didn't go out much after that, but it was impossible to watch TV because there was no TV. There was a device that might have had an iPhone as a distant ancestor. It could access any programme ever made, but it was operated by hand gestures that made Balinese dance look simple. The next-to-last straw was when the cars went away. Literally overnight, cars were replaced by slim archways with a keypad that allowed you to step through to any other arch. Only, the keypad had 164 keys, none of them English. But there was always someone to enter their destination for them – and offer to hold their hand as they stepped through. The very-last-straw was when each archway acquired a second keypad, in bright primary colours with cartoonish pictures showing where an immune might want to go.

The survivors spent a lot of time together after that. First via the internet and then in a graceful, hundred-storey tower that the Enhanced Men grew for them using tiny machines that manipulated individual molecules. The top floor had stunning views over the city, but it was still a city that changed radically every day and to set foot outside was to invite offers of help.

Matthew first heard of Eriskay Island from the introduction to an old black and white film that he found on the TV by accident. The same way he found everything on TV in fact. Seen through a fog of alcohol, Matthew was only vaguely aware that the film had something to do with a wrecked ship and whiskey, but it was in English and he settled down to drink himself into unconsciousness. Then one of the characters said how remote the island was, how used they were to governing themselves, and Matthew stopped drinking and starting thinking. He tried the idea out on a few friends, who liked it so much that they told their friends, until everyone in the graceful, hundred-storey tower wanted the same thing.

Matthew presented the idea to the Enhanced Men, using carefully rehearsed phrases – community cohesion, common vision and positive dynamic relationships. At first they were confused, but once they reluctantly agreed that it would be possible to let the saviours of the human race have their own territory, they suggested a beautiful tropical island with bathtub-temperature sea. Eriskay Island was a three-mile wide, two-mile long strip of metamorphic rock two hundred miles north of Glasgow, where the temperature was sometimes cold and the rest of the time cold and wet.

Matthew considered their offer of pure white sand, crystal-clear waters and hot sultry nights – and rejected it. He recognised it as a bargaining chip and knew that if he played along, 'beautiful tropical island' would become 'an island' and finally 'graceful hundred-storey tower'. In the end, the Enhanced Men made a great show out of dedicating the island to the survivors, grew each of them a mansion using their tiny machines and then reluctantly left them alone.

The few days were wonderful. Nobody talked down to them. There was TV they could actually operate. They even had cars. Jeremy said that this was their chance to enjoy themselves and be who they wanted to be. But as the days passed, they realised that they were 'The Men That Had Saved

The World' and that job was over. Their moment had passed and so had their chance to be relevant. They had no role in the new world, no useful purpose other than to exist. The books they never had the time to read turned out to be the books that were painful reminders of the world they had lost. Watching TV was even worse. But the cars were great! Absolutely amazing ... for the first few times that they drove them up and down Eriskay's five miles of road; after that it got a bit boring, but that was okay. They could manage.

They realised that they had a choice. They could either re-join the world and be treated like Gods – but simple-minded, very stupid Gods – or stay and feel like spare parts for an obsolete machine. While they decided, they began to drink. First just in the evenings and then at lunchtimes that so easily merged with evenings. Every day was a party where they could toast the world they had lost, drink until they almost couldn't remember what life had been like. And every night they went home alone. Even their parties were just people just sitting around drinking. There was no slow dancing, or any dancing at all, because there was always that sense of being watched.

Outside, there were birds in the sky never seen before in nature. Inside, ordinary objects would catch the light, as if cameras the size of a human hair were recording in full HD. Jeremy said that their benefactors were either watching them to make sure they were safe or they were starring in their own reality show.

And in tonight's episode of Let's Laugh at the Stupid People, *Matthew starts thinking about some*

406

hoochie smoochie action with the hot blond from Spain. So prepare for hilarity when the trousers come off!

But that was okay; they could manage. Sometimes people got a bit down, depressed even, but that just meant it was time for another party. They were having the time of their lives.

Every month, the shuttle delivered anything they wanted. Gold bars? People built walls with them. Precious jewels were as common as grit. But the shuttle also delivered only the best food. There was no need to dig, plant, weed and cultivate a vegetable plot to produce a wizened carrot when the shuttle delivered beautifully presented meals that would have made a cordon bleu chef throw his knives away.

They had reached the end of the rainbow and as long as the shuttle brought enough booze, they could manage.

At least this time the shuttle had brought something new and Matthew managed to secure two bottles of champagne before the locusts had stripped the container bare. On his way back to his compressed mansion, he decided on a plan for tonight. He would drink both bottles and then start on the vodka until he passed out. It was a simple plan, but it had worked every night so far.

Jeremy was waiting for him at his front door and Matthew thought he managed a very credible smile. "Hi! How's it going?" he said, although he already suspected the answer.

"Could I have a word?"

"Have several! Come in."

The entrance hall to Matthew's mansion was a fifteen- by sixty-foot room with high stone walls, solemn portraits, and a mansion's worth of furniture had been packed into it. Paths that had been clear, but were now strewn with discarded clothes, had been left between antique desks, tables and chairs that were too crowded to actually use. His bedroom was a bed-space, an opening between wardrobes that he couldn't open with a mattress on the floor and a thick blanket of yet more clothes. There was a toilet on the ground floor, but no shower. But there were always plenty of wet wipes.

"Take a seat. Tell me what's bothering you."

Jeremy shifted clothes until he had excavated an overstuffed easy chair, sat down and held out his left arm, the one he'd been so conspicuously scratching on the beach. "It's my arm."

Matthew examined it carefully. "Yes, yes it is. Have you hurt it or something? Looks okay to me."

"But that's just the point. Last night I was making myself a sandwich and cut myself here." He used a finger to slash a line across his wrist. "I suppose I should have contacted someone, but I'd had a few drinks and taken some headache tablets so I wasn't thinking too straight and just went to bed."

"How many tablets?"

Jeremy looked at Matthew under his eyes. "A few, maybe more than a few. But the thing, the important thing, is that this morning I woke up and my wrist was fine. The sheets were a mess, but there wasn't a mark on my wrist."

Matthew nodded thoughtfully. "Well isn't that strange. Because just this morning I cut my finger on some glass and the cut just healed up while I watched."

"The sea air is making us heal quickly?"

"Jeremy, Jeremy, Jeremy, you used to be so smart! What happened to you?" Matthew tapped his fingers thoughtfully. "Let me put it this way. How much have you had to drink today?"

"What's that got to do with anything? I might have had a small drink before I came out, but that's not significant."

"Small drink!" Matthew snorted. "By now you're probably putting vodka on your cornflakes. You should try it with muesli; it makes it taste less like cat litter. So how much have you really had to drink today?"

"A bottle."

"Of vodka?"

Jeremy nodded.

"That's pretty much what I expected. But try to remember those far-off days before we saved the world. If you'd drunk a whole bottle of forty-percent spirits back then you'd probably have spent the rest of the week in bed, or possibly hospital. Alcohol is fatal in large amounts. And yet here you are, walking and talking without a single slurred word. Don't you get it? We're being repaired. We can't hurt ourselves anymore. We certainly can't kill ourselves. I think we are full of the same molecule-sized machines that they used to make our mansions, but these are fixing us just as quickly as we can damage ourselves. A little bit of alcoholic poisoning? That's nothing; they fix up the kidneys and most of the booze is probably routed straight to your bladder anyway. Ever noticed what a funny colour your pee is in the morning?"

"I thought …"

"But you didn't. Even before your half-assed suicide attempt you must have had a paper cut or something, and you never noticed just how quickly you healed."

"No! And when did you get so smart?"

"Because I had a pet once. He was a little, short terrier called Rocky. I bought him toys and special treats – and then one day he died. I don't remember what of, probably my parents didn't tell me, but what I do remember was how much I wanted him to live again. It didn't matter how tired he was, or how much pain he was in. What was important was how much I loved him. And if that meant filling him with tiny machines then I'd have had the syringe loaded and be calling him in for a special treat before you could say self-replicating nanometre machines. Don't you get it? We are their pets. They bring back nice shiny things from space for us to play with, make sure we have plenty to eat. The obvious next step is shots to keep us heathy."

"They hate us don't they and this is their hell. We survived while the cones made them stupid and they hate us for that."

"Hate? Haven't you seen the statues? Weren't you awake though the parades? They love us! We gave them the universe, and this is what pure, unconstrained love looks like. They want us fit, alert and alive. And I think their tiny machines are as advanced as their owners and can deal with anything, even the most common type of cell damage."

Matthew looked expectantly at Jeremy, who looked dazed and confused, as if everything was happening too fast for him. Matthew sighed imperceptibly and carried on talking, but much slower now.

"Don't you remember all the TV adverts? 'Use our miracle cream to repair the cellular damage that comes with age'. The cream didn't work, but their machines do. Rafael from South America was eighty-four when we saved the world; he still looks eighty-four now and I think he's going to be eighty-four for a very long time."

Jeremy's face went paper white. "The guy from the ship said we'd be able to see the supernova in a thousand years' time, but I just thought it was a figure of speech."

"Nope! He was telling us the exact truth, and I bet he didn't think we were smart enough to notice. We are going to be fit, healthy and live forever."

"We'll go insane. There's no way we can spend eternity on this island, watching the sea, talking about the weather and drinking ourselves into a stupor every night."

"That's what I thought for a while, but didn't you notice how lucid everyone was this morning? There were people I haven't seen for weeks, up, around and looking very happy. I think our firmware has been upgraded to look after our mental health and the tiny machines are busily adjusting our brain chemistry to keep us smiling. But they're doing much more than that. Our owners want us to be happy and know that we need something to do. So the tiny machines are whispering to us. Some of the people this morning were talking about starting a book club or making a film of our experiences." Matthew looked side-eyes at Jeremy. "Some of them were talking about organising parades. When did you come up with that idea? Did it just come to you?"

"I just woke up with it this morning."

"They're probably managing our dreams for us. I wonder how many people have been waking up with brilliant ideas for a nice little hobby to pass the time."

"Is that what you've been doing? Waking up with ideas?"

"Nope, because I've already got a hobby. Every morning I get two bottles of vodka and a six pack of beer and walk down to the beach."

"Doesn't sound much of a hobby."

"Hang on! On the way down to the beach I collect as many fist-sized stones as I can carry. Then I sit with my back to that large rock, finish one of the beers, throw the empty out to sea and use it as a target for the stones while I work my way through the rest of the booze. The water is about five-feet deep at the furthest point I can reach, so it should only take a hundred years or so to build a little jetty out that far. After that, the mainland is only sixty miles away. Say a thousand years and we'll have a bridge we'll be able to walk over."

"That's … that's silly. That would need thousands of tonnes of rock. There's no way this little island is big enough."

"Well, that's the funny thing. Every morning I find my route to the beach just littered with stones exactly the right size. I think our owners approve of my hobby."

"Well they can approve as much as they like, but once I tell people what's happening their little machines can whisper, but nobody will be listening."

"Well, you can try, but judging by the number of people this morning that seemed positively ecstatic about forming a group to discuss Jane Austen's immortal classic of romance and manners I think most of them already know."

"And they're still doing it? They're going to just accept the machines inside them and a suggested hobby to keep them alert and happy?"

"Because they've seen the alternative. What happens if you give someone medication and it doesn't cure the problem? You try something new. And something new might be that our benefactors decide that we're overthinking our problems and the solution for overthinking is less thinking. Maybe with an IQ of eighty we'd think the shiny things they bring us were really funny. Maybe an IQ of sixty would make us nice and docile." Matthew smiled and patted Jeremy's hand. "Perhaps you need to find a hobby before it's too late. I hear there's a basket weaving course starting in the village hall. You'd be able to make lots of nice things and they use some very pretty colours. You'd like that wouldn't you."

Jeremy smiled, and his smile was open, trusting and completely childlike.

THE END